DATE DUE

OCT 1 1 1990		
NOV 1 2 1990		
JUN		
JUL 2 4 1991		
JAN 2 5 1993		
MAR 1 3 1993		
GAYLORD		PRINTED IN U.S.A.

CHERNEVOG

Also by C.J. Cherryh
Published by Ballantine Books

RUSALKA

CHERNEVOG

C. J. CHERRYH

A DEL REY BOOK

BALLANTINE BOOKS · NEW YORK

A Del Rey Book
Published by Ballantine Books

Copyright © 1990 by C.J. Cherryh

All rights reserved under International and Pan-American Copyright Conventions. Published in the United States by Ballantine Books, a division of Random House, Inc., New York, and simultaneously in Canada by Random House of Canada Limited, Toronto.

Library of Congress Cataloging-in-Publication Data
Cherryh, C. J.
Chernevog / C.J. Cherryh.—1st ed.
p. cm.
"A Del Rey book."
ISBN 0-345-35954-2
I. Title.
PS3553.H358C47   1990
813'.54 dc20   90-559
Sci Fic
CIP

Manufactured in the United States of America

First Edition: October 1990

10   9   8   7   6   5   4   3   2   1

CHERNEVOG

1

Snow fell in the woods, drifted deep, a pristine, starlit world in which a single winter hare made significance—slow advance from a wandering, footprinted time past into a white, unwritten time to come. One wondered where it had come from. One wondered where it was going.

Wings snapped. A white owl stooped and rose, flapping heavily with its burden. The track stopped in a circle of wing-flailed snow, a dark splash of blood—

Sasha lay with eyes open, heart thumping, unable to move, unsure where he was or what bed he was in. He did not know what should be so ominous in such a dream, or why a spatter of blood should seem so terrifying. He lay listening to the house timbers creak above and below him, gained courage to put a chilled arm beneath the covers, and knew he was in his bed at his uncle's place, in Vojvoda.

It was forest snow, river snow piled up and making the roof creak. He was safe in his own bed in his friends' house, where nothing evil could come.

Nor would come, so long as the forest grew.

Springtime, and a whisper went through the old woods, a rustling of dry, dead limbs, a rattling and cracking of branches aloft that came on like a rising gale and made Sasha look up from the seedling he was planting. The commotion stopped virtually over him, a last snapping of small branches, a hail of twigs and bits of bark on Sasha's head.

He stood up, brushed the detritus from cap and coat,

shaded his eyes from further such falls and peered up into the sunlight. A huge, particularly brushy limb seemed to detach itself from among the branches and fall—not a plummeting fall, to be sure, but a rapid floating downward that broke more twigs and showered more bark. A massive, brushy creature settled like living growth onto the bole of a long-dead tree.

"Misighi?" Sasha asked. It certainly looked like Misighi, lichenous and bristly and very, very old even as leshys reckoned years.

"Yes, Misighi." Its voice was the deep whisper of the woods. With another rustling it stretched out its multitudinous twiggy fingers and ran their quivering touch over Sasha's shoulders. They gently closed on his arms to draw him to the scrutiny of a vast, slightly mad eye. "Health," it rumbled, "health. Young wizard, you smell of birch trees."

"You look younger every spring," Sasha said, patting Misighi's rough trunk. It was true, Misighi flourished like an old tree with a heart suddenly greening, a wild old tree that took unexpectedly well to a little help now and again from the garden next to the woods.

"Birches," Misighi said. "This is a place for birches."

"All down this streamside." Sasha pointed, thinking of the stream the way it would be, when he was many more years than sixteen. It was all dead trees now, a stream flowing through roots that no longer had a hold on the soil. But hard work reclaimed the woods, grove by grove from the heart outward; and last fall, tall saplings had arrived, rescued from deep shade upriver.

"Roots to hold," Misighi rumbled. "Birch and pine. Root and branch, yes, young wizard."

"Is everything all right, Misighi?"

"Root and branch. Promises kept. All kept."

One wondered, sometimes. Sometimes, at night when doubts grew most naturally, one thought about a grove and a stone in a ring of thorns, and on that stone a young man sleeping . . .

Sometimes, when leshys came visiting so suddenly and by daylight, one felt a certain anxiousness about that place, and about the safety of them all.

But Misighi came calling for no reason, it seemed, beyond friendship and curiosity. Misighi briskly detached himself from the tree, moving at one instant so rapidly the eye could scarcely see him striding and at another so slowly he seemed no more than to drift above the seedlings he leaned close to examine.

It was true, a leshy's feet were backwards.

"Well set, well set," Misighi said of the young birches. And: "Him, yes. He sleeps. Sleeps."

Sasha brushed dirt from his hands, hooked his thumbs in his belt with an uncomfortable twitch of his shoulders and a guilty, long-held question he had never asked Misighi. But he whispered now, thinking of the rain, the winter snow, the passage of time, "Is he suffering? Does he feel the cold at all?"

Misighi rattled his many fingers, a sound like the shiver of wind through brush, and Sasha immediately had a waking dream of a young man's sleeping face, snowflakes touching and melting on dark lashes, settling delicately on colorless cheeks and nose and lips. The sleeper showed no sign of change or wasting.

One might have wished for change, one might have wished to see only the white of rain-washed bone, and to know by that, that all danger was gone. He felt guilt for that hope; but that there should be suffering, he could not wish, and he was unreasonably relieved to be sure that there was none.

But both pity and curiosity were so terribly dangerous.

"Disturbance," Misighi said. "Why?"

"Seeing him," Sasha said. "Thinking about him. —Misighi, why did you come?"

"The smell of birch trees," Misighi said, which most likely was true: Misighi had evidently had the notion, no more, no less, to see what his neighbors were up to since the snows had melted. Misighi came and Misighi went in this forest, and spring and a streamside with new birches was a momentous thing to the old creature, whose woods so nearly had faded altogether. Misighi cared for every leaf.

And quite as suddenly, "Goodbye," Misighi said, having seen what he had come to see. He climbed blindingly quickly

5

up and up the dead trunk and left with as great a commotion as he had made in coming.

Misighi was still a little mad, one had to remember.

"Goodbye," Sasha called after him, waving his cap, and perhaps Misighi heard.

After which Sasha gathered up his basket and his digging stick and moved on down the stream, to plant more seedlings.

"I saw Misighi," he told his friends that evening, when he came home to the river house. He told them how well Misighi had looked.

But the vision Misighi had given him he kept to himself.

Snowfall. There were hares in the woods, the first since the forest had died. Pyetr spied a fox hunting, and Eveshka nursed a half-frozen fieldmouse in a nest of rags beside the hearth.

Quite marvelously, kindling and firewood piled up near the old ferryman's house, as whole logs had done so long as they were useful. Leshys brought what they culled from the dead forest: one could see them some nights, tall as trees themselves in the moonlight, tricking the eye quite easily if one had not been accustomed to Forest-things and their tricks.

"We could build a bathhouse," Pyetr said, stamping in from the porch, his face stung with cold, his fair hair an ice-rimed fringe below his cap. "We certainly could use a bathhouse. There's plenty of wood for shingles . . ."

Mist hung over the river, and over the path past the old ferry, where the trees stood like ghosts.

Come back, she heard her father call to her, and she knew that if she ignored his warning she would die. But in this dream she kept walking, toward the cloaked man on the riverside.

Why have you followed me? he always asked her.

And she said, always knew she was going to say:

To ask you to come back . . .

—

Eveshka waked with a start and settled again, lay shivering against Pyetr's side, under piles of quilts. "Are you all right?" he asked, stroking her shoulder.

"Only a dream," she said. And shivered until he took her in his arms.

There was a book in the other room. Sasha kept it. Sasha read it, and she wished he would not.

She wished it burned. But that would not undo a single wish in it.

We'd better know what he did wish, hadn't we? Sasha reasoned against her fears. In her better sense Eveshka knew that he was right.

But tonight she kept thinking about the man in the mist, the young man sleeping on cold stone, ice on branches, and white flakes sifting down through a ring of thorns . . .

Snow-melt and greening then, the fieldmouse went free and birch seedlings leafed, saplings of three years rising tall and substantial across the disused road, above banks of bracken fern and moss. The dead trees that once had completely shadowed the forest floor were fewer than the year before . . . falling to the wind, but never crushing a sapling; to lightning, but never spreading fire; and never lying long, except as a shelter for hares or young foxes.

It was, said the grandmothers in Vojvoda, a magical woods where backwards-footed Forest-things lured the unwary to disasters and untimely death—a terrible woods, grandmothers in Kiev might well say, where wizards lived, and against them not even the Great Tsar and all his army would venture.

A girl—a wizard-daughter—had drowned in the river that ran through that woods, and in the way of such unhappy dead, dwelt in a willow, a heartless rusalka who drank up whatever life came near her. She haunted the shore of that woods, a girl with long, pale hair—

Quite likely now the rumor had gotten south (since even near such worldly places as Kiev there were surely grandmothers with their sources) that the old forest had been growing livelier of late, that a new wizard had taken old Uulamets' place on the riverside and broken the dreadful rusalka's spell.

But whether this was a good wizard or bad, the rumors failed to say.

In fact Sasha himself sometimes wondered what he was, being now eighteen and inclined, his good friend Pyetr insisted, to think far too much about responsibilities . . .

His friend Pyetr being of course a worldly and married man of all of twenty-and-six—married to the rusalka of the rumors, as happened: there was a great deal truly odd about their household that even the rumors of banniks and House-things and grandmothers surely must fall short of.

That Eveshka Uulametsova was no longer a rusalka, for one thing, nor even dead these days—and that the fey and mysterious boatman who traded with freeholders in the new wizard's name was that very scoundrel Pyetr the whole town of Vojvoda most gladly would have hanged.

Most of all Vojvoda would be amazed at the changes in The Cockerel's former stableboy: at least a handspan of height and a good breadth of shoulder—Sasha having done his share of wood-splitting and shingle-making in the remaking of his house, right along with Pyetr—

Whose hands, the god knew, were to this day more adept with the dice than with hammer and saw.

Notwithstanding which, over the last several years the old ferryman's cottage had quite well doubled its size, was comfortably (if eccentrically) shingled, with a fine, (though slightly tilting) shed built onto the back, a bathhouse at the side, (it did perhaps spiral a little out of true) and, in the front and on the left, a garden springing up in green shoots, without a single weed. The last was Eveshka's doing, the carpentry was Pyetr's and Sasha's, and only proved, as Pyetr said, that not even wizardry could make a corner-post stand true.

Still, all they built held strong and snug through the winters and the summers, a house weathered and patched with lichen, added on to with gray, weathered logs, rustic outside—

Ah, but *in* . . .

Inside were clean wooden floors, rugs from the Indee, cupboards and beds and tables and chairs likewise polished. There were golden cups and pewter plates. There were silk curtains and brass lamps and a wonderful samovar, besides a well-ordered cellar full of apples and nuts and dried mushrooms, bunches of herbs and pots of honey and sacks of good down-river grain—not mentioning, besides, the domovoi who was well-content there, and the shelves at the newly excavated end of the cellar, which held hundreds of well-dusted, well-marked little pots of herbs, simples, powders, and earths that a wizard or even a good householder might find useful.

Not a single mouse. The domovoi got those.

In truth, Sasha found himself so happy in this cozy house it frightened him, because nothing of the gold and the silk and the jewels had ever really seemed to belong to him: it was only a cup to drink from, was only a curtain to keep the draft away; these things had come to him in a night and they could go the same way, for all he cared. It was his welcome with Pyetr and Eveshka that mattered to him, and Pyetr's happiness with Eveshka, and their willingness to put up with him, who was no longer the fifteen-year-old boy they had started with.

This spring in particular it had begun to seem to him that he was a great deal underfoot for a married couple, though Pyetr and Eveshka had willingly set a room apart for him: Pyetr had in fact built the house twice as large for his sake, so that he could have his bedroom and his own clothes press at one end of what had once been the whole house and now was only the end of the kitchen. Pyetr and Eveshka had the big new room at the back, on the other side of the opened hearth, and Eveshka's cupboards. It *was* after all Eveshka's house: of all else her father had passed on to him, Sasha had never claimed the house Eveshka had grown up in, nor ever doubted it was hers. Yet here he was, always at their breakfast table, always in the middle of their evenings when work was done.

Most of all in those late hours when a not too naive boy was very acutely aware that man and his wife would want a little privacy, they often as not put that off for his sake, so as not, Pyetr had said more than once, to leave him alone by the fireside—all of which said to Sasha that he was a nuisance to them, even if he was company for Pyetr, and even if a wizard had no choice but the solitude of this woods. The house rightfully was Eveshka's, Pyetr certainly was; and that

9

left Sasha Misurov lately feeling all his own happiness so fragile a misaimed wish could shatter it.

It was so hard, for instance, not to wish them happy together. But a wizard generally got his wishes, in one shape or another: that was exactly the problem. He dared not wish a thing like that for Eveshka, who being a wizard herself could perfectly well feel it happening and angrily bid him mind his own business; and he dared not wish it for Pyetr, either, who would not feel it, but who certainly trusted his best friend not to meddle.

It was hard, too, not to want to be loved and wanted, despite one's inconvenience: and the knotty question of whether not-wishing could possibly be a wish in itself kept turning over and over in Sasha's mind, waking him at night and setting him for long hours to writing in his book, to which he added page after page as the months passed; it set him to reading master Uulamets' battered, rain-stained record, too—which warned him plainly that a wizard who loved anyone was in danger, and a wizard who wanted love from any creature was a thief at best.

That caution applied to Eveshka and him equally, of course; and however they tried, he was sure they were both guilty in their own ways and for their own reasons.

But Pyetr only laughed and said, when once Sasha confided to him his inmost, most terrible misgivings in his case,

"I'm not worried."

Wherewith Pyetr poured another cup of water over his head—they were sitting in the newly finished bathhouse at the time, sweating in the heat of the stones.

"I worry," Sasha said, and looked about him in the dim light and the steam—one would be cautious in a bathhouse at any time one was saying something serious, because of banniks. "Pyetr, if you ever think I'm wishing something—"

"What I wish," Pyetr said, "is a cup of water down my back."

Sasha poured it.

"Still," Sasha began again.

"You worry too much," Pyetr said, resuming the careful scraping of his chin. "You look at a clear sky, you worry it'll rain; you wish for clear weather, you worry it'll be drought across all the tsar's lands—and he'll come and burn your house down—"

"It might happen."

"Might happen. It won't if you wish not."

"If I wish not—"

"The tsar could fall dead. A fine reasoning. Why should you care? The damn tsar's going to burn your house down!"

"I never wished it to rain in the first place!"

"Oh, pish, you wish me up winds on the river, you wish me safe in the woods, god, some poor bear might starve to death for your sake. —Aren't you worried?"

Sasha scowled at Pyetr. Pyetr winked at him.

"Hush with your jokes," Sasha said. "How will we get a bannik if you don't take it seriously?"

"I'll say if there's a bannik he should have a sense of humor."

"Hope he doesn't!" Sasha said, and wished if one was listening he would be patient. "Bannik, excuse him. He really means well."

"Probably," Pyetr said, "he's still looking at the roof, thinking he could get a better job in Kiev."

"Pyetr,—"

"I know, I know." Pyetr gave careful attention to the spot under his lip, shaving by touch. "But if there's an ill-tempered bannik about we don't need him and if he's a decent fellow he won't mind a joke."

"They're not a joking sort."

"That's a grim idea."

"What?"

"Seeing the future and finding nothing to laugh about." Pyetr dipped a cloth in the bucket and wiped his face. "A body's always got that, wherever he is. Here in the woods, for instance—one needs that, in the long winters . . ."

"You miss Kiev, don't you?"

"I wouldn't know if I miss Kiev, I've never been to Kiev."

"You always said you'd go."

"Well, I will, when I want to."

"That's the point, isn't it, I mean, if we're really wishing you to stay, and not knowing it—"

"I like it here. I'm fine. God, what should I complain

11

about? We've got the house roofed, there aren't any more leaks—"

"You weren't a farmer. You were never made to be a farmer."

"No, I was a fool on his way to a hanging, with a flock of double-crossing scoundrels I thought were my friends, to tell the truth—who'd have seen me hanged as soon as lift a finger to help me. What's Kiev to offer? More scoundrels."

"You never thought so."

"Well, I think so now. I might go to Kiev someday, but I don't see doing it this year. I've no time to do it. I *like* it here."

"It's not Kiev."

"Well, thank the god it's not Vojvoda either, where I'd likely be hanged, if the boyars were in an especially good mood!"

"It's livelier."

"Not if you're dead. God, why should I complain? What started this? What do you think I'd want that I haven't got?"

Sasha tried to stop himself, but he did think of something Pyetr lacked. He thought of it so instantly and wanted it so clearly he knew it was dangerous, but for some reason he could not collect his wits to know what to do next. He felt the sweat running on his face, mopped at it, his heart thumping.

Pyetr said, flinging a dipperful of water at him: "Come on, out we go, we're not used to this. I think we're both getting a little light-headed."

Cold air did help. Sasha breathed deeply, leaned against the bathhouse wall and tried to think exactly what he should do about what he had just wanted.

That was the trap a wizard so easily fell into: if wishes worked, and if a wizard had a friend, then one wanted everything that could make his friend happy.

Of course one did—

Especially if one felt oneself constantly in the way of that happiness as it was.

That was the danger a wizard ran in having friends.

12

Sasha knew that absolutely—one evening a month later, when a black horse turned up in the garden, nibbling Eveshka's infant cabbages.

"God!" Eveshka cried, on the porch, wiping dusty hands; while Sasha, in the doorway behind her, said with all contrition, "I'm sorry," and wished the horse out of Eveshka's garden.

"Sorry!" Eveshka said, and looked back at him in wide-eyed indignation, which only made him wish—

But Sasha stopped himself in time. He said, in a very small voice, "I think it's Pyetr's horse."

2

✠ ✠ ✠ ✠ Pyetr eased the old ferry in, not scraping the dockside buffers too hard. Townsman and landsman he might have been born, but the river ran quietly near the house, the hand at the tiller could also work the small sail they used for this stretch of the river (Eveshka's clever notion, to extend the ropes that far) and since two wizards could easily wish him up a favorable wind, he took the boat out alone now and again, when his foresting and his foraging and his sometime trading took him upriver or down.

Today was one of those days, wizards being the peculiar folk they were, inclined to long stints of reading and writing in the books they kept—or, the case in the house today, to long, laborious grinding and brewing and boiling of things some of which were delightful and most of which were not. One supposed that wizardly noses got used to it: his certainly had not.

So off he had gone on his own this morning with pots and boxes of willow seedlings and herbs and packets of seeds of all kinds to plant upriver, where willows had once grown; and back he came gliding up to the dock in the evening, pleasantly recalling Eveshka had promised him honey-cakes in recompense.

He jumped ashore with the rope, made fast, returned aboard to gather up a bag of mushrooms he had found (Eveshka knew everything that grew in the woods, and saved them from his fatal mistakes). He took up his empty lunch-basket, in which he had tucked sprigs of several things he did not recognize, along with an interesting double oak gall:

14

Eveshka was always interested in curiosities, some of which became part of her recipes.

"Babi!" he called out, whistled sharply, and a black furball bounded ashore after him. It might have been a dog: it scampered around his feet, panting, doglike. Then, not at all doglike, it grabbed his trouser-leg with small black hands, making a thorough nuisance of itself.

"Go on, Babi," Pyetr said, shaking the dvorovoi loose, and dropped the lunch-basket, which Babi, sitting upright, caught neatly in his hands. "Don't eat it, hear?"

Babi hugged the basket in his arms and trotted on small bowed legs beside him, more basket than Babi, up the steep path to the house. Boats and riversides were not a dvorovoi's proper place, of course: a Yard-thing had an important duty in the world, keeping rabbits and birds and less common marauders out of a house's garden, and warding garden gates from going maliciously unlatched to strangers. But Eveshka and Sasha alike had wished their dvorovoi to keep an eye on him when he was off alone in the woods (they had separately confessed it) and Babi offered no objection at all: Babi seemed thoroughly to enjoy the outings, even the odd meetings with leshys, at which he growled and hissed and bristled. The leshys forgave him, even old Misighi: one had to grant Babi had the same manner with everyone.

Babi hissed too when they reached the top of the hill; and growled and bristled, growing rapidly and ominously larger as they walked—and that was not his habit at a homecoming.

In the same moment Pyetr saw the horse beyond the hedge and had the immediate apprehension of some visitor, though the god knew no visitor had ever come to this house in their tenure, nor was likely to, nor was welcome.

But as the black horse lifted its head and sniffed the wind in his direction—it looked very like a certain black horse Pyetr had once owned. Besides which, it was loose in the yard, which was a careless thing to allow any horse with a growing garden nearby.

So one supposed that Sasha and Eveshka knew the horse was there and that they had wished it safely out of the vegetables.

And one supposed that if they both knew it was there, one of them had wished it to be—and if one of them had wished it to be, then one could surmise on the instant it was a certain rascally young stableboy-now-wizard who *liked* horses.

Damn, it looked like Volkhi, it truly did, and the sight reminded Pyetr what he had lost when he lost that horse.

Still, Babi's behavior did give Pyetr a chill thought of shapeshifters, too, some insidious attack getting into the house past Sasha and Eveshka, and this—creature—standing here only to lure him in. There was the smell of baking honey-cakes on the breeze, but lies came with utter plausibility, if wizardry was in question, and traps came baited with things one most dearly wanted, whoever was doing the trapping.

"Babi," Pyetr said, quietly, "don't bother the horse, if it is a horse. Go to 'Veshka, there's a good Babi, go into the house and see if it's all right."

Babi went, growling, ducked through the hedge and shambled in plain sight and with a good many looks askance at the horse, up the slanting wooden walk-up to the porch of the cottage.

So it was safe. Babi knew.

And if the black horse did look like Volkhi—and since Babi had not startled it off outright as an imposter—

Pyetr picked up the basket Babi had left, squeezed through the same gap in the hedge and walked up to the horse, which stood watching this noisy traffic with ears pricked and nostrils working.

God, absolutely, it was Volkhi. He knew every line of this horse.

Babi popped into the house without using the door, a very put-upon and disturbed Babi, meaning, Sasha was sure, first, that Pyetr was back, second, that Pyetr had found the surprise, and third, that the surprise had found Pyetr—and indeed by the time Sasha had walked outside there was loving tryst in progress.

Sasha put his hands into his pockets and stood on the porch watching, earnestly hoping (but hoping was perilously close to wishing) that he had not done something wrong or dangerous.

Eveshka walked out and stood beside him at the porch rail, dusting flour from her hands onto her apron. He felt a very powerful wish from her side of a sudden: and Pyetr looked up, startled, as the horse shied off.

Sasha *knew*, perhaps because Eveshka did not truly exclude him from her wish, that Eveshka wanted attention from a husband coming home, *wanted* it, quite conscious of her selfishness and quite justifiably angry at a boy's thoughtless interference in their lives.

"Don't," Sasha whispered, not looking at her. "Eveshka, you promised. Don't wish at him like that."

"Everything was perfect," Eveshka said to him in a small, hurt voice; she wanted him to know she did entirely understand her own shortcomings; and his.

With which she turned and went inside, violently wishing him and Pyetr to leave her alone for a little while.

People in neighboring Vojvoda and maybe Kiev would have felt that one.

A disappearing flurry of skirts and hip-length blond braids, definitive slam of the door; and Pyetr stopped with his hand on the rail of the walk-up.

"What in hell's going on?" Pyetr asked, he thought quite reasonably, with his wife in tears, his long-lost horse in the garden, and his best friend looking as if he would gladly be elsewhere.

Sasha walked slowly down to him, and Volkhi tossed his head up and shied out of the cabbages: this assuredly meant (Pyetr understood these things by long experience) that someone's attention had slipped and come back again.

And a man used to wizards could equally well reckon that the slammed door, Volkhi's arrival, and the rueful look on Sasha's face were not entirely coincidental.

"I'm terribly sorry," Sasha said, looking more boy than young man at the moment. "I brought him. I wished him here. Eveshka's mad at me: she really didn't mean to wish you just then."

17

Pyetr looked up at the door, where, despite the upset of his stomach, he could reckon that Eveshka must be getting a stern hold on her temper.

But a man hated to feel obliged only because his wizard-wife had not wished him in the river; and hated to be angry at Sasha for probably meaning the best and kindest things for him in all the world.

Give or take horse theft . . . because Volkhi, sleek and well-fed, had surely acquired another owner in three years and more.

"I was thinking how to make you happy," Sasha said in a small voice, "I truly was. I thought you probably missed having a horse, and I must have been thinking of this one."

"Who said I wasn't happy?" Pyetr muttered, wondering if he dared go into the house just now. "—'Veshka! Come out here! What have I done, for the god's sake?"

On second thought he did not *want* to go up to the porch right now. He did not want to open that door and talk to his wife, because she was not being sensible at the moment: she was mad at herself for being selfish enough to be mad in the first place. In rusalka-form, she had done terrible things. Nowadays she had a body as well as a heart to trouble her, and sometimes she did not deal well with surprises and things that went against her wishes. Most of all she did not deal well with an eighteen-year-old boy who confused himself with her father—all of which came at Pyetr in half a blink and with a force that left him short of breath. His wife was decidedly upset.

"God." Pyetr rested his head on the rail of the walk-up while Sasha blithered on about how he had no idea why the part about the horse had worked and the part about him being happy had gone so terribly, awfully askew.

"It's not your fault," Pyetr said, looking at the twilight above the woods, the hedge, and black Volkhi snuffling wistfully in the direction of the garden. "It's none of it anyone's fault—unless some boyar comes looking for him with his guard. Who knows who bought him, after me? I left a lot of creditors."

"I'm sorry!"

"Sasha, I swear, I'm glad about the horse, I don't know

why anybody's upset, I don't know why I can't go inside and have supper, and I don't know why my wife isn't speaking to me, except the cabbages."

"I don't know," Sasha said miserably. "Pyetr, I'm—"

"—sorry, I know. —For what? What for the god's sake is anybody upset about? I've got my horse back. What's she mad about?"

"Because you don't know what could happen!"

"Because you didn't mean to want something." Sometimes a rational man felt his sanity in question. "And it trampled Eveshka's garden." He shouted up at the house: "Eveshka, for the god's sake, everybody's *sorry* about the garden! I don't *mind* you wanted me to look at you first, it's not a crime, Eveshka, I'm not mad, I swear I'm not, I'm sorry I didn't notice you! I would have, except I didn't expect the horse!"

Silence.

" 'Veshka, it's getting dark and I want my supper, dammit! Open the door!"

There was no answer of any sort. His wife was jealous of a horse. And in the gathering dark, Pyetr sighed heavily, let the basket and the sack of mushrooms to the ground and sat down on the rim of the walk-up, under the rail, that seeming to be where they might both spend the night.

"It's me she's upset with," Sasha said, settling on the split logs beside him, while Volkhi came up to investigate the contents of the basket at Pyetr's feet. "She just wants to think. To figure things out. A wizard has to—"

Pyetr looked darkly at Sasha, not particularly wanting a boy's advice at the moment.

"God," Sasha said, and dropped his head into his hands. "I truly am sorry."

"Don't tell me that. Everybody's sorry. I want my supper." Pyetr rubbed Volkhi's persistently intrusive nose; the horse jumped, threw his head and calmed again quickly under Sasha's offered hand.

Which for some strange reason gave Pyetr a most uneasy image.

A man married to Uulamets' once-dead and wizardly daughter, a man who daily dealt with wizards and leshys and the like got used to small, cold thoughts, some of which were not even his own to start with—and suddenly Pyetr had the wildest, most unreasoning impulse to stand up, wave Volkhi off to run back to whatever honest, safe stable he had escaped—

Even if Sasha loved horses and his touch was as true as his heart was.

But it was only one small cold thought. It was foolish to coddle his wife's skittish temper, still more foolish to leave her alone with her hurt feelings and odd imaginings: the wizard breed was only scarcely sane, Sasha and Eveshka both confessed that quite freely—scarcely sane especially when they kept their hearts, which all the rest of their kind seemed to think impossible to do; and particularly when they tried to use those hearts and live like ordinary folk. Both the wizards he loved had warned him outright that loving him, that loving anything at all was very dangerous to them and to everything around them.

The dead trees were witness enough to that.

" 'Veshka," Pyetr called out, grabbing the rail and hauling himself up under it onto the walk. " 'Veshka, dammit, it's getting dark, it's getting cold out here, and I want my supper, do you hear?"

There was quiet, serene simple quiet from the house.

He walked up to the porch and knocked on his own door. " 'Veshka? Let's have some sense, shall we?"

Silence.

" 'Veshka, I love you. Am I going to stand out here all night?"

The door opened. Without her touching it.

Pyetr looked back, then, earnestly hoping for Sasha behind him, looking for a way to make light of things, make a joke, and lift Eveshka out of her perilous despond. But Sasha, the coward, was still sitting down at the bottom of the walkup, with traitorous Volkhi nosing his hand.

So he went inside, to the hearth where Eveshka was stirring up their supper cakes, squatted on his heels beside her and rested his arms on his knees.

"Smells good," he said, and had only her profile, downcast eyes, pursed lips. Her pretty blond braids.

"Your father wanted me to be a toad," he said, touching one of those braids, moving it for a better view. "It didn't work."

She did not find that amusing. Her mouth set quite firmly, she flinched aside, and she flung a dollop of batter hissing onto the griddle.

"I think you've frightened Babi away," he said, "or he'd be here begging." He stole a swipe off the side of the bowl, and put the finger in his mouth, getting this time a threat from the spoon and a thunderous blue-eyed scowl. "Mmmn. You *don't* want a toad for a husband, do you?"

"It's not funny, Pyetr!"

"So what's the matter? You're not jealous of a horse, are you? That's silly."

"I'm just—" The spoon went back into the batter, and Eveshka wiped her eyes. "Sorry. I'm selfish, I can't help being selfish, I wish—"

"For the god's sake, don't!"

She rested her mouth against her hand. Shook her head, not looking at him.

"I want too much," she said. "And it's not fair to you. It's not fair. It's never been fair!"

Time was, he had been going cheerfully from trouble to trouble in Vojvoda, where ordinary folk lived and where wizards were, if gifted at all, hardly fit to cure warts. Now here he was, the god have mercy, with a wizard-wife who could have her way with passing thunderstorms.

He tipped her chin up, gently, tried with a quirk of his mouth to coax a smile from her. "Now in Vojvoda there was this girl who wanted too much—"

Her lips trembled while she looked at him, scowling. There was the distinct smell of cakes well-done.

"But her papa wasn't a wizard," he said, tracing a line down her cheek. "He was a tavern keeper. And she wanted to live like a boyarina. She never wanted to work. She wanted the clothes, the jewels—any fellow who'd have her, she wanted to order around. So she settled on this handsome rich lad named Ivan—"

"Are you sure his name wasn't Pyetr?"

"I wasn't rich. Besides, I was too smart for her. And we

21

figured out, some other lads and I, what she was up to. She'd gotten this potion from this wizard to slip into his drink—which had this dreadful effect. It didn't make him fall in love at all. But then, we'd switched drinks. She was dreadfully sick for a week."

"You don't make love with potions!"

"Wizards do in Vojvoda. But then, they're not very good wizards. I tell you, Sasha could set up shop—"

"My cakes are burning!" she cried, and escaped him to snatch for the spatula.

"A little dark," he said, as she turned them.

"Oh, they're ruined!"

"Wish them unburned."

"Wishes don't work like that, you know they don't. Damn!"

"*That* won't help the cakes, either."

"God." She clenched her fists, bowed her head against them. "Pyetr, don't."

He sighed and put his arm about her. "What do you want?"

"Nothing."

"Do you want Sasha to chase the horse back to Vojvoda? Is that the trouble? Will that satisfy you?"

"I don't want that!" she cried, pushed free of him and got up, her wonderful hair all shining in the firelight—

"God, 'Veshka—"

"Don't look at me like that! Don't love me because I want you to! Oh, god, I knew, I knew you weren't safe from me!"

"Dammit, *I* know what I want."

She went across the kitchen and began taking random things off the shelves.

"What are you doing?" he asked, scrambling for his feet. He very well knew what she was doing: it would not be the first time Eveshka had gone out into the woods alone for a day or so, and come back better for it, the god knew, after worrying him sleepless—saying nothing of where she had been or what she had done. But she had never taken off in the dark, in the middle of a quarrel. " 'Veshka, for the god's own sake, ask me what *I* want. Anything we both agree on, we can't have because you want it? That's crazed! That means

22

we only get what neither of us wants! That's damned stupid, 'Veshka!"

A piece of bread went into a basket; a handful of fruit. Eveshka stopped and leaned against the table, head bowed.

" 'Veshka? Is it something I've done?"

She straightened her shoulders then, took the things out of the basket, wiped a knuckle across her cheek and wiped the hand on her apron. The basket went back on the shelf.

He came up behind her and put his arms around her, whispering, "I have exactly what I want."

The grease scorched, meanwhile.

"My cakes!" Eveshka said, "oh, damn, Pyetr, —"

The cellar-supports shifted, the much-taxed domovoi getting the smell of smoke, perhaps, as Eveshka rescued the overheated griddle and the blackened cakes.

The house settled, then. Everything seemed to.

"Babi?" he said, remembering the dvorovoi. "Honey-cakes, Babi."

Babi did not put in an appearance. Perhaps Babi was waiting for higher bribes. Like vodka.

So Pyetr went to the door, put his head out and told Sasha there was a good chance of supper. Then he got down the jug.

Babi appeared not even for that, as happened.

While the horse was still in the yard. Dammit, a dvorovoi was supposed to like livestock, and take care of things and keep the horse out of the garden, for the god's sake, not have his nose set out of joint.

But Babi had him for a personal responsibility, two wizards had told Babi so, and quite probably, Pyetr thought, Babi was somewhere out around the hedge feeling jealous, rejected and sorry for himself.

Damn, he thought, and went to put the dishes on.

3

✠ ✠ ✠ ✠ Supper was quiet, everything was calm, not
a stray wish or an ungoverned thought flew
across the table, just Pass the cakes, please; more tea, Sasha?
Only Babi still seemed to be sulking, put out about the horse
in the yard, Sasha surmised distressedly, and neither honey-
cakes nor vodka would bring him.

"He'll come around," Pyetr muttered. "At least by breakfast."

So Pyetr and he made up a bit of grain and honey for
Volkhi, they curried him down, the two of them, by lamplight, and they built a sort of a pen around him at the back
of the house, where afternoon sun let wild grasses grow. It
was a hasty sort of work, but Sasha wished the posts to stay
put—much easier than wishing the horse, to be sure, which
had a mind of its own and which could not be wished out of
a taste for new spring vegetables for more than a few moments at a time.

Eveshka came out to help lift the bars into place, and
helped wish them to stay. She even brought Volkhi a bit of
honey-cake.

"I'm sorry about the cabbages," Pyetr whispered to her in
Sasha's hearing, across a fence-rail; and Eveshka whispered
back, leaning to take Pyetr's kiss on the lips:

"Hush, it's all right, I don't care about that; nothing is
your fault."

Another kiss. After that Pyetr ended up on the other side
of the rail and the two of them went walking arm in arm
around the corner of the house.

Probably, Sasha thought, they did not need a house guest to turn up in the front room any time soon.

So he shrugged his coat back on, the night being somewhat cold since he had stopped hefting rails about, and lingered to test the posts they had set, figuring that Pyetr and Eveshka would not linger long in the kitchen.

Eveshka had been sixteen when she had died: she had been a sixteen-year-old ghost for better than a hundred years before she had gained her life back and gone on with living it. Sometimes it seemed to him she was still sixteen when someone crossed her—and, god, Sasha thought, resting his arms on the rail, if she caught him thinking that, best he find a bed somewhere in the deep woods tonight, perhaps for several nights.

She had had all those years of Uulamets' personal teaching and all those years of being both a wizard and a ghost . . . but she had spent so long as a rusalka and so comparatively few years dealing with the simple pain of burning a finger on a pot handle, or dealing with a husband who sometimes, being Pyetr, did things not even a wizard could predict—

(*Say* what you want, Pyetr would remind them both cheerfully: just speak it out loud, it's only fair: tell me what you want me to do and let *me* decide, is that so hard?)

Sometimes, for Eveshka, it truly was. Sometimes it seemed the hardest thing in the world for her.

And then, just when everything seemed possible and they had everything in the world they ought to want—Pyetr's best friend had to do a stupid thing like this, and bring this poor horse into the question.

The horse was looking at him quite warily as it might, now that they were alone with only a rail between them. One misgiving equine eye shone under a black thatch of bangs. Its nostrils worked as if it could smell something unnatural about the place and the night and about him.

Poor fellow, Sasha thought: one night in a snug stable, by the well-cared-for look of him, and the next bolting through a woods full of dangers of very terrible sort.

"Volkhi?" he said gently, ducked under the rail and held out a hand to the horse—not cheating, this time, simply letting the horse make up its mind about his character. A few steps closer. "There's a lad. Come on. I'm a friend of Pyetr's. I'm really not a bad sort. See, not a wish one way or the other."

Volkhi eyed him a moment more, then stretched out his neck and breathed the air about him.

"Don't be afraid, there's a good fellow."

The horse investigated his fingers, carefully. Sasha felt warm breath on his hand, and the touch of a soft, interested nose, while the lamplight showed their mingled breaths like fog.

A wizard once a stableboy could be a great fool for something like this, could ask himself how he had ever gotten along without such feelings—a warm and friendly creature snuffling his fingers on a nippish night and nosing his face and his coat, looking for possible apples.

For a moment, defending his cap from the search, he was no wizard at all, only his uncle's stableboy, who had found his only true fellowship in his charges, in the black and white stable cat and old Missy and the various horses that had come and gone with the rich young men of the town. Pyetr had seemed only one of that wild crowd in those days—once upon a time and only, it seemed now, yesterday: The Cockerel's stable came back so vividly for a moment Sasha wondered just for whom he had really wished up a horse in the first place; or how he could be so warmly drawn back to days he wanted to forget.

But he had been a great deal safer then, he had been so very good in those days about not wanting things of people— not wanting things at all, except where it concerned his four- footed charges. He had never been sure he was doing it, for one thing: they had never accused him for his small sorcery, second; and he had never felt guilty about loving them, nor been reluctant, whenever he had gotten on his uncle's bad side, to come to the stable to lean on a comfortable warm shoulder and pour out his troubles to a patient friend like old Missy, that he could miss so much of a sudden—

He was that boy again, tonight, the town jinx, that no one wanted around, he had made a mess of things again and Eveshka had every right to be put out with him, on top of which, he had just come recklessly close to wanting Missy here for himself—knowing very well that she was Andrei the carter's horse, and that Andrei Andreyevitch in no wise deserved to be robbed by some selfish, self-pitying young wizard.

Missy. For rides in the woods, no less—himself and Pyetr out and about together, the way he had dreamed of it being when the three of them had settled here on this riverside.

God, he thought. The cat, too, why not? The house needs a cat. Why not the whole stable, fool?

That was how helplessly unreasonable he was being, longing for ordinary, common things a wizard could never, ever have, and, like a fool, thinking he needed something all his own to love. So things were more complicated in the house than a callow fifteen-year-old had once thought they would be. A man loved his wife. It did not mean he stopped being a friend. A wife took time, especially Eveshka, who had her own difficulties, not least because he was, dammit, too often under Eveshka's feet, in Eveshka's house, with Pyetr the one who ended up with a burned supper and an angry wife and Babi not speaking to any of them.

Maybe it was time that he did think what else he could do, such as, perhaps, talk to Pyetr about building another house, over on the hill.

A damned, lonely, solitary little house, without even Babi for company in the evenings.

Maybe he knew he ought to, in all justice. Maybe that was why he was all but shivering of a sudden, despite a good coat and a night none so cold, and why he had a growing lump in his throat, and why he decided he had best get himself inside immediately, away from horses and all such temptations, to read and think a good long while by himself without wishing anything at all.

The front door opened and shut. Pyetr lifted his head from the pillow, and Eveshka whispered. "He's perfectly all right."

There were other small, reassuring sounds, the domovoi settling again in the cellar, Sasha walking about in the kitchen, a log going on the fire, which sent up a small flurry of sparks on their side of the hearth.

But Pyetr heard the sound of the bench pulled back in the

kitchen and thought distressedly that Sasha was at that damned book again, scribbling and studying.

"That's no life for a boy," he said, "reading all day and writing all night."

Eveshka said nothing. He had only her shoulder.

"He's eighteen," Pyetr said. "He's not going to find everything he needs in that damned book, Eveshka."

"He made a mistake," she said. "He's trying to find out why."

"A mistake. The boy wants a horse. Why shouldn't he?"

"A wizard shouldn't."

"God."

"It's very serious."

"Can you help him?"

She shook her head, motion against the pillow. "It's his business. His question. He has to answer it."

Eveshka's father had given more than a book to the lad. Eveshka's father, when he died, the black god take him, had worked some sudden spell or another and magicked everything he knew into the boy's head, things a boy could have lived quite happily without, things far, far more than reading and writing.

No real memory of things, Sasha insisted. Nothing I can't deal with, Sasha said.

The double-damned, unprincipled old scoundrel.

"It's not natural," Pyetr said. "It's not natural, 'Veshka."

But she seemed to be asleep. At least she offered no conversation. So he lay there thinking about his own misspent years in Vojvoda, not regretting many of them, except the quality of the company.

Maybe he would sail down to Kiev after all. Maybe he would finally sail down to Kiev of the golden roofs, with Sasha in tow, just himself and the boy—

Shop around a little. Find a tavern. Do something thoroughly reprehensible. Or at least mildly riotous.

If he dared leave Eveshka.

He could not, not that long: Eveshka was far too prone to melancholy. The god knew she slipped too readily toward that state of mind.

So, hell, they would take Eveshka along—show her the

golden roofs, the rocs and the crocodiles and the palaces, which everything he had ever heard assured him were abundant in Kiev.

Not forgetting the elephants.

It would do the boy a world of good. Do good for Eveshka too. Show her how ordinary folk lived, show her that people *could* live together, more of them in one place than she could ever imagine.

Wish the boy up a tsarevna, she could, one of the Great Tsar's nieces or such.

No. A pretty beggar girl, who would be ever so glad to fly off to the deep woods and live like a tsarevna for the rest of her life—

A girl who would, wise as wizards, keep her wishes modest.

Sasha pulled the lamp a little closer on the kitchen table, going over the page again which, as best he remembered, ought to record his wish for the horse—which he did very well recall, but he had not even written the matter down, nor made any entry at all for that day, that was the puzzling thing. One hardly wrote down every little thing one did: even in the quiet of the woods there were days one got busy and let records slip a day or two, but he did not remember what could have gotten in the way that day, or why he had forgotten it entirely—when he recalled now how it had upset him at the time.

The day they had first fired up the bathhouse—and all of them had been wondering about banniks . . .

But they had felt nothing banniklike since but the slight spookiness a dark bathhouse might have: a whole (if slightly twisted) roof was not an invariable guarantee of banniks, by all he knew. Uulamets' book recollected a shy, slightly daft old creature that had sometimes provided visions—but it had hardly been a happy Bath-thing: Uulamets' bannik had deserted the place after Eveshka had died, Uulamets pursuing it relentlessly for foreknowledge—

About his hopes of raising the dead.

Not a happy creature, not a happy parting, and, Sasha had

thought from long before they had put the roof cap on, certainly nothing he really wanted to provoke to anger. It surely must have been glad, as Pyetr had said, to find some more cheerful establishment to haunt, say, down in Kiev—if (and this was the most substantial of his fears) repairing the bathhouse had not by some law of magic called it back against its will.

He recalled he had thought about that possibility, that day.

They had talked about Kiev. He had gotten quite lightheaded from the heat—had been quite, quite giddy when he had thought about the horse. They had had to go outside.

God, he thought, what was I thinking then? About banniks? Or was it remembering the bathhouse at uncle Fedya's that made me think of the horse?

Vojvoda. Pyetr and Volkhi and the butter churn—

He rested his eyes against his hands, elbows on the table, asking himself: Or was I worrying about Pyetr? Was I afraid he'd go off to Kiev and leave us and not come back once he saw the gold and the crocodiles and all? Or was I thinking about him and 'Veshka—because I'm afraid I am messing things up with them? Maybe I really should build that house on the hill over there.

But if I'm not right here with them when they argue, to say, 'Veshka, don't wish at him—then who's going to say it? He won't always know until it gets really plain—and she does it, damn it, she doesn't mean to, but she does it all the time.

But maybe my not wanting to leave the house is a wish too, and maybe that's why things are happening that shouldn't, maybe that's what's putting things out of joint.

God, why am I so confused?

Uulamets' teaching said, uncompromisingly: Write down everything you don't understand, —fool.

He certainly had enough to write tonight, about Missy and the black and white cat, along with, the god forgive him, shapeless, resentful, thoroughly dangerous thoughts about his aunt and uncle . . .

He squeezed his eyes shut a moment, got a breath and concentrated deliberately on writing a simple reminder to himself: Unwish nothing. Start from where you stand and *trust only to specifics*—with a shivery thought toward all the peace they had here, balanced on Eveshka's resolve to forget all too many grim things, his, to grow up without foolish mistakes; and Pyetr's, to be patient with two wizards trying their best to keep their wizardry and their hearts out of trouble.

For most of three years he had found one excuse and the other not to rebuild the old bathhouse, for fear of banniks—for fear of one showing them the will-be and might-be in the life they had chosen here, so long as Eveshka was still so fragile and it was still uncertain whether wizards could really live with each other at all. But Pyetr had kept after the matter till it had begun to seem silly and inconvenient not to have it. So one particularly frozen, icy day he had given in.

But what was I afraid of? he asked himself, pen in hand. What specifically was I afraid of learning?

Of seeing myself alone? Or Pyetr changed?

Eveshka wanted Pyetr to herself, of course a new wife would—but 'Veshka was not just any wife, Pyetr had a right to his friends, too, damned if he should build any small, lonely house up on the hill and live in it in exile.

He had a right to have something to love him.

Was *that* why I wanted the horse?

Everything was perfect, Eveshka said.

At least Eveshka was happy. . . .

Or at least—we got along.

Dammit.

He did not understand his own temper. He did not understand why he had a lump in his throat, but he intended to have no patience with it. He rested his elbow on the table, his chin against his hand, and kept writing, merciless to himself and his notions: *Having a heart is no protection against selfishness in that heart—mine or hers.*

I don't know yet what I should do to help the situation. I don't know how much is my fault, or how much I dare try to help, or even how much I'm imagining because I'm upset. Master Uulamets taught me all he could in the little time he had, but thank the god, Eveshka had more than that, and maybe I ought to listen to her. I understand how to do things, but I don't always know whether I ought to do them, or

*why. She does. I need her to tell me where I'm wrong, I need
her to keep me from her father's mistakes, most of all, because master Uulamets did make them, he made terrible
mistakes . . . and I don't want to be him. Father Sky witness
I don't want to turn into him . . .*

He had taken to the rebuilding of the house with more
enthusiasm than Pyetr could possibly understand, clearing
out Uulamets' cobwebby past, changing the very outlines of
the house Uulamets would recall, pushing master Uulamets
and his wishes and his memories further and further into the
past. The old man, dying, had wanted a boy wizard to know
all he knew; and have all he had, and a boy who desperately
needed that knowledge—fought back as much as he could,
knowing his master's mistakes as well as his virtues.

Old memories still attached to this place . . . chaotic, frag-
mentary recollections, the river when the ferry had been running, travelers on the road; the forest before the great trees
had died: mere curiosities, those—

Excepting memories of a woman in this house, one on
whom Uulamets had sired a daughter he did not, could not
trust.

Excepting his student, Chernevog—also in this house,
who had wanted that gift he had gotten, and tried to steal it.

I wish for bodily comfort, Chernevog had written in his
own book: *I wish for gold—why not?*

*Old Uulamets sitting in his shabby little house, old
Uulamets teaching foolishness, mistaking cowardice for virtue—*

*Uulamets talks about restraint—restraint in a world of
cattle, who know nothing, have no power over their own
wishes, understand nothing that they want—while we live
apart, all for fear of damaging these peasants. Foolishness.*

That was Kavi Chernevog, whose reasoning twisted back
on itself like a snake—whose reasoning was founded on as-
sumptions totally selfish and shortsighted.

Sasha dipped his quill and wrote, mindfully pushing Chernevog out of his thoughts: *The things master Uulamets
wanted me to know, like writing, I have to use, and I don't
forget. But what I didn't use right off just faded, and the
things that just come up less and less, I forget. And don't*

entirely forget, of course, because there's his book to remind me, but there are things that used to be very strong; and now they're just less and less likely to occur to me—I think as much as anything because it's not the house he knew any more and we're not the way he expected us to turn out.

Mostly he'd be surprised, I'm sure he would be. He'd be mad about Eveshka marrying Pyetr, I have no trouble thinking what he'd say about that.

Maybe that's why I keep worrying about them. Myself, Sasha Misurov, I certainly don't want to have bad thoughts about my best friends in the whole world. I think I have to watch that, and stop being upset with Eveshka, because Uulamets really didn't like people much—not since he married his wife, anyway, and after he found out she was after his book: Draga made him distrust people and then Chernevog came along—

Chernevog was his really big mistake.

But what might mine be? Letting myself remember too much? Letting what happened to him make me suspicious?

And selfish. What about the horse? What about me wanting Pyetr to myself again? I'm feeling lonely, and I've got to stop that. There's no good in it. There's not even any sense in it. Uncle's house was awful and nobody ever liked me till Pyetr did. So what do I want to change? Eveshka's mad at me, and she's right: nothing's good that upsets us this much, nothing's good when a wizard starts wanting love from people, it's not fair to them.

I knew that once, when I lived in Vojvoda, I was so good about not wishing things, till I came here and master Uulamets took me up.

But he didn't want my welfare, or even Eveshka's; he wanted his daughter back before she could join Chernevog: he died with this wish I still can feel—

His heart was beating so he could almost hear it. He could imagine the old man *wanting* to go on living—*wanting* his way with them and with his daughter, because Uulamets had held this woods more than a hundred years, and Uulamets was not the kind to give up on anything, least of all his life or his purposes.

Maybe that wish is still going, god, maybe I'm still part

*of it, and it's still going, because I can't not wonder. I won-
der what will become of us, and whether we're right to hold
on to our hearts and whether we'll be good wizards or bad—
and what if I didn't like the answer? There's so much that
could go wrong. Or even what if it was good? How can you
enjoy what you've got if you can see everything that ever
will happen to it?*

*But Uulamets wanted to know what would come after
him. And I'm scared to know even where I'm going. Maybe
that's why a bannik's never come. He used to say, Don't-
know and afraid-to-know always wins a tug of war—*

The pen dried while he was thinking. He dipped it again
in the inkpot and made his crabbed, unskillful letters, writing
so no wish could make him forget what he had thought tonight, hoping to the god that Eveshka was not awake and
eavesdropping.

*So in one sense the horse might not have been a mistake.
I need something to get my mind off all the might-be's I've
been worrying about since we built the bathhouse. When
you start worrying about might-be's, that worry is wishing
about things that aren't even so yet, and then it wishes on
what you've changed, and the god only knows what kind of
damage you could do. I'm afraid master Uulamets did a little of that. So maybe wizards have to be very careful with
banniks. But wizards wish on their guesses, too, and their
guesses might be a lot less reliable than that.*

*It does disturb me that I forgot wishing for Volkhi—but
then, if I had remembered, I'd certainly have done something to stop it; so maybe after all even forgetting was part
of the wish. Maybe I had to forget so it had a chance to come
true, and it's good after all.*

*Things change that can change and wishes only take the
shape they can take. Never wish things against nature or
against time. . . .*

Wish a stone to fly, master Uulamets had said—then beware the whirlwind.

Wish a horse from Vojvoda . . . god, one could imagine
dreadful things that could have brought the horse to them: a
rider falling and breaking his neck, a stable burning—the

whole town of Vojvoda going up in smoke or being put to the sword. . . .

A whole host of might-be's like that—while a draft twisted the lamp-flung shadows at the end of the kitchen; and he thought with a sudden shudder of the worst thing in the world to disturb, that forbidden, thorn-hedged place where leshys watched, patient as the trees themselves. . . .

Something cracked, the whole shelf above him tipped on one end, books and pottery came crashing down onto the table and off it in a thunderous tumble. He scrambled back, the bench scraping as he caught his balance against the table edge and overset the oil-lamp. He grabbed for something to smother the spreading fire, feverishly wished it *out* and flung a towel over it, trembling in fright as the last bits of pottery rocked and rattled to a stop.

The threatened House-thing, roused from sleep, shifted among the cellar supports and made the whole house creak. He heard Pyetr and Eveshka getting out of bed, Pyetr calling out, asking him what was the matter; and he felt Eveshka's frightened wish that the house be safe even before they could cross the room.

He had seen his own house burn. He had been all of five, but he remembered the neighbor saying, The boy's a witch—

The door opened. "What happened?" Pyetr asked, arriving in the kitchen. "Sasha?"

"The shelf fell." Still shaking, he found wit enough to pick up Uulamets' book and Chernevog's, both of which had fallen to the floor.

"The peg must have snapped," Pyetr said, examining the place on the wall where the shelf had been . . . while Eveshka was mopping up the spillage from the lamp and picking up the pieces of pottery. Pyetr said, then, and it rang in Sasha's hearing as if it had come from the bottom of a well: "Just split, that's all. I'll fix it."

Sasha remembered the books in his arms and laid them on the table atop his own, with the most terrible apprehension in his heart. It might be—surely it was what Pyetr had said, old wood, a shelf already old when Uulamets had held the house. There was a perfectly natural explanation, the making of the new wall, the opening of the archway, the weighting of the shelf with three books instead of the one which had stood there so many years; even and especially— the several jars he had added some days ago. The shelves and the counters in the kitchen were virtually the only things left the way they had been—

But everything assumed an unnatural importance tonight. A sense of panic came over him. His impulse was to ask Eveshka whether she felt any disquiet—and he shut that thought down quickly—

Because what he feared was so foolish and so deadly dangerous, even doubting in the least the power of the forest to hold the sorcerer who had killed her.

Doubt had always been Chernevog's weapon.

And Chernevog's book was *here*, on his desk, where he himself had never wanted it. It had sat here among spice cannisters and bits of old fishing tackle, sprigs of drying herbs and a curious bird's-nest . . . this dreadful, dangerous thing, fraught with memories of its own, a hazard that made his heart jump when old wood broke and an overloaded shelf fell.

"It's nothing," he said to Pyetr and Eveshka. "Go back to bed."

He wished them pleasant dreams. He wished—

But Eveshka stopped abruptly in the doorway and looked sternly back at him, with anger, he thought. Certainly disapproval.

What are you thinking? he asked her in that way that wizards might, *wanting* that thought to come into her mind. She scowled at him.

He saw himself, then, constantly reading, a boy hunched gracelessly over her father's book. Uulamets had not meant good at all to Pyetr, no more than he had meant good to Eveshka, nor trusted her—

Nor any woman, nor any daughter, nor any man nor creature that might possibly make alliances against him. It was having his own way that had mattered to Uulamets, it was all that had ever mattered, and he deceived himself if he thought Uulamets meant any one of them any good, if it crossed his purposes.

He had that thought, after she had gone through the doorway after Pyetr, and the bedroom door slammed definitively shut. He shivered when she had gone.

She was not all sixteen in her heart. In some things she was very, very old, and he was not. In some things she had experience and he did not; and he ought to listen to her advice, for reasons not least of which was the fact that Eveshka remembered only what Eveshka had seen, and was sure of what she remembered . . . which was more than he could say.

He was not entirely sure that that was his own thought. But he might have thought that.

What's happened to me? he asked himself in cold fright. What's going on in me, if what she sees is Uulamets?

4

Rain dripped from the brush, drops formed on thorns and hung and fell, splashing onto puddles that reflected other branches.

Water pooling on stone . . .

"He was white as a sheet," Pyetr said, touching Eveshka's shoulder as she lay abed. " 'Veshka, is there anything going on?"

She shut her eyes, said, trying to think of nothing and not to wish at all, even for peace in the house: "No. He's still upset about the horse, that's all."

Gray sky and branches. Iron-gray stone, iron-gray trees, and rain . . .

Rain running down the stone, to the earth, down to a shallow stream, and the stream flowing into the river, dark water, deep and cold . . . wolves drank from that spring, and looked at her with yellow eyes . . .

"I'm worried about him, 'Veshka."

"It's his problem. He can handle it. Just go to sleep."

He rubbed her shoulder, pulled the quilts up higher. She stared into the dark, fists clenched, thinking about the books, the boy sitting and reading by the hour, believing all the same damned things her father had believed, when they were only guesses the same as Kavi Chernevog's. Guesses were all anyone had to go on, because a wizard only touched the magical world, he did not live in it: he lived above the surface and tried to make rules for what went on in that place only creatures like Babi could get to.

Things came out of that place, too. She had seen them.

38

She had dealt with things whose thinking flailed this way and that of what a living soul called reason.

River flowing southward, through a forest of gray branches, dripping rain.

She did not want to dream of water, god, she did not want to dream tonight. . . .

Sasha lay watching the lamplight on his bedroom ceiling, afraid to blow the lamp out, afraid to sleep, for fear of what might come into his dreams, or, worse, go out of them—

Damn, a shelf dropped, that was all. A fool loaded the shelf up with books, a peg had gotten brittle over the years, and quite naturally it just—broke.

But two very considerable wizards had wished this house sound while they were sanding and polishing and waxing and building: they had as a matter of course wished things not to break or go wrong, and if anything did break, if something untoward happened to the household, from Volkhi to the broken peg—it seemed more than an omen, it seemed a symptom of things failing.

How did one, even days ago, put a new load on a shelf and not quite naturally hope it to stay up? From him, in the absence of someone else's wish to the contrary, that should have been enough. And certainly he wished himself well, and not to be bashed on the shoulder by falling books, or to have his fingers burned with a lamp-spill, god, he *hated* fire!

One thing and another since Volkhi had arrived had frightened him out of all proportion to the events, certainly making his behavior no wiser and his wishes no better aimed: he knew that, and he knew he might be contributing to the problem: he was sure at least he was not thinking clearly, and Uulamets' memories spilled up at random tonight, the river, the house, Eveshka in her childhood, the woods when the old trees on the river shore were alive, all mixed with memories of The Cockerel, aunt Ilenka, uncle Fedya, the old lady next door—the one who had called him a witch . . .

That so-named wizard in Vojvoda, a smelly old man his uncle had taken him to, the way folk took children suspected of wizardry, to apprentice them to someone who might make them safe and useful: but that old man had refused to take him, saying he had no gift, he was only unlucky. Then the old fake had sold uncle Fedya an expensive spell for that un-luckiness, to protect the roof that sheltered him.

He tried not to be angry tonight with that old liar, or with uncle Fedya. Wish no harm, Uulamets had said, above all, wish no harm; but Uulamets' anger kept turning around his own, Uulamets' anger at his own teacher, Uulamets' anger at his wife, at his daughter, at his wife's lover, his student Kavi Chernevog—

Like trying to rest in a bed full of snakes, Sasha thought distressedly, all the while guessing which one was dangerous.

He might perhaps talk to Pyetr: they had been able to talk straightforwardly about the most difficult things, and Pyetr being wiser in the world at large sometimes had very good instincts for right answers.

But how could he ask Pyetr to keep confidences from Ev-eshka, if it was about magic, if Eveshka might well feel any upset in him and want to know why?

He rolled onto his side and stared at the pattern in the boards of the wall, trying not to think things like that or entertain suspicions: a wizard was so liable to wish com-pletely crazy things—as apt to self-delusion as not, even about what his interests really were, and having an old man's mem-ories tumbling around in his head, mixing with his own . . .

In Vojvoda, patrons in The Cockerel had looked askance at him: That's the witch listening, they would say, nudging each other with their elbows. Be careful what you say . . .

Or the baker's daughters, whispering to each other in the corner, Don't look in his eyes, he can't bewitch you if you don't look in his eyes—

Aunt Ilenka, when a dish broke: I know who's the jinx around here. . . .

Maybe there was truth in that, after all.

Certainly Eveshka wanted what she thought was right for Pyetr: that was one constancy he could believe in; that was, perhaps, part of the trouble with all of them. And perhaps, he reasoned, if he could only retrace not only the business with the horse, but a number of small quarrels, and recover the kind of peace with Eveshka he had had at first, if he only could get her to trust him and if he could avoid making some other foolish, selfish mistake to make her angry with him, Eveshka knew him in ways even Pyetr did not—being a wizard and knowing in her very bones what he meant when he said certain things, which Pyetr might well hear completely differently.

If, he thought, if he could get Eveshka to sit down and listen to him, really listen, just once, and listen—if that was truly what she was worried about—as if it was only himself who was talking to her, and nothing to do with her father and his advice . . .

If, please the god, he could know that himself, and be sure his thoughts had no one else's wish behind them—including hers.

He lay abed until the birds nesting in the eaves began to stir, then quietly got up, built up the fire from last night's coals and started breakfast with as little noise as possible, a special breakfast, as he intended, cakes of the sort aunt Ilenka had used to make, the best flour, sweet dried berries. . . .

Sun rising beyond the branches, dew gathering on thorns—

Reddening with the dawn—

He chased meandering, chaotic thoughts away with the soft rattle of the spoon against the bowl, one of Uulamets' wooden ones, pinch of spice, pinch of salt, a recipe against unwanted memories . . . spice and salt and grain they got from a freeholder downriver, an old man who had trouble, Pyetr said, in recalling it was no longer Chernevog or Uulamets living in the woods upriver—an old man who wanted mushrooms, simples, medicines for a cough and a good wish or two in the bargain, which Sasha gave whenever he thought of it.

So much the world knew of their doings: the old man felt safe from wizards and their doings, and had no notion what had happened up here in the woods, except herbs grew in the woods again.

That was all it meant, all that they had ever done, wizards had changed, the dreadful rusalka was gone, and herbs helped an old man's cough.

41

River water, dark and deep . . . Eveshka's ghost drifting above the waves, part of them . . .

Eveshka had so much skill with growing things, she always had had: she could wish a garden to perfection, protect the seeds they planted, the creatures that ventured back into this woods. She had all this love of life—even when foxes by their nature preyed on rabbits and on fieldmice. And she was wise about nature. He got attached to the mouse, he thought about foxes, and he wanted it safe—because it was one particular mouse. But Eveshka had said to him, quite soberly, *If you do that, he won't be free.*

He thought about that. He told himself he should have listened to Eveshka long since, that she had given him good advice, over all, much of which counseled him plainly to want as little as possible and to ignore her father.

He heard voices from the bedroom, people he loved, people who did truly, in differing degrees and to their own capabilities, love him: "Tie that, will you, Pyetr?"

We'll be all right, he had argued with Uulamets. *We'll manage; Pyetr can make the difference for us, because neither of us would ever hurt him.*

To which Uulamets' ghostly voice still said: *Fools.*

Fool, Uulamets whispered again, plain as plain, while he was sitting on the hearth, stirring up the cakes and heating up the griddle. It was never Uulamets' advice that had brought them to live under one roof. In very fact, if one thought honestly about it, it was Chernevog who had thought wizards could live in the company of other folk. Chernevog had argued that a wizard could use wealth, rule cities—*a wizard can do more good in the world,* Chernevog had written in his youth, *than tsars can ever do; and work far less harm than tsars have ever done.*

But at the very time Chernevog had been writing that, he had been deeply under the spell of Uulamets' wife: had become, boy that he had been, Draga's student and very soon after that her lover—

Draga ate him alive, Uulamets had said when he had found out.

Uulamets had written: *Two people can't have the same interests. They can't have the same wishes, not a man and*

*his wife, not a father and his daughter—not a teacher and
his student.*

And the end of Chernevog's book said: *Generations of
cattle. . . .*

"Up early?" Pyetr hailed him, opening the door beside the
fireplace. Sasha rocked in startlement and spilled a big splash
of batter off the griddle, making the fire throw ash.

"Thinking," Sasha said, rising, dusting ash off his knees
as Eveshka followed Pyetr into the kitchen. "Breakfast is almost ready."

"God," Eveshka said, "how many berries did you put in
those cakes?"

"A fistful." Eveshka had her ways in the kitchen, her very
precise ways, and he was instantly concerned about the things
he had not yet cleared from the counter, wanting no offense,
god, no quarrel in the house this morning.

Pyetr said, sharply, "They're just *fine*, Eveshka."

"It's quite all right," Sasha began to protest, in Eveshka's
defense; but Eveshka was already stacking the spice-pots and
the berry-cannister back the way she wanted them, rearrang-
ing things he had disarranged, saying, "God, Sasha, you must
have used half the stores. Let a man in the kitchen—"

"For the god's sake, Eveshka!" Pyetr cried, turning around;
and Sasha quickly said, handing Pyetr the spatula: "Pyetr,
watch those, will you?" The shelf Eveshka wanted the berries
on was too high for her convenience: Sasha hurried over and
put them up himself.

"Thank you," she said quite pleasantly, and smiled at
him, seeming not to have noticed any upset in her wake,
perfectly cheerful and intending to put her kitchen and both
of them in the order she liked, too.

Which left him standing there numb, wondering if he
were the one losing his senses. Of course he could talk to
Eveshka, he talked about a great number of things every day
with Eveshka, they worked together to make their medicines
and do simple householder things that Pyetr, not having
grown up doing an aunt's various chores, had no notion how
to do.

He was Eveshka's friend, dammit, he trusted her; he did
not know why he had suddenly begun to fear dealing with

her, or how he had ever started thinking he could not make her understand his concerns.

Of course she would give him good advice. He had just failed to listen to it, since it mostly said, Do nothing; stop worrying over things; let things take their own course. He found that very hard to do.

She said, mercifully shoving plates into his hands: "Set the table."

He did that, while Pyetr started to turn the cakes, but Pyetr tended to miss his mark and sometimes even the griddle. Eveshka shooed him to the table and took over *her* fire and *her* hearth, thank you, bidding the two of them make tea, do something useful this morning and stay out from underfoot.

Pyetr gave him an apologetic look, a shake of his head, as glum as Sasha had seen him in months.

Which was not at all what he wanted, if he dared wish anything at all without upsetting the house.

"God," he said to Pyetr, "it's all right, it's her kitchen, don't worry about it, Pyetr. Please."

Pyetr gave him a second distressed look.

Sasha bit his lip till it took his mind off wishing, while the domovoi made the timbers creak under the floor. He poured the tea and Eveshka slipped the cakes onto their plates. "They do smell wonderful," she said brightly, a peace offering to one or the other of them—now that she had her way, Sasha thought; and sternly chided himself not to be so contrary-minded.

We fight about things like that, we fight about cakes, but that's not what we really fight about, it's never what we should fight about so we can ever really settle things. She scolds Pyetr about her kitchen, but that doesn't matter to him—nothing like that matters to him, he really is an awful cook. It's when she does it to me that bothers him, and she knows that, absolutely she does. Why does she do that?

Charred timbers against gray sky. Chernevog's house. Rain washing half-burned beams. . . .

"Sasha?"

He blinked, his heart skipping a beat, realized she had sat

down and said something about the honey in front of him. "Excuse me," he said, and pushed it into her reach.

She put honey on her cakes and passed it to Pyetr, who wondered whether it was the new pot or the old—

God, Sasha thought, what's the matter with me?

Is it my doing?

"Isn't it?" Pyetr asked him about something, he had no idea what. He became aware of Eveshka and Pyetr both looking at him, aware of Eveshka wishing him to get his wits about him, not to upset Pyetr with his foolishness.

"Did you get any sleep last night?" Pyetr asked.

Sasha took a breath, trying to recollect what the two of them had been saying most recently, mumbled, "Some."

"Liar. Eveshka, —" Pyetr laid his hand flat on the table. "Sasha. Both of you. Answer me, a simple question: do we send the horse back or not?"

"No," Eveshka said firmly.

"Sasha?" Pyetr asked.

"No," Sasha said, because it was too late for any such thing.

Pyetr just stared at one and the other of them, as if he was sure it was conspiracy.

"It's done," Eveshka said. "It's all right, Pyetr. Done's done. Nothing's wrong. Believe me, nothing's wrong."

Another moment of silence. "God," Pyetr said.

"It's all right," Sasha said earnestly. "It really is, Pyetr. We'll take care of it, I promise you. There's no chance of anybody coming after him, nobody in his right mind would come in here looking for him, would they? We'll make a stable shed, put up a solid pen, we'll be sure he stays out of Eveshka's garden . . ."

"There's nothing to worry about," Eveshka said, got up, walked around the end of the table and kissed Pyetr on the forehead. Kissed him twice more—not on the forehead. "No, Babi's just sulking, just jealous. He'll get over it."

Sasha saw Pyetr's little hesitation, then, the little frown before Pyetr said, as smoothly as if he *had* said aloud what Eveshka had just answered, "Well, dammit, still, it's not like him to take off this long."

Maybe she answered Pyetr then without a word, too, pressing some point about her privileges with him. Sasha found distraction in his plate, in the reflection of firelight on gold. Their plates, spoils of Chernevog, were mostly gold, the platter silver, with jewels, but the teacups they used at breakfast were the old ones, Uulamets' plain pottery . . .

His had a crack which Uulamets' casual wish probably still kept from breaking.

All these years.

Sasha murmured, getting up as Eveshka started taking the dishes away: "I'll help you clean up."

Pyetr caught his arm. "Too much thinking going on here. Forget the dishes. Let's see if there's a carrot left, see if the rascal got out last night. Both of you. —Veshka? Come on. It'll do everybody good."

"I've notes to make," Eveshka said, over a clatter of plates in the washing pan. "Too many changes yesterday. It's all right, go on, go on, off with you."

Pyetr looked at Sasha.

"Later I will," Sasha said, ducking his head, gathering up the teacups, sure that he had to pursue what he had started with Eveshka. Now. It was all getting too strange and felt too unreasonable.

"Later. Later. God. —You spend too much time with that damn book, boy." Pyetr was put out with him: he was put out with both of them, with reason, Sasha was sure. Pyetr said, again: "Come on. Clear the cobwebs out of your thinking. Get your hands on a horse again. It'll do you good."

Volkhi muddled his thinking even without his touching him. "I can't," Sasha said unhappily, to which Pyetr flung up his hands and said to Eveshka: "You reason with him."

Eveshka only looked back over her shoulder with a sober, enigmatic: "Don't you know? You can't argue with him."

"God," Pyetr said, "I'm going to talk to my horse. Books make you crazy, you know." A motion at his head. "Thinking all those little crooked marks mean real things, that's not sane, you know." He waved the same hand toward the front door. "Out there is real. Don't lose track of that."

"Don't forget your coat," Eveshka said.

"I don't need a coat. I plan to work. Like honest, ordinary

folk. It's sit-abouts that need coats on a day like this." Pyetr took the bucket they had put the honeyed grain in, opened the door on daylight, went back to take a remainder of last night's honey-cakes, and went back a third time to pick up the vodka jug from off the kitchen counter. "Bribes," he explained. "The whole world works on sufficient bribes."

"Don't trample the garden!" Eveshka called out to him.

Pyetr made a face, swept his cap off the peg, gathered up his bucket from beside the door, the vodka jug in the other hand, and pulled the door to behind him with his foot.

Sasha started dipping water into the pan to wash the dishes. Eveshka said not a word to him, wished him nothing.

Sasha said, aloud, "I didn't sleep at all last night. Eveshka, I keep thinking something's wrong."

"Let's not talk about it. Done's done. It's all right."

"It's not about the horse. It's about us fighting."

"We don't fight."

"We're fighting now."

"I'm not fighting. I don't know what you're doing, but I certainly don't intend to fight." Eveshka went back to the fireplace after the griddle, then took a cloth, got down on her hands and knees and started cleaning up the ash he had gotten on her floor.

"Let me do that."

"I'm perfectly fine. Everything's perfectly fine. I'm not mad, dammit!"

"Listen to me." He got down on his knees and took the cloth away from her, but she would not look at him. She got up and went away to the counter, so he scrubbed the boards and the stone where the ash had landed, and got up to hang the rag on an empty peg to dry.

Stop, she wished him, so violently he looked at her. "Not with the good ones," she said. "Hang it by the fire. I'll get it later."

He hung the offending rag where she wanted it, on the spare pothook, anxious to keep the peace any way he could. Aunt Ilenka had been that way about her kitchen. One supposed it came with marriage.

He did not want to think that, either. Eveshka eavesdropped; she was doing it now, he felt it plain as plain. She knew he felt it and wished he would go outside with Pyetr and leave her be.

"I think," he said aloud, standing his ground, "I think our not getting a bannik must have been my fault. I think with what happened yesterday—we need one, badly, and we ought to try. But I don't want to be wishing it on my own, I don't want to be wishing things about the house that you don't want."

"What does a bannik have to do with anything? Or with the horse? That's *done*, that's all. We don't need anything else muddying the waters. Just stop worrying about it, Sasha!"

"It might stop things we haven't done yet. It might tell us—"

"It won't."

"It might stop things from going wrong."

"Who said they were going wrong?"

"They're not going exactly right, are they?"

"Banniks don't like wizards. They don't talk, any more than Babi, any more than the domovoi: they show you things, and they never make sense."

"But if we had the least idea where what we're wishing might take us—"

"It never helps. We change things, we're constantly changing things and you can't tell, you can't tell anything by what they say and *they* don't like it. Papa used to say." Every time Eveshka mentioned her father she would frown guardedly and look at him as if she were looking for echoes. "And we don't need it."

"I still think—"

"Our bannik didn't help us. I didn't see what was going to happen to me. We didn't see anything about Kavi Chernevog." She never talked about her dying. She scrubbed furiously at the last dish, bit her lip and said, "I'm sure I'll like the horse. If it makes Pyetr happy, I'm happy."

She hardly looked happy. Sasha said: "Is there some reason not?"

"What?"

"About the bannik. Is there some reason not to want one?"

"It doesn't help. It didn't help, I'm telling you! Why don't you go help Pyetr?"

"Eveshka. Why wouldn't you want it here?"

"For the god's sake why should I care? Why should I care if we do or if we don't? What's that to do with anything?"

"Things just aren't right," he said, thinking of the shelf, thinking of—

—the stability of everything. Everything in balance. Chernevog, in the leshys' keeping; Uulamets; all the hundreds of wishes that might be loose about this place and all the dangers for as long as they lived and worked magic here.

"Things have been perfectly right," she said, drying the bowl. "Things have been perfectly right for years before this, and what you did is done, and there's not a thing we can do that doesn't make a bigger thing of it than it is, so just let it be, Sasha Vasilyevitch, for the god's sake, just forget about it, you're the one who's making an argument out of it."

"I want your help."

"If you want a bannik, if you want a horse and a pig and a goat besides, god, I'm sure I don't care. It's your house."

"It's not my house."

"I'm sure papa intended it."

"Your father gave me the book. Nothing else."

A spoon clattered onto the counter. "Papa gave you a lot else."

There was long silence.

"Not as much as you imagine," he said. He had been wanting to say it for years. He had tried to say it that way for years. But it fell short, he saw the set of her chin.

"You don't know what I imagine."

"Eveshka," he said, treading further and further onto dangerous ground, "Eveshka, you don't want me here, do you? Not really."

"I never said I didn't want you here. I don't want you here *now*, that's all, I don't want you in my kitchen and I don't want to talk about that damned horse. I'm sick of talking about the horse!"

"You're mad at me."

"I'm not mad at you!" She flung down the dishtowel. "You're being stupid, Sasha Vasilyevitch, I don't know what put this idea of a bannik into your head, but you're acting the fool—you've been acting the fool for a month, and I wish you'd stop it! If you want a bannik, wish up a bannik, wish up whatever you like."

"That's what I'm worried about," he said. He wanted her to know he was confused, and scared, because he was not her father, he was not even sure he knew what her father would have wanted except to keep them out from under the same roof, and he did not even know if it was his idea to leave the house and live elsewhere or if it was Uulamets'.

That set Eveshka off her balance. She wanted him outside, wanted him to quit bothering her with his wishes and his worries, forbade him to talk about building another house, wanted him not to upset Pyetr with his ideas and never to talk to her about her father—wanted three things and four all at the same time, and stopped wishing at all, folding her arms tightly and biting her lips before something else escaped her.

"I'm inconvenient," Sasha said carefully, "and even if none of us wants that to be true, it is, I know it is. It's very hard to get along just with Pyetr—"

"I've no trouble getting along with Pyetr!"

"But I do," he said, wishing she would be honest. "At least enough, and I've lived in town with people . . ."

"I'm not a fool! Don't treat me like one!"

"I know you're not."

"I'm tired of hearing about that damned horse! I don't want to want anything, I just want peace—"

She stopped herself and bit her lip, and hoped that wish desperately to safety. He tried to help.

"Please."

"—peace with all of us," she said firmly. "Leave it at that."

"Eveshka, I'm not sure about things, I'm not sure about what we're doing."

"Leave it alone!" Eveshka said. She turned away from him and started straightening up the counter.

He said, "Will you help me find a bannik?"

"I don't see why. I don't see why it matters, I don't see how it can stop you from anything you want to do. Certainly nothing else does."

"That's not fair," he said.

"What isn't fair?"

"You're very strong." He knew it would make her mad: every time he told her she was stronger than she knew it made her mad, but he intended she think about that. "You can do anything you really want in this house, you know that."

She wanted him not to say that. Her mouth made a straight, unhappy line.

"It's true," he said. "You'd probably be stronger than I am if you really wanted something."

"That's papa's damned nonsense. I'll tell you what I have my mind made up to: I don't want to be stronger than you, I don't want to be stronger than anybody, and that's finished, then, isn't it? I have everything I've ever wanted to have, and there's nothing else I need or want, Sasha Vasilyevitch, which is more sense than Kavi had, and between you and me, more sense than my father had! If you want a bannik, fetch one. I'm sure I'm not standing in your way!"

"Don't you want to know where we're going? At least don't you want to know where our wishes are taking us?"

Eveshka scowled at him. No, she did not. That was clear.

Maybe he should go outside with Pyetr, find something hard to do, like splitting wood, something that gave him little time to think, but he was so damned scared of what was going on in the house—

Lack of sleep, he thought.

I want all I love to be safe?

But that's not responsible, any more than Eveshka wishing peace. The dead can be at peace. The dead can be safe.

She said, "It's nonsense, anyway, my wanting you to leave. I don't know why you'd think that—I certainly don't want it."

"I hope not," he said, and dared not wish anything else, like being welcome in the house for his own sake and not only Pyetr's. He kept thinking about the shelf falling. He kept thinking about the fight they were having, that he had above all not meant to have. He thought of burned timbers, and stood there tongue-tied, not even able to agree with her enough to wish their safety or their peace in the house.

So he went quietly to his books, and left Eveshka to her own, hoping desperately for banniks and foresight.

5

There was no mayhem in the garden, the rails had held, and Volkhi was in a frivolous mood this bright morning, trotting around his small pen and kicking up his heels.

There was also, Pyetr had a very strong feeling by now, another, invisible, and, since yesterday, very put-upon observer.

"Come on," he said, setting the piece of cake down on a stray bit of shingle. "Honey-cake, Babi."

There was no answer. There was, however, when he looked around, at least the ghostly impression of two reproachful dark eyes in the air at his left.

And, having had experience of, as his detractors would agree, every tavern keeper's daughter in Vojvoda, he knew it was not a good idea to make any great amount of fuss over Volkhi while Babi was feeling slighted.

So he stood up, unstopped the jug and poured a little vodka into empty air.

Not at all strange to say, the vodka never hit the ground.

There were very definitely eyes.

Then the honey-cake disappeared, and one could see the least suggestion of a black button nose and a mouth.

So Babi got the vodka, Babi got fussed over, Babi got his invisible back scratched, and little by little Babi became a blacker and more substantial shadow in the air, a suspicious Babi, a most put-upon and grumpy Babi—

A most canny and still dutiful Babi, one suspected, who had been watching the horse very carefully since yesterday. Being a Yard-thing and a keeper of livestock at least by ancient habit, Babi had only to be coddled a little and coaxed a little, and convinced things were still in approvable order in his yard—adding, of course, reassurances of his great importance.

And lo and not completely surprising, a mostly visible Babi wound up sitting by Pyetr's feet once he had given Volkhi his grain and sat down to watch him eat it.

"You know," Pyetr said, pouring another dash of vodka which Babi did not let reach the ground, "the yard's looking quite respectable these days, isn't it? It's got a garden, it's got a much larger, *much* finer house, and all, and now it's got a horse to look after, probably a stable this year—it's a very good job you're doing."

Much of this. Babi grew more visible and more cheerful, and eventually Babi, a quite tipsy and much happier Babi, trotted round the perimeters of their makeshift fence—a very good thing, Pyetr understood from Sasha, who knew all about such matters, to have Babi's approval of that fence, a Yard-thing having a certain magic of his own.

And magic, he had found, could have its uses around the house. Else the corner-posts would be far worse than they were.

So by midmorning, Babi was sitting sunning himself, if Yard-things indeed felt the sun, on the rail of the pen, content to watch him fuss with Volkhi. Not a sign from Eveshka or Sasha, to be sure: one supposed they were at the books again, most probably at the books again.

Volkhi would get the boy, Pyetr was quite sure of that. Volkhi would get him sooner or later, and Pyetr intended just to let the matter go along as it would: the stableboy who had wished up the horse in the first place was certainly not going to resist temptation forever; and the sun and the wind would put a little color into the boy's face, absolutely it would.

A tight straw-bound bundle of broom stalks made a fair currycomb, and Volkhi took the attention for his due, always quite the glutton for pleasure. Certainly someone had taken good care of him: there was no fault to find with his feet nor the condition of his coat, but the old lad had certainly not unlearned all his scoundrelly tricks—such as backing up on a man trying to comb his tail, then looking around with a soft, innocent eye to wonder whether that was indeed his master's foot he had almost trod on.

Not the perfect horse, not at least where it regarded manners, but he was certainly the handsomest thing Pyetr Kochevikov had ever owned in his life; and sure of foot and willing to go wherever a good rider took him.

"No tack," he chided Volkhi. "Lad, while you were making off with yourself, you might have been considerate enough to have snitched a saddle, or at least a bridle."

Another look of wise innocence over Volkhi's shoulder, a mostly obscured dark eye.

"I suppose," Pyetr conceded, "you did the best you could."

So he went and got a bit of rope in the storage-shed, and sat down in the sunlight beside the pen to braid a sort of bridle, which decidedly drew Babi's interest.

And when he had his makeshift bridle and put it on Volkhi, and when he swung up onto a horse's back for the first time in three years, Babi was perched up on a rail to watch, chin on manlike hands.

But there was no point to riding circles around a pen on a day like this, so Pyetr leaned over, let the top bar drop, circled away and jumped Volkhi over the lower rail, not having forgotten his seat after all.

He was quite pleased with himself. He rode Volkhi a wide circle in the back and side of the yard, then rode around to the front of the house and stopped in front of the porch, looking, he was quite sure, a very fine figure on Volkhi's back.

" 'Veshka, Sasha!" he called up to the house, "I'm for a turn up and down the road!"

The door opened. The shutters of the kitchen window moved. Eveshka appeared in the doorway looking at him.

"Go for a ride?" Pyetr said and, realizing it quite possible Eveshka had never been on a horse, held out his hand for encouragement. " 'Veshka, come on. I'll take you up. Nothing fast at all. It's absolutely safe."

She stepped back a pace, definite dislike. "I've work to do."

"Oh, 'Veshka, come on, just down the road and back."

Eveshka shook her head, frowning, and stepped back entirely within the doorway. "You," she admonished him, "be careful."

"Sasha?" he said then, looking to the window where Sasha was. "Want to see how he goes? Take a turn on him yourself?" Bribes again. It was the highest he had. He was sure it would win.

But: "I've work," Sasha said. "Or I would."

"Work can wait."

"Maybe tomorrow," Sasha said.

"Stick-in-the-muds," Pyetr said. Sasha puzzled him. He turned Volkhi full about, giving them both a chance to change their minds.

But Sasha did not. Certainly Eveshka would not. Both of them, he was sure, were using a great deal of ink this morning searching after answers that would make sense to wizards—all for a stray horse, for the god's sake, which only proved how far the boy had gone down the old man's track. And Eveshka—the god knew she was difficult to win.

But give it time. Sooner or later, he thought, he would get them.

For himself it was sedately out the front gate and sedately down the ghost of a road that ran into the dead woods, with Volkhi all to himself, and nobody calling after him Be careful, Pyetr, don't take chances, Pyetr, —

He kept it quite tame until he was out of sight of the house.

Eveshka was worried when she shut the door; and wished something quite strongly, Pyetr's safety, Sasha was sure, against the unknown dangers of horses.

"Babi was with him," Sasha said.

Eveshka only shook her head.

"Pyetr won't fall off," he said. "Saddle or no saddle, I've seen him do really crazy things—"

This seemed not to reassure Eveshka at all, so Sasha instantly changed his mind about telling Eveshka the story about Pyetr and aunt Ilenka's front porch, or how Volkhi had broken the butter churn. He amended it quickly: "But it only looks that way: he really does know what he's doing."

"I don't trust that creature," Eveshka muttered, and went back into her own room, to her own studies.

Sasha was not up to arguments at the moment, with a dozen things from his book and Uulamets' all floating about in his head. He went back to the kitchen table, sat down and turned the pages one after the other, looking—

—looking for reconciliations.

He wrote, *Eveshka and I like each other as well as two wizards can. We want no harm to each other and certainly we want things for Pyetr's good: but that's very tangled, unless we want the same thing in exactly the same way. One never dares be too specific in that kind of wish.*

Could Eveshka's wish for Pyetr's welfare harm me?

Only if—

He stopped writing, feeling a slight chill in the air, a stray wish, perhaps.

He went on: *—I threatened Pyetr, and if that were ever the case I'd certainly want her to—*

To do what?

The answer seemed overwhelmingly dangerous. Everything did. Anything he could set down could have consequences.

Rain on stone . . .

Wind shaking branches . . .

Eveshka dipped her pen and wrote: *The dreams don't stop. Papa always said I was scatter-witted. But papa didn't hear the river in his sleep—*

If wishing could make me someone else's daughter, then I would. If it were only me, alone, I'd wish I had no gift and maybe that would stop it: papa always said that was possible. Maybe if I believed that absolutely that we'd always be safe here, that would be the spell papa always said a wizard could cast once in his life, the spell that can't be broken—

Her heart jumped, her hand moved the pen against the flow: ink flew across the page, a spatter like blood—

He heard Eveshka push a bench back in the other room, heard her running across the floor. She flung the bedroom door open and stood looking at him, in a hush in which the whole woods seemed to participate.

"Sasha?" she said.

He pushed his bench back, rose with the feeling of a terrible presence standing behind him—no, farther away, beyond the wall, from a very precise spot at the far side of the yard—a bed of stones—

"The bathhouse!" Sasha exclaimed, "the bannik!" as he headed for the door. He banged it wide on his way out onto the wooden walk-up, with Eveshka crying: "Wait! Wait!" and racing behind him to the yard.

But when they had gotten to the ground she rushed past him and ran, braids flying, out the front gate into the road, calling out, "Pyetr!" Terror was swirling about the yard behind them, Eveshka's wild apprehensions flying out into the woods far and wide, wanting Pyetr *back* here now, within her protection, immediately—

"Eveshka!" Sasha shouted after her, and ran as far as the hedge himself. "Eveshka! Wait! We don't know what we're changing, you could *make* something happen, don't call him back!"

She hesitated in the weeds of the lane, still gazing in the direction Pyetr must have gone; and all Sasha could think of was Eveshka's summons going out, out into uncertainties, agitating everything that was hitherto stable. She clenched her hands and called again, with a silent, panicked force. "God, I can't find him! I can't find anything out there, it's all gone!"

" 'Veshka! If you don't know, for the god's sake, don't wish! We don't know what we're calling him into! Come back here!"

She stood with fists clenched, cast an anguished look down the way Pyetr had gone, then came running back through the gate, pale of face and breathless, falling in beside him as he turned and struck out for the bathhouse.

"I can't find him," Eveshka muttered as they went. "I

want to know where he is, dammit, and I don't know. I don't know where Babi is, I don't know where the leshys are—"

"That's not unusual," he said. He could feel the malaise too, silence like a smothering snow settled over the house and yard, in which there was no sense of any presence but that cold feeling from the bathhouse. He was tempted to try a summoning himself, to see if it was his own apprehensions stopping her; but unease was growing in him with every stride he made, and he was more and more convinced he did not want Pyetr near this thing, did not want any recklessness near this thing. Danger, he kept feeling: danger both in doing and not doing, danger in every word they spoke and every question they asked at this point . . .

"Sasha, this thing doesn't feel right, dammit, nothing feels right—"

"Don't swear! And don't wish anything. We don't know there's any trouble at all where Pyetr is, it could all be here and we could wish him right back into it."

"It *won't* be to us, use your head, Sasha! It doesn't have to come at us, Pyetr's out there alone, he's always the one anything would go for."

"He's got Babi. He's got Misighi if he gets in any real trouble. You know they're the hardest thing to feel, even if they don't mind talking to us. Just calm down, let's see what we're dealing with."

She was frightening both of them, anxieties flying back and forth between them as they reached the bathhouse. She flinched from his hand on her arm, wanted him to stop interfering with her, in all respects—and she was so strong in her fright, so terribly, dangerously strong—

"Calm down!" he begged her, catching her hand.

Calm won suddenly, a quick clasp of fingers, a meeting of eyes at the bathhouse door. "I know my question," she said on a breath, thinking determinedly of Pyetr, and pulled the door open.

The presence inside retreated into shadows on a gust of wind, an oppressive dread slipping farther and farther from their hold, circling around the edges of their magic. It whispered, it muttered, it racketed suddenly about the walls and shrieked at them.

"It's not ours!" Eveshka cried, collided with Sasha in the doorway and caught his arm. "It's not the one I know—look out!"

Sasha pushed her behind him, demanding of it to know why it retreated from them, wanting to see with his own eyes the shadow that moved around the walls, a crooked shape that might have been a boy and might have been something far less savory, leaping with blinding quickness from bench to bench to firepit.

It hissed at him. It lunged for him with long-nailed fingers and raked his arm: Sasha gasped and jumped back with the impression of wild eyes and spiky hair and a feeling of cold and damp—

And the most terrible premonition about a place of thorns and branches.

6

✠ ✠ ✠ ✠ Very little was left of the old road: it was getting increasingly overgrown, most confused where the fall of old trees had let in the sun, stretches rife with new bracken, saplings as apt to grow in the roadway as in the woods about. There were the occasional deadfalls, there were washes and slips where the death of trees had let streams run unchecked—rough ground and unpredictable, and Pyetr had had every notion of taking it easy on himself and on Volkhi this first outing, simply seeing, sedately and sanely, how Volkhi had fared these last several years.

But Volkhi's traveling stride, sure-footed and sensible, ate up the distances, made little of the obstacles, and in the shadowed places, the barren ground beneath the old trees, Volkhi threw his head and danced, never minding Babi turning up in his path—actually not odd at all, Pyetr thought, reckoning that a horse probably knew a dvorovoi when it smelled one. Babi skipped and trotted and panted along quite briskly, crossed right under Volkhi's feet, and Volkhi never made but a skip and a kick like a colt.

Pyetr laughed aloud, dusted Volkhi's rump with his cap, jumped him over an old log and, Volkhi taking it into his head just then to race, ran Babi a wild course for a long stretch down the old road—but Babi cheated: Babi kept popping up just ahead of them.

Sweet oils and pine, bay for foreseeing: it was not what one burned so much as the thought one put into it, master Uulamets would say. They filled the bathhouse with aromatic

61

smoke and steam: they flung herbs into the small stone furnace and wished for visions in the firelit dark.

"Bannik," Sasha asked it, most respectfully, "is there a danger to anyone of this household?"

"Not is!" Eveshka said. "It only knows the future. Bannik, excuse us and show us the fireside this evening."

But they had nothing from the bannik beyond that first vision, only the creak and pop of settling timbers, ask though they would, however politely and respectfully.

Not their bannik, Eveshka had said: and Sasha was sure it was not, not the Old Man of the Bath of Eveshka's childhood, not even the angry creature that had fled from Uulamets, but something much darker—something which, so far as Sasha had seen it, resembled nothing so much as a ragged, feral child—

With claws that had left bleeding scratches on his arm.

"Ours never had eyes like that," Eveshka said, hugging her arms about her as she paced the circuit of the bathhouse. "Ours never attacked anyone, it never made sounds at all, it was just this little old man who sometimes left footprints in the snow—especially when we left him vodka, and he'd get drunk, and you'd go into the bathhouse and he'd sit in the corner and give you visions—but they never made sense. They never were about anything important. This thing—"

"I'll get the vodka jug," Sasha said, willing to try anything, and opened the door and hesitated in sudden doubt of Eveshka's safety.

"I'll be all right!" Eveshka said, and waved him out. "Go! Let's just for the god's sake do something, shall we?"

He wished *he* knew why Pyetr was not back. He wished—

He ran out into the daylight and got the vodka jug from where he was sure Pyetr had left it, beside Volkhi's pen, and raced, breathless, back to the bathhouse and inside.

Eveshka stood waiting, arms folded. "Nothing," she whispered to his anxious look, as he shut the door again. "God, just let's get it to show us whatever it wants to show us . . ."

He unstopped the jug, splashed a generous dash into the furnace along with the bay and the pine bark and the moss. Fire roared back into his face, dazzled him with light—

62

—

Drops falling from thorns, splashing into water . . .

Droplets red and spreading in puddles on the stones . . .

"Where's Pyetr?" Eveshka cried, wishing truth from the bannik, feeling the silence on the woods like suffocation, like drowning. . . .

The River-thing sleeping deep in his burrow, old Hwiuur, coiled like the snake he seemed . . .

She caught at Sasha's sleeve as he staggered upright. She stood there trembling, teeth chattering, saying, though she could hardly hear herself speaking in that silence, "I can't make sense of it. Blood and water—blood and water's all I can see of it—Sasha, I don't like this."

And Sasha, between breaths, holding her sleeve: "I don't see anything at all. It's not speaking to me."

Pyetr reined back at a brushy deadfall across the road, walked Volkhi around its end to the other side, then slid off for a rest— god, a little ride and already he felt the first hint of soreness that might, by tomorrow, have him walking very carefully.

More than that, Sasha was going to laugh—wish him well and cure the ache Sasha might, but he was certainly going to have his amusement beforehand.

So if one was going to suffer for it, Pyetr thought, rubbing Volkhi down with old leaves, and if one was bound to be sore before the day was done, there was no degree to that kind of ache: as well enjoy the day. Sasha would understand, Sasha would tell Eveshka there was no reason to worry about the horse—

But it was probably not wise to press the point too far, Pyetr told himself on a second thought: just a little way down the road. Eveshka was already upset, and if he was determined to cure her of her fear of horses, he could hardly afford to have her worrying.

So he swung up again to Volkhi's back, wincing a bit as he landed, and started off at an easy pace, Babi trotting along at one side and the other by entirely unpredictable turns.

It was too good to give up quite this early: aches to come and all, there was not a tsar in all the world he envied at the moment, not for his wife, not for his court, not for any horse a tsar could own.

He'll surely come to some bad end, they had said of him in Vojvoda. Pyetr Ilyitch, the gambler's son, was bound, they said, to be hanged—to which he had come quite frighteningly close, as happened, but for Sasha. And here he was, Pyetr Kochevikov, who never had believed in magic, living with wizards, married to a rusalka who really, truly, was alive again; and riding in a woods with a dvorovoi for company.

Sometimes it all did take a little getting used to. Sometimes he did think of Vojvoda, where there was doubtless a price on his head, and where none of his old friends would ever believe the sight of him hale and well.

And he most particularly hoped his old friend Dmitri Venedikov had bought Volkhi back from the innkeeper to satisfy his debts—because if so happened that Sasha's innocent wish had indeed committed horse theft, he sincerely hoped it was from 'Mitri, and by the dumping of 'Mitri in some muddy street—not that he was bitter, god, no, he was too well-content for bitterness toward his old friends, else he would wish (being no wizard and free to do such things) for 'Mitri to break a leg or two, for all the help 'Mitri had not been to him.

In truth, outside of Volkhi's original owner, who had been no good master in the first place, he could think of no one else more likely to have bought Volkhi from his creditors— 'Mitri having said, loudly, in his cups, that he had thought his friend should *give* him a horse like that, his friend having being lucky enough to win him with borrowed money—

'Mitri being a boyar's son, after all, and entitled to all that was fine, and Pyetr Kochevikov having inherited nothing from his father except a bad reputation and a close acquaintance with the dice.

Pyetr found himself thinking for the first time in years how the road that had led him to this woods equally well led back again, and how quickly Volkhi could carry him—just far enough for a sight of Vojvoda's brown, shingled roofs above its wooden walls, just for a satisfyingly remote thought of those same muddy streets where he had grown up and almost died, and particularly for the imagination of his old friends' faces.

God.

He reined Volkhi in, suddenly aware that his thoughts had turned in very foolish directions, that he had been riding for some little time oblivious to the road, and most alarming, that somewhere along the way Babi had stopped running ahead of him. He looked back to find the dvorovoi, reckoning Babi had reached the end of his patience or his boundaries, and saw that the old road, clear enough ahead, was a maze of gray, peeling trunks and leafy saplings behind him.

"Babi?" he called, but the forest was so quiet except for Volkhi's snorting and breathing that it seemed hard to speak at all. "Babi, dammit, where are you?"

"Down the road and back," Eveshka muttered, pacing up and down, wiping the sweat from her face. Her hand was shaking, Sasha could see it. Eveshka paced another course, said, looking toward the north wall of the bathhouse, "He should at least be turning around now, don't you think?"

"Probably." He knelt, adding wood to the fire. His nose was running from the herbs, his eyes stung. "But he's on a horse for the first time in years. Don't worry. He's probably just taking a turn or two—"

"Oh, god, Sasha!"

"Don't worry about him. Babi's with him."

"We don't know he is," Eveshka said shortly. "We don't know anything." She paced half the circuit of the bathhouse, stopped, hand over her eyes, wanting simply to know what was going on in the woods, Sasha could feel it up and down his spine, wanting till it echoed around the walls—

But there was no answer at all.

"Don't," he said, "don't doubt, 'Veshka, just think about the bannik."

"Banniks don't know what's going on *now*, it's tomorrow they live in, and wizards keep changing that—it's likely we've changed it even walking in here. We ought to be down that road, Sasha, that's where we ought to be! We ought to be

65

seeing where he is and what's going on out there, because we're not going to get anything here!"

Sasha wiped his nose again, and passed his arm across his forehead. "We could equally well bring trouble right to him. We don't know what we're doing."

Eveshka shook her head violently, fireglow making her pale hair and her underlit face all one color in his swimming vision. "It's not going to give us anything: if it was going to, it would have by now!"

"Maybe we haven't asked a right question, yet," Sasha said, and shut his eyes and tried to find that question, but all he kept getting for vision was Uulamets' memories turning over and over in his head, images of the river shore, a foggy morning, Eveshka walking into that mist, ghost among ghostly trees—

Memory or prophecy? God, did Uulamets foresee 'Veshka's drowning—and not even known he'd seen it? Or is it some morning still to come?

"It's a trap," Eveshka said, "papa always said, prophecy's a trap."

"Don't offend it, 'Veshka!"

She hugged her arms about her ribs, looked up at the rafters with a shake of her head. "I've bad feelings. I don't trust this place. I don't like what I'm feeling—I don't like what I'm feeling from the woods—"

Wind skirled through the open door, hit the fire, flung ash and embers, whipped at them.

The door banged shut and open again, once, twice.

Sasha stood up, looking about him. His shadow and Eveshka's trembled in the rafters and against the wooden walls.

"Bannik!" he shouted. "Answer us!"

Everything seemed fraught with possibilities, yea and nay equally balanced. He felt a sudden sense of suffocation, all the wishes successive wizards had ever made in this place hovering and circling—other, older wishes, mostly impotent, unless they should brush up against a strong new one, and that touch should set some old wish spinning, bring it into new motions, bring it into the current of things—

Leaves in the current, leaf brushing leaf—

Motions more and more violent—the whole pattern

swirling and changing as the current changed—the leaves madly whirling among the bubbles, a small whirlpool and a greater and greater one—

"Bannik!" he whispered, wishing with all his might for true answers this time, feeling the currents move around him till they bid fair to disturb everything in the world that was fixed.

"Bannik, answer me! You've come here for a reason. What question are you waiting for me to ask, bannik?"

A shadow jumped from one bench to the other, and to the rim of the firepit. A stone rattled.

The ferry on the river, by daylight, headed north under all its sail.

"Is this the future?" he asked. "Bannik? Is this what will be, or is this what we ought to do?"

Pyetr's face, ghostly pale, lit by lightning . . .

"Is this now? Is this someday? —What are you telling me, bannik?"

A stone rattled. Of a sudden it sprang at him, grabbed his arm with long-nailed fingers, drew him close to its face, growing more and more visible.

Thorn-branches. An overwhelming sense of danger. . .

Eveshka gazing at him out of shadows, with a face cold and unforgiving as death.

"Bannik! Will Pyetr need our help?"

Spray flying under the bow, canvas cracking—

A young man walking toward him, out of shadow. It might be the bannik itself, it had that feeling of danger and omen. Moonlight touched dark hair, white shirt—

The bannik hissed into his face, and sprang back into shadows, a figure all elbows and angles as it scuttled under a bench.

"Bannik!" Sasha shouted at it.

Again that sense of smothering in this dark, of a presence surrounded by chaos, might-be, could-be, must-be constantly changing position with every wish that brushed it.

He wanted its name. He wanted power over it. He wanted to stop this future from being. He stood still and shivering and tried to stop wanting anything in its presence.

Leaves moved more and more slowly in the current, bub-

*bles on dark water, that seemed now to stand still, every-
thing seemed to stand still, waiting for a single wish to steer
it—*

The door banged open again, admitting stark, gray daylight.

Raindrops pocked the dust outside.

Pyetr looked about him, reining Volkhi around. It was as if
some veil had come down between himself and the road home
again—the way magical things could look quite otherwise
than the truth, tricking an ordinary man's eyes and lying to
his senses.

"Babi?" he shouted to the woods around him, and it
seemed to him that the very daylight was grayer and colder,
that the trees were shifting at every glance away and back
again to look less familiar. Volkhi moved under him, tossed
his head and snorted as if he did not like the breeze that was
blowing to him, rustling the young leaves and rattling dry,
old branches.

"Babi?"

A prickling touched between his shoulders, a sensation of
something watching him from behind. He looked back,
looked up into the branches, hoping still for Babi. Nothing
was there.

He was increasingly tempted to call out Misighi's name.
If one was in trouble in the woods, leshys were a very good
idea; but they were odd creatures too, especially Misighi, who
was very old, impatient with fools, and apt to ask embarrassing questions, such as precisely what *had* he seen to be afraid
of?

Nothing, precisely. He had, like a fool, ridden without
watching the shapes of the trees, and just as soon as he did
see some familiar shape, some oddity he had observed riding
past it on the way out, then he would know precisely where
the road was.

In the meanwhile the sun gave him a general direction
toward home, the lay of the land gave him an indication
where the road ought to be—so he started riding again, paying
close attention to the trees this time, looking deep into the

woods on either hand for the sight of the peeled limb or odd trunk that might give him a clue: he was sure he could not be far off the track.

But when he looked behind him, where the road toward Vojvoda had once looked quite recognizable, what he had just come from seemed as much a maze as the way home did.

"Babi!" he called. But the silence when the sound died was stifling.

He could not believe Babi would have left him intentionally. He told himself that Babi was quite probably still there, and that it was only his nonmagical perception of things that was making it difficult to see him. For some reason magical things had started hiding themselves from him, the way leshys could look like leshys one moment and like trees the next. He had been thinking very hard of Vojvoda and his old life, and he felt a guilty apprehension that he should not have done that: that being so stupid as to want Vojvoda again, he might have—the god only knew—broken some spell or something, separated himself off from whatever let him see magical things, because there had been a time he had not been able to, there had been a time he could look straight at Babi and not see him at all for what he was.

Sasha would not have set such a trap without telling him, but Volkhi's arrival was proof enough that Sasha could make mistakes, and there was absolutely no knowing what kind of visitor-confusing spells that old curmudgeon Uulamets might have set and forgotten.

God, he had not been afraid in the woods for years: he had been up and down the river, past the place where he knew quite well a vodyanoi might still lair; and poked into all sorts of places no sensible man would go without protection. But he had been able then to see where he was going, and he had had his sword with him, and, not inconsiderable, he had always had Babi to guard his back.

Now Volkhi walked as if he suspected devils under every bush. His ears flicked this way and that, his nostrils tested the wind, he seemed to float more than to walk—

Volkhi shied off from something, a quick sidestep and another before he came back under his hand, trembling, snuffing the air and snorting at what he was smelling.

"Good horse," Pyetr muttered, patting Volkhi's sweating neck, himself sweating and his heart thumping while he tried to decide whether Volkhi could perceive something his senses could not. A fool was out in the woods on a skittish horse with no saddle, with the day well along already and the road, if it was the road, going into deeper and deeper shadow under a clouding sky.

He sincerely hoped Eveshka was worried by now. He sincerely hoped his wife and his friend were wondering where he was by now, and were wishing him home before dark. He certainly wished so; but if his wishes worked in the least he would not be out here wondering where the road had gone.

Volkhi shied up and aside: he recovered his seat, kept Volkhi under the rein and got his heart back from his throat, patting Volkhi's neck, telling him lies, how it was all very fine, they were going home, wherever that was.

7

Rain spattered the boards of the porch outside, a cold rain with a cold wind driving it. "He didn't take his coat," Eveshka said, at Sasha's back, inside the cottage. "He didn't even take a coat—"

Sasha lapped his belt about him, took his cap from under his arm and pulled it on. "He can take care of himself. He'll either find cover till the worst of it's past or he'll be coming as fast as he can—I'll probably meet him out there, probably slow him down, truth be told. I'm not sure—"

"The woods is *wrong*! Everything is *wrong*—"

He looked at her. He said, "I agree with you. But that's no assurance he knows anything about it, and if he doesn't know, he's safer than we are. 'Veshka, please let's not argue, please don't be wishing him anywhere on his own. He won't melt in the rain; he can build a shelter."

"Build a shelter! He'll be soaked to the skin—don't tell me he's out there now because he doesn't know there's anything wrong!" She was wrapping dry clothes into Pyetr's coat, making a compact bundle of it. "We shouldn't have waited, dammit, we shouldn't have let him stay out there."

"There's every chance he's with the leshys."

"There aren't any leshys, I'm telling you!" She was near to tears. She tied the cords tight. "I tried!"

"Maybe they've heard you. Maybe they've answered and gone straight to find him. They don't need to tell us. It may not occur to them to tell us."

"Use the sense my father left you! There's nothing out there, there's simply nothing out there, it's as if the world ends at the hedge. We can't even make the rain stop!"

"It's a big rain, it's had a long time to get going, for the god's sake, rains do have natural causes."

"Don't talk to me as if I was a fool! Something's in our way out there!"

Doubt upset Sasha's stomach, made Eveshka's hastiness seem a threat more than the forest was. " 'Veshka, I'll find him, just for the god's sake stop wishing *anything*. As long as we don't know what's out there—"

"Don't know, don't know, you don't know the sun's setting unless you look out the window! Use your head, Sasha! There's the vodyanoi, for one, there's ghosts!"

"He went the other direction, and neither one travels far from the river." He took Pyetr's sword from the peg where it hung and slung it from his shoulder. "I've wished him well, I've made wishes for him every day we've lived here, the same as you have, and if those wishes are working at all then they're still taking care of him, and if something's gotten around them, then it's better one of us go where he is so we know what we need, isn't it?"

She said nothing. She took a small clay pot from the counter and tucked it into the bag he was taking. Then the coat. "Just be careful," she said, giving him the bag. Her face was pale in the gray light from the doorway, pale and terribly afraid. "That's salt and sulphur. —You've got the fire-pot . . ."

He reached out, pressed her small, cold hands tightly in his own. "Listen, I'm *not* that worried about him. It's probably the weather. He won't take chances with a storm. *He can't wish the lightning.*"

"He can't wish anything else, either. Can he?"

He felt afraid of a sudden, profoundly, unreasoningly afraid of his choices. Everything seemed to tilt one way and the other, changeable, perilous. "I'll find him," he promised her on a breath; and ducked out into the storm, down the rain-washed boards of the walk-up. He splashed along the puddled path to the front gate—stopped there on impulse, feeling Eveshka's strong wish behind him, and saw her standing in the doorway, pale as the ghost she had been. Haste, that wish said; and he caught a breath, shoved the gate open and hit the lane at a run, through rain-laden weeds, where wind and water had swept away the trail Pyetr had left.

Most likely, he reasoned, Pyetr had just taken out for the afternoon, had tossed that down-the-road-and-back promise completely out of his head the moment they had left him to his own devices, Pyetr having never a qualm about going off on his own, no more than he had worried seeing Pyetr ride off into a forest he knew.

But Eveshka had worried from the start, Eveshka had told him he was a fool about the bannik, and he had still trusted it, sight unseen . . .

Ordinary man Pyetr was, and blind and deaf to some influences. Illusions and compulsions had less power over him than over a wizard—until the source of them came close enough to lay material hands on him.

He wished he had listened to Eveshka, he wished he had listened to her from the beginning. *He* had called the bannik, it had come at the same instant this silence had descended, and it was as twisted as the house they had built for it, changing with every wish they made and every action they took, flinging up bits and pieces of vision that might be imminent or might be years away—one looked, and guessed, and doubted, and had to look again: a wizard had to know— wanted to *know*, kept wanting to know until there was no doubt. By that very wanting there were changes; and by those changes there were always doubts—

Beware my daughter, Uulamets' memories said: Uulamets had continually mistrusted her; but he had looked for Eveshka's advice and not taken it when she had given it to him, not even heard it, he had been so set on being right . . .

Think things through, Uulamets' teaching advised him. Do the least possible. Don't move till you're sure. . . .

Things were going wrong and it might only be a rainstorm and it might only be a stray horse and their own fear of what he had conjured up in the bathhouse, but there was a terrible feeling of wishes going askew, and along with them all their safety in this unsafe woods. No time, he kept telling himself now, no time for prophecies, no room for thinking things to the bottom and back again. He made only one clear, unequivocal wish—to get to Pyetr in person before something else did.

—

Rain perfectly well capped the situation, in Pyetr's estimation. He rode along in a driving gale with his shirt and breeches soaked and no idea where he was going in this woods. "God," he muttered, teeth chattering, and yelled, "Misighi!" as the rain became a gray, sheeting downpour. "Misighi!" —having lost all reservation about appealing for help the moment the rain started.

But there was no sign of leshys. And no sign of friends either. The rain gusted at him, the only warmth he had was Volkhi's wet, moving body, not the surest seat one could wish; and Volkhi kept turning his head, laying his ears back to protect them from the water, shaking his neck and snorting protests at this lunacy.

Another gust, cold-edged and water-laden, and Pyetr ducked from it, spitting water, wiping it from his nose and his eyes. It was not only rain pelting them, it was dead bits of leaves, bits of bark, dirt, the god knew what. He said, patting Volkhi's shoulder, "That's enough, that's quite enough, lad."

It was deep, aged forest about them now, nothing but dead trees about, hardly a sapling or a bit of brush big enough to strip for living branches to shelter them, but a rocky outcrop finally offered a windbreak; he slid down and led Volkhi close up against that shelter, such as it was, next a couple of dead, dry pines that afforded relief from the wind coming at them sideways.

Volkhi snorted and protested, doubtless accustomed to a warm stable and a generous helping of good dry hay on a day like this, not to stand chilled and chilling after hard going, and Pyetr's own teeth were starting to chatter. So he took to rubbing Volkhi down with twists of fern, work to keep both of them warm so long as his strength held.

Lightning flashed, turning the woods winter-white for a moment, making him and Volkhi both jump. "Easy," he said, and shoved against Volkhi's shoulder to hold him, thinking that the last thing he needed was to lose Volkhi in the woods. "Just Father Sky in a bad mood tonight. I promise you he has nothing personal against horses."

C. J. CHERRYH

Volkhi grunted, shifted, tried to nose his ribs, as if he did truly hope there was supper coming after all this work, from some magical bottom of his master's pockets. Pyetr scratched under a wet chin and said, "There's none for me, either, lad. I do promise to do better than this in future."

Another flash and clap of thunder. Rain poured down their necks. Somewhere nearby a dead tree gave up a branch that crashed down and took others with it.

"Not a nice evening," Pyetr muttered, pressing himself against Volkhi's shoulder. "I don't know what's going on, lad. I truly don't. —Sasha, dammit, have you noticed it's raining?"

Granted neither of them liked to meddle with the weather more than the raising of a breeze, for fear of droughts and floods and other disasters wizards had to think about; and granted they might not go so far as to stop the rain for his sake—but they had surely noticed he had not come back.

"For the god's own sake, Sasha, not wishing at me doesn't mean I want to spend the night out here!"

Surely two wizards with their minds made up could manage to let him know where home was—unless—

Something's wrong at home, he thought, clinging to Volkhi's warm shoulder, scared and suddenly chilled inside as well as out. They had enemies: there was always the River-thing. And the leshys were not answering, no matter he called Misighi's name till he was hoarse.

Things seemed less and less clear to his mind . . . first Babi, then his memory of the woods—slipping away from him so persistently he had to think hard to keep his wits about him, so pervasively that from moment to moment he began to think there *was* no such place as the cottage by the river, or, completely crazy notion, he had somehow not come there yet, but would; now and again he had escaped the tsar's justice on his own, riding Volkhi out of town. There was no such thing as magic—anyone who thought so was crazy, and everything he had remembered in these woods was yet to happen . . . or never would happen, and nothing good would ever be true for him for long: it never had been.

"Misighi!" he shouted, desperately, making Volkhi fret— but if there was a thing altogether elusive in the woods it

75

was the leshys themselves; and if there was a thing first to turn invisible to an ordinary man, it was not something so plain and substantial as an old ferryman's cottage on a river-bank, it was the Forest-things that a man's eye had trouble enough seeing in the first place.

"Misighi!" he called until his voice cracked, until he was half ashamed of himself, standing here shouting at nothing but his imagination. But if he was a fool he had no witnesses. "Babi," he made himself say, confidently and loudly to the empty air, "dammit, go home if you can't do anything else! Go home and bring Sasha here."

The wind gusted, shifting direction, slipping around the hill to find them. Under Volkhi's mane was the warmest place to keep his hands, and against Volkhi's side was the only warmth for a man in soaked clothing. He pressed himself there as closely as he could, and kept thinking about home, the very outlines of which were starting to shift and elude him, as if a veil were coming between him and that, too. He had to be crazy to keep thinking he had known such creatures as leshys or had a wife and a friend waiting for him.

He was the gambler's son, the one the law wanted.

He had gotten away through the streets.

Gotten past the guards at the gate.

Gotten lost on the road, somehow, and ended up alone and freezing in the rain—in a woods he did not understand, looking for an escape that had never existed—or did not yet exist.

He squeezed his eyes shut until they ached, and until he stopped seeing the woods and the lightnings. Dammit, yes, there was a house, and there was a river, and he remembered someone saying—he had no idea who or when—that if ever he was lost there was always a way home: follow the river, no matter how far off true he had wandered, no matter how some subtle turning of the road and the obscuring trees had confused him, he had to believe the river lay east and the morning sun would show him the way. As long as he could remember that one thing and not lose it—

"Something's very wrong," he said to Volkhi. "Something's very wrong with us, lad."

He clung to that direction, held to the mere imagination

of a house that shifted outlines, friends waiting for him, a warm fire . . .

An old man there had threatened him with knives when he was sick. The river ran by the house. It might be all his imagining. But it was what he chose to go to, it was the only warm place in the world, and there were people there he could trust, he had no idea why—

The vodyanoi was there, coiled in his cave on the riverside, one knew . . . one knew he was. Eveshka paced the floor, knotted her hands together till they ached; and it whispered while she paced, the old snake did, Eveshka, Eveshka, listen to me . . .

It said, Fool, to trust a heart. They're so breakable.

It said, You could do so much, you always could, and you fall so far short of that—

Shut up, papa, she said, because that last was not the snake at all, that was her own memory: the room said it to her, the walls said it to her, the cellar echoed with it: Fool, fool, you won't take advice. Trust no one, least of all anyone who says he has your interest at heart . . .

Want nothing. Need nothing. Wishes do come back on you, young fool, don't you understand that? And when the wizard wishes himself, then everyone's in danger.

She wished for leshys. She wished for Pyetr. She wished to break through the silence.

But something else whispered back: Listen, Eveshka.

8

✠ ✠ ✠ ✠ Streams were over their banks: trees were down—reason enough to hope Pyetr had settled in to wait out the storm, Sasha told himself, with the dark coming and the rain still falling. His own coat was soaked, his boots were soaked, probably the fire-pot in his bag was drowned, and he had had to leave the road again, edging out onto a flooded log for a bridge to the other bank, holding to willow-wands overhead.

He reached a point he had to jump for it—hit the slick far bank, grabbing for handholds among the new bracken and wishing the roots to hold in the sodden earth—no testing whether his magic was working any more, except the fact that the bracken-fronds held and he did not dump himself into the flood. Such small proofs gave him both hope and fear—hope that his gift still might find Pyetr; and fear that Pyetr's vanishing from his awareness might mean something unthinkable.

But he was fast running from daylight to a starless, stormy dark, in which he had to trust his wizardry absolutely. He was north of the road, he was sure of that; he kept wanting to know where Pyetr was, and what Pyetr was thinking, and something kept convincing him of direction—but whether that was his wizardry working blind, he had no idea. He had no sense of Pyetr's existence.

I'm here, he wanted Pyetr to know, I'm looking for you: if you're safe, don't leave where you are, just wait for me.

He struggled calf-deep through rain-wet fern, brushed thickets that caught at the sword and the pack, in a twilight so deep the fern could mask an abrupt edge, anything. He caught a stitch in his side, kept going, shaking water from his eyes, in the erratic white flicker of lightning.

And in that flickering the fern moved on the hill opposite, rippled in a swift line headed straight for him.

He wished his welfare and drew Pyetr's sword, for what good it was to him: the disturbance streaked at him and flung itself with considerable weight onto his leg, scrambled with a frantic strength up his body despite his grabbing to stop it, reached his neck and clung there with all its might—a most familiar grip, perfectly reasonable that his wish had not fended it off.

"Babi?" he said, still shaking. "Babi, thank the god, where's Pyetr?"

It hugged him the harder, burrowed its head against his collar, a most desperate and rained-on Babi, in a dark nearly complete now, except for the lightning flashes.

The rain settled into a drizzle, at what point in this interminable night Pyetr had no idea. He thought if he had the strength he would try to gather such weeds and fern as he could and make a pile of it to keep the chill off; but he kept putting that effort off, thinking how cold he already was, hoping for dawn to bring him warmth: very soon now the sun would come, he thought as he clung close to Volkhi's side, any moment now the sun would come up—it was only the storm clouds making the dawn late.

But when the weather did settle, and the sun had not come, Volkhi shook himself and started to wander out into the open despite the cold sprinkling from the trees. "Whoa, lad," Pyetr murmured, held him, and Volkhi stood for a while, but restlessly.

So, he decided, he had kept Volkhi warm, and Volkhi could return the favor: he found purchase on the rock with his foot, got the reins and a handful of Volkhi's mane and shoved himself up to sprawl out flat on Volkhi's wet back, to travel again in the dark, wherever Volkhi took the notion to go.

East, he reminded himself, trying to draw from his muzzy wits which way that was or what he was doing in this place,

79

or whether he had only been dreaming about going east and finding a river. He was stiff, he was sore, he could not remember why, or why he was riding half-frozen in the woods with no saddle nor proper bridle.

But eastward he had a wife waiting for him. A warm fire. Sasha, The Cockerel's fey stableboy, the one nobody wanted—Sasha was there, too. He could not imagine what they all had to do with each other, but he had a conviction that they were friends—that they all lived together in a house—

Which had a garden, a porch, a bathhouse he and Sasha had built—

His wife had wonderful blond braids, hair like light when it flew free, so much of it she could wrap in it. . . .

She liked blue. She had a favorite gown with leaves embroidered down its sleeves, and petticoats with flowers on their hems. They were spells she stitched, she had told him so. She had a garden, and little plots she tended in the woods, where she grew trees and plants that would not grow in other ground.

But he could not see her face now, except details that would not fit together—and he fought to keep them, even if they did not match what he thought was true any longer, everything he loved slipping away from him faster and faster—

He was in a room with Sasha; Sasha was (but that was wrong, Sasha could not read) writing something. Sasha had grown up. His face had lost its boyish look—become a young man's face—

And the river would lead him—

Home, somehow. He knew so little for certain. Things in woods, the old folk said on winter nights, wore their feet backwards and led travelers astray; Forest-things shifted shapes, and Things that looked like trees could move and change a man's path, leading him to disaster.

How did I get here? he wondered, finding his lids heavier and heavier as he rode—until of a sudden Volkhi shied sideways, came full about under his hand, bringing an old man into his sight—a white-bearded, scowling old man in the lightnings and the crazed patterns of the brush, who looked, the moment Pyetr thought about it, like someone he had known very well, and, crazily, had trouble seeing quite right—

Because he had never in this life looked to see that face again.

"You're dead," he said to his father-in-law, as all sorts of things came flooding back to him—the inside of the cottage, the cruel old man with his knives and his damnable singing . . . the old man whose daughter was a cold-fingered ghost . . .

"You're lost," Ilya Uulamets said, leaning on his staff. "Not that I'm surprised. And here you are. My daughter's choice. God save us."

Volkhi was still fretting and trying to turn. Pyetr kept a tight rein, jostled this way and that. His heart was thumping hard from the start the ghost had given him . . . but Eveshka had died and haunted the river shore, he remembered that: he had seen ghosts, and recalling that his wife should be a ghost ought to pain him, but it seemed only a fact to remember, nothing he should be entirely distressed about. The oddness was Uulamets, who had no business being dead yet . . . or was; god, he had no idea what had happened and what was going to happen, or what was happening to him now.

"I need to get home," he said to Uulamets, patting Volkhi's neck, himself trembling while he reassured the horse, and feeling as if he were doing all this in his sleep, completely numb. "I think something's wrong. I think something could be very wrong."

Uulamets leaned on his staff and glowered at him, no less pleasant than he ever had been. Then he said, "Follow me," and walked away through the shadow.

Volkhi showed no inclination to go. Pyetr argued with him once, twice, before Volkhi started picking his way down the rough hillside, following the old man in the same direction that they had been moving. More bits and pieces started coming back to him—how Eveshka was waiting at home, how Uulamets was dead, upriver, how he had left the house riding and somehow lost himself in the woods . . . so far lost he had not even recognized his father-in-law for a moment.

That Uulamets' ghost should come to his rescue did not seem entirely incredible: they had not liked each other, the god knew, but one could certainly believe Uulamets might stay around as a ghost, if anyone would—the old reprobate had never trusted anyone to do anything right, least of all his daughter: Eveshka had abundant reason for her secrecies and her touchiness.

Still, it did seem to him that Uulamets, being dead, should be paler, glow in the dark like a proper ghost, not just show up in the lightning flashes with shadows and all. . . .

Follow me, Uulamets said.

But what did a ghost mean by that, looking more and more solid?

God, he did not like this. "Grandfather?" he said, respectfully.

Uulamets might not have heard for all the sign he gave. Certainly that was no different than in life.

He urged Volkhi to a faster pace at the bottom of the hill, fought Volkhi's misgivings until they were close at Uulamets' back.

"Grandfather, do you know what's going on? Do you know what's going on back at the house?"

No answer. One naturally expected a ghost to be peculiar—angry, perhaps, especially this one. But there were definitely shadows about this figure which one did not expect in a ghost, except a rusalka when she had stolen a bit of one's life . . . or unless, frightening thought, he had somehow strayed over to the ghostly side of things himself in the cold last night and never known it.

He did still have a heartbeat. He felt his chest, to be sure. He felt Volkhi's warmth under him and he heard the crunch of last year's bracken under Volkhi's hooves: if he was slipping over some line, somehow, he damned well ought to have some sense of crossing a boundary. Even if he had frozen in the rain, certainly Volkhi ought to be alive.

He missed ducking. A branch caught him across the face and he clapped a hand to what felt like a bleeding scratch across his cheek. He heard Uulamets' staff disturb the ground, heard Uulamets' body move the brush, the same as he and Volkhi did—but Eveshka in her ghostly form could never disturb a leaf. Neither sun nor moon could touch a rusalka—

unless she had gotten strength from somewhere . . . and a rusalka only got it from living things.

Rusalkas were drowned girls, that was what he had heard, drowned girls unhappy with their lovers. Surely crotchety old men only turned into ordinary ghosts, the sort with cold fingers and dead, awful eyes, the sort of ghosts that only wailed and blamed people—not half so dangerous.

"Grandfather," Pyetr said faintly, less and less sure he knew what he was dealing with.

Uulamets just kept walking; and of a sudden Pyetr was sorry he had called out to what was moving in front of him. He hoped to the god it did not turn around. He pulled Volkhi quietly to a stop, turned his head—

Something in the brush crashed toward him, growling, and he ducked flat and hung on as Volkhi shied and scrambled for footing, breaking them uphill through branches, through vines, up a slope too steep, too slick with recent rain—he felt Volkhi start to slide, stayed on somehow as Volkhi veered off on a downward slant. A limb hit his shoulder with numbing force as they passed under, all but took him off Volkhi's back. Branches whipped at his shoulders. He had no more wish to stop than the horse did, he only saw a way through and steered for that sole black gap in the brush.

A pale shape loomed up in front of them. Volkhi reared, came down again, uncertain, bemazed and still in a way nothing natural could stop a panicked horse.

The apparition held out its hands, saying, in Sasha's voice: "Pyetr, are you all right?"

Pyetr held on to the reins, shivering as much as Volkhi was. Sasha walked a step closer, making a soft, very welcome sound on dead leaves. But Pyetr reined Volkhi back from him.

"It's me," Sasha said.

"I sincerely hope so," Pyetr said shakily, "because just now it was Uulamets, and I don't know what's going on."

"Babi's after it," Sasha said, and shed a sack he was carrying from his shoulder to his hand, then started searching into it. "I brought your coat. Eveshka sent some bread and sausages. . . ."

A shapeshifter could be that plausible, and a shapeshifter

in Uulamets' likeness was surely what he had been dealing with: there had been flaws in Uulamets' appearance, there were always flaws with a shapeshifter, Eveshka had told him—and he saw none in Sasha.

Sasha came closer, offering him up the coat with one hand, calming Volkhi with the other, and Volkhi stood still for it—that was what told Pyetr who he was really, truly dealing with. He hoped to the god it did.

"Is everything all right at home?" he asked, taking the dry coat, deciding Volkhi would stand still a moment while he let go the reins and put it on.

"Eveshka's terribly worried," Sasha said, keeping his hand on Volkhi's neck. "A bannik came. And we couldn't find you anywhere."

Sometimes Sasha's accounts of events seemed to leave out essentials, especially when a man was having trouble following things in the first place. Pyetr said numbly, "I lost Babi. Then nothing looked right. I don't know where I've been."

"Are you all right?"

"I'm fine. Let's get out of here."

"Fast as we can," Sasha said, patted Volkhi's neck and started walking.

So they were going home. That was quite all right. That was exactly what Sasha would do. That was entirely the way Sasha would talk.

It was still a better sign that of a sudden there came a panting in the dark, a quick pad-pad-pad in the wet leaves beside Volkhi's feet and Sasha's—no visible sign of the dvorovoi, but that was Babi, Pyetr had no doubt of it.

Then he began to believe he was safe.

Go home, Sasha wished Babi silently, as they walked along, himself and Pyetr leading Volkhi on this level ground, where they had come on the road again. Go back to the house, let Eveshka know everything's all right—

But, perverse as everything else magical, Babi obstinately stayed with them—for promise of more sausages, or because of some wish, his or Eveshka's—Sasha had no idea.

"I don't know what's the matter with him," Sasha said. "I don't know what's going on. Babi won't listen, or can't, I don't know. Nothing's worked right, except finding you."

"Thank the god you did," Pyetr muttered, and asked, after a moment, "What in hell's this about a bannik?"

Sasha shook his head. "I don't know. It showed up just after you left. I don't know why. I hoped it might help."

"Help *what*?"

Sometimes Pyetr's questions seemed so clear and his own answers so abysmally stupid. "I don't know. It only showed up, and after that—or about the same time—everything stopped being there . . ."

"What do you mean—stopped being there?"

"Things. People. They're *there*." He was not even sure how ordinary folk felt the world around them. He had thought he knew; he thought at least he had known once, before he had taken up with Uulamets and started listening to the wizard-gift he had been born with; but lately he doubted he knew anything about ordinary folk. Lately he doubted he understood himself. "Right now it's—like seeing the trees move and not hearing the leaves."

"That's stupid!" Pyetr said, but Pyetr looked worried. "What do you do, eavesdrop all the time?"

"It's not like hearing. It's . . ." Anything he could say sounded stupid. "Knowing they're there. The way you know the forest is there with your eyes shut. It sounds like the wind stopping. Quiet. And it's not like that. Ever. It's not natural."

Pyetr gave him a look, Sasha saw it from the tail of his vision; Pyetr said, "So it's quiet. You couldn't hear me. I couldn't make Babi hear me either. Or the leshys. Why? What's going on?"

"I don't know," Sasha said, with his eyes set on the road ahead of them, the confused track through the regrown woods. "A lot of things that shouldn't. I don't know everything I should. Pyetr, I swear to you—'Veshka thinks her father left me a lot of things, but that's not so. She thinks I remember, but I don't, not—not as if I ever feel her father being there. He's gone. It's not like she thinks it is. I can't make her understand that."

"I've told her. I've told her, myself. It's not you. She's just worried, she worries about everything—I get myself lost, I start thinking about Vojvoda, the god knows I could have strayed into some damn trap the old man set, and it's not the first time you couldn't hear me. . . ."

"It's not just you. Something's wrong, I've felt it going ever since Volkhi came—"

"Volkhi, Volkhi, what for the god's sake does Volkhi matter to anything? A horse strays. So what's going to happen? For a stray horse, the tsar's going to come?"

"I'm not talking about the tsar. I'm talking about the bannik."

"I'm sure all of this is going to make sense."

"I can't hear the woods," Sasha said. "I couldn't find Babi, I can't hear a thing except 'Veshka when she's close, I can't even hear you when you're right next to me, and it has to do with the bannik, it all started with the bannik, the same as Volkhi coming here."

"You're not getting enough sleep," Pyetr said. "It's that damn book, you know, those little crooked marks you stay up all night staring at—"

"Things are going wrong, Pyetr, they're just going wrong!"

"Because you can't hear the trees."

"I don't mean hearing the trees. It's not like a sound, Pyetr,—"

"God. I don't care what it is. You say yourself once you start doubting you can do something it won't happen, so maybe you're tripping over your own feet, did you ever think about that?"

"I think of it."

"So wish it right again."

"I do! But there's nothing I can reach, Pyetr, and the bannik just showed up and I'm not sure I even wanted it myself, I know Eveshka didn't, and nothing's right."

Pyetr put his hand on Sasha's shoulder, walked with him that way, Volkhi trailing them of his own volition. "Listen. Maybe 'Veshka's right. Forget Uulamets. Leave his damned book alone. Leave everything a while. Quit trying so hard to think of trouble before it happens. Aren't you likely to wish it up that way? Forget it. We'll take the boat out, maybe even sail down to Kiev, you, me, 'Veshka . . ."

The very thought touched him with sudden panic—all those people, all those wishes and needs weighing on his heart, unstable as things were. Not now. God, not now, and Eveshka certainly could never bear it. Even dealing with two people she loved was hard.

"There's girls there," Pyetr said. "Girls who'd think you're a damn fine catch."

"No!"

"Life doesn't go on in a damn *book*, boy!"

Sasha caught a breath, stopped thinking for a moment, stopped even trying to listen with his ears or his wizardry, so that everything Pyetr said became only sound to him. He had used to do that when his uncle had upset him—go away until his heart was quiet.

"Boy?" Pyetr said, shaking at his shoulder as they walked. "What's the matter?"

"I just want the woods back, Pyetr, I just want things to go right." He tried not even to think about Kiev, or the people and the girls and the idea of escape Pyetr was talking about. They frightened him, they brought him to the edge of wishes, and he could not let himself want the things ordinary folk might—Uulamets had made that mistake. And Pyetr would not understand that. Pyetr only let him go after a moment, unhappy and worried, he needed no eavesdropping to know that much.

He said to Pyetr carefully, reasonably, "I want everything we've done to hold."

"It's going well enough. You found me, didn't you? I didn't break my neck. Whatever that was, it was scared of you. It ran. If the old snake's at his tricks again, we can deal with that, we always have."

"We got the bannik, and when Eveshka wondered where you were, all it said was thorns and branches."

"Well, that was the truth, wasn't it? But it didn't take any damn prophecy to know that. . . ."

Blood on thorns . . .

"Did it?"

He was afraid to answer. An answer meant nothing. An answer might change before he could so much as think of it. "Will-be is always moving," he said faintly. "Everything we do changes what's going to happen. That's why banniks don't like wizards."

" 'Veshka says. At least the last one didn't like Uula-mets—but I can understand that. So we've got a bannik. And the forest is quiet and you're seeing thorn-bushes and it scares you. —You don't make sense all the time, you know."

The quiet was absolute.

Leaves on the current, the current stopped . . .

Waiting . . .

"Sasha?"

"I want us *home*," Sasha said.

"Why? What's wrong?"

"I don't know." He faced Pyetr about and pushed him at Volkhi's side. "I'll just feel better when we get there."

Pyetr gave him an anxious look, then swung quickly up to Volkhi's back and offered him his hand.

9

✠ ✠ ✠ ✠ They came in sight of the house at twilight, both of them staggering tired, in muddy, chafing clothes that had dried on their backs, and with Volkhi so weary they were both afoot and leading him again. But at last there was the gray roof in sight, the hedge, the garden, their own porch, all safe and waiting for them, and Pyetr had no inclination to upset Eveshka twice. He opened the gate, shoved Volkhi's reins at Sasha, calling out dutifully as he came running up onto the porch, " 'Veshka, I'm home!"

He opened the door into a dark, cold house.

" 'Veshka? Where are you?"

Sasha came thumping up onto the porch and walked in behind him.

"She's not here," Pyetr said, thinking, Well, damn! Now *she's* gone out looking! Then he thought about the horse and the quarrel yesterday morning and had another opinion.

"She just might be out at the bathhouse," Sasha breathed, and ran back down into the yard. Sasha's voice drifted up distant and distressed: "Volkhi, get out of there!"

Hell with the garden, Pyetr thought, looking around a shadowy, supperless kitchen. He threw wide the kitchen shutters for light, opened the door into their bedroom and bashed his shin on a bench, opening the bedroom shutters.

Her book was gone from the desk.

He looked in the clothes press, found clothes missing, her walking boots gone; and slammed the wardrobe door so hard the piece rocked against the wall. "Damn!" he said, hit it with his fist and sulked out into the kitchen to find out what else was missing—and by that just how long she intended to be off on her little pique this time.

He was finding blank spaces in the spice shelves when Sasha came running up onto the porch and inside to report breathlessly that she was not in the bathhouse, and he had found neither sight nor sense of the bannik, either.

"No need of any bannik," Pyetr said. "She's off again. She's just mad and she's left." He pushed his cap back on his head, remembered Eveshka disapproved of caps in the house, and took it off, as if that could patch things. "She took her book with her this time. Damn her." Then he added, with the least little remorse and no little worry in his heart: "Though I honestly can't say I blame her."

"I don't like this."

"Well, I don't like it either, but it's hardly the first time, is it?" He waved at the door, in the general direction of the woods. "Trees make better sense to her than people do. They always have. Myself, I'm for supper and a bath. She'll be back. Not my fault I got lost, not her fault she does things like this, is it?"

"I don't think she'd go off like this. Not—"

"I do. I see absolutely no reason she wouldn't. She's done it too often. —Let's get a light in here, have supper, get a bath. —Babi? Babi, where are you?"

Babi turned up at his knee, tugging at his trouser leg, upset, one could reckon, at finding no supper waiting.

"Go find her, Babi. Get her back here if you want your dinner. Or you'll have to put up with my cooking."

Babi dropped to all fours and walked the circuit of the room in a decided sulk, all shoulders.

"I really don't like this," Sasha repeated to himself, shed his cap and coat onto the kitchen bench and started sorting the books and clutter on the side of the kitchen table, the survivors of the broken shelf.

"Well, hell, I don't like it either! But we haven't any choice, have we?" Pyetr went to the fireplace, poked up the ashes and thrust a little kindling into the banked coals. Flame shot up quite readily, yellow light. He lit a straw, stood up and lit the oil lamp, which threw giant shadows about the walls and made Sasha's worried frown disturbingly grim.

90

"She didn't leave any note?" Sasha asked him. "Nothing on her desk, no paper or—"

"No." It frustrated him, this leaving of vitally important messages on arcane little bits of paper. He jammed his hands into his coat pockets and set his jaw, thinking about the silence in the woods, the shapeshifter that had taken Uulamets' likeness. "I don't know why she would bother. Does she ever leave one when it's important? —Damn it, Sasha, you know exactly what it is, she's mad and she's off to talk to the trees or whatever she does out there, I don't see we should worry."

Sasha ran a hand through his hair, left his books, went and pulled up the trap to the cellar.

"She's not hiding down there, for the god's sake," Pyetr said, at the end of his temper, embarrassed, even though Sasha was their closest and only friend, at having a constant witness to their private difficulties. He knew he would end up, he always did, defending Eveshka to a boy who had more sense than Eveshka in his little finger. Then Sasha would end up, inevitably, telling him the same old things, that he just had to understand Eveshka, Eveshka had to have time, Eveshka had to be alone with her thoughts—

"It's not safe out there," was what Sasha said, on the first step of the cellar stairs.

Pyetr gave a twitch of his shoulders, uneasy at this urgent searching and poking about in dark places, as if something truly grim could have happened. "I know it's not safe out there, we both know it's not safe out there, but she's a wizard, isn't she? —What in hell do you want in the cellar?" Pyetr had a sudden, most terrible imagination that Sasha knew beyond a doubt that something was amiss—with a girl who could stop a man's heart with a wish.

Certainly there was no chance any intruder could get past the front door—

Except a shapeshifter, except someone that she knew . . . or thought she knew.

Sasha said to him, casting a glance over his shoulder, "Is there bread?"

Pyetr glanced at the counter, where loaves of bread sat wrapped in towels—Eveshka had left that much for them, in

91

its usual place, evidence she had planned for them coming home. She had at least done her usual baking. . . .

But damn her, he had searched the woods for her on her earliest disappearances, spent sleepless nights and called himself hoarse, all to no profit. She came back when she wanted to come back. There was no reason to think it was more than that, no matter the scare they had had.

He brought a loaf to Sasha, on the steps, waist-deep in the dark. He guessed by now what Sasha was thinking of: the domovoi, down in the cellar. The House-thing favored homey gifts like fresh bread: it had gotten fatter and fatter on Eveshka's baking in the years they had lived here; but whatever wisdom it had, it sat on. It never offered them a thing but to stir when quarrels disturbed the peace, and to make the house timbers creak on winter nights like some old man's joints. "What can it tell us?" he asked sullenly. "It's only Eveshka it talks to."

Sasha ignored his opinions and ducked down the stairs into the dark. What floated up to him was,

"Just stay there, don't block the light and don't say anything!"

Meaning that a magic-deaf fool was apt to open his mouth at the wrong moment and offend the creature. He was outstandingly good at that. If he had ever made sense to Eveshka she would not be off in the woods right now, and they would not be worrying and wondering if she *was* just off on a sulk or a soul-searching or whatever she did to keep herself, Eveshka would say, from her damnably dangerous tempers.

He paced. That was all he could do.

Then of a sudden Babi growled, leapt up and vanished right through the shut door to the outside.

"Babi!" Pyetr crossed the room hardly slower than Babi, jerked the door open, hand on his sword—

And saw Volkhi head across the neat rows of vegetables with Babi in pursuit, wreaking equal havoc in Eveshka's rain-soaked garden as they went.

"Damn!" Pyetr whistled, loud and sharp. "Volkhi! —Dammit, Babi, get him out of there!"

Volkhi swung off toward the side of the house, with a kick or two in his gait. Babi followed. Pyetr set his arm against the doorframe and leaned his head against it, thinking, god, Eveshka had worked so hard on that garden, Eveshka had weeded and watered and taken pride in that garden, and if she saw it before he smoothed that rain-soaked ground he would have to go and live with the leshys, that was all there was to it.

Nothing was wrong. She would come back, please the god Eveshka was only angry at him. He deserved it for his fecklessness and his stupidity: no one in Vojvoda had ever counted him a responsible type, the god knew 'Veshka had had a great deal to put up with. He only wanted her back safe, that was all he asked.

The domovoi did not like the light. It hated disturbances, it wanted peace, and if one ever wanted to see it, one might search the shadows at the end of the shelves, among the bins and barrels of the cellar. It stayed as far as it could get from the stairs and noisy comings and goings. So at the very limit of the dim light that came from the kitchen above, Sasha unwrapped his offering, squatted down and broke the bread for the domovoi, setting the pieces on the floor.

Timbers creaked at the end of the cellar. A shadow moved there. It was hard to see its real shape. Sometimes it was a bear. Sometimes it was a black pig. Sometimes it was a very shaggy, very puzzled old grandfather, which was what Sasha had seen when they had summoned it to feed it and explain their plans for the house and the changes they proposed to make. It had simply wanted to know the roof would be sound, Eveshka had said: that was all it cared about, besides a loaf of bread now and again.

One hoped it forgave them for the corner-posts.

"Domovoi, little father—" Sasha bowed very respectfully from where he was kneeling, and edged backward to give it room. "Pyetr and I are back, but now Eveshka's gone off somewhere and we're worried. Do you know where she's gone? Do you remember her leaving?"

It moved, the shifting of a large, heavy body; it came out of the shadows and sat on the dirt floor looking at him, which was more attention than it usually paid.

It was a very old domovoi, by any account, and very odd.

It blinked at him. It remembered things, Uulamets' knowledge told him: it knew very little about today, less about tomorrow, mostly dreamed about the way things had been, glossing the bad and exaggerating the good—at least a healthy one did, in a healthy house. The god only knew about one a wizard owned.

It hunched closer. It looked a lot at the moment like an old bear, the oldest bear anyone had ever seen, and the fattest. It swiped a half a loaf up in its paws and sat up to eat it like a man . . . completely unconcerned, it seemed, at Eveshka's disappearance, which might be a good sign.

But of a sudden a memory came very strongly—a young man stood like a ghost on the wooden steps, very like the figure in the bannik's vision—no feature visible, light falling on dark hair, white-shirted shoulders. . . .

It might be himself. It was so real Sasha turned his head to see if it was there, or perhaps a recollection of his recent presence on those steps.

But there was nothing. He looked back at the domovoi, hands sweating. He imagined the room upstairs the way it had been. He imagined violent anger in the house, Uulamets shouting till the rafters rang, Young fool! And Eveshka sobbing, Listen to me, papa—you never listen to me!

He was trembling. He took hold of the post beside the steps, looked up into the twilight of the room above, hearing Eveshka say, plaintively—

I don't believe you, papa. You're wrong! Doesn't it ever occur to you that you might be wrong about someone?

Years and years ago—when Kavi Chernevog had come and gone on these steps, gotten herbs from this same cellar, slept by the hearth upstairs, while Uulamets and his daughter had had their beds at the end of the kitchen . . . and Chernevog had had his bed close to where he slept now.

God, why is it showing me this? What's Chernevog to do with anything now? He can't be awake, please the god it doesn't mean Chernevog has anything to do with this.

"Little father," he whispered to the domovoi, "what are you telling me?"

The house rang with ghostly voices:

Fool, love's got nothing to do with him! He's got no heart, he hasn't had one for years! Good riddance to him!

Eveshka, furiously: You never give me a chance, papa, you never credit me with any judgment! Why should I ever be honest with you? You never trust me to know anything!

And Uulamets, then: Trust you? The plain question, girl, is whether you can trust yourself! The plainer question is whether you're my daughter or your mother's! Answer that one! Can you?

His heart was racing. He recalled a scratching at the shutters in the night, the raven that had held Uulamets' heart prying with beak and claw to get inside . . . while Uulamets sat alone at the table by lamplight—reading and plotting and writing, night after night, wanting his daughter back . . .

Lonely nights, silent days, the scratching at the window— and Uulamets never listened to it. Uulamets had reason enough to want his daughter alive again, and a heart had very little to do with it. Eveshka was absolutely right about that.

Leaves on the river . . .

Spray flying from the bow . . .

Sasha broke out in sudden, sweating terror, scrambled up and ran up the steps, shouting at Pyetr: "The boat—"

The dock was empty, Pyetr saw that well enough from the top of the path: the boat was gone, and he went running down to the weathered boards, to stand there like a fool and look helplessly up the river—up, because he knew it was no trip down to Kiev that Eveshka had undertaken without him.

"She's gone," he said as Sasha came running up beside him. "It's a bad dream. It's a damn bad dream! What in hell does she think she's doing with the boat? Where does she think she's going?"

"I don't know," Sasha said.

"I thought she was worried I wasn't back, I thought she had this notion something just damn well could have happened to me out there! I don't mind if she's mad, I can understand if she's mad, but taking the boat—"

"She could have heard from the leshys."

"Oh, god, fine, she could have heard from the leshys! Then

she could damn well have had the leshys talk to *us*, couldn't she?"

Sasha caught his arm, pulled at him to bring him up the hill again to a house Eveshka had deserted, along with everything else she had a responsibility to think of. "She cares," Sasha said, "Pyetr, I know she does. I'm sure whatever she's doing, she can take care of herself, she's thought it through—"

"The hell!" he cried, and tore from Sasha's grip. He climbed to the top of the hill, he stood there catching his breath under the old dead trees looking out at the house and the yard in the gathering dark, with a lump in his throat and a cold fear in his stomach.

He heard Sasha climbing the trail behind him. He was in no mood to talk about Eveshka, or to wonder aloud what kind of danger she might be in—he could think of all too many right now without a wizard's help. So he shoved his way through the gap in the hedge, stalked up to the porch and inside, into the kitchen, where he snatched a basket down off the rafters and started searching for flour and oil.

He was aware when Sasha walked in the door, was aware of Sasha standing behind him, upset and wanting to help.

"I'm taking Volkhi," Pyetr said, "I'm going after her, I'll find her, don't worry about it. If she's on the river, I'm not going to get lost following *that*."

"Pyetr, I know you're in no mood to listen to me—"

"It's not your fault. —Where's the damn flour? Did she have to take all of it?"

"It's under the counter. It should be. —Pyetr, please, just think this through with me: she's on the boat, she's not out in the woods—so at least we know something; and I didn't know exactly where you were, either, so long as I was any distance from you. It's this quiet out there. . . ."

He turned and glared at Sasha, expecting him to use good sense and shut up. But Sasha set his jaw and said, without flinching:

"We'll find her. I promise we'll both find her, let's just not do anything rash, Pyetr."

"Rash! God, let's not do anything rash while she's out there on the river, shall we? Let's not take any chances while she's out there alone on the water in the dark with the god

96

knows what! There's a shapeshifter loose! Who knows what shape it's got right now? Who knows what she's sailing with?"

"Pyetr, I don't want you going without me, you understand me? I know you're mad and I'm sorry, but I don't want you running off out there!"

"The hell! *Don't wish at me, dammit!* I know you mean well, Sasha, but just stop it! Stay out of my way! Stay the *hell* out of my way!"

"Pyetr, —"

He found the flour. "You give me advice, boy, when you've got a wife. I'm not sitting here while she's out there begging for trouble and you can't tell me what's going on."

"Pyetr, *listen* to me!"

He felt the wish hit him: he felt his thoughts scatter, his hands shake with an intention he suddenly had trouble recollecting, even when he knew what was happening to him. He slammed his hand down on the counter, leaned on it, because sleeplessness and cold and the rest of it were suddenly making his knees weak. "Don't do that to me, dammit!"

"Pyetr, we're going, I absolutely agree with you, we're going after her as fast as we can, but we can go off with what we need or we can go without it—I don't just throw things in a sack, Pyetr, and magic doesn't win by luck and it doesn't work by generalities!"

"Tonight it seems it's not working at all!"

"I can wish her well—but that's no good at all if somebody else wishes something a lot more specific, does it?"

"Somebody else. Somebody else— Is that what we're talking about? Is that why we're not naming names right now?"

"Pyetr, don't doubt her, don't doubt *us*! Doubt undoes magic, and that's the absolute worst mistake we could make."

"Doubt's when you start to know you're off the mark, boy, doubt's when you start to figure out you'd better do something—and the stupidest thing we can do is sit here and let her sail off on the god knows what hare-brained notion while we *believe* things are going to be all right! North, Sasha, north is where she's going right now, and if there's something wrong down here, then it's a good guess there's something going on up there with the leshys, and if the leshys can't stop it then I doubt my *wife* is the one of us who has any business up there!"

"If it's not old magic," Sasha said quietly. "And we don't know: it could be. It could be a hundred years old—it could be anybody who ever lived here."

That made no sense at all. He was not in a mood to listen to obscurities. But Sasha went on, with that worried, earnest look he had when he was trying to explain the unexplainable:

"A wish lasts. Like that old teacup that ought to break. We don't want it to break either. I think we might keep that wish going. But I'm sure it's still Uulamets' wish keeping that cup in one piece. He's dead and it still works because we use it. A lot else he wished just doesn't matter to anybody now he's gone, so it just fades away and doesn't do anything—but there might be all sorts of old wishes floating around these woods that we don't know about. There was Uulamets before there was Chernevog, there was Malenkova before there was Uulamets, the god only knows who taught Malenkova, hundreds and hundreds of wishes could still be working, for all we know, and we don't know what we're messing with or what it's aiming at, or if it's completely harmless until it bumps into something else and starts it moving."

"God," Pyetr said disgustedly.

"It's all complicated, Pyetr, magic's always complicated like that, and we can't go off to the north rattling everything that's settled and risking the god knows what, going right for what we're most afraid of—"

"Well, *she* is, isn't she? Who knows what 'Veshka's going to do? —God, it's Chernevog we're talking about, not some damn village fortuneteller—not mentioning the ghosts in the woods up there. He murdered her! He had her heart in his hands once! Tell me again she's got any kind of business going up there!"

"We don't know for certain that's even where she went."

"Well, it damn sure wasn't to Kiev market! What's going on out there? What's making the forest look different every time you look at it and why's my wife off on the river in the dark if it isn't his doing?"

Sasha bit his lip. "It could be. But—"

"Could, could, might! —I'll tell you what I'll do, *friend*, I'll go up there and separate him from his *head*, that's what I'll do, and then we won't have to wonder! The god only knows why we didn't do it in the first place!"

"If you ever get there—if you can find your way through the woods—"

"I'll get there!"

"You couldn't even find the house!"

"Well, I don't need a guide to find the damn river!"

"And what happens when we get up there without what we could have brought if we took time to think? —All right, all right, I don't like what Eveshka's done, I don't think it was smart, I don't think it was the best thing to have done, I want to catch up with her as much as you do—"

"I doubt that!"

"—but it's no help, scattering like sheep all through the woods with no idea what we're dealing with!"

"Fine! Pack! Let's move!"

"Pyetr, god— Go take care of Volkhi, take care of Babi, go outside, just for the god's sake give me time to think! Maybe I can reach her. Out! Please!"

Pyetr bit his lip. All certainties went sliding away from him—which could as well be Sasha's doing, even without Sasha's intending it: that was the kind of thinking that could drive a sane man crazy, especially facing a second night of no sleep, so tired and so scared for what Eveshka might be doing he was all but shaking. Sasha was in no better state, his voice was a hoarse shadow of itself; and without wizardry there was no hope they could overtake the boat tonight.

Pyetr flung up his hands. "All right," he said, "all right." He went to the washbasin, threw water into his face and toweled off the dirt, went to the grain bin and slammed it open, to do whatever Sasha wanted, trying not to wonder what might be going on elsewhere or what trouble the boat could get into with Eveshka sailing blind and alone. "I'll get Volkhi rubbed down," he said, throwing grain into the bucket. "Talk to her. Turn the wind if you can. If you can't reach her I want to be out of here tonight, I don't care if it's only an hour along the shore, I'm not going to sit here waiting for word and I'm damn well not going to sleep."

"Volkhi's exhausted," Sasha said. "I'm exhausted. Two nights now I've had no sleep, for the god's sake! —Just—let me try. I'll do what I can."

"I know. I know you will." Pyetr filled the bucket, did the mundane things a plain man could. All his life he had known a run of luck only lasted till a fool believed it enough to commit himself. Then the god tipped the dice and everything went to hell.

But, but, he argued with himself, he still had throws left, Sasha was saying he still knew things to try. Sasha and Eveshka could load anybody's dice.

Only hope to the god it was not Chernevog responsible, or if it was, that Eveshka was not going up there to handle matters alone—because it seemed always the last thing in the world to occur to Ilya Uulamets' daughter—that she was not the sole competent in a world of fools and strangers.

—Oh, leave that alone, Pyetr, let me do it!

—Here, stop, you're making a mess!

—Don't touch that, Pyetr!

And when, too often lately, she would frown and stare into nowhere, chin on fist—and he would ask: What's worrying you, 'Veshka?

She would say, Nothing. Nothing at all. . . .

As if she were looking past the walls, past everything he could see or think of seeing . . .

"When I left her here," Sasha was saying at the edge of his attention, a hoarse and weary voice, "she kept wanting to hear from the leshys: maybe she got an answer. Maybe she just felt she had to go get one. She left the bread. So she knew we were coming back."

Pyetr refused to be comforted. He said, tight-jawed, "Anything's possible," got the vodka jug from the shelf and cut down a couple of small sausages to take along with it. For his supper. And Babi's. "I just wonder what the hell answer she did get, myself. Or whose. —I'll take care of outside. I'll wait out there till you call me. But for the god's sake let's not just trust to wishes. Do what you can and let's get closer to her where we can do some good."

"I'll hurry," Sasha promised him, "as much as you can hurry magic, I promise you."

It was an eerily uncomfortable feeling Sasha had, entering Pyetr's and Eveshka's room—carrying the kitchen lamp into a behind-doors privacy he had never entered since the day he and Pyetr had moved the furniture in. He felt strangely furtive and guilty here—as if Pyetr would object to him being in this room, as if Eveshka herself might have set some wish here that he was crossing. He would never have expected that of her.

But he had his own specific purpose in this room, and wishing nothing else he searched the floor around the washbasin and the table where one would expect her comb and her brush to be, if she had not taken them with her—a woman thinking of necessities, he thought—and searching by lamplight under that table and against the wall he found the leavings he was looking for—perhaps a last, hasty brushing as she was packing, a few pale strands broken and disregarded on a floor otherwise immaculately swept. He wrapped them around his finger and tucked them into his pocket: that was the link that he wanted, the single personal tie to her, be it ever so slight.

Everything indicated a point of decision, quick packing, reliance on the provisions the boat always had: a very worried young woman who likely had not slept baked bread, slow work, and left it neatly wrapped, two loaves, all the rising tray would hold, for menfolk she surely, desperately, wanted home; then, evidently suddenly, with book, inkpot and scant personal things—she went down to the boat.

He had herb-pots of his own to bring up from the cellar. The bread he had left the domovoi was gone, neither crumb nor track showing on the smooth-worn floor: "Little grandfather," he called, but the House-thing made no appearance even when he brought his lamp into that area of the cellar it most haunted. He searched the shelves there for feverfew and woundwort, willow bark and yarrow, salt and sulfur, little pots he and Eveshka had neatly labeled, everything to Eveshka's exacting sense of order.

Her touch, her presence was strong in this dark place, in the depths of the house she had grown up in, died near, returned to as a wife . . . He told himself there was nothing in the world to fear from Eveshka's lingering wishes, there was nothing she would ever do or want that might harm him or Pyetr . . .

But he kept remembering—Chernevog came and went here, often.

He heard Uulamets shouting, heard her saying, in tears:

—You never give anyone a chance, papa. You never trust anyone! Why should anyone be honest with you?

Eveshka walking on the misty river shore, among the ghosts of trees long dead—toward a cloaked man waiting for her—

"God." Sasha all but lost his breath, caught his balance against the shelf, pottery rattling against his arms.

Cold and dark, roots above a hollow bank, where the vodyanoi lived, Chernevog's old ally—

Eveshka's grave, such as it was, whatever it still contained. . . .

He wished with all his heart for her to hear him. But that smothering hush fell like deep snow. He stood there smelling age and preservation, and listening to the distressed creaking of old timbers.

One never knew how long wizardry was going to take once it got started, Pyetr knew that, and there was no telling what Sasha meant to do in there, but a body was well advised not to walk in on things, no matter how tired he was or how desperate, no matter that it was dark out in the yard and he had no lamp.

A wizard did not have to think about such petty things. A wizard could talk about packing damned little pots while a man's wife was in danger, a wizard could talk about reason while the sky was falling and then still cast about to be sure and double sure before he did anything.

So Pyetr had himself a supper of cold sausage, and poured a drink for Babi while Volkhi lipped up the last of his grain

C. J. CHERRYH

in the moonlight, under ragged cloud. Babi had zealously done
what a proper Yard-thing should do: he had gotten Volkhi out
of the garden and into his pen, Volkhi none the worse for a
few greens on the way, and not at all disturbed about Babi,
who had been, when Pyetr had arrived in the back yard, sitting in the gap he had left in the pen—insisting something at
least behave itself and stay where it was supposed to.

Now Babi was a small black furball tucked as close to
Pyetr's boot as he could get. "Find 'Veshka, can you?" Pyetr
had asked him, and maybe Babi had tried, silently, in whatever way a dvorovoi might know where his people were. Certainly Babi was not his ordinary cheerful self tonight—he
moped, drank his vodka and dropped his chin on his small
hands with a sigh.

"We'll find her," Pyetr said, and stroked Babi's shaggy
head. Babi growled then, which might mean almost anything.

But Babi had his head up staring across the dark yard; and
Pyetr looked at the bathhouse, where Babi was looking, with
the most uneasy feeling there was something in the shadows
staring back at him.

Sasha fed kindling into the fire in the hearth, flung in herbs
that master Uulamets had recommended; salt, baneful to certain wicked things; lastly a few strands of Eveshka's hair: that
was the essence of the spell he was casting. He looked for
patterns in the light, he leaned close and fanned the smoke
to him, taking whatever thoughts the smoke brought.

The spell was not the smoke, the spell was not *in* the
smoke, it was in thinking about the things it held, not in
one's own order of importance—

It was in letting the smoke mix everything equally and
spin out a new order of things—no one thing and no one
question, momentarily, in greater importance than anything
else—

*A willow leaf balanced on a still current, a bubble
stopped in the act of breaking—*

In the quiet, think about hearth and house: Pyetr and
Uulamets and Eveshka. Think of Vojvoda and Kiev; think of

ordinary folk, oblivious to what existed beyond their fields and over the hills, think of all the tsars in all the kingdoms in all the world, because the currents went that far—

Everything poised motionless and waiting—

Think of a butter churn and a mud puddle; a house far north of this house, all in charred ruins—

Chernevog's house. Malenkova's house, once. Even Uulamets had lived there, when Uulamets had been himself an apprentice . . .

Be rid of hearts, Uulamets' voiceless voice chided him: never rely on them; love nothing and nowhere above everything and all places.

Nothing more than anything, everything passing like the river passing the house. Uulamets' wife was in that river and his daughter was in that river, Uulamets' life was in that river: everything flowed past him, everything was always there, the paradox of leaves on the water—

Breathe in the smoke, boy, breathe in, breathe in, breathe *in* . . .

Head above heart, boy. Head always above heart.

He pressed his hands against his eyes, thinking: Head without heart—that made Chernevog. Heart without head—what can that make anyone, but the town fool?

Thank the god, Uulamets had said, most wizards lose their gift young, most smother it, most wish the power of wishing away—

Always that choice was available, until the power grew too great, until one dared do nothing—not even retrace the steps leading to that one frozen moment—

'Veshka saying: I don't want to be stronger—so that's that, isn't it!

He sat in front of the fire, he listened to the shifting of the domovoi in the cellar, bound to the house, lost in its memories; he thought about Pyetr out there alone in the yard.

Babi was with him. But there were things Babi could not deal with, there were things Babi had no power to fight—nor did he have. God, if it was Chernevog at the root of this, and if the leshys were failing to hold him . . .

A ring of thorns . . . where Forest-things wove in the danger that Kavi Chernevog had been—

He got up, shaking in the knees, he got all the books from the kitchen table and sat down again cross-legged in the heat and the light of the hearthside. He breathed the smoke, he asked himself what he was doing here, in Uulamets' place, alone . . . it was Uulamets' book he wanted, it was Chernevog's he profoundly dreaded—but dread seemed like doubt to him, and wondering whether he was a fool even to contemplate what he was doing, he wished for answers from Chernevog's: let it fall open to any page it would and let his eye find anything that stopped it—

Today Draga is dead. She had begun, I think, to worry about me.

Another skip of the eye:

. . . But she wanted me more than she wanted power: she had so much of that she didn't want any more, so she settled for her own indulgence. That was her mistake . . .

—I don't want to be stronger—so that's that, isn't it?

Learning it, I surpassed my teacher; understanding it, I despised her; using it, I killed her. . . .

God, what's it saying? Is it about 'Veshka?

Or does it mean anything at all? It's like the smoke, it's not what's in it, the spell's not in the smoke, it's not in the words—

Chernevog's not a wizard any more, he's a sorcerer, whatever that means. Uulamets had to use real magic to stop him—he had to do it and the god only knows what he paid for it or how he got it or what helped him. That's not in his book. That's not in anything he left me.

He sat there in the smoke with the book open in front of him and felt colder and colder despite the sweat on his face: he thought of Eveshka out there on the river, Eveshka wanting Pyetr safe with all her might—

Uulamets saying: A rusalka *is* a wish—

A wish to live, a desire so strong it stole every life in its reach, up and down the river, leached life out of the woods, destroyed everything but what her father could keep from her grasp . . . until her wishing set itself finally on Pyetr—

Things change that can change—

Always at the weakest point.

That was, they had always thought, Pyetr . . . but—

God—no, he did not want—

Leaves moved, the bubble burst, dark water swirled aside from the bow—

What have I wished? he wondered, cold through and through. Father Sky, what did I just wish besides her getting home again?

He shut Chernevog's book, he took up his own, desperate to recover his wits and remind himself of his own recent wishes. He opened it to the page last written.

There was Eveshka's fine writing, the very last line. *Take care for Pyetr. I know you'll follow me. But I beg you don't.*

The spookiness from the bathhouse came and went. Pyetr took to glancing at the ground, talking to Babi, soothing Babi's upset with a constant touch, then abruptly stealing a glance in the direction of the bathhouse, in hopes of surprising whatever was lurking in the shadows of its doorway, no matter that the door was shut.

Banniks, Sasha had said. Magical things. He had no pressing desire, in Sasha's absence, to go over there and open that door: he did very well at believing in magic these days, even in dealing with it face to face—but this thing, bannik, ghost, whatever it was, made him sure if he opened that door it was going to dash out at him, and maybe get away from him altogether—along with everything it might tell them if he could only keep it for Sasha to deal with.

But it might be what Sasha was trying to raise with his magic, it might be the very answer he was conjuring—and in the completely unreasonable way of magical creatures, it might not stay long enough for Sasha to realize it was there.

He stood up, uncertain in the persistence of that feeling; he walked a few steps toward the bathhouse, stopped then in an increasingly unreasoning dread of that door, asking himself, on second and third thoughts, what a bannik might want with an ordinary man—the one of them hardest to bespell and most vulnerable if something actually got its hands on him—

Of a sudden something hit his leg, strong arms locked tight about his knee, Babi clinging to him and growling deep in his throat—while as strong as the terror of that closed door now was the idea the bannik might not intend to talk to anyone else, it might not wait for Sasha, it truly might not wait and they might lose every wisdom it might have for them.

But just then he heard the door of the house slam open, heard Sasha running hard down the boards, calling out, "Pyetr!"

He waited, while Babi let go of his knee and growled, with stay and go shivering through his exhausted wits. Sasha reached him, out of breath and he said, "There's something in there." He pointed at the bathhouse, expecting Sasha to find that of major significance, but Sasha caught his arm, saying,

"We're going. Right now. Come inside, help me get the packs sorted out."

"There's a bannik!" Pyetr said; and Sasha:

"Let it be!"

Perhaps he was entirely muddled from lack of sleep, perhaps he expected Sasha to make clearer sense than he was making. Sasha held him painfully hard by a slack arm and drew him back to Volkhi's pen, Babi growling as they went. "Just let it be! Don't ask me anything, don't argue, just get Volkhi around front."

"What's wrong, for the god's sake? What did you find out?"

"Hush. Just bring Volkhi. Now!"

"Sasha, for the god's sake—" Pyetr stopped and made a furious gesture back toward the bathhouse. "Did you even hear me? Are you listening? It wants something. It's been trying to talk to me and I was waiting for you, before I did anything—Why are we suddenly scared of it?"

"Never mind! Just do it. Come on!"

There were times the boy showed a disturbing tendency to Uulamets' habits—or it was wizardry that made one sit for hours and then, of course, immediately, the moment an ordinary man just momentarily began to believe the last piece of advice was sane—it was face-about in the other direction, and hurry about it—even though he had a gnawing feeling now that he truly *wanted* to open that door yonder, and he truly *wanted* to know what was in there and hear what it had to tell him. Eveshka was in trouble and that Thing in the bathhouse was the only creature in the world who knew precisely what was going on—it *wanted* to tell them—

"Come *on!*" Sasha hissed at him, and pulled at his arm. He hesitated, looking back—

But in any case of magic, he did exactly what Sasha asked.

The wind sang a steady song in the rigging, shifting only as the river turned, and Eveshka sat on the bench Pyetr had made beside the tiller, her arm over the bar, her eyes on the dark ahead. She distracted herself with recollections and precise reckonings, wished herself calm: Fear lends a certain strength to your wishes, papa had been wont to say, but does it ever make them wiser?

Papa's advice. Always. She said, coldly, to the rushing wind and the dark, "Does arrogance, papa?"

And the dark said back, You're right, of course. You couldn't possibly have that fault yourself.

The answer disturbed her. There were ghosts aplenty in these woods, ghosts that haunted her solitary walks, ghosts she met in anguish and in guilt—but of all the ghosts that could exist, this one she had decided by now would never come back.

And it had no right to turn up now, god! he did not, slipping up on her quiet as a memory. She still was not sure the manifestation was not exactly that: overwrought imagination—and dammit, she refused to flinch. This ghost owed *her* an apology, by the god he did!

It said, so faintly it might have been the wind, Do I owe one to a fool? Just what are you doing up here, daughter?

She tossed her head, shook the blowing hair out of her eyes—aware in the same instant that the wind was changing, the pitch of the deck decreasing, the sail about to slat, uncertainty in every motion, her wishes all overwhelmed.

"Papa?" Fear struck her for a moment, her heart tottering unstable as the boat, but the wind came back to the sail, steadied the deck, carried the boat on its way, a wish as sure as the arms that had used to carry her. Her heart settled with a familiar, infuriating confidence—fluttered then, the whole world seeming to reel and pitch in the smothering silence and the humming of the ropes and the hull. One could sleep in that sound.

Going north? that whisper said to her. The tiller rocked and swayed beneath her arm, and the water hissed under the thrumming hull. —Young fool. I expected this. Sleep now. I'll keep us steady.

She did not want to sleep. She hated her father taking things out of her hands, damn, he always did that to her; and she hated the quiet tone he took, as if she were a little girl again—god, she had even forgotten he could use that voice: papa tucking her in at night, kissing her on the forehead, walking away to bank the fire and blow out the light, in the single room the house had been in those years.

Good night, he would say then, out of the dark. Good night, mouseling. Safe dreams.

She tried to keep her eyes open. But the hiss and the hum ran through her bones, made her eyes heavy. Her head began to droop, the motion of the tiller rocking her to sleep.

The voice said, more substantial now, rough as she remembered him: Shut your eyes. You've taken on far too much this time. You need help. If you've not discovered it yet, young fool, that's my grandchild you're carrying.

10

✶ ✶ ✶ ✶ One could wish a wound to heal, one could wish strain and heat to leave tired joints—but unless one did something both reckless and foolish, that wish had no resources but the body in question—and a body had only so much to spend: it always paid afterward, in profound, watery-kneed exhaustion.

But Volkhi had to stay sound at least to get them away, please the god, and Sasha rubbed Volkhi's legs down, wishing up new strength in himself and in Pyetr, too, while Pyetr was shutting the door and bringing his packs down. Volkhi, evidently inspired to appetite, ducked his head and unconcernedly cropped a mouthful of something that interested him.

"You ride," Pyetr said, carrying their several packs off the walk-up, Babi trotting at his heels. Pyetr set everything on the ground and offered Sasha a quick hand up to Volkhi's back, insisting, "I'll take second."

Pyetr was doing very well at the moment, Pyetr was not asking questions and Pyetr wanted no arguments. Sasha took the lift up, settled astride and took the packs Pyetr handed up to him, his own bags of books and breakables, the grain and the blanket-rolls. "I think we should take the old path," Sasha said. "It's longer, but you're right, at least the river can keep us going right, no matter if something tries to confuse us—and there's at least a chance of spotting the boat that way."

"The wind's been out of the south since noon," Pyetr muttered, shouldering his own packs. "It's a damned long start she's had already. —Can't you do anything? Stop the wind, maybe?"

There had come a sighing in the trees just after the sun had passed its height—just when, while they were walking home, Eveshka must have taken to the river and wished herself up a wind that . . . he was not sure . . . might be blowing a little less for his efforts.

"I've tried. Weather takes—"

"Time," Pyetr finished glumly. And then looked alarmed. "She *planned* this ahead of time? Is that what you're saying?"

"We don't know she raised it." He was pushed to say that. He did not want to say anything else. He wished Volkhi to move, so that Pyetr had to go ahead quickly and open the gate.

"You're saying—" Pyetr began.

"Don't," he said. "Pyetr. Later. Please. Later."

No need to lead Volkhi, Pyetr had found that out: the boy just wanted, and Volkhi had as well have no rein on him.

Wizards wanted this, they wanted that, and everything moved, horses, people, friends—Eveshka was off to the god knew what, and Sasha first insisted they stay and then insisted immediately, now, in the next few moments, they be off into the dark with a wizard's clattering pharmacopeia and a load of books—

Which told him nothing except that Sasha had found something in the house that scared him out of good sense, something he did not want to talk about in earshot of the yard or even in the house—whatever banniks had to do with it. And the wind that carried Eveshka away from them had gotten itself together in whatever time it took a wind to gather.

"What's going on?" Pyetr asked once they were on the downward pitch of the road, beside the dock. "For the god's sake, what are we running from? What did you find out?"

Sasha said, from Volkhi's height beside him:

"She did leave us a note. I found it in my book. It should have been the first place I looked."

Pyetr looked up at him, but against the night sky Sasha was shadow, and out of the dark Sasha's voice was hoarse and thin, telling him less than it might have.

"She wanted to go looking for you, right off," Sasha said. "But I didn't think we should: I was afraid we might be calling you back into something, and she was going to stay and try here while I went looking—"

"You said that already. What else did the note say, dammit? What's she up to?"

"Finding the leshys. She was worried, the way things were going."

"Worried about the leshys?"

"About the quiet. So she was going to try from the house. . . ."

"What? Try what? Sasha, don't make me ask every damn question: spit it out! What did she write? What did she say she was doing?"

"She didn't say. If she knew, herself, which I'm not sure of."

"God! Wizards! Then *guess*, is that so damned hard? Tell me what goes on between you two! I live in the dark!"

"Things don't go on between us."

"The hell!" He never wanted to shout at the boy, he never wanted to be unreasonable. He was losing his mind. "Dammit, just give me a guess, give me anything, I don't care! Tell me what goes on in my wife's head. And what's the bannik got to do with it?"

"It showed up just after you left. She called you to come back—but this quiet—"

"You said that! What about the bannik?"

"We both asked it, and it showed us thorns and branches. She didn't trust it."

"Showed you thorns."One resisted the urge to drag Sasha off the horse and shake him. One just kept asking, reasonably, patiently, shivering with the chill of wet weeds soaking one's legs as they left the empty dock behind and started along the trail, "What do you mean, showed you thorns?"

"It doesn't really talk when it answers. You see things."

"So why in hell didn't we ask it a question? Are we afraid of it? Maybe it showed her something you don't know about, maybe—"

"It wasn't the same bannik that used to live there. She

didn't trust it; but you're right, that's not saying she might not have gone back in there after I left. She could have asked it something on her own."

She certainly would, Pyetr thought desperately. Nothing was ever right unless Eveshka did it herself.

"—Or maybe she got an answer from the leshys," Sasha said. "That's just as likely. She packed, we do know that. She left around noon, we can guess that by the wind and the bread and all, and I really think she might have heard me last night telling her I'd found you. That'd certainly make her feel better about leaving."

"Fine! That's really fine, Sasha!"

"Not because she wanted to."

"Is that what the note says?"

"It just says she knew we'd follow her and she didn't want us to—which is saying she knew she couldn't wish us not to, because she wasn't that sure she was right."

"Eveshka doesn't think she's right. The river'll run backward first. Where's she going?"

"It didn't say."

"Didn't say. Didn't say. She left you the note, for the god's sake! She had to have said that."

"I told you what it said."

"There's got to be something else. You didn't read it right."

"Writing doesn't mean everything."

"Well, it's damn useless, isn't it? What the hell good is it if it doesn't tell you the important things?"

Sasha had no answer for that one.

"I'll tell you the first thing I want to know," Pyetr said after a moment more of walking and gathering the bits and pieces of his temper. "I want to know where our old friend under the willow is, and I'll lay you odds he's not in his cave right now."

"I think it might be a good place to look," Sasha said. "That's another reason I wanted to go this way."

"For all we know the damn Thing's in our bathhouse! The bannik talked about the river, did it? It probably wanted me for its supper!"

"I don't think it was the vodyanoi. But I don't trust it.

113

I'm not that sure it's a proper bannik. They're supposed to be old. This one isn't."

Shapeshifters, Pyetr thought. In the god knew what shape. One could come up to the house in Uulamets' likeness. Or Sasha's. Or his. And Babi, who could recognize such things, had been with them. Babi had growled at the bannik, if that meant anything. He slogged through a boggy low spot, keeping his balance against Volkhi's side. "I'll tell you," he said, between breaths and struggles after footing, "you say you daren't doubt anything. I can, remember? Doubting's a talent of mine. I doubt everything's all right. I *doubt* we know what we're doing. I *doubt* we're going to find anything in the old snake's hole, and I *doubt* my wife's in her right mind, does that add it up?"

"It seems to," Sasha confessed.

The river trail dwindled to a track under dead trees and degenerated into a brushy bog. Sasha clung to Volkhi's back, his head buzzing with exhaustion and river-murmur. Time seemed muddled. He wished Volkhi and Pyetr to sure footing where it existed—there was no hope of following Babi, who had no sense about taller folk or obstacles Babi could pop past. Blink! and he was the other side, or halfway up a hill, or wherever Babi wanted to be, puzzled because no one had followed, no matter they were half dead of exhaustion and snagged in thorns.

"Babi!" Sasha called, wishing him to find 'Veshka, if nothing else, go to her, stay with her—but Babi paid no attention. Babi kept coming and going in his usual way, regardless of wishes. And from time to time he turned up on Volkhi's rump, when the going got damp, to sit until they reached drier ground.

Wrong, Sasha kept thinking, desperately wrong to have come this way: recent rains had made the trail worse than the maze it was. He desperately wished them strength to keep going, wished Volkhi not to take him under branches, wished ways through this maze of dead ends and soft ground where Pyetr swore and stumbled knee-deep in water.

"It's worse and worse," Pyetr complained. "God, it's a damn swamp!"

"I'm sorry," Sasha said; but it hardly helped now. He called up more and more of their strength, telling himself he was more use on Volkhi's back than struggling along afoot— he scarcely had his wits about him now as it was, and bit by bit the well-wishing he could do, using up strength and warmth from their bodies, would wear them down to cold and chills; it would kill them if he kept it up.

"I think we should stop," he said, and let go his wishing slowly, argument enough, he was sure, for Pyetr to feel the truth of it in his bones. But:

"We can make the cave," Pyetr said.

"The cave! God, we can't get that far! If we did we can't deal with him tonight." He let everything go, and ached like winter in every bone. "I can't keep us going, Pyetr."

"I can," Pyetr said, and took Volkhi's reins in hand and led him, to Sasha's dismay. The god only knew what strength Pyetr was going on now, swearing and struggling for footing in the morass he had advised them into, while he sat safe and dry on Volkhi's back.

"Wait," he said, wished Volkhi to a halt and slid down from Volkhi's bare back into ankle-deep water. The baggage came off with him. "God," he muttered in disgust and heaved the dripping packs up onto Volkhi's back—but lifting them took more out of him than he expected, and he leaned trembling against Volkhi's shoulder while his head spun, the whole due of his well-wishing suddenly come down on him with a vengeance.

Pyetr walked back, laid a heavy hand on his shoulder, slapped Volkhi commiseratingly on the neck. "We both walk," Pyetr said in a ghost of his own voice. "Volkhi's done enough the last two days. Let him carry the packs, that's all."

"He can carry you," Sasha objected, struggling after Pyetr as Pyetr led Volkhi ahead of him. "At least you don't have to lead him! I can wish him, just let him go!" But even such simple wishes came with difficulty to his muddled wits, confused and scattered like so many birds. "Pyetr, we're both taking for granted 'Veshka's being a fool—but what if she's not? What if she knows something we don't? Maybe we ought to trust her. We don't know what we're walking into. Stop!"

"We're not assuming anything," Pyetr's hoarse voice said out of the dark ahead of him. "We're going up there to find out, aren't we?"

Pyetr never had blamed him in all of this; Pyetr had never asked anything of him but answers he did not know how to give, and help he could not find—at least not in themselves any longer; Pyetr just assumed his wizardry had failed and did not blame him for that either—

"Damn," Pyetr gasped, and caught his balance, bent over as Sasha reached him, hauling his foot free of some underwater hole or root. He leaned against Volkhi a moment shaking his head and catching his breath in a coughing fit before he began to walk again.

Thorns and branches closing about them, leshys standing still and tall as trees . . .

Leaves falling in sunlight, a golden carpet on the ground . . .

Visions crowded in, brighter than the real night around him, filled with omen. Sasha panted after breath, tried from moment to moment to summon up strength where they most needed it. A night might seem to go on forever—but it had an end. This trail did. Only get to higher ground and they could rest, Pyetr surely thought they would get their second wind, Pyetr was that much stronger, he would go as long as he could push himself—

But Pyetr coughed, Pyetr swore in gasps and staggered and hurt himself and said, finally: "Dammit, Sasha, can you possibly give us some help here?"

"I can't. There isn't any more. We've gotten as far as we can, Pyetr."

Pyetr just kept walking. Sasha did. His sense of direction was going, and he fended brush from his eyes in one long giddy confusion of hills and branches. He wished Pyetr's cough to stop, stealing a little of his own strength and Volkhi's to do it: dammit, he was nine years younger than Pyetr, at least his legs ought to hold up—if only he had spent less of his recent years at the books, if only, somewhere, he had learned to draw on himself the way Pyetr did, the only magic an ordinary man had to keep him going—while a wizard learned only, desperately, how to stop that kind of wish.

A wizard could never want things beyond reason: a wizard could kill someone . . .

He hated his failure. He *hated* being less than Pyetr. That found a little more strength in his body than he had thought he had. He tried to find advice in Uulamets' memories—

But he recalled Chernevog's instead: *Nature can't work against itself. But magic, pure magic, has no such limits.*

It took all a wizard's magic to move so much as a pebble against nature: once or twice in a lifetime, master Uulamets had said, a wizard past his childhood could work a real spell—

If—

If he wished something magical with a child's simplicity.

Or a rusalka's ruthless single-mindedness—

God, I do know how. I *do* know how—

And we can't, we daren't, I won't.

They climbed a bank to dry ground, moved as shadows in a starlit maze of white, peeling trunks, came down again to bog and brush. River-sound grew distant, a faint murmur out of the dark, beneath the dry rattle of limbs in the wind. "You ride," Sasha urged Pyetr, again, panting for breath, but Pyetr refused—the foot was fine, Pyetr said, he had not hurt himself, he was only glad to get Volkhi to solid ground. "Can't be that far," Pyetr said, leaning on his knees a moment. "I don't ever remember it being this far."

Sasha thought, We're not going to find Eveshka tonight. She doesn't want to be found, she doesn't want us to catch her.

Not when Pyetr's with me. If Chernevog breaks free—Pyetr's the way to her heart. She told me—take care of him. Don't follow her.

God, I'm a fool! Eveshka, Misighi, *hear* me!

"We're being fools," he called out to Pyetr, but Pyetr

said, in a rasping voice, "Is that news? Come on—" and came back and tried to help him, taking his arm, holding to Volkhi's mane to keep his own balance.

"Damn," Sasha said, surprised into tears, "dammit, Pyetr!" But he could not say he was right arguing with Pyetr's judgment: he had no idea any longer what was right or wise. It was Pyetr's heart drove them both, and it was his own heart muddling up his thinking, he knew that it was: his own heart, his own doubts, his own weakness.

Everything's going wrong, we're falling into a trap, my wishes aren't working. It's magic we're fighting—and I'm not Uulamets, I'm not even Eveshka, and I don't know any more what to do. I can't even be sure enough to stop Pyetr, Pyetr's the hardest of us to work on, and maybe he's the only one of us still in his right mind—

"Damn," he heard from Pyetr. "Damn! —Volkhi! Stop!" as Volkhi stumbled in water and lurched wildly off and aside, trying to get a forefoot free—

Volkhi made it, on a terrified wish Sasha hardly felt. Sasha stood, gasping after breath while Pyetr got down on his knees in the water, feeling after the leg that well could have snapped.

"Is he all right?"

"He's all right."

Sasha clenched chattering teeth, wished the leg sound and wished Volkhi not to be in pain, or tired as the poor creature was—surely Volkhi was worth more than the trees or the bracken, more than foolish hares or any stupid jay. The leshys might not agree: in the leshys' reckoning they and a nest of sparrows might be equal—but the whole forest might perish, god, the leshys themselves might be lost if a young and ignorant wizard lacked the moral courage or the wisdom to break their rules for their own sake.

He made his wish not wholly rusalkalike, to draw one life till some creature died—but, in the way Eveshka had discovered to do, drew life from everything, all the woods far and wide—

"Forgive me," he said to the leshys, then, and deliberately widened that theft, wished Volkhi well, wished Pyetr and himself well. Magic flooded strength into them, at least enough to serve.

"What are you doing?" Pyetr asked. "Sasha?"

"Something I can't go on doing. Something Eveshka would have my hide for."

Pyetr might not have understood. Maybe Pyetr was too distracted to understand. "God," was all Pyetr said; and Pyetr did not question the need for it, he only led Volkhi through to better ground and kept walking.

Sasha followed him, aches fading, breath coming, frighteningly easy. The whole forest was there to draw on, all the life they had nursed back into it.

For all their replanting—surely they could steal a little. It was not, after all, for themselves he stole. It was nothing selfish.

The leshys had to understand . . . please the god they had to understand.

Something glided off through the trees, ghostlike, pale. Eventually an owl called.

A ghost drifted past—one of the shapeless sort, no more than a cold spot.

"Damn!" Pyetr cried, and swatted at it. "Out! Away!"

It made a faint, angry sound. The god only knew what it said. It dogged them for a while.

But ghosts did that sometimes, in the worse places in this woods.

"Papa?" Eveshka said, feeling the change in pitch. The deck tilted sharply and something splashed.

Hush, the whisper said. Everything's all right.

The old mast creaked against its stays, the rush of water past them grew faster and faster. The ropes hummed, or it was her father singing spells, in his tuneless way.

Remember, the ghost said to her, remember when you were five, and wanted the snow?

She did. She rubbed her nose, tucked up in her cloak and ruefully thought of the storm she had raised, that had piled up drifts high as the east eaves of the house and made the roof creak.

Snow deep and white, snow like a blanket, lying in tall,

precarious ridges on the branches, branches that wishes could shake, making small blizzards . . .

You remember, the ghost said. You do remember. You weren't afraid of magic then . . .

Maybe it was a spell on the place, maybe only that their eyes were tired enough to take the ridge in front of them for more dark behind the trees. They had crossed the small ravine and were almost on the slope before the land began to make sense, and Volkhi snorted and Babi hissed at the rotten stench a skirl of wind carried to them.

"It's the mound," Sasha said, and Pyetr, slinging his sword around where he could get at it:

"No nicer than it ever was."

A smell of rot and earth hung about the side of the ridge as they climbed, up and up to a barren top where the south wind blew unchecked. Water-sound whispered to them out of the dark as they walked the crest toward the river, with the hollow, ruined mound on their left, until the ridge ended in a long slope to a flat grassy edge and black water beyond.

"No sign of the boat," Pyetr said quietly, and after another moment: "I'm honestly not sure whether that's good or bad. —Is the old snake in his hole down there?"

"I don't know. But I can't rely on anything, either. The quiet's still with us."

"One way to find out."

"Don't even talk about it!" Sasha said. He tried not to draw any more from the trees than kept them going; but when he slacked off his thievery, he felt so cold and weary his knees began to shake. Or the place frightened him that much—the mere thought of the cave down there, and the deep pit on their right, that had been part of the cave once: he wanted to know where the vodyanoi was, and was sure of nothing, as if he had his ears stopped and his eyes shut. "We'd do better to sit up here tonight and wait for daylight. The boat's not here, that's all we need to know, it's all we can find out tonight."

Pyetr said: "I want to have a word with the snake, myself."

"Not in the dark!"

"Well, god, he's not going to come out in the light, is he? You've got the salt."

"I've got it."

"Good." Pyetr took Volkhi by a shorter rein and started leading him downhill. Babi growled, hissed, then bounded after, a small moving black spot in the starlight.

"We're not up to it!" Sasha protested; and Pyetr ignoring him: Stop! Sasha wished him, and saw Pyetr hesitate in the same instant, set his feet on the slant and look up at him with a look he imagined as indignation.

"I'm taking from the forest, Pyetr, I can't go on doing that!"

"You can keep on doing it till we know what we're dealing with!"

"Not against him! I'm stealing what I've got—I don't know, I can't hold on to it—"

I find no limit—

"Long enough for questions!" Pyetr said. "Dammit, Sasha, don't doubt! Isn't that what you tell me?"

Eveshka's grave, beneath the willow—

I've seen this, he thought. The bannik showed me this, god, we've arrived exactly where it said we would be.

"What are we going to do," Pyetr asked, "camp here, go to sleep, not knowing whether he's here or not—not knowing whether *she* is, more to the point?"

"I don't know. Pyetr, I just don't know, I'm not sure—"

"God. All right, wait here if you want to. Just keep wishing, all right?"

"I can't!" he cried, feeling everything slipping. But Pyetr had already turned and started downhill, intending to go into that cave below the roots of the dead willow—with the bones and the dead things—

Eveshka's bones, for all they knew, the irresolvable paradox of her existence—

"Wait!" he cried, plunged into a reckless, weak-kneed descent. Pyetr never so much as slowed down, that was what his wizardry was worth at the moment. He reached the flat strip along the water, seized Pyetr's arm. "Wait!" he said, and Pyetr was going to resist him until he said, breathlessly, "Let me try."

"Do it," Pyetr said. And he was trapped, looking into Pyetr's face—not *up*, nowadays. Eye to eye. Pyetr believed in him, Pyetr *wanted* him to produce thunder and lightnings, the tsar and all his horses: Pyetr, who did not always believe in magic, had an absolute faith in him, at least, and no belief in limits.

Eavesdropping had its penalties. He was trapped, en-spelled by a man without a drop of magic. He felt in his pocket to be sure, in all the rain and the stumbling about in the woods, that he still had the little packet of salt and sul-phur, while his wits were still wondering why he was doing this and telling him that they both were fools.

But he started walking toward the old willow down the shore—and stopped at once as he heard Pyetr leading Volkhi behind him. Pyetr nudged him in the ribs, saying, this man all Vojvoda knew for wild risks and breakneck escapades, "Go on. I'm here in case the magic doesn't work. Babi's right with me."

Sasha clenched his teeth to keep them from chattering . . . chill and exhaustion, perfectly natural, he told himself. He was not sure any longer whether Pyetr was wrong, whether he had been right, whether in approaching the vod-yanoi with stolen strength they were not doing something supremely stupid. It was certain at least that doubt was fa-tal: he tossed alternatives to the winds and resolutely wanted the vodyanoi out of his cave as they reached the willow.

"Can you feel anything?" Pyetr asked, and he jumped, losing his concentration.

"Shush!" He waved at Pyetr to be quiet, gathered his cour-age and, deciding the willow itself might afford him some feeling of the cave below its roots, he worked his way along one large root and leaned against the trunk, almost over the water as he wished down, down into the earth, where the River-thing collected bones and wove his own magic—he could feel that magic, now, dark and snaky and many-turning as its wielder, but he found nothing at the heart of it, as if the dark down there were vacant.

"Hwiuur!" he called to the vodyanoi. "Answer me!"

But there was no response under the bank. He heard the random lap of the river against the roots, smelled the dank breath of the cave under his feet as he balanced there—with very mixed feelings about finding the creature not at home. But the arm that supported him was starting to shake and, with the growing conviction that Hwiuur was not, wherever he was, asleep, he was very anxious to get off his precarious perch and away from the water edge. He pushed away from the trunk.

The tail of his eye caught a shape swinging in the willow branches beside him.

"God," he gasped, afraid for an instant it was some drowned body snagged there.

It hissed at him, Babi hissed, and Volkhi shied up, as the creature suddenly took on an elbows-out outline, moving spiderlike toward him.

Blood on thorn-branches—

Pyetr's sword rang free of its sheath. Pottery crashed. Volkhi thundered away along the shore.

Fall of rain . . . gray sky, gray stone . . .

Burned timbers . . . and lightning . . .

Pyetr's sword crossed his vision and Sasha put out his hand to restrain him from that recklessness.

Black coils slipping into dark water, flowing and flowing into the deep . . .

Eveshka sitting at the rail, pale hair blowing in the wind . . .

The shape vanished from the branches in the blink of a night-confused eye.

"What in hell was that?" Pyetr breathed.

"The bannik. At least—it's what showed up in our bath-house. It's not supposed to be out here. It's not supposed to do things like this!"

A gust of wind blew willow-strands against his cheek, feathery and chill as the touch of a ghost. He faltered in his balance on the roots, snatched at the branches and immediately let them go—then grasped them again to be sure, while

123

his heart thumped so hard it all but stifled his breathing. "Pyetr, it's alive. The willow's alive."

Pyetr caught a handful of the willow switches in his left hand and let them go again as quickly. "Maybe some green left in the roots," he said, his voice none so steady either. "Trees do that."

One prayed the god it was only that—or at least that it meant something good, this life returned to dead branches, to Eveshka's willow, Eveshka's dreadful willow—that had been the last thing alive when the woods had died.

"What did you see?" Sasha asked him. "Did it show you anything?"

"No," Pyetr said. Then: "Damn. Volkhi!"

Sasha looked. There was no trace of the horse but the baggage he had dumped on the grass—in which he held out little hope for the jars of herbs and powders.

The fire-pot at least had survived. And the vodka jug—which, by the one real magic of a very foolish young wizard, had no possibility of breaking or of emptying. Driftwood gave them convenient kindling. They shared a portion of bread and sausages, while Volkhi grazed on the margin at a good distance from the willow and the cave.

"Can't blame the poor horse," Pyetr muttered, while Sasha sorted broken pottery among other surviving pots, to tell what had spilled in the bottom of the bag.

Comfrey and their other pot of sulphur and salt—that was the real disaster: one wondered what comfrey did in a mix that repelled River-things.

"Probably," Pyetr said, "he's thinking life might be better with 'Mitri, after all." He broke a piece of wood in his hands, a crack muffled by the river-sound. "Probably he's right. —I'm not going to sleep, understand? I don't want to sleep tonight, in this place, I don't care if the River-thing's not at home, it's not safe here, it spooks Babi, and don't you dare work any of your damn tricks on me, hear me?"

"I'm not," Sasha said.

"A wonder he didn't break a leg out there."

"He's all right. Some of our wishes stuck, didn't they? So it's not everything that's not working. We did get here, didn't we?"

"Whose wishes?" Pyetr asked.

"Fair question," Sasha said, glumly, and tossed a bit of broken pottery into the river. Splash. Firelit ripples spread.

Pyetr unstopped the vodka-jug, took a drink, stared off into the dark where the tree stood and said,

"We should be out of here. We're not going to find him—"

"Pyetr, I can't keep doing what I've done, I can't!"

"You can do it a few damn days! 'Veshka did it for years! Pick on some scrub for the god's sake—it needs thinning anyway!"

"It's not like that. It's not like that, Pyetr, you don't—"

"Don't what?"

"You don't understand. I don't use magic, I'm not really magical, I don't deal with it! There's a difference between being a wizard and being a sorcerer."

"Nothing's happened yet!"

"Pyetr, —"

"I *don't* understand," he said. It was a challenge. It was hurt and frustrated expectation. "I feel *fine*, we can keep walking. . . ."

"And wear ourselves down again. Pyetr, I've hedged terribly close—terribly close to something I shouldn't do—and the leshys won't like what I've already done—"

"We haven't got damn many choices!"

"Pyetr, I'm killing things!"

That seemed to reach Pyetr. His frown changed, as if he were really looking at him for a moment.

"The vodyanoi's not here," Sasha said. "Eveshka's not. We can't do anything tonight and I can't keep us going at this pace if we have to go all the way—all the way north. . . ."

"Let's say it."

"Let's not. —*I* can steal a little." Even that promise sent a shiver through his bones. "I can keep us going faster than we might. But I can't take and take and take, Pyetr."

Pyetr rubbed the back of his neck, looked up. "All right.

All right. But if you could steal enough, just once—once, to make 'Veshka hear you—"

He thought about that. It scared him. He said, still thinking about it, "I'm not sure that's a good idea."

"The leshys?"

"I'm not sure of that either."

Pyetr shook his head in despair, rubbed his neck again and looked at him with tired, desperate eyes, saying, "No one's ever sure. No one's ever damn well sure."

"I have to be."

"Then nothing's damn well going to get done, is it? My *wife's* evidently sure."

"Pyetr, I'm scared. I'm scared it's all coming undone up there. I don't know magic. I understand wishes. They only work natural ways. You can't wish something against nature."

"Things change that can change," Pyetr said. A muscle worked in his jaw. "I've seen 'Veshka come back to life, I've seen shapeshifters run like puddles . . . Babi, over there. Is that *nature?*"

"Magic's different. Like that jug we can't break. Things don't always turn out what you'd expect. It's hard enough to think about consequences with wizardry. Magic just doesn't make any sense to me. If there are rules I can't figure them out—Chernevog didn't find any. Uulamets just said that *why* you do something has something to do with it, but it doesn't make any difference, if something like the vodyanoi gets a hold on you, because he's older and he's smarter and he *is* magical. Your body can wear out when I use it the way I was using it. Trees can die. Magic can't. Magic's a whole other thing, magic's that place Babi goes to when he wants to get out of the rain, but it's where the vodyanoi comes from, too. And if he's wishing on *there* and not *here* when he changes shape, if that's the way it works—"

"You're not making sense."

"Would you bet against Dmitri Venedikov's dice?"

"No!"

"Well, I won't use magic on the River-thing, either."

—

Pyetr fell silent then, rested his elbow on his knee and a hand on the back of his neck.

Sasha said, desperately, "I'm doing all I can, Pyetr."

Pyetr nodded, jaw tight. And did not look at him. Eventually Pyetr said, in response to nothing Sasha remembered, "She never plans on anybody else doing anything right. —Maybe when you're a ghost that long you stop believing in people, do you think?"

"Eveshka loves you."

"I don't know what that means," Pyetr said after a moment, and sighed and bent his head and poured Babi a drink from the jug, Babi leaning expectantly on his knee. The liquid went down Babi's throat. "I truly don't know."

"You don't know what *what* means?"

"Her loving me."

"She does. Of course she does!"

"I had a lousy father. I had lousy friends. Women all over town said they loved me, while they were cheating on their husbands. I don't know what the hell it means, loving somebody."

"You don't mean that."

"I'm not so sure."

"Because 'Veshka's doing something we don't understand?" This turn of Pyetr's thoughts frightened him—it was a pain he had never dealt with, this whole mystery of wives, that turned a light-hearted man to hurt and constant worry. He *resented* 'Veshka's hurting Pyetr. He tried not to make judgments. He said, "What's that to do with anything? We've been wrong before. She might be right, do you think of that?"

"I never can make sense of her, you know. She never thinks I understand anything. Maybe she thinks ordinary folk are stupid."

"She knew we were going to follow her. She knew you would."

"Is that love—because she knows I'm a damned fool?"

"Pyetr, I swear I don't know if she's right or wrong; but I do know that whatever she's doing, she's got a reason. She thought she was doing the right thing—"

"What reason? What reason, for going off where she's got

the least excuse in the world to be going? The ghosts, the vodyanoi—she's no business dealing with anything to do with him, for the god's sake! Let alone Chernevog! Why in hell doesn't she turn the boat around and come back and find us if she's so damn sure I'm following her?"

"She doesn't want us in trouble. I don't think she's being smart in going alone—but I don't know how she'd get me to go and argue you into staying at the house. You know how that would work." That came out saying 'Veshka would think him helpless. He tried to patch it. "She's not in *love* with me."

Pyetr drew a long breath and let it go slowly. He said, staring out at the river, "Keeping her heart wasn't really a good idea, was it?"

Pyetr always managed to get past him—far past him, to ideas he did not himself want to deal with. "It may not have been," he said. "But you've given her a lot, a *lot*, Pyetr, you don't guess how much. Wizards are lonely. You make her think of someone besides herself. Uulamets always said—that was what she needed most."

"Uulamets." Pyetr said the word like a bad taste in his mouth, and his jaw clenched, making shadow. Pyetr refrained from speaking about the old man, for his sake, Sasha supposed—hated him passionately; blamed him for Eveshka's faults, but he never brought the matter up of his own accord. The god only knew what it took Pyetr to keep his calm tonight. He had already blundered into sensitive spots, but something had to be said, now, while there was a chance to say it so Pyetr would understand it:

"Pyetr, don't think she's weak. She doesn't like to use what she's got: I think what she's been through makes it hard for her, maybe in ways nobody understands. But she's so very strong she was terribly hard to teach. Even her own father was afraid of her."

"Well, then, we don't have to worry about her, do we? She'll handle everything. No need of help. We shouldn't have left the house. We can go back home and sit and wait."

"Pyetr, you know what the truth is: she's scared to death for you. Yes, she's got her heart, and she knows anything that wants her or me is going to go straight for you, that's why she didn't just ask me to go, she wants us looking out for each other. She can't work with people. She can't even work with me. She gets scared. Sometimes I think—" He had never brought it up. He took a breath and took the chance with Pyetr. "I think maybe she's scared of slipping back again."

Pyetr looked straight at him this time, with all his attention. "To being a ghost?"

"To wanting things. To wanting things so much she can't stop."

"She could stop. She did stop. She could have killed me, and she did stop."

"With you she did, because you were the first person in all the world who made her think of somebody else. But if she weren't alive, if she hadn't come back all the way to life and she were with you every day—I'm honestly not sure she could have been that good, this long. I'm not sure anybody's that strong, not to have a selfish thought sometime, even if you know it's going to hurt someone—and sometimes if you have hurt someone—if you've done something really, terribly awful—your wishes won't work very well." He was thinking of his own house, seeing the fire in the windows and hearing the voices. "I can put out fires a lot better than I can wish them to start. And if she's thinking of using her magic—I don't think she wants anyone she loves near her."

Pyetr stared grimly into the fire and took another drink. A big one. Then he capped the jug. "Well, I know what I'm going to do, friend, it's very simple. No magic. Nothing of the sort. I just want within reach of Chernevog. The leshys had the right idea in the first place. Old Misighi was for breaking him in little bits. I should have helped."

Chernevog's own wishes might well have prevented that, Sasha thought; but he kept that unsettling thought to himself; he had poured enough into Pyetr's lap tonight, and he was not at all sure he had made Pyetr understand him, about magic and rusalkas. He could wish that Pyetr did. But that broke promises—and that wish itself might go astray, Pyetr having no way to feel what it was to have wishes work— what it felt like to wish while one's enemy wished, faster and faster, until there was no time to think and no time to mend things . . .

129

Until the power grew so much and the confusion so great—

Sasha shivered, a twitch of his shoulders. Across the fire, Pyetr settled down in his blankets. Sasha lay back on his own mat and pulled his blanket to his chin, staring up at the sky, and listened to Volkhi moving nearby.

Thank the god most of the baggage had survived.

Thank the god they had Babi with them to guard their sleep. Babi had posted himself between them and the water, as good a watchdog as they could have.

He only wished he knew where the vodyanoi was tonight; and recalling the bannik—why it had come here or why it had power here. Maybe, he thought, the bannik's behavior was like Babi's: Babi had no reason to leave a dvorovoi's duty either, faring off with them about the woods, except that being a wizard's dvorovoi seemed to make Babi different. Certainly being a wizard's bannik—might account for almost any odd behavior.

Insoluble by any reason. His thoughts were growing random and chaotic. He worried whether Pyetr had understood anything.

He could still change his mind about what he had said, at least he could wish Pyetr to forget specific things he had said—but that was meddling, too; the god only knew what damage it might do—even put Pyetr off his guard and endanger his life. One could not find a path without a trap in it, and he was scared to the bottom of his soul that he had said things that Eveshka would not forgive and Pyetr might never, ever forget.

God, he did not want to hurt them. Either one.

"Watch us, Babi," he whispered, before he set his own mind to drift, and deliberately breaking a promise, began to wish them both disposed to sleep . . .

After which the earth seemed to move and pitch under him like the river.

A ring of thorns . . .

A cold bed, a hard one—he felt the breeze and knew the touch of sun and moon; was aware of the movement of the stars. . . .

It was the motion of the horse he still felt. It was the dizziness one got from gazing into the heavens—

Sky overhead, blaze of sun through branches, stars glittering through a net of thorns, a long succession of days and nights, careering madly across the heavens . . .

He sat upright, caught himself on his hands as Babi hissed and barreled into his chest, holding him and burying his head under his chin. He hugged Babi back, still trembling, not wanting at all to think how close that had been.

God, he thought, that was Chernevog, the thorns, the stone, the days and the nights. I'm dreaming his dream.

I nearly did it, I nearly waked him myself . . . God, I'm a *fool*!

In the same instant he felt a prickling at his nape, looked toward a sudden sense of presence in the dark at his elbow, fearing the slither of something large and snakelike—

There was indeed a shadow, in which eyes shimmered gold-filmed red, reflecting firelight. But the shape was human, a spiky-haired, ragged urchin.

What do you want? he asked it, while Babi clung to him and hissed like a spilled kettle. The bannik shifted forward, grinned at him, resting bony arms on bony knees. Squatting there in the likeness of a starveling child, it made a rippling move of its fingers.

Sound of hoofbeats . . . pale horse running under ghostly trees.

What are you? he asked it. Bannik, what's your name? Are you our bannik—or are you something else?

It grinned at him. Its teeth were sharp as a rat's. It spread its fingers again.

Spatter of blood on a golden leaf—a single drop, shatteringly ominous. . . .

Perhaps he dreamed that he had dreamed. Now he rode through woods, trees rushing past him, a horse's pale mane flying in his face. Everything was twilight and terror, and falling, golden leaves. He was not sure where the horse was carrying him, or what pursued them, or where hope was, except in getting away from this place before the light finally failed.

—

The leaves fell, the sun came and went in patterns of dark and light, following a curve across the sky.

Trees stretched their branches, thorns wove like serpents—and slowed to graceful leisure. Leaves unfurled, more slowly, so slowly finally the eye could no longer see them move.

Then one droplet hung still, still, on the thorn, impaled there . . .

Eventually it fell.

The next drop gathered. One began to think, if one wished, it might stay a little longer, fall just so.

One would know by that small sign, that one was no longer quite asleep.

11

✠ ✠ ✠ ✠ Pyetr put water on to boil—tea, Sasha
asked for this morning, late as they had
waked, *tea*, for the god's sake, in this damnable vicinity, a
delay hard to bear, considering the vodyanoi missing from his
den, and Eveshka on the river—

In spite of which considerations he himself had slept like
a stone last night, suspiciously like someone's intervention,
while Sasha complained of unrestful dreams and wrote furiously. But if one dealt with wizards, patience was a necessity,
and if the lad wanted tea while he did some quick scribbling
in his book, tea Sasha got: it was at least something for a man
to do who had no choice but to wait.

So Pyetr delayed the questions that were churning in him
this misty morning. He made the requested tea, and set a cup
by Sasha's foot and a lump of honeyed grain on Sasha's knee.

Without a glance, Sasha reached after the grain-and-honey,
stuffed the whole into his mouth and drank with the left
hand—alternate with holding the inkpot, god hope he did not
confound the two. An elbow braced the pages open, the quill-
tip waggled more furiously than it had on the goose. Clearly
Sasha was hurrying as fast as he could and an ordinary man
could only hope he was coming to useful conclusions.

Pyetr washed his own breakfast down—asked, eventually,
in case spells required it, "Are you going to need the fire?"
and, Sasha answering with what he thought was no, Pyetr
drowned the embers with river-water and packed as far as he
could, except Sasha's book and the ink-pot.

He thought, while he was doing all of this: 'Veshka's not
a fool, either. Sasha's right: she at least thinks she knows

what she's doing. If she only bothered to tell a body what she's up to—

Or why in hell that tree's alive again—

It had upset him last night. It worried him this morning and occasioned glances down the bank to where it stood, lithe limbs blowing in the wind. He did not understand why it should matter that an apparently dead tree had returned to life, or what obscure connection there should be to that tree and Eveshka's disappearance—except he most emphatically recalled it dying, shedding its leaves out onto the water while Eveshka became alive again. And certainly it had looked dead for all the three years he had sailed back and forth past this place replanting the forest upriver.

Eveshka cared about the woods. She bespelled her seed-lings with fervent wishes for their growth. She talked about this tree and that tree as if it was a person. This willow had held her soul once, whatever that meant; and it had survived the whole forest dying, died at the moment she lived, and come back to life suddenly after all this time, and she had never, ever, with her magic, noticed that curious fact?

Or noticing it—happened to mention that trivial matter?

God, he had never even imagined she might come *here* in her flights into the woods.

Surely not.

Sasha closed the book.

"Are we going now?" Pyetr asked.

"We're going." Sasha put book and ink-pot into his bag. "You ride. Your turn."

"What are we going to do?"

"We're going to go up there," Sasha said, "and find out."

"Good. Finally something makes sense. —Move, Babi." He swung up onto Volkhi's back as Babi, perched there, vanished out of his way. He set his cap on as Volkhi ambled over to Sasha in a very unnatural attraction for a horse, and he reached down to take Sasha's pack up. "Do we know anything? Have we learned anything in all this reading and writing?"

One hoped. One did hope.

134

Sasha dashed that notion with a worried shake of his head. "I only think somebody wants us here. Don't ask me who."

"I am asking. Or is it that name we're not saying?"

"I don't know," Sasha said, and shook his head again, starting Volkhi walking without laying a hand on him.

"Well, what?"

"I don't know what."

"Sasha—"

"I'm afraid he's waking. I don't know how, I don't know why, I don't know if it's something he wished a long time ago or it's just one of those accidents that happens with wishes. Maybe something made the leshys' attention slip. It doesn't matter why. I don't think it matters, at least."

"Don't say Don't know. God, I'm tired of Don't know, Not sure, Don't know why. Just for the god's sake let's make up our minds how *we* want things and dig our heels in, isn't that the way it works?"

"It works best," Sasha said, "if what you wish is of no possible use to your enemy."

They traded off from time to time, from time to time let Volkhi carry the baggage alone to rest from both of them—in a pathless region, Sasha thanked the god, both higher and drier than the boggy ground south of the den, and further from the river now, but not often out of hearing of it. Sasha slogged along during his turns afoot as fast as he could, catching a stitch in his side he wished away, stealing only so much as kept them moving and wishing the while for some wisp of a thought from Eveshka, some break in the silence that went around them—most of all for some sign that the leshys were even aware of their difficulty.

But there was no answer from any source, except that foreboding which had been with him in his nightmare, that they were running out of time and running out of luck, that Eveshka when she had taken the boat had effectively stranded them so far behind there was no hope of catching her on the way, not so long as the wind blew from the south— and blow it did, against all his wishes.

Pyetr in his own turns afoot spared little breath for conversation, made no demands, offered no recriminations for his shortcomings or his bluntness of last night.

Only once: "Damn mess," Pyetr said, when they lost time wading a substantial stream, and once again, when, immediately after, Pyetr slipped and took a ducking—"I know you've got other worries just now," Pyetr said, standing up dripping wet, "but could we have a little attention here?"

"I'm sorry," Sasha said in all contrition. It *was* his fault. But Pyetr frowned up at him on the horse, put his hand on his knee and shook at him. "Sense of humor, boy. Sense of humor. Remember?"

That was the way Pyetr got through things, no matter his friend was a fool. He realized then Pyetr was trying to cheer *him* up and make him quit a very dangerous brooding and woolgathering.

"I'm sorry," he said, and only by Pyetr's face realized it was still another damnable Sorry. He tried to joke too, and winced. "Sorry."

"Lend me a canvas."

"Why don't you ride?" Sasha said, though he had only just gotten up, because Volkhi's bare back afforded some warmth to a man in wet clothing. But Pyetr refused and only asked for the canvas, saying walking kept him warm, and that Volkhi had no need for another soaking.

Within the hour it thundered.

They kept traveling in rain and dusk, lightning flashing white above the trees—a miserable night, Pyetr said to himself, but they had their shelter canvases to wrap about them as they walked—soaked as he had been when it started, it still kept him warm; and at least since that ducking they had better ground underfoot—wide spaces between dead trees and new saplings, more new fern than thorn brakes, which let them keep traveling well past sundown.

But for some reason about sunset Sasha had taken to looking over his shoulder as they went—and once Pyetr realized it, then he began to have a prickly feeling at his nape, and began to cast his own anxious glances at their backtrail.

"What are we looking for?" he asked. "That spook of a bannik?"

"I don't know," Sasha said. "I just have this feeling."

Came a sudden crash over the woods, white glare lighting up the puddles, glancing off wet branches and leaves and bracken. Sasha looked white as a ghost himself: it might perhaps be the chill.

But the light was failing them fast by then; and they put up their canvas in the near-dark with ropes between two trees, got a fire going at the edge of their shelter in spite of the rain, and had a fair supper, themselves and Volkhi and Babi.

Comfort, as far as it went.

Only now that they had stopped there was time to think, and Pyetr stared into the fire wondering if Eveshka might know he was thinking of her right now, and asking himself for the thousandth time—he could not help it—whether if he had done better for Eveshka she might just once have trusted him when it counted.

"Don't give up," Sasha said, perhaps eavesdropping, he had no idea. He began to think he had no shame left, or privacy, and sighed.

"I'm not," he said, chin on forearm. "I only wish I knew what she thinks she's doing. Or what we keep looking for, or why in hell—" Sasha always chided him about swearing, never mind that master Uulamets had never stuck at it. And it helped the knot in his throat. "—why we can't reach her."

"I don't know," Sasha said, "I honestly don't know."

"Are you trying?"

"Pyetr, I swear to you—constantly."

He ran a hand through his hair, an excuse to look elsewhere, because his eyes stung. He had no wish to distress the boy. So he said, tight-jawed, the only hopeful thing he could think of: "I trust you." And again, after a sigh, because he felt a little better for that, and it crossed his mind that Sasha might find some things easier to explain without words, "I really don't mind you wishing at me." It was different from just living in the house, he told himself, there were things he needed to know in a hurry, the god help them, even if it made him crazy for the rest of his life—even if Eveshka had scared hell out of him doing it.

Sasha winced visibly, looked embarrassed, and he was sure Sasha had overheard him. Finally Sasha said, faintly, "Wish me to mind my own business when I do that."

"It upset Eveshka," Pyetr said, and after recalling what he had not told Sasha, once upon a time: "That was one of the times she ran out of the house."

Sasha looked upset. Finally Sasha said, "She never said. Pyetr, she makes mistakes, I make mistakes—"

"She said she'd had a hundred years to learn bad habits. She said once—" He did not like to remember it. He knew 'Veshka would kill him for telling it to Sasha. But he thought too, now, if there was one person who ought to know . . . "She said she thought sometimes she ought to be dead again, she said sometimes she almost wished she was—"

Sasha's face grew grim and worried.

Pyetr asked, because for three years he had wanted to ask someone: "Can she do that? Wish herself to die?"

"She doesn't mean it," Sasha said. "Or she would die. That's *not* what she wants, that's absolutely sure."

"What, then?" His wife talked about suicide—and he had to ask an eighteen-year-old boy what she meant. "Dammit, what can I do for her?"

"Make her happy."

"I'm not doing that very well." The knot was back in his throat. He picked up the vodka jug, pulled the stopper.

Sasha said, "Better than anyone could."

He thought about a drink. He decided that was a coward's way. He looked at the fire instead, wishing Sasha would drop the whole thread of conversation, talk about something else now. He had found out all he wanted.

"It's hard to grow up," Sasha said. "It's terribly hard. I killed my own parents."

"Oh, hell—" He knew it: he did not want Sasha going off into those thoughts.

"It doesn't matter whose fault it was. It's just hard to grow up if your wishes work. She hates her father. But her father had to keep her from burning the house down or wishing him dead or something, and he was strong enough to stop her. Mine wasn't. What 'Veshka wanted that made her run away—that's why wizards can't live with each other. That's

why bad wizards can somehow grow up in town. But Uulamets' father just took his son into the woods and left him on
a wizard's doorstep."

"Malenkova." He had heard this story, too.

"Uulamets said most really powerful wizards just go
crazy—and most of the rest just wish not to be able to wish—
and that's the cure, if you can really want that. But 'Veshka
doesn't really want that either, or she would. Malenkova's
dead, Draga's dead, Uulamets is dead, Chernevog—the god
only knows about Chernevog; and as far as I know 'Veshka
and I are the only really strong wizards alive. It's—"

For a long few breaths there was only the sound of the
fire burning, the wind whispering in the leaves.

"—very difficult sometimes," Sasha said. There might be
a shimmer in Sasha's eyes. Sasha's knuckles were white, his
arms locked around his knees. "Scary. But when you've been
able to do anything you want—and you learn to use that—
it's scarier to think of being helpless. So you don't do anything. When you do move, you try to be right."

Pyetr did not know what to say. Finally he said, "You're
better than Uulamets."

"I hope so," Sasha said, and put another stick on the fire,
clenching his jaw. Something happened. Pyetr felt his aches
suddenly stop.

Another theft, he supposed. A man got used to these in-
terferences.

"You think she's scared," he asked, "she might do what
you're doing and not stop?"

"I think she's terribly scared of that." A second stick. "She
had terrible fights with her father. Not just shouting. Wizard
fights, wishing at each other—back and forth. He stopped her.
He was always strong enough to stop her—until she ran away
that day. I don't think she understands yet how scared he was
of her."

"Why? She can't have outfought him."

"Because a wizard's never more powerful than when he's
a child. Only thank the god no child wants very much. He
can want his mother. She has to listen. Has to." Another of
those pauses, Sasha's eyes downcast in the firelight. "Which
might not make her love him much. And if she doesn't love

139

him he's going to want her to. He's going to want her to do what he wants till, the god only knows, either the baby burns the house down or wishes something really dangerously stupid or some day his mama runs off or his papa picks him up and takes him to a wizard who can deal with him. 'Veshka's mother was a wizard, her father was, she got her gift from both sides. If there was ever somebody who was born like her, I don't know, and Uulamets didn't hear of anybody like her either."

"What are you saying?" He honestly had no idea, except that it seemed nothing good.

"I'm saying I wonder now if Chernevog was even thinking about revenge on Uulamets. It's possible he killed her because he was that afraid of her."

He had no idea how to put that together, whether it was good or bad. Eveshka going up there alone—suddenly might have a completely different interpretation. "You think she *can* deal with him?"

"I don't know. I don't think 'Veshka herself knows."

"What does that mean? Dammit—either she can or she can't."

"She doesn't like to talk about it, but I think—I think she's learned a bit about herself since she came back. I think she's gotten a better idea why certain things happened, and maybe she knows now why she and her father came to odds— even if she does hate him. I think she's afraid he could have been right. And then this business up north—if this has been coming on, and she felt it—she *was* linked to him once . . ."

"That's wonderful. That's damned wonderful. So he's calling her up there. You think she's got any chance whatever against him? He *killed* her, for the god's sake! How much more can you lose than your life?"

Sasha gave him a strange, troubled look. Pyetr suddenly wished he had not asked that question.

Sasha said, stirring sparks from the fire, "She might beat him. The one thing she has to do is know exactly what she wants."

"God," Pyetr said before he thought, and having said it, shook his head and added, his honest thought: "Then we're in trouble, aren't we?"

The forest lay still under the stars, not a breeze stirring.

An owl swooped, talons struck; a hare squealed sharply into silence.

Sasha waked with a jerk in the huddle of blankets, caught his breath and, to shake himself free of the dream, sat up to feed another stick into the embers.

Pyetr stirred and mumbled, "Need help?"

"Go to sleep," he said, wishing the dawn would come. The stick took light, a line of small bright flames in the coals. "It's all right."

Pyetr leaned on his elbow, looking at him with concern.

An owl called, somewhere near. Sasha fed a second stick in and tucked down again, not wishing to discuss it.

"The rain's stopped," Pyetr said.

It had. There were only the droplets the wind shook loose from the trees. Thunder walked far to the north.

Near him, Sasha could not help thinking tonight. Near Chernevog.

God, Eveshka, listen to me . . .

He felt vulnerable tonight. Perhaps it was the dream. He thought of the hare—the swiftness of the strike. . . .

He had never thought overmuch about carrying weapons, he had never even thought of wanting a sword for himself: a wizard with his art was more than armed. A wizard wishing to kill . . .

Could.

Pyetr trusted him to do the wise thing, the right thing to save them; he was terribly afraid that he had been making wrong choices all along, and he wondered if it was so much virtue or wisdom had made him hesitate at killing Chernevog as it was his fear of uncertainties.

Or the force of Chernevog's own wishes.

He shivered, listening to Pyetr settling back into his blankets. He thought, I haven't Pyetr's courage. I'm scared of consequences I can't even think of, so scared I can't think straight. Like a damned rabbit—of some shadow in the sky.

If the leshys let him wake—and if Eveshka's gotten herself into something I can't get her out of, god, Pyetr believes

141

I know what I'm doing, and who am I, for the god's sake, to deal with a sorcerer in the first place? Uulamets was scared of him, *Uulamets* couldn't beat him, except with magic . . .

He thought, then, clear and cold, God, what am I doing? Magic against Chernevog?

Dmitri Venedikov's dice . . .

Fool, *fool*, Alexander Vasilyevitch!

He came free of his trance, scrambled up, looking for his pack.

"What's wrong?" Pyetr sat up and grabbed at his arm. "Sasha?"

"It's all right, it's all right, Pyetr, I just for the god's sake woke up." He dragged his bag into reach and set out pot after pot of herbs. "I haven't been reading what I'm writing all these years, that's what. Words. Words and words. They don't mean anything unless you listen."

"What do you mean, reading what you're writing?—What are you looking for?"

"Mullein, golden-seal, and violet."

"Violet?"

"I like violet."

He found the jars he wanted, he unsealed them and flung a pinch of each into the fire, added moss. The fire leaped up. "More wood," he said.

"Sasha?—" Pyetr seemed to think better of questions then, and got up and fed in three more sizeable sticks.

"I don't promise," Sasha murmured, trying to keep his thoughts together, examining that Don't-promise for hidden doubt. He amended it, absently: "But it's a mistake to go at this with magic."

"Can you talk to 'Veshka? Can you find her?"

"Maybe. I don't know." He added more violet, breathed the smoke, tried to shut Pyetr's questions out of his mind and keep his thoughts joined, like holding so many skittish horses at once. "Magic doesn't belong in nature. Nature's shutting us out, the harder I try to use it. That's what's going on. Nothing against nature."

"What for the god's sake are you talking about?"

"Dmitri's dice. Magic and nature. They don't like each other. Leshys are something special. Magical as Babi. Natural as the trees. Like wizards, more than anything else, part this, part that—but they don't know us: even if they like us they can't tell us apart except they smell us over. They never do know us one from the other by our faces. Us, him, no difference, no difference at all to them, if it's wizardry they don't want happening in the woods—"

"God. You think the *leshys* are doing this?"

"I don't know. I honestly don't know. It's a question of moving pebbles."

"Pebbles?"

"The little things. Hush, please, Pyetr, hush!" He put his hands over his ears, in danger of losing his thought—the exact way Misighi felt when he was speaking, the things Misighi loved and noticed by choice . . .

Misighi and birch trees. Misighi leaning close to smell and touch. Misighi, who heard the least twig break in his woods—*his* woods, long before it ever belonged in any wise to wizards. . . . He leaned close into the smoke, under the drizzle from the trees, held his hands to the warmth, filled his eyes with the leaping flames, unblinking.

Wood and fire. Natural as the forest. Natural as the fall of rain that snuffed it, the seeds that sprouted after it. —Natural as the fall of a single pine cone somewhere unseen— and the wish that Misighi hear it.

"Misighi," he whispered, "Misighi, 'Veshka's out on the river and we can't find her—can you talk to us, Misighi?"

He expected that the answer would be faint when it came. He rested there in the warmth of the smoke, he rested his eyes against the heels of his hands till he saw lights, he thought with guilt of the borrowing he had done against the woods, not trusting wizardry, not thinking of Misighi as Misighi truly was—

And maybe, in that thought, Misighi was chiding him for his mistakes: he did feel the woods again, distant and trying to escape him.

But he clung to that elusive sense of presence: he remembered birch trees, he made all his thought simply of birch trees. "Misighi," he whispered, and somewhere far away dropped another pine cone.

One had to look ever so carefully to see a leshy when it

wished otherwise. One could so easily mistake them. One had to listen ever so carefully to know a leshy's voice—and one might never, ever hear it, if one had one's mind already set only on what one expected to hear . . .

It was truly amazing how long the boy could sit still: Pyetr tucked back in the narrow shelter, wrapped up in his damp coat and his blanket. The magical smoke had no effect on him but to make his nose run—but he saw the concentration in Sasha's attitude, and he was sure something was going on: if it took building fires in the middle of the night and if the boy suddenly said he understood something, then, god, if belief could put some force behind the boy's efforts, then he *did* believe, damn, he did, he would believe in old friends before he believed in anything.

Misighi, he thought on his own, if you're listening—we need help. 'Veshka does. Maybe you do. We're trying to get to you. Listen to the boy, he knows how to say things . . .

Babi screeched of a sudden and bounded out of the shelter: Pyetr's heart jumped. Babi took refuge on Volkhi's back, eyes glowing gold in the dark above the fire. But Sasha never flinched.

Is it going all right? Pyetr wondered. Am I fouling things up?

Then he heard something saying . . . he had no idea. It sounded like the sighing of leaves. It felt like a clean wind. It smelled like spring.

It passed, slowly.

That was Misighi, Pyetr thought, with no sane reason in the world to say he had heard a thing. He wiped his nose furiously, stifled a sneeze, found the arm he was leaning on trembling violently and the fist that had been in his chest let go.

Sasha said, a whisper, "He's listening. He knows we're here."

"I heard."

Sasha sat there a long time on his heels, elbows on knees, firelight shining on scarcely blinking eyes. Pyetr held himself on the shaking arm, dared not move, hardly dared breathe, thinking, eventually,

God, is he all right? Ought I to wake him up? What use am I, except to keep some bear from eating him?

Sasha murmured, finally, scarcely a movement of his lips, "The quiet *is* the leshys' doing. They want us up there, fast as we can."

"They damn near got me killed!" Pyetr whispered. "Don't they know that? They've gotten 'Veshka off alone, the god only knows where she is— If they want us up there, why didn't they damn well *say* so?"

Sasha said, in the same hushed tone, "They're preventing things, that's all. All magic. They're allowing only what agrees with them. I think they're in some kind of trouble."

"Fine. Fine. We know what kind. Is Misighi hearing from 'Veshka? Did you ask him?"

"I asked him. He said—he just said hurry."

God, he did not like the sound of that.

"We've got to go," Sasha said. "Now."

In the dark. Of course. Now. Immediately.

Pyetr grabbed up mats and blankets and started packing. Fast.

Daylight found a wholesome woods, wide-spaced growth. A fox crossed a hillside, stopped and wondered at them.

They were out of the vodyanoi's woods, Sasha said; and in small truth, whether they had suddenly passed within the leshys' healthy influence or whether it was the sheer relief of knowing Misighi was at least aware and answering, Pyetr felt as if they had some real hope: he kept moving as fast as he could possibly walk, despite the occasional stitch in his side, keeping Volkhi's pace and insisting Sasha ride more than he did—"It's all right," he said to Sasha. "My legs are longer."

Ride and walk and walk and rest—the latter only by short stretches: time to splash water in one's face and wash the dust into some spring. Walking warmed wet clothes, wet boots wore blisters, and the whole day became one long confusion of leaf-strewn hills and bracken patches.

But the change in the woods itself was heartening. Leshys' work, for sure, Pyetr told himself: there was hardly a fallen branch in their path, no reason not to go on after dusk and into dark; and when the dark got too deep, they simply un- rolled their blankets, tucked down and rested without a fire, with the branches sighing over them.

"It feels safer here," Pyetr murmured dizzily, on the edge of sleep: "It feels healthier. Thank the god."

"You've got to ride tomorrow," Sasha said.

"Faster otherwise."

Sasha said nothing to that. Pyetr had second thoughts then that maybe it was only that his walking *felt* faster, the god knew Sasha pushed himself as hard as he could—

"Besides," he amended it, "you don't think when you're busy watching your own feet, and my thinking doesn't help us: yours does."

Further silence. Then, a shaky: "I am trying, Pyetr."

"I know you are. Did I ever say not?"

"When I was little," Sasha said on a sigh, "when I'd burn myself or smash a finger—I'd want it to stop hurting—and it would. And that would scare me. So I'd want it to hurt again. And then I'd want it to stop, because it hurt. I feel like that sometimes."

He thought about that. It was more like Eveshka than he wanted to think about at the moment. He said, "I can under- stand that."

"Can you?"

"Nobody knows what they really want. Everybody has doubts. That's the point, isn't it?"

"I think it's the point."

"You should have dumped that skinflint uncle of yours in the horse trough, you know that? You put up with too much."

"I was scared."

"You were too damn polite, you truly were. You always have been."

"That's what I mean! I'm not—not like you."

"Thank the god. What do you want? The boyars after you for a hanging?"

"I'm not as brave as you are. In a lot of ways."

"God, what does that mean? —Because I said I walked faster?"

"You take chances. Chances don't scare you."

Walking a balcony railing. Irina's upstairs window. An icy porch and a prodigious icicle. "They scared hell out of me! I was a gambler, I knew the odds. I wasn't brave. I was broke."

"But you did it. You always knew what you were doing."

"I guessed."

"I wouldn't have had the nerve."

"You're a wizard. You wouldn't have to."

"No. I could cheat."

"Ridiculous. Fedya Misurov was the cheat. And you wouldn't even dump him in the horse trough."

"I was afraid of him."

"No." Pyetr lifted his head off his arms and looked at Sasha, who lay with Babi sleeping on his chest. "You were afraid of *yourself*, friend. You were afraid when you did dump him, it wouldn't be a horse trough."

A sigh. "You're right about that."

"Better damn well do something, hadn't you? You can't do worse than nothing."

"But that's it, Pyetr, that's exactly it—if somebody's wishing me into mistakes."

Pyetr leaned on his elbow. "Maybe doing nothing's a mistake. You think of that?"

Sasha turned his head and looked at him. "If you were a wizard," he said, "I think you'd be a good one."

"God, no, I wouldn't." The thought appalled him. "Not me."

"What would you do?"

"I'd wish him dead! I'd wish the woods safe and 'Veshka back home. That first."

Sasha scratched Babi's head. "How?"

"What do you mean, how?"

"That's too general. How are we going to make that happen?"

"You tell me."

"I'm asking you. —I'm serious, Pyetr, you've a good head

for right wishes. You think of things. Think of getting around what somebody else might have wished—think of something he won't have thought of. You always were good at that."

That was a hard one. Pyetr rolled onto his back and looked up at the dark branches.

"I wish—I wish 'Veshka to make right decisions, for a start."

"Not bad, but too general. Specific things win out."

"What, then?"

"I'm asking you. You're good at getting around things."

"Tavern keepers. Creditors."

"Are wizards smarter? —What would you wish?"

"I want 'Veshka safe! Can't you wish that, with no equivocation?"

"Safe could mean—"

One lived with wizards, one learned such simple truths. "God," Pyetr sighed and put both arms over his eyes. "Get some sleep, boy, just for the god's sake, get some sleep." He thought a moment more. The idea would not turn him loose.

The fact was, what he truly wished was embarrassing—but he thought it might help if Sasha threw it in. "I wish her still to love me."

"Is that fair?"

"To protect her—absolutely it's fair!"

Sasha said nothing to that. Pyetr thought about it, and worried over it, and Eveshka's damnable independence, and said, finally, thinking that by morning he was going to be embarrassed about this: "Then wish me to be someone she'd rely on."

"That's already true," Sasha said.

"Wish it anyway. I do. —And while you're about it, wish us smarter than our enemies."

"I don't think you can do that. You either are or you aren't. That's how you win and lose. You have to be specific."

"Then—" He thought of Vojvoda's upstairs windows, of balconies, latches and shutters. "Wish us not to forget the little things. Wish us—" He thought about the years of his boyhood, that he had gambled his way up from tavern cellars to the fellowship of young gentlemen—and deluded himself about their loyalties. "—to see through our most cherished self-deceptions."

"That's good," Sasha said. "What else? What about Chernevog?"

Pyetr shook his head slowly. "I don't know." God, he found himself don't-knowing, the same as Sasha. But there was so damned much to keep track of. "Wish a snake to bite him. Wish a bear to eat him."

"Awake or asleep? Now or later? You can't put much complication in a wish. There might not be a bear in the neighborhood."

"Well, find one! God, what can you predict? What use is the damn bannik, if it doesn't give you that? —Get some sleep, for the god's sake. We're crazed, we're getting nowhere closer, talking all night."

"Uulamets used to say, Never ill-wish."

"Well, it never damn well stopped Uulamets. Did it?"

"No," Sasha admitted, and then said, on another sigh, "A bear isn't really such a bad idea."

12

★ ★ ★ ★ *Slow thump of hooves on earth, quicker
and quicker—an ominous sensation of
presence behind him—*

*Sasha looked over his shoulder. Eyes shone out of the
dark. Babi hissed, or something did.*

*White mane flew in his face, dead branches rushed past
him. He was riding he had no idea where with something
clinging to his back, riding double on the horse—*

Volkhi made an odd noise, and Sasha waked with a start in
fog-bound daylight—with the pale horse of his dream leaning
over him.

A white and brown spotted horse, actually, looking at him
down a very familiar bowed nose.

He scrambled up, sending the horse shying back in offense; he asked, wobbling on his feet, "Missy?"

Ears pricked forward to his voice—and switched back
again as Pyetr staggered upright. "God, boy, where are you
getting them?"

"I didn't intend to. I honestly didn't intend to—"

"Isn't that the carter's horse?"

"It's Missy, yes."

"Well, god, don't let her get away! —Here, Missy. Good
Missy, here, girl, Volkhi's a gentleman, I swear to his behavior."

Missy shied back from Pyetr's enticements, even from
Babi; but Sasha cheated, afraid she might indeed bolt back

into the woods. He wished and whistled softly, stood with his hands held out as Missy took one cautious step and another, until he had her soft nose smelling over his fingers.

Old friends, old memories, in the midst of troubles—god, it was good to see her. It was wonderful to put his arms around her neck. "Poor old girl," he said against her warm, broad cheek. "Poor old girl, I'm sorry, I wouldn't have brought you here. This is a dreadful place."

Missy distractedly butted him with her head, cracking his teeth, looked up and surveyed Volkhi and Pyetr and Babi with a worried eye, doubtless asking herself what this odd gathering was, or what an honest working horse might possibly have to do with present company.

But that something had gone right suddenly began to seem too improbable. Missy's presence, however loved, became a threat. He had dreamed about a white horse: he had never thought of white-maned, white-rumped Missy.

"I wished for her the night Volkhi came," he said dazedly, holding Missy's cheek-strap while Pyetr was busy throwing the packs together. "I knew I'd done it. I thought I'd stopped it. That was why I was up writing, when the shelf fell. I wished other things—god!—about my uncle—"

"The black god take your uncle. And I doubt Missy had much to do with the shelf."

"It doesn't. But she had to have come straight up from town—to where we were *going* to be this morning . . ."

"Well, damn little use her coming to the house today, is it? Your wish just took care of us, friend, it crossed a flood getting here—"

"But that's just it. She didn't go the way we did. There wasn't time. The only way she could have gotten here since I wished is straight across from Vojvoda, not even *by* the road, no path, nothing—since that night."

"So maybe she got a head start. Maybe for your wish to work she had to."

"You don't do things like that. Things don't happen before they happen."

Pyetr looked at him under one brow. "Good. I'm glad. The world should work like that."

"I mean I honestly don't know. Pyetr, I don't like it, I don't like any of this. I'm telling you I don't think it was my wish that got her here."

"Maybe it was 'Veshka wished it."

" 'Veshka didn't even want Volkhi!"

"Which means you did it. I damn well don't think Kavi Chernevog did." Pyetr gathered up two of their packs and flung them over Volkhi's back, shaking his head. "Just let's get moving this morning. Whatever it came from, whyever it came here, isn't it what we *do* with it that counts? Let's just wish not to be fools."

"Wishing's never helped that," Sasha muttered. "Babi? —God, where's Babi?"

"There," Pyetr said, indicating about head-high. Sasha looked over his shoulder, ready for disasters, and found Babi perched comfortably on Missy's rump, a ball of black fur for all the world like a slit-eyed and comfortable stable cat.

It made him feel better about Missy being Missy.

But not about the other things.

Andrei Andreyevitch's mare having had the decency to run off wearing a halter, it was only a spare bit of rope she needed for a rein—if she even needed that, Pyetr thought, considering Sasha's peculiar talents. "Hauling turnips may be safer," he murmured into the mare's white ear while he knotted the rope to the ring. "But the lad's all right. Do what he tells you. He's not all crazed. Now and again he's even right."

He had no notion himself why he felt in better spirits the last two days—as if, somewhat like the night he had fallen off The Doe's shed roof, this whole business with Eveshka running off had hit him hard and left him dazed; but eventually, even after a fall like that, one started walking straight and realizing nothing he had done lately was sensible.

He got saner and Sasha got crazier—precisely the trouble with wizards, Sasha and Eveshka both.

Hell, she needed him, absolutely she did—she was doing something crazy and she needed both of them. They *would* catch her. . . .

He swung up to Volkhi's back and Babi scrambled out of

152

Sasha's way as Sasha tried the same trick getting up on Missy.
—And failed, his booted heel sliding down Missy's flank
while Babi watched from the ground.

"Not as light as you used to be," Pyetr observed, leaning
on Volkhi's shoulders, watching the second attempt, Missy
wincing, standing quite staunchly still through this. "Taller,
though. Wish, why don't you?"

Sasha gave him a dark look and made it, not elegantly,
hauling himself up belly-down while Missy started to travel.
He managed in a most remarkable way not to dislodge the
baggage.

At which Pyetr found himself chuckling, as if there were
truly hope in the world, as if—

—as if he had had a right to laugh, without Eveshka to
approve it.

As if he had no right to a joke with Sasha, that she would
not approve—that he had not had certain rights—for a very
long time.

God, he did *not* want to feel what he was feeling, damn,
he did not! He wanted 'Veshka to be happy: he had done everything to make her happy. . . .

. . . which mostly seemed to mean giving up one and the
other habit of his that 'Veshka could not abide, considering
her delicate state, until there were bits and pieces of himself
just . . .

. . . dying, until this morning.

Damn, he thought in panic. No, that's not so, that's not
so, I've never been happier in my life. . . .

Granted my misspent youth; and 'Mitri and all the rest,
not to mention all Vojvoda wanting my neck in a noose. . . .

—That's not altogether a happy life, is it?

"Pyetr? Is something wrong?"

His hands had gone cold. Volkhi was wandering under
him without direction. He looked at Sasha with a sudden,
acute fear that Sasha might have eavesdropped just then. But
Sasha only looked puzzled.

"Pyetr?"

"I'm fine," he said, knowing that had not come out as
reassuring as he had hoped. He took up Volkhi's reins. "Fine.
I'm absolutely fine."

153

Up one foggy hill of ghostly young trees and down another—Babi jogging briskly ahead, the carter's mare going
along at Volkhi's side, her ears up, her nostrils working, a
constantly worried look in her eye, as if she were still looking
for a familiar street, or trying to figure what dangers hereabouts particularly relished horses.

But the mare kept up very well on the climbs, sturdy legs
carrying her quite resolutely—straightforwardly trampling
down the sort of nuisances Volkhi danced over.

Precisely when and why she had started from town and
whether they had indeed only arrived at a place that the mare
was headed for before any of them knew they were going to
need her . . . that was the kind of thinking a sane man left to
wizards; but if some of Sasha's wishes were looking out for
them before they even knew they needed it, then maybe their
other wishes would come true. Maybe that was why he could
feel as if—

As if a burden that had been on him for years was falling
away from him on this dismal trail—as if, away from the
house, with all the rules upset and his life in danger, he could
breathe again.

He never, ever thought ill of 'Veshka, he swore to himself
he never, ever begrudged her what he gave up to please her . . .

But he still thought, God, what's the matter with me?
What's happening to me? And why am I so damned angry
with her?

"What did she write?" he asked Sasha that night when, after
a little hot tea and a bite to eat, Sasha opened his book and
got out his inkpot. "Show me where she wrote."

Not that he knew what good it would do him to see it.
He mistrusted writing, he suspected books of contributing to
their troubles, but Eveshka set great store by writing things,
and her curious ways of thinking had been turning over and
over in his mind all day. Her likes and dislikes made him so
angry that for small, frightened moments today he had not
even been able to remember anything but her frown—stupid
of him, he knew; and self-centered; and all the reprehensible
things he knew he had been before Sasha and 'Veshka had

reformed him. So it suddenly seemed to him that, writing being magical, maybe—just maybe, Sasha doing the reading, and Sasha not knowing her quite so well, or not having the right spell on him, Sasha might have missed something essential.

So he overcame his apprehensions and asked to see the very writing; and Sasha carefully opened the book and canted it to the light while he shifted his shoulder to see past their single shadow.

He knew where her work was before Sasha ever pointed it out—marvelous as it seemed to him, the same as he could tell 'Veshka's fine stitches from their coarser repairs, he knew precisely the two lines she had done. He did not touch the page: he had no idea whether that might disturb the spell; but he squatted on his heels looking at it, while Babi snuggled up as a warm lump in his arms, and he listened while Sasha ran his finger along the line and said what he read in it.

But it was only the same thing. "You said that already."

"That's what it says."

One hated to accuse Sasha of inability. But it was a desperately serious point: "Try. I really think it ought to be more than that. Try again."

"Pyetr, I swear to you, ink is ink, and not even a wizard can play tricks with what's on that page. It doesn't change."

"Are you sure?"

"Pyetr, it doesn't ever change. You can burn it, maybe, scrape it off, but nothing can make those letters into something else. It's there, exactly what she said, as long as the book lasts."

"What if some other wizard wishes it?"

"Not that easy. Not in any wizard's book. Letters don't shapeshift. What's there is there. She wanted me to understand things by what she said. But I'm sure of exactly what's there, too. She was worried about us coming after her."

"And getting in her way."

"Yes."

That did sound like 'Veshka. He pointed at the blank space at the end. "Then write one about her being careful, too," he said, and Sasha not forbidding, he watched while Sasha did that—because he saw a use for writing, finally, that

155

no matter how his thinking shifted around, and no matter what happened to him, still, ink being ink, the way Sasha said, that wish if Sasha wrote it might stay and take care of her, even if he failed her, or some spell on him made him forget everything he loved.

He wished with all his heart he could think of a better wish than that. He sat there looking into the fire and trying to think of one, but it seemed to him that anything beyond that doubted Eveshka, and he knew that was no help to her at all.

So he poured Babi a generous bit from the jug, he had some himself, and lay down to sleep, thinking, Well, we're ahead by one horse, aren't we? Things are looking better.

Pyetr did sleep, finally. One learned to be deft about magic, when one was cheating. Sasha spun sleep like wool, wished it soft and deep while he worked, all promises to the contrary—

Water curling white about the bow, ropes creaking—

One tried—even with one's skin crawling, one snatched at thoughts like that the instant they came, tried to speak to Eveshka if it were at all possible . . . but all that echoed back was that sound, over and over, just when he thought he had the thread.

He kept wishing, he leaned his head against his hand, fighting sleep himself, and wrote, simply, with all the wisdom he had, *I wish Eveshka may see Pyetr with her heart, and never doubt him.*

That might be interfering. He was afraid that it was. It might in some unpredictable way be dangerous. But, doggedly unrepentant, he went on writing:

If there's anything common about everything that's gone wrong with us, it's not the silence, it's our losing touch with what's going on around us.

Things happen that can happen. Pyetr reminds me: It's the things we take for granted that we most of all mustn't forget.

—

It was up before the dawn and roll the blankets, pack half-blind in the dark and the chill, and move again, one long half-asleep confusion—a bit of sausage by daybreak as they rode, and a drink from the jug, while Babi sometimes perched on Missy's rump and sometimes Volkhi's, and occasionally, the mood taking him, jogging ahead of them.

Pyetr gave up asking questions, reckoning he knew as much about the leshys' reasons as Sasha did—which was very little: no one knew what went through leshys' minds. But they were moving, gaining ground with the steady rhythm of the horses' stride, up one hill that looked like another hill and down this one that looked like the last, slow down for the horses to rest, pick up the pace again, stop for the horses to recover their wind, rub their legs down with salves one could thank the god Sasha had brought plenty of, and on and on again.

Sometimes he completely despaired, fearing he would never see 'Veshka again, that events were combining against them, and that the short rest of his life was aimed straight for a disaster even leshys could not deal with. At such moments he was in no hurry at all to get where they were going, or to discover what was waiting there.

Then quite as suddenly all such thinking would seem completely unreasonable to him: they were riding up north simply, grandly, to deal with wizardly matters Sasha and Eveshka would realize quickly how to deal with: then all his fears seemed ignorant and foolish.

"Are you wishing me?" he asked Sasha suddenly.

"Sometimes," Sasha admitted.

"Thank the god. I thought I was losing my mind."

"I'm sorry."

"It's all right," he said. But he began to shiver then—want of sleep, perhaps, or the sense that in one way or the other—he was constantly being lied to.

"Pyetr?" Sasha said.

It kept coming and going . . . extreme despair and foolish, unreasonable hope.

"Are you still doing it? Stop it!"

"I'm not. Things keep shifting. Do you feel it?"

"What in hell is it?"

157

"I don't know. I'm not doing it. I—god!"

They came through a curtain of young trees and the afternoon sun hit the young woods ahead of them in a blaze of transparent gold—green-veined gold on sapling boughs, all shot through with sunlight, gold leaves covering the ground. . . .

Pyetr was struck dumb as Sasha, first by the color and the beauty of it—as if they had ridden magically from spring into a golden autumn.

Then he thought with a chill, It's not a healthy color. The trees are dying here . . .

Sasha said, in a hushed voice: "I've seen this place. I've been seeing it for days, in my dreams."

Something strong and heavy hit Pyetr's boot and climbed. He caught his breath and realized it was only Babi, clambering up not to sit on Volkhi's rump this time—but to cling to his side like a frightened child.

"I don't like this," Pyetr said, for what it mattered to anyone.

13

Falling leaves, trampled under
the horses' hooves—
Dream of riders in a golden wood, nearer and nearer—
Dream of a boat, where another sleeper lay, arm over
the swinging tiller, pale hair like a veil—
Dream of blood, a dark wall of thorns—
Wolves . . . whose eyes were gold as the falling
leaves . . .

Every brush against a branch, every gust of wind loosed leaves about them, a constant drift against the sunlight, both beautiful and dreadful.

This is the way the old woods must have died, Sasha thought. *But it's not Eveshka's doing this time—surely not.*

He said to Pyetr. "I think we're going straight to the heart of this."

"Fine," Pyetr said with an anxious look, and patted Babi, who clung to him. "Fine. How far, and what's there, and do we go on going straight to it?"

"I don't know. I'm not sure what we ought to do."

"Babi's not happy with this, you know." There was an unwonted pitch of anxiousness in Pyetr's voice. "It's not many things make Babi afraid . . ."

A sudden spate of golden leaves where the riders
passed . . .
Light faded, the gold dimmed . . . cloud drew across
the sun.
Time moved now—the heart beat, faster and faster.

159

"God!" Pyetr said as a sudden gale hit their backs. The horses snorted and ducked their heads, leaves and twigs pelting them. Grit of some kind went down Pyetr's neck, Babi hissed and vanished out of this sudden inclemency, and Sasha said,

"He's waking. I'm terribly afraid he is."

"Wish him not to!"

"I am!" Sasha said. "I'm just not sure it's doing any good!"

"Don't doubt, dammit!" The blizzard of golden leaves dimmed suddenly with a shadow over the sun. Pyetr looked up and back, shielding his eyes from the wind-borne debris. A single rain-dark cloud loomed over the treetops in the west.

"Rain and thorns," Sasha said faintly—which made no sense, but a man got used to that.

"I'm very tired of rain," Pyetr said, set his cap securely on his head, and looked about him for wherever Babi might have gotten to—but there was that Place that Babi could go when the going got unreasonably uncomfortable; and at the moment he wished he were there, too, if it was out of the coming rain and whatever worse they were going into. "Damn. Damn. Damn."

"Don't swear," Sasha chided him, and he kept his mouth shut, hoping Sasha was wishing something such as Chernevog staying where he was, such as them living to see the river again—such as 'Veshka and the boat safely waiting for them on that shore.

Thunder rumbled. The sky went to iron gray, not unlikely weather for spring: storms came whisking up over the forest horizon, spat a bit and swept on again—and one did truly hope this one was that sort, and not someone else's wishing. Wizards had a knack with lightning—at least the real ones did—and the rumblings and flashes overhead could make a man very uneasy.

"I do hope," Pyetr said, "you're noticing the sky. And the thunder."

"I do," Sasha murmured, "I have," —as if a thousand other things were more important. Sasha pointed ahead of them, where, if one squinted through the rain, one could see a gathering of leafless trees far taller and stouter than the saplings they had been seeing.

That seemed strange, on a second thought, that the leshys should have cleared and replanted these woods so completely—and left such a grove standing.

Tall, aged trees, Pyetr thought as they rode closer—old trees of that generation that had died with the south woods, all standing in thorn brakes and weeds, dead and dry, in springtime . . .

Volkhi viewed it askance, pulling at the rein; but that was the way they had to go, and Volkhi settled with a snort, shaking his head—while poor Missy kept her steady, wizard-wished pace.

Pyetr was about to lodge his own objection when it came to him what they were seeing in the peeling, brushy trunks ahead of them. A chill went through him.

"Leshys!" he said on half a breath. "God, what's happened to them?"

"I don't know," Sasha murmured. "I honestly don't know."

"Leshys can't die!"

"They're not dead."

"They're not doing damn well, are they?" They came to the last edge of the gold, in among thorn thickets, thorns and vines twining round leshys standing so very still, in this desolation—

The horses stopped suddenly, and stood—Sasha's doing, Pyetr was sure; and he looked around with the strongest, most uncomfortable feeling of something ominous all about them.

A whisper of brush surrounded them. He saw the stirring of twiglike fingers, the slow opening of vast, strange eyes in trunks all around them.

"Wizard," a voice rumbled, deep as the grinding of millstones.

And another, deeper still, "Promises broken . . ."

Twigs rustled, thorns bent and snapped as that leshy slowly stretched out its arm toward Sasha. It grasped Sasha's coat and dragged him from the mare's back, Sasha holding desperately to its twiglike fingers.

"Be careful!" Pyetr shouted at it. Misighi had warned them of the wild ones, leshys from woods unaccustomed to visitors—leshys which had no appreciation at all what discomfort flesh and bone might suffer in a stone-breaking grip. "Be careful of him!"

Foolish, he thought in the next breath. Of course Sasha was quite capable of taking care of himself—a fool going after a leshy with a sword sheathed or unsheathed was only likely to annoy the creature.

But: "Promises," the leshy said, and Sasha said, in a voice which clearly said he was in pain:

"Pyetr, Pyetr, don't do anything—don't argue with them—please!"

That was not right. Nothing was right about these creatures.

"Let him down!" Pyetr yelled at it, waving the sword to attract its attention. "Damn it, you're hurting him! Let him go!"

It paid no heed. It began to move, striding through the thorns, bending and breaking them, Sasha's coat snagging, the god only knew about his face and hands.

Volkhi was not moving, spell-bound as he was. Pyetr pulled his head around and waked him with a kick, rode after the leshy that had Sasha—straight on into branches that raked him off Volkhi's back and caught him up and up in a painful grip.

"Misighi!" he yelled. It was all there was left to do, as it snatched him along. "Misighi, dammit, help!"

Twigs wrapped him about, the sky and the ground exchanged positions more than once, and his ribs were creaking.

"Misighi! —Sasha! Let go, damn you!"

Maybe it listened. At least the grip let up, and it handed him on to another and another, a confusing wrapping and unwrapping of twiggy grips about his body and his face, until one took him painfully by both arms and held him in front of its huge, moss-green eye.

"This one," it said, in a voice like rolling stones. "Yes."

It let him go. He flailed out, hit the ground on his feet, and staggered into Sasha's steadying hands. "What in hell—" he said, and caught sight of the stone and the sleeping man beyond Sasha's shoulder.

Then he knew beyond a doubt where they were.

"Promises," a leshy said, and the murmur from the lot of them was like the sound of stones in a river.

"Killing the trees," another said.

And another: "Trust no wizards. Break bones, crack limbs."

Twigs reached toward them, quivering, grasped them both and drew them close, folding about them.

"Misighi!" Pyetr yelled; and the one who had them rumbled, above the other voices:

"Stone and brine, young wizard, fail the root, fail the leaf, fail the tree. Foolish, foolish wizards."

"Is it Misighi?" Sasha asked.

"Misighi, yes." Brushy arms extended, rustling in the hush that had fallen, and set them safely back on the ground. "This root goes deep, deeper than leshys drink, young wizard." Twigs felt them over, twigs grasped and curled and faced them both about, toward the sleeper on the stone.

"What do we do?" Sasha asked, turning about again; and Pyetr turned, seeing nothing but a grove of trees.

"Misighi?"

Nothing stirred. There was nothing but the grove, the thorn hedges around them—the young wizard lying pale and still.

"God," Pyetr said, catching a breath. "*Is* he asleep?"

"He certainly seems that way," Sasha said, and walked closer to that stone, and to Chernevog.

Pyetr overtook Sasha and caught his arm. "Close enough. Don't touch him."

Rain glistened on Chernevog's pale face and hands, soaked his dark hair and his clothing. Like wax, he seemed—but he breathed. His clothes—white shirt, black breeches—were weathered and scattered with bits of twigs and leaves. That seemed to Pyetr the most disconcerting sight—that cloth should have faded, while Kavi Chernevog remained so apparently alive.

This creature—who had murdered 'Veshka once, and caused so much harm—slept like nothing so dangerous or evil. He looked so young and so incapable of the things he had done.

"So we're here," Pyetr said, with a breath. He looked

around the circle of leshys, that looked like nothing so much as aged, weathered trees. "Here before she is, I hope to the god. —Misighi, where's Eveshka? At least tell us that!"

Not a branch moved, not an eye opened anywhere around the grove.

Sasha said, "The way the river bends—it's entirely possible we've beaten her here."

"I don't like this, damn, I don't like this at all. What's the matter with the leshys? What in the god's name are we going to do with him? What do they expect?"

"I don't know," Sasha said.

Pyetr shoved his cap back and raked his hair out of his eyes, set it again and looked at Chernevog, thinking how in his impoverished, cellar-pilfering boyhood he had killed a rat once; he had even pinked a rascal in a duel once, and he could, not enthusiastically, behead a fish; but that dreadful thump that had put finish to the rat resounded in his dreams; and the god knew he had never killed another.

So here he was contemplating killing a sleeping man— even if it was Chernevog and even if he deserved a hundred times over to die.

"I think you should go get the baggage," he said to Sasha.

"It'll be—" Sasha looked at him suddenly if he did understand. "Pyetr,—"

"I'll take care of things. My business. Something we should have done long since. Go on."

Sasha walked off slowly, shaking his head—stopped then and said, "Pyetr, I'm not sure about this."

"I'm hard to wish. You aren't. Get out of here!"

"The leshys could have killed him: they don't mind killing trespassers, they've no conscience at all about it—"

"So maybe they figure it's our job. Fair enough. I'll accept that. Go on. *Go.*"

"Just—"

"Sasha, go see to the horses, dammit!" That Sasha lingered to argue frightened him and something shook his conviction. There were wishes loose, he was sure that there were, wishes to make them make mistakes, doubts to bring them to disaster and to set this creature free again. He clenched his hand tighter on his sword. He waved at Sasha, insisting he leave.

"Pyetr!"

He saw alarm flash into Sasha's eyes, turned as an owl glided to a landing at Chernevog's feet.

"So he does have a heart."

"Be careful of it!"

"Damned careful! —Which should I go for, him or the bird?"

"Not the owl—not the owl! It can't die while he's alive."

"Just stay back!" He shook the sheath free, walking toward Chernevog, to spit him; but the owl spread its wings and launched itself at his face.

"Look out!" Sasha cried.

He cut at the creature—but the owl evaded his blade and flung itself at his face. "Damn!" he yelled, swung and tried to fling it off, but it clung to his sword hand with its talons, beating at him with its huge wings and tearing at his hand with its beak as Sasha struck at it barehanded to distract it.

It flew up again. Pyetr cut at it with a wild effort, hit it to his own dismay, and slung it to the ground off the edge of his blade.

"Pyetr!" Sasha cried.

A leaden blaze of daylight and a net of thorns—pain stabbed deep across arm and shoulder, settled in the heart—and in that pain, Chernevog flung himself off his bed and ran . . . wished sight, wished warmth, wished strength from the woods around him—

But it resisted him, and the hunters were close behind.

He was the boy again, fleeing the house, Draga's wolves loping on his track, sharp-toothed and yellow-eyed. Thorns tore his hands as he fended brush aside. He ran free a moment, always a moment to think he might get away—but a thorn hedge loomed up in front of him, thorns hemmed him in on every side, and when he turned, his back to the thorns, the hunters were the riders from his dream, closing in to kill him.

He wanted to live, truly wanted to live, but the power failed him, and he could not remember where he was, or why the wolves had shifted into human shape. He was shivering so he held to the barbed branches to keep himself on his feet. He remembered names: Sasha, Uulamets' student: that was the one he most feared, though it was Pyetr Kochevikov who had the sword, it was Pyetr who would kill him and send him back to Draga's bed again, Draga saying, Young fool, did you ever think you could escape me?

"God," Chernevog said, and sat down against the thorn hedge, holding to its branches.

"Where's my wife?" Pyetr asked him, with the sword against his heart. "Where's my wife, damn you?"

"I don't know," he said faintly, and it seemed to his confusion that he had no better friend in all the world than this man who would put an end to wishes, this man who of all men he had ever known had no further designs against him. He sat there waiting to die, Pyetr stood there looking at him, and the sword hurt, but not greatly. Neither of them moved, for what seemed forever.

"Damn you," Pyetr said finally. He thought that was the last thing he would hear.

But Sasha pushed the point away.

14

✠ ✠ ✠ ✠ Nothing had worked the way it ought, in
Sasha's reckoning: the owl ought not to
have died, the leshys ought not to be standing motionless and
unhealthy as they were, and Chernevog ought not to be
alive—but for the latter fact at least he had only himself to
blame. He could not understand what he had done—or why
he had not shoved Pyetr's hand the other way.

"Get up," Pyetr said, and Chernevog struggled to his feet
against the thorn hedge, grasping branches that stabbed his
palms with a cruelty that made Sasha wince. Blood came—
droplets shaken from the thorns spattered the leaves.

God, I've seen this, I've seen this, and now it's happening.

"Move!" Pyetr said, and Chernevog, seeming dazed and
lost, went where Pyetr sent him, back through the thorn-
hedge maze to the clearing and the stone.

We have to kill him, Sasha thought miserably. Surely
that's the only sane thing to do. Nothing can ever be safe so
long as he's alive.

"Misighi!" Pyetr called to the leshys, who stood all about
them, still as trees. "Misighi, he's awake, we've got him, now
what in hell do we do with him?"

The leshys gave no answer. Chernevog had knelt by the
owl, blood still dripping from his fingers, falling to the ground
between his knees—Chernevog wiped his cheek with the
back of his hand, looked utterly overwhelmed.

God, this is where it was telling us we'd be, this is what
the bannik meant. But he's not fighting us, he doesn't act as
if he understands anything—

"Don't put on with us," Pyetr said, "damn it all." He had

his sword in his hand. Everything about him said he was ready to use it: Sasha wished he would, before Chernevog recovered his wits and wanted their hearts stopped.

But Chernevog looked up, cradling his wounded hands one in the other, his face white with pain, eyes holding only bewilderment.

Pyetr's sword trembled, rose in a wide, glittering sweep, and with a sudden wrench of Pyetr's arm, hit the ground at Chernevog's knee.

"Hell!" Pyetr said in disgust.

Chernevog had never flinched, only looked at them with that terrible lost expression.

"Is he doing that?" Pyetr asked angrily. "Is he wishing at us?"

Sasha said, "I'm not sure."

Pyetr came back to him, and turned and looked again at Chernevog, the sword still in his hand. "He *is* doing it, dammit."

The books, Chernevog's with them, were all lying out in the brush somewhere—Sasha tried *not* to think about that. He caught Pyetr's arm, drew him half about and whispered, "The owl shouldn't have died, we've left my bags out there, and I'm not sure the leshys are watching anything right now."

"Let the damn bags stay there! Don't let's go off in separate directions like fools, all right? It's exactly what he'd want!"

"I don't know, Pyetr. I don't know! If the owl did have his heart, and it did come back to him— Maybe that's what the leshys wanted, maybe that's what they've been doing with him all these years—"

"We don't damn well know what the leshys have done, do we? They're not talking to us. They're not looking healthy at all right now, are they?" Pyetr's voice rose. Pyetr made an evident effort to keep it low. "Misighi's not the sort to draw off from us."

"Maybe it wasn't easy," Sasha said, "working a magic like that. If they *have* somehow cured him . . ."

"Cured him of what? Cure him of *life*, that would have been some help! What are we supposed to do now, take him home? Let him live in our house, eat at our table, wander the woods and talk to the foxes? Pay social visits to vodyaniye and the god knows what? There's a shapeshifter loose in the woods! Did Misighi send us that little gift? Did he sent us the bannik? Or did Misighi turn the house upside down and lose me in the woods? Where's 'Veshka, that's what I want to know! She should have been here ahead of us!"

It was a disturbing lot of questions, all of which nested ominously in that confusion Chernevog occupied in his thinking. "We don't know how far we are from the river," Sasha said. "I don't know. I don't know about the shapeshift-er. Maybe he did send it. Maybe it's the vodyanoi trying to stop us getting here."

"Fine. Fine. 'Veshka's on the river and maybe the vod-yanoi's loose—"

"Pyetr, he *has* his heart, I really think that's what hap-pened. He must have sent it away a long, long time ago—and he wasn't very old, then, he can't have been, he was a boy when he came to Uulamets and he didn't have it then. I don't know what it would be like—but I'm not sure it wouldn't still be the same as it was then."

Pyetr looked at Chernevog, scowling. "That's no damn boy."

"But his heart, Pyetr, —something brought the owl here and brought us here, and the owl shouldn't have died."

"Fine. The owl's dead. He *wants* us to feel sorry for him!"

"I don't feel him wanting anything right now."

"He wants to be free, is what he wants," Pyetr said. "He wants us dead, is what he wants, and just because he hasn't got his wish yet doesn't mean he won't if we turn our backs on him. 'Veshka's coming here—we hope to the god she's coming here—and we'd damn well better do something about him before she walks into this. I don't want him trying any of his damn tricks with her!"

"Don't—"

"—swear. I'll swear, dammit, I'll swear—Misighi, dam-mit, wake up and give us an answer!"

Something happened, then. It might have been a voice. It felt like a reassurance. It felt like a light moving around them when everything outside this grove was dark.

A leshy voice said, "No more, no more strength . . ."

"No more time . . . no more. Keep him safe."

Misighi said, deep as bone, "Trees die. This will not. Take him to Uulamets."

After which—Misighi stood as still as if he had never moved, as if not even wind could stir him.

"What does *that* mean?" Pyetr cried. "Misighi, what are you talking about, take him to Uulamets! —Uulamets is *dead*, Misighi! Uulamets has been dead for three years! Wake up and listen to me!"

Misighi did not move again. The only sound was thunder, the wind moving in the woods—

And the first few spatters of rain.

Owl was dead . . . he truly could not understand that. Owl was a ball of fluff, a hungry mouth—one had to feed him, one had to keep him in secret—Draga would kill him, else. He had taught him to fly, wished him safe and free and sent his heart where he had thought Draga could never catch it. It was not that many years ago.

But Owl was gone, without his ever knowing Owl was in danger at all—and everything he knew seemed to have changed. Lightnings flickered overhead. He could seize them—if he knew beyond a doubt that was what he wanted. He could free himself if he cared for one thing more than anything. But Owl was gone and Draga was dead and the pattern his own blood made, rain-washed on the leaves where he knelt, was of equal fascination with his warders' argument about whether it was wiser to kill him. He could have offered his own opinion, but it seemed superfluous: the leshys had given their orders, and he felt—truly, mostly numb now, the pain in his hands a welcome distraction from wishes. He could not gather the pieces of his magic up again. He dared not, and it was the same as being blind.

"Get up," Pyetr said to him; and he did, caught Pyetr eye to eye for an instant and with all his heart wanted this extraordinary man's goodwill . . .

He felt Sasha's instant intervention—turned his head and for a panicked moment it was Sasha he was looking at, Sasha wishing him helpless and quiet.

Then for no apparent reason things slid into order: he was aware of the ground they stood on, aware of the boundary of nature and magic, and for an instant of utter terror wavered this way and that of that line.

He clenched his hands, courted the momentary pain—he had that much sense left: think of running water when things went wrong: water and stones, no fear, change without change. He caught his breath and his balance then, looked back toward Pyetr—

And in complete simplicity cast his heart in that direction, quite the same as he had given it to Owl—because a man like Pyetr could no more use it than Owl could. He hoped it might appease Sasha—and no one had ever said of Kavi Chernevog that he was a coward.

But Sasha snatched it himself, before he could more than think of his own survival, and sent it back to him with a wish so strong he had no defense. He recalled the moment before he had given it to Owl, and tears came to his eyes— that was what Sasha did to him, while Pyetr said, completely extraneously to everything that was happening— "Find Uulamets! Misighi's lost track, that's what he's done—he's forgetting things the way I was forgetting!"

Sasha said, distractedly: "I don't think so. It's very possible there's something left. I'd be surprised if there wasn't a ghost or something."

"There's a damn shapeshifter!" Pyetr said. "We met that! No, thank you!"

Chernevog listened to the argument, remembering his house, remembering Uulamets coming to kill him, and how they had fought with magic the old man had all his life abhorred—

(Fool, Uulamets had railed at him, when Uulamets had first caught him at it, when he was a student in the riverhouse. Don't you know there's no creature wants to help you for free? The things that swear they will, want *you*, that's what they want, boy, don't ever think otherwise! Someday they'll turn on you—at first chance they'll turn on you, and then you'll have not a chance in hell, boy!)

It was true—and maybe if early on he had had the old man's advice he might have stayed with simple wizardry—

and had his heart in Uulamets' grasping hands instead of where it was now, in himself, causing him pain and threatening his very existence. So very many things might not have happened: Uulamets would not be dead and he might have been, like Eveshka, under Uulamets' orders, doing forever whatever Uulamets told him.

He thought of that, too. For some chances missed he could be truly grateful.

What Draga had dealt with had ultimately turned to someone cleverer and less indolent and less interested in pleasure and comforts. He had been there, when she had begun to fail.

Now it could find other possibilities, now that Sasha had him helpless as he was and exposed everything he had ever felt and wanted and dreamed of to, the god knew, anything that might happen by. He wanted Sasha to understand the appalling folly of what he had done—he tried, completely honest in what he offered, but Sasha wished him silent so violently and so angrily it stung.

Dammit, he had not had to bear that kind of rebuff since Draga's time. And this *boy* did it to him with impunity, refusing to listen, the way he had refused to listen, if he had ever truly had a chance—

"Fool!" he said aloud. "It's your own lives you're throwing away!"

Pyetr looked at him anxiously. But he felt Sasha take what else he would say and turn it into silence. He fought that back and forth with Sasha until he knew Sasha would not hear his reasons, nor would he let Pyetr hear him: Sasha doubted everything he would say and every argument he could possibly make, because Sasha knew his own ignorance of magic, and simply had to assume he was lying in everything.

He knew that defense too: it was one he had used when he had been that young and that foolish and that damnably, blindly ignorant, and not Draga nor Uulamets nor even Eveshka had ever gotten past it.

There were broken jars: pottery grated as Sasha picked up his bag: "The god only knows," Sasha said with a shake of his

172

head, and squatted down to investigate the damage, trusting him, Pyetr supposed, to keep an eye on their prisoner, all this in a leaden, drizzling rain, at the edge of the dying wood. The leaves were almost all fallen now, the wind had stripped the limbs bare: black trees, golden, sodden ground.

No Babi, no horses, and no sign of Eveshka. Pyetr kept his sword in hand and one eye on Chernevog: even an ordinary man knew enough to worry when, in wizardly company, he found himself doing stupid things or omitting to do smart ones.

"A snake," he muttered, standing guard while Sasha tried to put things to rights, "is still a snake. Whether his heart was in that owl or not, it's still his heart, and it's still a snake. —I hope you've noticed we haven't done what we came here to do, I hope you've noticed this viper is still getting his own way."

"Not all of it," Sasha said, "I assure you."

"I'd like to know what he's missed. What do we do, let him loose while we go searching after a damn ghost that's just as good let alone?"

All this while Chernevog was listening. He was acutely conscious of that. But privacy to speak meant leaving Chernevog unwatched.

Pyetr wanted to go down to the river, he wanted—desperately, on some premonition or someone's wish—to go down to the river. He said quietly to Sasha, "I've got this feeling, I don't know where it's coming from . . ." Chernevog had sat down with his head on his knees and his hands locked on the back of his neck, no longer paying any apparent attention to them—but a cold unease nagged him, a sense of disaster no matter what they did. "I keep thinking we ought to head for the river, however far it is."

"I think that's as good an idea as any," Sasha said.

It was not the kind of answer Pyetr wanted. He wanted the upset in his stomach to go away. "Are you sure it isn't him wanting it?" he asked. "Look at him over there, pretending he doesn't hear—dammit, he wants us dead! A heart doesn't make any difference in that!"

"He can want that anywhere," Sasha said. "I know what I want right now. I want to do exactly what Misighi said to do."

"Hunt down Uulamets?" It was stupid to listen to irrational feelings, sudden notions, or chills down the back of his neck. But Pyetr knew where to start looking for ghosts if one wanted to find them, particularly Uulamets' ghost—and that place was over on the other side of the river, the god knew how far from here, a burned house and a shallow grave. "Conjure him from here, can't you?"

"I'm not sure I ought to conjure anything—I'm not sure magic's a good idea right now. They said 'Take him.' So we'll take him where Uulamets is."

"I don't like this 'not sure,' you know."

Sasha stood up. "We've got no choice, Pyetr—"

"Damn right we've got a choice! How in hell are we going to cross the river? At least try calling him here, for the god's sake! If we go out of here and magic starts working again outside this woods, it works for him too, doesn't it?"

"It already is working," Sasha said, in a low voice. "I have this awful feeling—that we need to find 'Veshka. I need her myself, Pyetr, I really need her help—the books don't tell me everything—"

"God." He heard the fear shaking Sasha's voice, grabbed his arm and held it hard. He had loaded too much onto the boy, everything had, for days, he saw that. Sasha was exhausted, white-faced. "Let's not panic, shall we?"

Sasha got a breath. "I'm not Uulamets, Pyetr."

"Thank the god."

"I think," Sasha said on a second deep breath, "right now, you'd be a lot safer if I were."

He squeezed Sasha's arm. "I've every confidence in you. You're doing fine, boy. You're on your feet, he's not, you're doing perfectly fine."

Several more breaths. "I keep thinking about the boat. I keep thinking that 'Veshka . . . might look this way right now if she wanted to. But she doesn't. I don't know why."

Now Pyetr's stomach was truly upset, and he looked narrowly at Chernevog, wondering how far this whole thing went and whether the wiser course was not after all to kill him without warning.

But Chernevog lifted his face just then with a haunted

look the match of Sasha's, and said: "Eveshka's outside the leshys' spell. It's fading. It's only here, now."

No more damn sense than any other wizard. "Here," Pyetr echoed, "what, 'here?' " and looking at Sasha: "What in hell's he saying?"

But at the moment he had two wizards on his hands, both looking off into nowhere and murmuring things like, in Chernevog's case:

"They haven't the strength . . ."

And in Sasha's: "Pyetr, the horses are coming."

An ordinary man just gathered up the baggage and hoped for something very soon to make sense—but he could very well wish the two wizards in question were not unanimous.

15

Volkhi turned up first. Then Missy arrived out of the woods, looking at them across Volkhi's back as if she were none so sure now about anything she saw—ordinary trees having lately proved unreliable.

But of Babi there was no sign at all, and Sasha found that fact both understandable and worrisome. The leshys' silence was rapidly drawing in on itself, encompassing less and less, twining through this last small grove with a feeling angrier by the moment, and he kept thinking, while the horses were on their way to them, It may get worse here, it's only a handful of them will talk to wizards at best.

He said to Pyetr:

"They're down to protecting themselves now: we've got only so long to get to the river. After that, I wouldn't be near this place."

He scared Pyetr with his vagueness, he knew that he did, but he was thinking, desperately listening all around him: he had no reassurance to give and words came hard to describe things without substance or sense: there was foreignness, confusion as if whatever maintained the silence about them was also smothering the clear thinking essential to wizardry, the god only grant Chernevog was no less addled at the moment.

He thought not: Chernevog's wishes tumbled through his awareness, fear-crippled, wanting escape, wanting this, wanting that, going nowhere. Chernevog continually assailed him with promises: Chernevog swore he would defend them and Eveshka with his wizardry, Chernevog railed at him as a young fool who was confusing him and killing all of them—

176

Uulamets taught you! he could hear Chernevog saying, clear as spoken words. God, boy, he stifled everything in you he couldn't use, he *wanted* someone to use, don't you see it? He failed with me and he failed with Eveshka, and here you are in our place. He wanted his own way, and that damned wish of his is still going, Sasha Misurov!

"Let me alone," he muttered, taking Missy's trailing reins. He flung them over her neck, slung the packs up, wishing Missy to stand still. He kept trying to reach Eveshka through the silence, he kept worrying over the leshys' riddles—and wondering in a certain cold corner of his mind what it was going to feel like if they did find Uulamets: Eveshka already accused him of thinking her father's thoughts, echoing her father's advice.

"He set you to do what he wanted done," Chernevog said aloud, behind his back. "Uulamets was no one's friend, you surely knew that. Don't you remember?"

It was not childlike bewilderment he was hearing now. It was a harder, clearer presence. He looked at Kavi Chernevog.

"You're dealing with magic," Chernevog said. "He was. And the god only knows what might have taken him."

Sasha heaved himself up to Missy's back and looked down at him. "Let me alone!" he said, and Pyetr came leading Volkhi and roughly shoved Chernevog away from Missy, saying: "You walk. You're not getting your hands on either one of us."

Chernevog might have resisted that shove if sudden anger had given him clear direction: the thought gave Sasha a sudden chill—but Chernevog did nothing and Pyetr, unscathed, handed him up the sack with the pots and the books.

God, the books . . .

"Pyetr," he whispered, hugging that sack close, "be careful of him. Don't touch him. Don't do things like that!"

"I'm all right. It's all right, boy, just take care of us, hear?"

Pyetr turned away. Sasha settled the bag with the books and his little pots carefully in front of him. Chernevog stood waiting as Pyetr took Volkhi's reins and swung up to Volkhi's back—and in a moment's clarity Sasha thought of wishing Volkhi to go to the river, Volkhi's nose seeming a better guide for them than erratic wizardry in this numbing, angry hush. "Let Volkhi go," he said to Pyetr, then. "He knows the way."

"Good," Pyetr said with an uncomfortable look, and stopped holding Volkhi in.

One did try not to sound like Uulamets, one earnestly tried not to, but thoughts grew difficult and details kept trying to slip past his attention.

He thought, while Chernevog walked in front of Missy, was it me or was it Chernevog who thought of wishing the horse?

He thought of a ball of white fluff, a hungry baby-owl mouth—

He drove that image out of his mind with a deliberate thought of the stone and the ring of thorns. He knew where the thought must have come from. He listened to Missy a moment, smelled after some scent of the river—if he wanted, he could catch such things for a heartbeat or two, more wholesome than listening to mice and foxes, attention so flooded with smells and sounds and sights that a gust of wind was cataclysm—one dared eavesdrop only by moments, or one risked panic . . .

But Chernevog slid into his thoughts, wizard-fashion, walking beside Missy with his head meekly bowed:

Draga set Owl to catch me. I was a stupid boy. She wanted me to find that nest, I really think so. I suspect she killed his mother, all with the notion I'd set my heart on him, because she had a spell on Owl, and she had that until I killed her.

That's horrible, he thought, sorry for Chernevog, it was so ugly a trick: he thought of Vojvoda, and his own upbringing, at best neglected, never at worst, that cruelly used. He remembered all too vividly what it was to be unwelcome in a place . . . but never what it was to be trapped.

Chernevog asked: What do you suppose Uulamets wanted you to have, that you had to fear losing?

He wished Chernevog silent then, but with a sudden sinking remembrance of Uulamets threatening Pyetr, making Pyetr's life the price of his help—

A cup shattering, in Pyetr's hand, Pyetr doing nothing more than arguing with Uulamets—

Himself saying, terrified: Pyetr, that could as well have been your heart . . .

Uulamets had been a *good* wizard, virtuous because, although Uulamets had made his threats against Pyetr as plain as a shattered cup, although Uulamets had most particularly hated the idea of Pyetr being courted by his ghostly daughter—Uulamets had not, after all, killed Pyetr and he certainly had not wrung everything he could have gotten from his student.

Most of all Uulamets had renounced sorcery as foolhardy, wealth as useless to him, human company as dangerous—that was all the sum of Uulamets' goodness.

For a moment he did not know whether that last was Chernevog's thought or his own. Then he found a thought like flotsam in the flood: 'Veshka wouldn't let her father put any wishes on us, she'd know, surely she'd know, now. She would never let anything go on working on us—*I'd* know, for the god's sake, with his book and all—

(But we didn't know about the patch on the teacup. I didn't, until I started worrying about it. . . .)

He stared past that dark gulf of panic to the real world of misty woods, to Pyetr riding just ahead of them, Pyetr ducking to miss a branch, resetting his cap—Pyetr knew the world in ways he never would, had gotten along in Vojvoda's streets, fought actual duels—Pyetr could live anywhere. He didn't need to stay here . . .

Why did Pyetr stay if there weren't any wishes? It was Kiev he wanted, it was Kiev he dreamed of—but Uulamets stopped that. I did. Eveshka did.

Find Uulamets . . . god, I don't really want to find Uulamets, I don't want to meet him again, I didn't trust him while he was alive, until I knew he needed me enough to keep away from Pyetr.

Now I don't know how to keep him away from *me.*

"Shut up!" he said to Chernevog, thinking: Both of us had Uulamets for a teacher—both of us had to stand up to the old liar, and he's using that, damned if he isn't . . . he's asking about Pyetr, that's what he's doing.

Chernevog laid his hand on Missy's neck as Sasha ducked

the same branch in his turn. "Listen to me," Chernevog said softly, "listen—"

Pyetr turned around, leaning on Volkhi's rump. "Let him alone, snake. Get your hand off the horse!"

Chernevog said, "I'd look out for that limb."

"Pyetr!"

Pyetr made it, only scarcely, lying back on Volkhi; and looked around again, scowling.

"It's a mistake to go to Uulamets," Chernevog said. "The leshys can be wrong. Uulamets wanted nothing but his own welfare. Ask his daughter."

"For the last time, shut up!"

"She's alive, isn't she? The old man actually brought her back."

"Shut up!" Pyetr cried. "—Sasha, shut him up."

It was hard to hear what Pyetr was saying. Sasha ducked the same oncoming limb. He collected presence of mind enough to watch Pyetr's trail while Pyetr was looking back, watching Chernevog. The silence grew and grew. For a moment the constant wishing and watching ahead made his head spin and Missy's motion under him confused him—but Pyetr was stopping, Pyetr got off and led Volkhi back past Chernevog—

"No," Sasha said as Pyetr took Missy's reins too. Pyetr asked him something, but he was snared in a different kind of silence, one in which he could hear a deep, distant whisper, as if the whole forest sighed, the air growing colder and the world rapidly grayer—

As if a storm were coming—but the sky was already overcast, and the mist falling now was only the wind shaking drops from wet limbs—

He *knew* exactly where 'Veshka was, he *knew* there was something wrong on the river. He said, in panic no wizard should give way to—"Pyetr, Pyetr, 'Veshka's in a bad spot, there's something wrong out there and I don't think she knows it—I think she's asleep or something—"

"Tell her!" Pyetr said. "Wake her up!" and Sasha tried to do that with all the attention he dared take from Chernevog.

Chernevog seized at him with a fervent wish for silence. Pyetr grabbed Chernevog by the shirt and flung him away.

C. J. CHERRYH

But Chernevog was not the worst danger he was feeling. It was a different thing. It had place, but no course that he could find, it was neither good nor evil and might not even have intent. . . .

"Can you find her?" Pyetr was asking him, and it was strangest of all to him that the horses should stand so quietly in this storm, as if there was not a thing amiss in the world.

"Sasha!"

Pyetr had his knee, Pyetr was shaking at him, glancing anxiously back at Chernevog. "For the god's sake—Sasha, wake up!"

There was nothing wrong. In the daylight where Pyetr was, where Missy was, where his own body was, there was absolutely nothing wrong.

But Chernevog was saying, "God, get away from it—"

Everything came back to clarity again—the daylight, the slight mist of rain, Pyetr's worried face.

And with that came the slight, constant sighing of the trees and the small awareness of life in the woods and the sky and the river, as plainly, as constantly available to him as if there had never been a silence in the woods.

Nothing was wrong, nothing might ever have been wrong—except for Chernevog's face, pale and sweating, and Pyetr's worried expression. Missy sighed under him and ducked her head, like Volkhi, to examine the weeds underfoot for edibility.

"We're passed outside their circle, now," Chernevog said. "Or they've just stopped protecting us."

"What in hell's going on?" Pyetr asked, and shook at Sasha's leg a second time. "Sasha?"

" 'Veshka's across the river."

"*Across* the river—"

"I don't know why. There's something wrong over there. I'm afraid she's in the middle of it and I still can't make her hear me."

"God," Pyetr said with a disgusted shrug, as if it were some town squabble Eveshka had involved herself in. Pyetr walked a step or two aside, swept his cap off and stood there holding it, looking out in the direction of the river.

As if we're deaf to each other, Sasha thought desperately,

as if all of us are deaf to him, and he can't make anybody hear him, ever.

God, Pyetr.

Pyetr hit his leg with his cap, turned and motioned with it ahead of them, toward the river. "Well, we've got to go there, don't we? Find Uulamets! Uulamets is in the damn middle of this, that's what's going on. He wants us over there, hell! It's 'Veshka he wants!"

For a moment it made a terrible, clear sense. It was like Chernevog's warning. It was frighteningly like the things Chernevog had just been saying to him. "He brought her back from the dead, Pyetr, he died bringing her back."

"He died getting her away from *him*! He died making sure Chernevog didn't get his way in the world! That doesn't say he's happy being dead, or that he's through meddling!" Pyetr shoved his hair back with the cap, pulled it on and caught a breath while Sasha tried to think whether Pyetr was sane or he was. But Pyetr said then, quietly, hand on hip, with a shivery twitch of one shoulder, "God, I don't know. I don't like this. I don't like anything to do with him. —Why the shapeshifter? Why did it look like him?"

"Was there a shapeshifter?" Chernevog asked.

"You shut up!" Pyetr said; but Sasha was thinking that both of those questions were important. He said,

"There was. It tried to lead Pyetr off somewhere."

"What are we doing?" Pyetr cried. "Asking *his* advice now?"

"My advice," Chernevog said, "is exactly yours—don't trust Uulamets."

"God," Pyetr said, leaning on Missy's shoulder.

"The dead aren't loyal," Chernevog said. "You can't trust them. Uulamets had no idea what he was doing with that kind of magic, he didn't understand it. I do. Believe me, Ilya Uulamets was never on anyone's side but his own."

"God, of course, you're our lifelong friend, you want the very best for us!"

"Pyetr," Sasha said anxiously—but Chernevog said calmly, with a wave of his hand in Pyetr's direction,

"I can't blame him. I only hope you aren't as abysmally stupid as Uulamets was. He didn't know what he was doing, and if he's delivered himself to something that can use him— I don't know what he might be by now. I'm sure you don't."

"The leshys trust him."

"I don't know what the leshys understand and don't understand, and I doubt you do. I'm telling you—"

"You're telling us what you damn well want us to believe!" Pyetr said. "Sasha—"

Sasha pleaded for Pyetr's patience with a look and maybe a wish, he had no least idea, but he was afraid not to listen to what Chernevog might say, foolish and dangerous as that attention might be.

And Chernevog, bitterly: "You've killed Owl, you've put me in the same trap you've put yourselves in—dabble in wizardry to its limits, but you don't ever deal in magic with your heart in reach, boy! Magic can't wish on its own, magic can't imagine nature—but if you're fool enough to let my enemies get to me as I am now, then I'll remember you, damned if I won't, along with everything else I had to do with."

A chill went down Sasha's back; he forgot even to breathe—and Pyetr's hand was on his sword. But Chernevog said, further,

"Boy, let me free. Something's hunting us, now that we're outside the leshys' keeping—or if it's not yet, it will be, and if I fall, the first thing I'll trade them is two fools, hear me? I won't have any choice."

He remembered Uulamets saying, Doubt is Chernevog's weapon. . . .

He said, coldly, from Missy's height, "I'll bear that in mind."

"Arrogant young *fool!*"

"No!" Sasha cried, as Pyetr went for his sword: it occurred to him that dead, Chernevog was no more catchable than mist or water. He gave that thought to Pyetr, and said to Chernevog, leaning on Missy's white shoulders while she cropped a wildflower or two, "What would the vodyanoi give, I wonder, to know what I could tell him about you? I've read your book. I doubt he could read it for himself."

Chernevog went a shade paler, wiped his lips with the back of a finger. "You'd be an *absolute* fool to do that."

"Not if you're going to work against us anyway. You don't

want me dead, Kavi Chernevog, and let me tell you this: you don't want any harm to Pyetr or 'Veshka, either, because you don't want my heart taking over my good sense, now, do you? —Because when you care about something besides yourself, Kavi Chernevog, you take care of your friends, and you don't *want* anything happening to them. I don't need your magic. Wizardry is enough for me—because I believe you, I believe you made one terrible mistake and you'd give everything you have to be where I am."

"To be a young fool?"

"A young fool still has all his choices left, doesn't he?"

Chernevog said nothing then, only stepped back from Missy in angry, offended quiet. Sasha thought: God, I shouldn't have said those things to him, shouldn't have talked that way to him . . . whatever he looks to be, he's a hundred years older than I am and he knows things I don't even imagine. God, make him mad, Sasha Vasilyevitch, give him a reason if he needed one—he's nothing if not vain.

He said, with Chernevog scowling and Pyetr looking at him as if he had taken leave of his senses, "None of this is getting us to the river, is it?"

"Right," Pyetr said on a breath, as if that was all he could find to say, and took up Volkhi's reins and swung up again.

Pyetr rode closer to him after that, herding Chernevog in front of both of them. Pyetr was worried, that was clear, and Sasha thought in despair that if he had his choice he would stop right now and write everything down and study for days to see if there was a way out of the wishes he was making one after the other.

But things when they were going wrong never waited for slow wits. That was what Pyetr had been trying to tell him in these most important years of his growing up: Get out of the damn books, boy.

He thought, I had three years, I didn't know that was all the time I was ever going to have. I thought everything would come from the books.

Everything can't depend on me. God, this is all a mistake. . . .

He felt for the bag at Missy's shoulder, the precious one with the books, he laid his hand on the oiled canvas.

Woven branches. Branches over sand and water. . . .

They mounted a wooded hill. Gray sky showed between the trees, as if the world ended in nothing but cloud. The sound out of that gulf might have been wind in leaves, but it was the river whispering to them.

Chernevog stopped at the crest, silhouetted against the gray light. Volkhi took the last climb with a sudden effort and Pyetr reined back abruptly, saying, breathlessly,

"God . . ."

Missy made the hill at her own pace and stopped at Volkhi's side, giving Sasha his own look at gray river, gray sky, a thin, long ribbon of vines and logs that arched out and vanished into the mist above the river.

16

✠ ✠ ✠ ✠ "It's our way across," Sasha declared, as if that thin wooden arch were the most wonderful sight in the world. "I thought of logs, myself," Pyetr said, with a fluttering in his stomach, "maybe floating across—you know, keeping the horses up, rigging something with canvas and rope—the river's not that fast here . . ."

"It's leshy work. They made this for us. They planned for our crossing!"

"Good, it's leshy work. Tell that to the horses. —They're not going out on that damn thing, for the god's sake. Look at it!"

"You can do it. You rode The Cockerel's porch on the ice—"

"I was drunk, boy!" He saw Chernevog gazing out at that thread of a bridge, arms folded, with the god only knew what kind of ill wishes already shaping in his head. "It sways in the wind. Look at it! It's only wishes keep that thing up as it is!"

"The horses will go. It won't fall, Pyetr. We won't. I won't let us."

"God," he said, and turned and patted Volkhi's neck and apologized—for riding him across The Cockerel's porch, too, while he was at it.

But Sasha was preparing to lead Missy up that muddy slope. Pyetr took a deep breath, said, "Come on, Volkhi, lad," and motioned Chernevog to go ahead of them.

Chernevog shrugged and trudged up the soggy earthen mound to the head of the bridge.

186

The slope was hard enough for man or horse—Pyetr helped where he could, got out of the way where he could not, and reached the top where Chernevog stood in the wind and the mist.

It was split logs, whole trees torn lengthwise by main force, cobbled together with vines and wishes, and supported from beneath—god, one did not even want to think about the security of those braces—with whole trees set in the river-bed, their broken stubs of branches sticking out about the bridge at all angles.

Two logs wide—at most, and sometimes. Beyond Chernevog the arch of splintered wood disappeared outright into mist and distance.

"I'm coming!" Sasha called out from below.

Meaning there was another horse coming up and this one had to move.

"Come on, lad," Pyetr said, and tugged gently on the reins, coaxing Volkhi up to the logs while Chernevog turned and walked out onto that splintery, uneven surface.

Volkhi came, looking it over, a first few uncertain steps. Pyetr kept the reins slack, let Volkhi see where he was putting his feet, trusting wizardry would keep Volkhi calm—and the bridge steady. Personally he had no wish to look down, but he had to, at least as far as the surface of the logs, to be sure of Volkhi's footing, to ease him over the joints. Step by slow step, while sweat ran on his face and the wind chilled it.

Past one set of braces, like a shattered forest on either side of him, the pale ribbon of wood stretching in front of them into nowhere. He was all in gray now. Gray to either side, gray below and above, and on the bridge ahead of him, Chernevog, walking faster than he was. The wind blew. The span creaked.

God. . . .

I'm losing him, he's getting ahead of us. . . .

"Sasha!" he yelled, risking a look back past Volkhi's shoulder, where Sasha and Missy followed at a distance. "He's getting too far ahead of us—"

Another gust, cold and wet. He suddenly lost his sense of

up and down, felt Volkhi stop behind him, while the bridge quaked and swayed perhaps a finger-breadth, but it felt like it was going for a moment.

He got a breath, got his balance, started Volkhi forward and took a hasty look ahead to be sure where he was going.

Chernevog was gone, vanished in the mist.

God, god, god . . .

"Easy, lad, there's a good lad, nice grain and honey-lumps when we get off this damned thing—*god!*"

A cold spot went through him, left to right—a ghost, a haunt, flitting across the arch of the bridge.

"Seen Uulamets?" he asked it, while his heart fluttered like a trapped bird. In daylight, something as pale as a ghost seldom showed. "We're looking for him. Lost a wizard up ahead of us just now. Named Chernevog. You might want him. We certainly won't object."

Wherever it went, it did not come back. He kept going, nerved against more such encounters, and watched Volkhi's feet and his, taking his own time.

One could finally see the other shore, at least, stealing a quick glance ahead: it showed as a hazy green in the gray.

"At least it's alive over there. That's—"

A joint in the logs. Down to one width, here, knotty and uneven. Sweat was running down his neck, while his hands and feet were numb from the wind.

"—encouraging, isn't it? Lots of green things, I promise you, stay calm, lad, easy, easy—watch the feet, god, don't rush me—"

He could see the end of the bridge. He could see the other shore—

And a figure waiting in the mist where the bridge ended.

Chernevog. The god only knew his reasons.

A shelter against the misting rain, fire to boil up something edible—that was Sasha's job. A few sips of vodka to settle the stomach and Pyetr paid off the promised honey-lumps, curried Volkhi and Missy until his arms ached and his knees were shakier than they had been coming off the bridge. They worked—while Chernevog sat at his leisure and idly, with his fingernails, stripped a leaf down to its skeleton.

That reminded him of that damned bridge out there.

Pyetr wiped his hands on his breeches, put the straw curry brush away in the proper bag, came wobbling back to the fire for a cup of hot tea fortified with vodka.

He sat down next the fire, shut his eyes a moment to rest them and kept seeing gray, empty space and feeling the ground sway. He had done crazier things, he told himself he had: walked The Doe's rooftree on a bet—climbed any number of balconies in Vojvoda—with no wizard to steady him. It had been a sure thing, this time. Absolutely. Even with Chernevog involved. Leshys had built it.

God.

He shivered, let go his breath and took another drink. Sasha nudged his arm and passed him a plate: pancake and a bit of sausage.

There was a helping for Chernevog.

"Damn waste of good sausages," Pyetr muttered, in no mood for charity.

Chernevog accepted it, and the cup of tea—held the cup out to him, saying, pleasantly enough, "A little vodka if you please."

Choke, Pyetr thought. But outrageous behavior moved him to outrageous courtesies: a gambler's son, among rich young gentlemen, learned their manner in self-defense. He gave Chernevog his falsest smile, added vodka to his cup, saying: "Personally, I wish it were aconite."

Chernevog said, "Your health," and lifted the cup to Sasha. "Is it?"

"No," Sasha said quietly. "I promise you."

Chernevog smiled, ate his supper, drank his tea and vodka along with them, said, somberly, "I miss Owl. I truly do. You're very cruel, Alexander Vasilyevitch."

"How do you know my name?"

Chernevog shrugged, took a deep drink. "I have my sources. I did, at least. Now I'm content to be your prisoner."

"Liar," Pyetr said.

Chernevog looked him in the eyes, over the cup rim. "Your health, too, Pyetr Ilyitch."

"You were talking about Owl," Sasha said.

Chernevog's gaze went distant. Finally it dropped to the cup in his hands.

"I'll sleep now," he said in a subdued voice. "—Good night, Pyetr Ilyitch."

Pyetr did not look at him; he drank another sip of his tea and vodka, and listened to Chernevog settle down next the fire.

For a good long while afterward he held his peace, listening to Chernevog's breathing grow more regular. He thought how Sasha could as easily have poisoned the wretch.

Sasha saying—I'm not Uulamets—

Himself: Thank the god—

Sasha said, "He's probably asleep."

"Don't depend on it."

"I'm not. Tea and wishes. And a little something extra. He'll probably have a headache."

"Good." He remembered the muddy yard of Chernevog's house, none so far away, remembered unnumbered hours of hell. Eveshka crying: Kavi, don't! He made a face and took another drink, but he thought that should be his last, fearing too deep a sleep on this darkening, drizzly shore. The ground still felt as if it were swaying, every time he shut his eyes. "We should give him another one in the morning. I'll just put him on the horse like a sack of turnips. If we need him at all."

"The leshys had a reason."

"Doubting's my one small talent, remember? I doubt the leshys know that much what they're doing, where it doesn't regard trees. They don't understand us. For some reason he's waked up. For some reason something's wrong over here that has the leshys scared. —For some damn *reason* we haven't cut that scoundrel's head off!"

"I know, I know, I'm thinking about that. But he's worried, too."

"He's worried. Thank the god *he's* worried, I'm so glad to know that. I'm scared out of my skin. I'm worried about my wife, dammit!"

"I know, I know, Pyetr."

"No word, nothing."

"Nothing."

He shook his head, took another drink without thinking about the jug in his hands. He was thinking about Eveshka out there alone in the dark tonight, somewhere on this shore, if the leshys were right; and he thought of Uulamets in his grave, as strong as he had ever been—wanting to come back, wanting his daughter, every wish and want a spell to reach out into other people's lives.

The old man had passed some kind of legacy to Sasha— too much, Eveshka was wont to say. He sat here drinking himself to helplessness, like Chernevog, and the boy was under some damn spell.

The bridge is safe, Pyetr, leshys made it—

Two cat eyes opened in the dusk, in empty air—right in front of his knees.

"God!" He scrambled back against the canvas, before he recognized the small shadowy nose that appeared next, with the outline of a round belly.

"Babi!" Sasha said. "Thank the god—Babi. Come on, Babi. . . ."

"Vodka, Babi." Pyetr unstopped the bottle, tipped a little into empty air.

The eyes vanished. The vodka splashed onto the ground.

Sasha said, "He's upset."

"He got a good look at our company. Dammit, Babi, come on back, it's all right!"

But Babi did not come back. There was nothing but the crackle of their small fire, the occasional spit of a water drop as it dripped off the canvas into the embers.

"Babi probably had a terrible scare," Sasha said. "He's probably not far from us, right now. He may not have been, all along."

Sasha was trying to cheer him. Pyetr sipped from the jug, set his jaw and stared into the fire thinking—

No, dammit, he refused even to think about losing Eveshka. He refused to think how they might have been tricked from the beginning, and how, after the small inconvenience of dying, Ilya Uulamets might have something in mind for them after all—some spell he might have put onto the boy, to bring them all here when he was ready—

But there was Eveshka, for one very major point of resistance in any such scheme: Eveshka had fought lifelong for independence from her father, she had made most of her young mistakes trying to get free of Uulamets, and she would never be taken in by him now. Sasha argued that, by what was written in his book, Uulamets had never been a truly bad man—to which he had retorted: He was too smart to be bad. He wanted his way—and as long as he got it he was a perfectly wonderful man.

Uulamets had wanted Sasha, too. The old man had taken immediately to Sasha, said to himself, Aha, here's a likely, trusting lad—

So we go find him, Pyetr thought. Which gives Uulamets his daughter, his heir, and his enemy all in one basket. . . . And where does that leave me?

But, he argued with himself, Sasha won't see the old thief do me in. Neither will Eveshka. He'll have to take me with whatever deal he wants to make with them—and won't the old man hate that?

But what deal? What do wizards want, when they're not scared of causing storms and bringing the tsar down on them?

A man could get a headache thinking about wizards. He asked Sasha, whose firelit, pensive face was hazing more than it should in his vision, "You didn't give me any of that damn stuff, did you?"

A look of wide brown eyes. "No. Of course not."

Sometimes Sasha scared him. Sometimes he thought, I haven't got a chance. The boy can do any damn thing he wants. Someday he will.

God help us all.

Pyetr lay down on his side, tucked up like a child, forgetting his blanket. Sasha got up and spread it over him, threw their other canvas over Chernevog, then sat down and pulled his own blanket about his shoulders.

He did wish Babi would come back. But Babi was not answering him any more than Eveshka was, and he was becoming increasingly anxious about trying. What Chernevog had said echoed disquietingly off his recollections of what

Chernevog had written, with no ulterior motive—that hearts were dangerous to have when one dealt with magic, because magical creatures could understand hearts: it was wizards' intentions they could not fathom: and wizards could no more fathom them. Babi was one thing. Something like the vod-yanoi was quite another, and leshys did things for reasons that made no sense. What such creatures wanted was very, very different from what people would want—or at least from what good people would want.

He would not write that in his book. He wanted no more writing about magic in his book. He wanted not even to think about it, except—

Except there was something in common about their difficulties lately, and that, magically considered, argued for a common source of their troubles, a single *kind* of wish.

Whatever it was, it scared Babi, and absented Eveshka, and now that they were out of the silence where they might perhaps speak to her—kept her silent, absolutely cut off from them in a way he did not want to admit to Pyetr, not until there was no choice. He still hoped—but he grew more afraid with every assault he made on that silence, afraid that something unwanted might suddenly track him down the thread of that wish. He had no idea why he felt that way, or what it meant beyond a childish fear of bogles and bumps in the night, but that was the case.

The fear of an answer might prevent one, as effectively as the leshys could—that might be the reason; or it might be his own wishes saving a young and naive wizard from disaster. His thoughts kept going in circles like that—but he equally suspected that what Pyetr called his damnable worrying, laid on thick over the years, might be the protection that had saved Pyetr's life in the early stages of this trouble, a web of wishes that had not let a shapeshifter lead Pyetr to disaster in the woods, and that had gotten them to the leshys before Chernevog got loose altogether. Pyetr might ironically be the hardest of them for someone else's magic to get at, after all, seeing he had had two wizards anxious as hens over him for years.

Perhaps the wizards involved had worried too little, after all, about themselves.

One assumed, most particularly, that Eveshka had been taking care of herself; one assumed . . .

But Eveshka had grown increasingly fey and difficult as the years passed, had worried Pyetr and worried *over* Pyetr so very passionately that Sasha could see now, increasingly since Pyetr had been alone with him, that Pyetr was—

Was—finally—the man he had left Vojvoda with, a Pyetr, however distressed, all of a sudden thinking again about what he would do and how he would deal with things instead of, inevitably, always, what 'Veshka would think.

That idea scared him. It scared him terribly. He thought: What did she do to him?

He thought: 'Veshka's been scared all along. She wanted so much to make Pyetr happy . . . but her running off into the woods, her tempers—

She was so terribly scared about using what she knows.

Magic, rusalka magic, not wizardry.

God . . .

Both of us have kept our hearts.

17

There was a terrible crash, the boat hit something, the tiller bar jolted. Eveshka caught at it, looked up in a fright—in dark, in woods, with branches sweeping over the bow and breaking against the hull and the sail. She wanted the boat free, wanted some way left to extricate it from its predicament before it lodged itself where even wizardry could not back it out.

But her father was there, whispering, "It's all right, it's all right, daughter, This is as far as the boat will go."

"Where?" She saw nothing but shadowy trees, willows weeping into the water, a black tangle that ensnared the boat so completely she had no hope of freeing it. She wanted Pyetr with her—and desperately wanted Sasha—for the merest self-ish instant, with the most terrible feeling that she might not see them again. She was going deeper and deeper into some-thing that, in the night and on a strange shore, seemed to have no shape and no end, and if she had gone willingly at first, for Pyetr's sake—now she was no longer sure she had a chance at all. "Where are we going?" she asked. "Papa?"

Like a small child again, angry and betrayed.

"Don't doubt," her father's ghost whispered. "Haven't I taught you better than that?"

He was very real in the night, a shadow, a substance, against a curtain of black willow boughs. The boat moved slowly, its bow entrapped. That was real, too.

Her father's shadow-shape changed then, seemed to sink and flow away from her.

"Papa?" she said, and found herself alone, standing on the deck of a boat shrouded in willows.

"I never could advise you," the ghost whispered from some far distance. "That's a dangerous way to grow up, girl: you always assumed the right course was opposite my advice. You called it freedom—but you were still taking your direction from someone else without understanding it. Haven't you an idea of your own, daughter?"

"You never gave me a chance to know what I wanted!"

"You never could tell my wishes from yours. So you fought everything, even your own good sense. Do you understand now? You'd better."

"Papa, you're not making sense!"

"I can't stay. I can't—tell you—the most important— *Dammit!*"

"Papa?"

She could hear the creak and groan of the boat, the sighing of the leaves, the water breaking against the hull.

Nothing else.

"Papa, why did you bring me here? What do you want me to do, for the god's sake? —Damn you, papa, come back!"

The willows sighed together. Finally something else was there, a sense of direction, an ominous significance in the dark heart of the woods.

Magic was there. She knew the feel of it, subtle and quiet and dangerous, wanting her to leave the boat, come ahead. It assured her of her safety, it offered her—

God, she had left the house with the feeling of something wrong, she had thought she was going to deal with the leshys, but nothing after that had gone right. Papa showed up and papa left her here, papa said she had a baby and she had had no sense at all of it happening until he had said that. She had not thought of children: she was so young in her own eyes, and she had never planned for children. But it seemed one had happened, all the same, and her whole life was moving at someone else's whim, the way papa had done to her and Kavi had tried to do. Now an unplanned-for child did it, her own damned stupid fault. She had hardly even wished against the possibility, and babies did happen, given a chance.

She was in a terrible situation that she now began to think had never been what she had believed—and papa—

Papa steered her into this dreadful place, lectured her on

making up her own mind and then ran off somewhere. Papa wanted, papa wanted, and her whole life turned on his wishes—and then he told her to choose.

It was not Chernevog she had to deal with after all. Papa wanted this baby. Papa wanted something, and maybe it was good and maybe it was bad, one never knew with him—

But a wizard-child was a disaster to her and a terrible danger to Pyetr. It was the end of their lives the way they had hoped to live them.

No, dammit, *someone* had wanted this baby. It could not happen, it could not wreck her life this way, unless someone had wanted it against her wishes.

"Papa," she said, while the willows whispered against the deck and the hull, and tears spilled from her eyes. "Papa, damn you, what are you doing to me?"

Often enough in his life Pyetr had waked ashamed of himself, and more than once dimly surprised to be alive, knowing he certainly had not deserved to be—both of which were the case at this gray edge of dawn. To his profound embarrassment he had the vodka jug still in his arms, and poor, faithful-to-duty Sasha had fallen asleep sitting up, with a book in his lap and a pen in his hand—while Chernevog slept wrapped in their canvas, not so far away.

Pyetr capped the inkpot, took Sasha by the shoulder, saying, "It's me, lad, go to sleep," and, laying the book aside, pushed Sasha back among the blankets for whatever proper rest he could still get.

He kept a wary eye on Chernevog, stirred up the fire and heated up a few sausages and the rest of the water for tea and shaving, by touch, in the dark of the dawn. He did not want to push the boy this morning, no matter his own fever to be off. Just shave, take his time, no use breaking their necks in the dark—no matter that he had this most uncomfortable cold knot in his stomach that breakfast was not going to warm, no more than the vodka had cured it last night; and no matter that he feared 'Veshka was in some dire trouble: if it was Uulamets they had now to deal with, then 'Veshka herself was in no danger and that trouble would certainly wait for them: it had waited all these years. If it was something more than that, then resting was still the wiser course this morning: it was foolhardy and it was useless to her to walk into it too tired to think.

Speed when it counted and deliberation when needed: he much feared otherwise he had lost his edge, forgotten the lessons of a misspent youth and grown—well, to admit the fact, soft.

He had come to rely too much on wizards and not enough on his own wits, that was the trouble. Sasha himself said that wizards were most susceptible to wizardry and magic (which seemed, the god only knew why, from Chernevog's view and lately from Sasha's, to be two different things). They were prone to delusion, and someone in this company had to use his head.

Nature and magic. Moving pebbles, Sasha said. This pebble, by the god, did not intend to be easy.

The tea boiled over, hissing in the coals: he nicked himself on the chin and grabbed for it.

"Damn!"

He burned his hand and the tea spilled. Sasha came out of the blankets, asking, "Pyetr?"

"Just the damn tea boiling over." His chin stung, his finger was throbbing from the scald. He took a stick and fished the pan out of the sodden embers. "Sorry. There's sausages. No tea."

Sasha scrambled to his feet, looking at the lump of canvas where Chernevog was sleeping.

One hoped, at least, that he was sleeping. Pyetr looked that way with sudden misgivings and a scalded finger. "Well, if that was his best, he's lost a bit. And it's no tea for him." He sucked on the burn, shook the hand. "Hell, boy, accidents do happen, don't they?"

"They shouldn't," Sasha said.

Pyetr looked at him.

"Not against me," Sasha said.

Pyetr nodded toward Chernevog. "Think it's him? Think we ought to make another batch of that tea?"

"I honestly don't know."

"Have your sausages. His can go begging. We'll load him on with the baggage."

"Not my doing," Chernevog said, from the canvas across the fire. "I could plead I wasn't awake. But your clatter makes it unlikely."

"Tea," Pyetr said.

"Poison me and be done, damn you."

"Sounds like headache," Pyetr said brightly, and suddenly cherished the thought of slinging Chernevog head downward on a horse. He fished a sausage out of the pan, said: "Breakfast, snake."

"Damn you."

He said to Sasha, "I think he's sincere."

They could joke about pain—when his simplest wish for relief trod that boundary where wizardry stopped and magic answered. It had been so very long since it had mattered at all which did—and to cure a damned, piddling headache he had to remember past the pain what unassisted wishes were, had to retrace the earliest and most simple wish he had made, back even before Owl, long before Owl.

Some petty wizard—perhaps his grandmother, who knew? Or not. He had lived with her. She had hated him, he hated her, he had grown cannier and she had wished him lost forever. He had wished her dead; and he had run and run—

That was what wishes felt like—before Owl, before Draga: one simply trusted things to arrive in their own time, in their own way, no second-guessing, no calling it back—that was what it felt like: fear and anger and damnably unpredictable consequences.

His magic had drawn down lightnings, made the ground shake: and to cure his various pains he was reduced to a child's feeble effort—simply trying to believe in certainties, while magic denied they existed and a damned, ignorant *boy* did it effortlessly.

By their laughter, they realized how helpless he had become, and Sasha surely knew what coin he had in hand. Pyetr was still his hope, but even Pyetr confounded him. One could take the man for a fool, but that was subterfuge; he could take him now for hot-tempered and precipitate, but after everything was packed, Pyetr came to him and said he should ride a while, upright on the horse, though he did not, Pyetr added acidly, deserve any favors.

It might be his wishes working; it might be some reason of Sasha's; it might even be an ordinary man with notions of his own, more subtle than he could discover: Pyetr was not, one had always to remind oneself, a fool; and it did no good to work on one of them and not the other.

So he said, when he was riding alongside Sasha's mare, with Pyetr leading his horse, "I suppose you've both been thinking how to be rid of me."

Sasha gave him a suspicious look.

"I don't know what you want," Chernevog said. "But I'll agree to anything." He added, not without a certain queasiness at his stomach: "There's no trick in it, not at all."

"And a pig has wings," Pyetr said shortly. Chernevog ignored him, asking Sasha quietly:

"What will you do? Everything Uulamets wants? Forever? You could free yourselves from him. You could have anything you want."

"Like you?" Pyetr jibed. But he was patient and prepared this time, to deal with Pyetr: he said, directing himself to Sasha,

"You probably realize you have me to trade—but that's the worst thing you can do. You've won: you've put me in a terrible position, and you've won everything you could possibly want, if you'll only listen."

"Are we down to serious bribes now?" Sasha asked.

"Listen to me! Magic doesn't know anything, it isn't alive, it isn't dead, it just is, and the things that can give you magic don't know what they want in this world without us to show them. If you've any sense at all you won't give me up to them—"

"I'd trade you," Pyetr said darkly, "for a mouldy turnip."

"You're not understanding me! They can use us the way we use them. I'm telling you the leshys couldn't hold out any longer and you're being fools if you think you can. Things like that go straight for weakness—mine; and ignorance—yours; and the god knows who else."

"I don't use your kind of magic," Sasha said. "I don't want it. It can't touch me."

"It can touch Uulamets. It can touch Eveshka. A rusalka's whole existence is magical. It was sorcery brought her back. And it's *one* magic. It's all the same. Will you say you've nothing to lose?"

"We don't need you," Pyetr said.

"You'll lose her. You'll lose her first—Pyetr next; and yourself, inevitably . . ."

Pyetr turned and stopped the horse. "You murdered my wife, you damned dog, you're responsible for this desolation, you tried to kill me—and you want us to listen?"

"Pyetr," Sasha cautioned him.

"He's right," Chernevog said. "Indeed, he's right. All those things I did—and some you don't know. But now I need you. That makes a difference."

Pyetr's jaw dropped. Then he said, backing up a step: "I don't think I ever heard anyone put it quite that plainly before. —God, Sasha, we're dealing with an honest man!"

"Sasha," Chernevog said, "Alexander Vasilyevitch, . . . you know what I'm saying. Nothing's an accident. The leshys' fading wasn't an accident. I know what we're dealing with. It cheats, and it lies, and it doesn't give a damn for your wishes. But it does regard force. You have that. All you have to do is use it."

Sasha said nothing for a moment. The horses shifted restlessly.

Pyetr said, "It's a snake, Sasha. It always was, it always will be."

But Sasha was listening, Sasha was thinking. Chernevog said, so, so carefully, shivering between self-restraint and fear of denial, "Ask anything you want of me, Pyetr Ilyitch. There's nothing I'll refuse you."

"Get off my horse!"

He slid down, stood eye to eye with Pyetr, felt Sasha's fear wish him not—

Maybe Pyetr realized a danger, too. Pyetr's jaw set and he

201

ducked past him, flung the reins over and swung up with an enviable skill.

From that vantage Pyetr looked angrily down at him.

Chernevog said, with all sincerity, "You could save your own life, Pyetr Ilyitch —you could stop all of this; you could stop it in a moment—but he won't trust you."

Chernevog of course wanted him to ask Sasha how, and why he could rescue them, which was, Pyetr decided, good enough reason not to do it—for one thing because Chernevog was wishing at him and he thought it was time to worry about those wishes if he did one single thing Chernevog wanted; and for another because Chernevog plainly wanted to cause trouble between them, and he was not going to give Chernevog the satisfaction of seeing him worry.

So he ordered Chernevog to walk, he and Sasha followed on horseback keeping an eye on him, and he thought again that, whatever ties wizards might have on each other, a good bit of rope would make sense.

He said as much to Sasha. But Sasha said no, Chernevog did not want to escape them.

All of which sat in the back of his mind and rattled from time to time. It was the hardest thing in the world for him to have a question and not ask it, and it did occur to him to wonder why if there was no truth at all to what Chernevog had said to him, Sasha had not bothered right then to dismiss it as a lie. He knew Sasha's bad habits very well, one of which was taking all the blame for troubles, and another of which was a tendency—he had surely caught it from Uulamets—to keep his worry to himself, whether to save his friends anxiety or whether because he simply forgot he had not spoken out loud.

So he rode beside Sasha with never a word, but, damn, it bothered him.

"You can't hear anything," Pyetr asked Sasha, in the brief privacy they had as they stopped for water. Sasha splashed water into his face and down his neck, put his hands over his face and made one brief, futile try.

It was worse, that cold feeling, the further they rode into this young forest, and worst of all when he listened for some answer from Eveshka. He was a fool not to tell Pyetr outright what he was feeling: he knew he was; but the look on Pyetr's face, that both hoped and forgave him his failure—how could one say to that, I'm sorry, I'm scared, Pyetr, she's lost, she's gone and I don't want to go on rattling that door, Pyetr?

Pyetr would take that risk. He had no doubt of it.

—Head over heart, young fool. . . .

What if it is Uulamets, god, what if it *is* Uulamets that's after us? Eveshka said I think his thoughts, I do the things he'd choose—

What if, the way Pyetr thinks, he wants us all—back? Is that what we're following?

"I can't hear anything," he said, and saw Pyetr sigh and shake his head. "Possibly," he started to say, and Pyetr looked up and he had to go on, fool that he was, temporizing. "Possibly it's her choice. She could have decided—" The idea struck him as he was talking, and he blundered into it without time to think it through: "—She could just have decided the leshys had a reason for not talking, so she isn't going to, either. She might not trust what she hears from us. I'm not honestly sure—" He started to say—That I'd trust what I hear from her. It was true. But he swallowed it unsaid. And, oh, god, but Pyetr listened to what he surmised; he fervently wished he had kept his mouth shut.

Meanwhile Chernevog was washing his face a little upstream from them, dipping up water with torn and surely painful hands. Perhaps he was listening, one way or another, to everything they said and half they thought. One could think very easily of pouring another cup of tea down him, the way Pyetr said, just sling him over a horse and silence him and his offers and his arguments—at least until they found Uulamets.

"Time we got moving," Pyetr said, dusted off his hands on his knees and got up, looking at Chernevog.

But Pyetr stopped then, gave a deep breath, still staring

ahead of him, and put his hands in his belt. "The snake wants me to ask you," he said, "what he was talking about. I don't want to, if you don't want to say. But if it's 'Veshka's safety—and there is something I can do, you understand, Sasha, it's something I'd really like to know, myself."

Pyetr had never asked anything of him that way. Sasha did not want to talk about it, he did not want to discuss the matter with Pyetr and if Eveshka was in danger, he certainly did not want to let Pyetr make choices he did not understand.

But it would not really matter to Pyetr. Not where Eveshka was concerned. And not, he was sure, if he were the one in trouble.

"He's saying," Sasha replied in an almost whisper, "that whatever's caused this is magical; and it's not friendly to him. Whether that's true I don't know. He says if he uses his magic something can find him by it—that's something I don't know and his book doesn't tell me. But he's arguing that it might be using Uulamets and it might be after 'Veshka—"

"God." Pyetr's lips hardly moved.

"Pyetr, I don't know. What he's saying—is if magic gets a wizard in its hands, instead of the other way around, then it can do things in the natural world it can't do otherwise. He says that's what it's after, that if it gets him—it's got a way to get at the rest of us."

"Where do I come in?"

"He wants to put his heart in your keeping. He wants to work magic again."

"He's crazed!"

"I don't think he's crazy, but I certainly don't think he's our friend. I can't tell how much truth he's telling. His book doesn't give me any help. I don't know magic, not—not the way he does. Even Uulamets didn't."

Pyetr bit his lip. "Your magic, his magic—it doesn't make a lot of sense, you know."

"Every wizard works a certain sort of magic. A wizard's born with it. But whatever you were born with, you just—don't use as well when you grow up. Or you do it knowing more, and then it's harder to know exactly what you want."

"And he does? —He's not that smart, Sasha, heart or no heart, he's not that damn smart. Look at the mess he's in."

"That vodka jug . . . Uulamets said you only work a spell like the jug just once or twice in your whole life—and it is real magic, what I did. It's not natural and maybe in most points it's the same as sorcery. But I can't do it twice. Uulamets is right—you grow up and you see how complicated things are and you're not sure what's right . . ."

"Wizards have a bad habit of that."

"I'm sorry."

"Sasha, —just give me one plain answer. What's this hearts business, what does he want to do?"

"What he did with Owl. I don't know what that would do to you."

"Or what he'd try to do. If he thought I could hold on to him he damn sure wouldn't be offering."

"I don't know. I'm not sure—" He caught himself doing it again and ran a hand through his hair. "I'm sorry, Pyetr. —God!"

"I don't understand this, I don't damn well understand this. Magic that isn't magic—"

"I do use magic, Pyetr, it's just not—*magic*, the way he does."

Pyetr gave him a straight, bewildered stare.

Sasha said, helplessly, "We know what we mean."

"Good."

"I use what I was born with. I move pebbles—just the tiniest bit of magic. It's mine. He wishes for more than he was born with, *that's* what the difference is. He doesn't bother with pebbles, he just wants a whole hillside to come down—and it will. He doesn't care about consequences, either—because magic can keep them away from him, never mind the rest of the world."

"Ham-handed, you mean."

"It is, essentially. It certainly could be that—if he was stupid. But he grew up as a wizard. He can do the little things *and* the big ones. Like me stealing from the trees—only he can steal it from that place Babi comes from."

"Is *that* why Babi's staying clear of him?"

"Maybe. I don't know what he can do, I don't know what the rules are in that place. Uulamets said it was the worst mistake a wizard could make, to wish for more magic than he has. I think he was right, but—" There was a place in his reasoning that gaped dark and deep, that said—maybe. And he looked Pyetr in the eye, thinking that, in case things went very wrong, Pyetr should not be unwarned. "I don't know. I don't know that Uulamets knew. I've been thinking maybe I could do it better—maybe I could do the same thing, and do it the right way. Maybe I'm making a terrible mistake not to do it and just—take care of things. . . ."

Pyetr said, with a deep frown, "Sasha, —"

"I'm scared to do it. And you're right, Babi's hiding. I don't know whether he's hiding from him—or from me."

"Sasha, —maybe this one time you'd better listen to Uulamets."

"Uulamets could have been wrong, you know. He could just have been scared—the way I'm scared."

"He could have been right. I never thought I'd argue his side, but for the god's sake, Sasha, —"

"I'm scared of it. That doesn't make it wrong."

"Then any wizard could do it. Any wizard could—and Chernevog's the only one that did. Which is no damn good recommendation, is it?"

"Uulamets did say one thing about magic. He said that motives somehow do make a difference."

"Uulamets is dead. That's not a recommendation either."

"Maybe he wasn't as strong as Chernevog. Maybe Chernevog isn't as strong as he was, either. I'm not saying I'm thinking of doing it. I'm saying—whatever it costs—if he starts to get away from me, if we've no other choice, it could be the only thing I can do to hold him. *If* it happens—if he does something and that's all I can do—I want you to understand what's happening. I want you to get clear of it, find Babi—I think Babi would come to you. Not to me right now. Just for the god's sake don't hang around."

Pyetr drew a breath. A second one. He was disturbed, Sasha knew that. Finally Pyetr said, "Maybe this time we'd better wait to ask Uulamets. That was what the leshys said. They didn't say make yourself another Chernevog. Did they? That's not what you're supposed to do, is it?"

Pyetr had a knack for cutting through confusion. Pyetr

was not always right, but Pyetr had a way of getting back to solid ground.

"No," he was relieved to say. "No, they didn't say that."

"He *wants* us to do something stupid. You know that. It's him, dammit, it's him." Pyetr pressed his shoulder, a hard, bruising grip. "Just don't listen. And be careful with the old man too! I don't trust either one of them."

"I'm trying not to. I wish I knew what's right. I wish to the god I knew. I keep thinking we shouldn't listen to him— but then he says things that make sense."

"Good liars are like that. You should have known Dmitri."

"Things ought to be clearer, Pyetr."

Pyetr said, "Not when he doesn't want that."

"I'm scared! I don't know about my choices. I don't know I'm right!"

"Hell. So we could lose. Make a choice. Any choice. Better your dice than his. Just watch for switches."

He drew a breath, let it go again. "We can't be that much further from the house. I think I know where the bridge brought us. I think this is the same stream."

"I've had that idea."

"—But I don't know that Uulamets knew any answers. Pyetr, he left me everything he could, and I don't know that he was right about magic, I *don't* know that this is the answer. The leshys don't understand wizards . . ."

"Listen." Pyetr's fingers bit into his shoulder. "He may not have been right about anything, but let's not believe this fellow, either, not more than once a day and then only if he agrees with us. Just don't *think* about doubts, you know where they're coming from."

"I'm not sure they are, Pyetr. I think they're mine."

"Then let me do the worrying. And the doubting. I'm better at it. You wish up a bear or something."

"Don't—"

"—joke about it? Better than listening to him."

"It might be."

"Might. May. If. Make up your mind, friend! That jug never has broken. Or emptied. You're a hell of a wizard when you know what you want. Why don't you just wish Chernevog to love us dearly?"

"Jugs don't argue," Sasha said glumly.

"They don't put nasty thoughts in your head, either. Put a few in his. Can't you?"

"I don't—" He thought with embarrassment of his only enemy, of poor cousin Mischa, and a mud puddle, and one unbridled, purely malicious wish—and that, only after years of abuse. Pyetr's misdeeds had always seemed, to a young wizard trying desperately to grow up without killing anyone, gloriously, recklessly imaginative. "I don't want a fight with him—I can't—"

"God, what do you think we've got? What do you think's going on, boy? Wake up!"

He had no answer for that.

"Sense of humor," Pyetr said, and hit him on the arm. "I'll wager you anything you like—it'll confuse hell out of him." With which Pyetr took up Volkhi's reins and swung up, then looked to Chernevog, saying,

"Come on, snake, we're going."

I don't know, Eveshka wrote in her book, on the deck of the old ferry, *what to wish about the baby. Papa would say— you can undo anything but the past.*

Pyetr, if this book comes to Sasha, and you hear this, believe that I love you—but I can't come home until I know what brought me here and why. A wizard-child's nothing you ever bargained for. I won't do that to you.

I want you to know that. Maybe you hear me. But I can't hear you and I can't hear Sasha, no matter how I try. And I daren't come back till I know more than I do. So I've got to go and find out what I can.

She put away the inkpot then, and closed the book.

18

There were cold spots in the woods. That was always how it started. Volkhi and Missy hated them and Pyetr swore and patted Volkhi's sweating neck, saying, "There's a lad, it's only a ghost."

At times he heard himself saying things like that and wondered about his sanity.

Magic that wasn't magic and magic that was sorcery. Babi in hiding—and Babi, with Sasha and 'Veshka, was the only contact with magical things that this gambler's son wanted. Things were not going altogether well, in Pyetr's estimation, and while the ghosts were no surprise, they were nothing he wanted to deal with, and nothing Sasha needed, either—the boy was distracted enough; and there was a real danger in these flitting nuisances.

Despair, a cold spot whispered, brushing his ear.

"Shut up!" he said, swatting at it, small good that did.

Hopeless, another wailed.

"Go away!" Sasha wished it, and it wailed into silence. Another cried, Murderer! and flitted in front of Chernevog, who walked ahead of them. It gave Pyetr some satisfaction to see him flinch.

Chernevog! more of them cried. And, Chernevog! Chernevog! went through the woods like a whisper.

"Now we're in it," Pyetr said with a shiver. "Damn, Snake, you do draw flies, don't you?"

Chernevog turned a pale face toward him and Pyetr felt a moment's pain about the heart. Volkhi pitched of a sudden—

And stopped, throwing his head and snorting: it might have been Sasha's doing that a ghost went right through

Chernevog at that moment. Then a whole cloud of them surrounded him wailing and crying, and Chernevog, who had not been so mortal as to wave his arms and do natural things to ward them off, flinched and flailed out at them.

"Damn you!" Chernevog cried, and one said,

We *are* damned. . . .

As the whole horde of ghosts whirled around them like so many pale leaves.

"Uulamets!" Pyetr yelled. "Uulamets, you old liar, if you're out there, you're the one we want!"

There was sudden silence. Not a ghost to be found.

Sasha said, "God, I don't like *that*. . . ."

Eveshka, the ghosts mocked her, Eveshka, where are you going?

She shuddered. They were *her* ghosts that walked with her, in the deep forest twilight. They were her victims, hundreds of them. They were wayfarers, rivermen, travelers on the road. They carried packs, some of them, and looked lost.

Do you know the way—? they would begin, and then their faces, faint in the forest daylight, would grow horrified, as if they had suddenly recognized her, and they would flee shrieking into the brush.

Some leaped out to rob her—horrible men with shaggy hair, whose attacks ended in racketing shrieks of terror.

Worst was one that trailed her, calling out, Have you seen my mama? Please wait!

She would not look at that one. She felt it closer and closer, almost on her heels, felt it tug at her skirts.

Please, it said.

She wished it away, and it went, a child's voice wailing, Papa, where are you?

She forgot her resolution then, she forgot everything but remorse, and the ghosts took it and grew stronger. It was harder and harder to resist them. She felt their hands pulling at her.

Come away, they said, come away, you've no right to be breathing.

C. J. CHERRYH

You've no right to the sunlight. You're bones, you're only bones in a cave. . . .

"*Pretty* bones," something said, different than the ghosts, and she stopped, stood looking about the dark brush, her heart fluttering in panic.

"Oh, I'm here," the voice said, deep in the shadows, and everything grew quiet, except that sibilant voice. Brush crackled with the gliding movement of a heavy body. "I'm here, pretty bones. Don't be afraid of me."

"Go away!" she cried.

It hissed. She saw a rapid disturbance in the brush, the merest glimpse of its huge, slick body as it lashed through the bracken. It turned up to her left, and said, "That's not nice, Eveshka. We're old friends."

"Away!"

It slithered a ways further. She heard it stop.

"Go away!" she ordered it, but its persistence made her doubt it would go, and that was deadly.

"See," it hissed. "I don't have to do what you want. But if you're nice I will. I won't say pretty bones any more."

"Leave me alone!"

Another slithering movement, a voice further away this time: "He's followed you, pretty bones, the man's come up-river. But do you know who he's traveling with? You'll never believe it."

Curiosity was a trap. She tried to refuse it. But her thoughts went scattering after the lure, and it said, the old snake did,

"Kavi Chernevog."

She went cold through and through.

"Isn't that odd?" it said. "If you listened very hard just now you might hear him. Sasha's with him, of course, and I've no notion what they're going to do with Chernevog. Why don't you call them here? I'm sure they'd be glad to see you."

"Shut up!" she cried.

"It's getting dark fast, pretty bones. And don't think of salt. Surely you don't want to drive me away. You know where I'd go, first thing."

She knew. She took a deep, shivering breath. One talked

211

aloud to a vodyanoi, if one had the choice. She said in a trembling voice, "I know. But I'd be careful, Hwiuur. I'd not come too close, either."

"To a wizard as powerful as you? I'd be very foolish. Where were you going? Is it interesting?"

The light was going. Night was the worst time for ghosts—when the eye had less detail to distract it: you don't see them with the eye, Uulamets had said, you see them with the mind.

But there had not been a one since he had called after Uulamets, and Pyetr himself had a bad feeling about that, whether it came from Chernevog or Sasha or whether it was his own suspicion.

"Nastier than the lot of them," he muttered as he rode, in the cold misery of a light, misting rain. "Even in this neighborhood the old man's got his reputation."

It was all saplings now, young trees, some knee-high to the horses, others, fewer, rising slim and tall—leshys had brought those from outside, to this region that had been barren, stream-cut ground. There began to be upthrusts of rock, gray, rain-glistening in the twilight, rising out of a knee-high forest of birches and half obscured by taller growth—when he had last seen those stones standing in eroded, barren land.

Pyetr remembered that landscape with a cold feeling in the pit of his stomach, a memory of pain.

And Chernevog, panting after breath, hard-driven by their pace: "God, this place is changed! —We're near the house."

Chernevog's old holding. Damned right he knew where he was.

"We shouldn't go any further tonight," Chernevog protested.

"Night's a fine time for our business," Pyetr said. "You want a ghost, you might as well look after dark."

"No," Chernevog said, and turned and took Volkhi's reins, at which Volkhi threw his head. "No, listen to me . . ."

"Let go my horse, Snake."

Missy had stopped. Chernevog kept his hold and looked

up, his face waxen pale against the rain-shadowed dusk. He put a hand on Volkhi and Volkhi's shoulder twitched. "Make camp," Chernevog said. "Now."

It seemed for a moment quite reasonable, even prudent. Sasha said, "Why?"

"Because you're being fools. Because we're already too close. Listen to me—"

Both horses started moving abruptly, shoving Chernevog off his balance, but Chernevog grabbed at Pyetr's leg, held onto the reins, stopped Volkhi a second time. Pyetr laid the other hand on his sword, but Chernevog's look stopped him—or something did. He hesitated, suddenly thinking Chernevog might know something worth hearing, while Chernevog said, "Pyetr, please Pyetr, for the god's sake, listen to me—"

"Chernevog!" Sasha said, but that seemed far away, and Chernevog's hold unbreakable as the gaze of his eyes.

"Be my friend," Chernevog said. "Pyetr Ilyitch, *believe* me! I won't betray you."

Sasha hurtled down off Missy's back and seized Chernevog by the shoulder with a violence that spun Chernevog back against Volkhi's side. Pyetr caught up the reins and kept his seat, amazed to see Sasha with a fistful of Chernevog's shirt, saying very quietly, "Don't touch him. Don't you touch him," in a way that Pyetr thought he would take very seriously if he were Kavi Chernevog.

But in all truth—he had not felt Chernevog's appeal to him as an attack: he had felt Chernevog's distress, felt Chernevog had just tried to explain something direly important to him.

Dangerous, probably, to feel that. He watched Sasha let Chernevog go, Chernevog standing with his back to Volkhi's side.

"Move!" Sasha said.

"I'm not sure—" Pyetr found himself saying Not sure and plunged ahead. "I don't know if we shouldn't listen this time. The way the ghosts took off—"

"Pyetr, that's him wanting you to say that."

"I'm not sure it isn't my idea too. —If some Thing or other is really looking for him, isn't it going to start there?"

213

"I thought time mattered."

Eveshka. God. He felt a sudden deep embarrassment, to be so foolish, and Sasha was unwontedly sharp with him. Deservedly. He said, "Come on, Snake," and offered him help to climb up.

Chernevog cast an anxious look at Sasha over his shoulder.

"I'll take him," Sasha said.

Time was when he had felt obliged to stand between the boy and any sort of trouble. It was a strange feeling, to watch a sudden, stern-faced young man climb up (however ungracefully) onto his horse and offer his hand—and see it was Kavi Chernevog who looked afraid to take it.

"Following a notion," the voice said from the brush and the deepening twilight. There was an intermittent long slide of a massive body, a crackling of small branches. "And where will this notion take you, I wonder? Did you know your willow's greening up this spring? I wonder why."

Eveshka ignored the vodyanoi as much as possible. It was time to stop soon, and to make a fire, and to ring herself with protections the River-thing could not pass, but there was nothing savory about this thicket. The forest here might never have died, but it had not prospered either: there was no clear spot to build a fire, and no clear spot either to build her protections.

"I smell smoke, pretty. Do you? I'll bet if you go much further you'll find what you're looking for."

She smelled nothing. But she felt a chill all the same. Old Hwiuur had his wicked ways, and he lied, but he loved tormenting someone in trouble, too, and one got to know when he was getting to the point of things.

"Never been this far up the river, pretty?"

She clenched her jaw and kept walking, breathing at a measured pace, thinking if she could find a place to build a fire and boil water, she might give the damned creature a salt-water bath. That might send him elsewhere awhile.

But she dared not believe it, she dared not do anything

that risked sending the vodyanoi south, not even that she believed Pyetr and Sasha might not deal with it—

But if Kavi was with them, god, the leshys had surely failed, if that was the case, and Kavi might use the vodyanoi, might be using him now. Hwiuur would by no means tell her any straight truth. Kavi was with them—how?

The scent of smoke reached her, very faint. She said, "Hwiuur, who lives hereabouts?"

"Oh," the vodyanoi said, "now are we polite, pretty bones?"

She wanted to know, unequivocally. But Hwiuur was hard to catch with one intent, or two, or three. He said,

"If we're not polite, I'll leave, pretty. I'll tell you. Better yet, I'll show you. Just a little farther."

He was moving away from her for a moment. Then she heard something at her left, looked and saw her father standing there.

"Not so much farther," he said, this gray, shadowed figure that was no ghost.

Then it dissolved and flowed down onto the ground, rushing past her like a runaway spill of ink.

A damned shapeshifter . . . in her father's likeness.

Recent lie? she asked herself. Or a lie from the start?

She stood very still for a moment. She heard Hwiuur's slithering progress in the brush, coming from the other side now. It passed behind her.

"Stop playing games," she cried. "Hwiuur, damn you!"

Movement stopped. The whole woods was still.

But the feeling—the assurance that had been with her from childhood, of something especially, uniquely waiting for her—was with her again in that quiet.

Perhaps, she thought, Hwiuur had been trying, in his malicious way, to mislead her from what was essential for her to find.

Or perhaps, in the presence of such malicious creatures, it might mean something utterly dreadful about her childhood longings—that mysterious assurance of special worth somewhere, most private and most central to her heart.

She walked forward, down a slope and past an old, old tree, found herself facing a strange hill of sod and logs.

Set in that hill, dim in the last of the light—was a door.

It was a most uneasy feeling Sasha had as they rode into view of the ruin, and he wondered if Chernevog was somehow to blame for that uneasiness: Chernevog had scared him terribly, going at Pyetr as he had a while back, and he had no idea what was the matter with him since, that had his hands trembling with anger and his heart racing—whether it was Chernevog that disturbed him or whether it was some other abrading influence in this place.

He was not one to let feelings get away from him, no matter Pyetr's advice to let his temper go—no matter Pyetr thought him weak and indecisive . . . he was not Pyetr, he had all but panicked with Chernevog, and he could not ride into this place as Pyetr did, looking as if trouble had better watch out for him and not the other way around. He was frightened, he was angry at Chernevog, and most of all—

Most of all he did not really want the meeting they were here to get, which might well prevent it happening at all. He kept thinking, What do I do if the old man does want me?

"Not much of the place left," Pyetr said. It was true—ordinary luck might easily have missed the house entirely in the almost-dark, the planting of trees was so thorough. Only the burned beams above the trees showed them where the old building had stood, fire-charred timbers standing stark and washed with rain.

I've seen this, too, Sasha thought, uncomfortably aware of Chernevog's presence brushing his back. Missy moved at her deliberate pace, constant movement of muscle and bone beneath him: Missy was smelling rain and young leaves and old fire—nothing in the way of dangers that horses understood.

"Looks as if the leshys flattened what was standing,"

Pyetr said. "The big tree in the yard is gone. Trees must be planted right over the grave."

"We'll find it," Sasha murmured distractedly. He felt nothing precisely amiss about the place, but it seemed far more haunted than the woods, full of memories and old wishes. He said to Uulamets' ghost, if it chanced to be listening, Master Uulamets, it's me, Sasha. We've got Chernevog with us: don't be startled—

"Sasha," Chernevog said. Chernevog had not held to him in their riding together, had avoided him as much as two people could avoid each other on the same horse, but of a sudden Chernevog touched his arm. "For the god's sake we're close enough!"

"Shut up!" he said.

The ruin stood in seedlings that made a deep green deception in the twilight, level as if it were some knee-deep lake the horses waded. The dead tree that had stood in the yard was indeed gone, there were only scant traces of a wall and the tumbled foundations, except one wing. They passed the remains of a wall, a charred round ruin where the bathhouse had stood, all half-drowned in infant birch trees.

He stopped Missy, bade Chernevog get down, and slid off as Pyetr did. They were virtually over the grave, as best he recalled it. The light was fast leaving them, the green birches faded to faint, moist gray, the edges of the forest lost in rain, the burned timbers black against the clouds. The only sound was their breathing.

"Master Uulamets," he said aloud, defying all that silence. "Master Uulamets?"

He waited. He wished earnestly for the old man's good will, he tried earnestly to remember that Uulamets had also saved their lives, and not to hold Uulamets' motives against him.

"Damn stubborn old man," Pyetr muttered after a fruitless time of standing there, during which the horses stamped and shifted and idly pulled leaves off the young birches. "It's wet, it's nasty, and he doesn't like the company. —Come on, grandfather, dammit, 'Veshka's in trouble and there's something using your shape. I'd think you'd like to know that."

There was a sudden chill in the air. A wind sighed along the sea of leaves.

That passed. Sasha let go the breath he had been holding, stood a moment in the quiet trying again to convince himself he truly wanted the old man to speak to him personally.

He trusted Misighi. That was the only advice he was willing to take where it regarded the welfare of the woods—which was their welfare, too: he trusted that the way he trusted the ground they walked on and the food they ate and the water they drank.

What harmed it, harmed them; when it was well, they were: that was the bargain they had made—using nature kindly, working with what magic agreed with it—like the Forest-things themselves.

That was where he had to stand. That was the safe magic.

"Watch him," he told Pyetr, and got down his pack from Missy's back, knelt down and bent back a couple of seedlings to give himself room, searching after rosemary and the herbs he recollected Uulamets using in his spells.

Chernevog wanted him to stop—a weak, a desperately frightened wish for his attention and his patience to hear him. "For the god's sake," Chernevog said, and Pyetr grabbed him by the shoulder, "—it may not be only Uulamets that answers."

Doubt, Sasha thought, and stood up and looked Chernevog in the face with an angry suspicion what Chernevog was trying to do to them.

"Sasha," Chernevog said, "Sasha, —oh, god—"

Dark and fire . . .

Hoofbeats in the dark . . . inexorable as a heartbeat . . .

Eveshka, sitting at a hearth, drinking a cup of tea.

Sasha felt that sense of presence that had haunted him from home. He turned his head toward it and saw, like a bad dream, the bannik squatting in the charred skeleton of the bathhouse doorway, a dusky, spiky-haired shadow, like a sullen, bored child, staring at the steps beside his feet.

One did not want it to look up. One did not want to look it in the eyes.

Sasha thought with a chill. —It lied . . . it was always his . . .

But Chernevog tried to retreat behind them, fighting Pyetr's grip on his arm.

"No!" Chernevog cried.

The bannik stood up, frowning at them with eyes like dying embers. Then it looked skyward, lifted its hand as something filmy white swept down on broad wings to settle on its wrist. The creature folded its wings and stared at them in its own moment of sharp attention. Then ghostly owl and ragged shadow of a boy faded together into the dark.

19

 "What in hell was that?" Pyetr asked of Sasha. "That was the bannik! Wasn't that the bannik?"

"It's what showed up at the house," Sasha said.

"It's *him*," Pyetr said. "Is it my eyes, or what's it doing with the owl?"

"I don't know," Sasha said.

"He damned well does," Pyetr said, and took a new grip on Chernevog's shirt, wanting answers. "What kind of tricks are you up to, Snake?"

Chernevog said on a ragged breath, "I told you, I told you, and you won't listen—"

Pyetr shook him. "Told us, damn right you've told us— one damned lie after another! Sound asleep, were you? Innocent as morning snow, are you?"

"I'm not lying!" Chernevog cried, and it sounded both desperate and fully in earnest.

Which meant nothing, with wizards. Pyetr shook him a second time, saying, "Bannik, hell! Call it back!"

"I can't!" Chernevog said.

"Can't, hell! That's you. That spook's you, Snake, don't tell me it's not."

"It's a shadow," Chernevog said faintly. "A piece. A part. A fragment . . ." Chernevog shivered, put a hand on his arm, eye to eye with him in a twilight so deep that his eyes had no center, only dark. "The dead can fragment. . . . That's what ghosts are: pieces, fragments, sometimes a single notion—"

"You're not dead!"

"I don't know what made it, I don't know why it happened, I didn't know it could happen and I don't know where I lost it—"

"Damned careless of you!"

"It's the truth, Pyetr Ilyitch!"

He worried every time he believed Chernevog. He had memories aplenty to remind himself what Chernevog was, and had done, and still might do; and certainly enough to remind him why he wanted to kill this man; but he could not find the man he wanted to kill, that was the trouble: this one held to him, teeth chattering, and said things like,

"For the god's sake don't go on with this tonight. Don't invite any damned thing that might be listening. Build a fire. Lay down lines. It's not nature you're dealing with: put some limits to this, don't leave it to whatever comes."

Sasha said, "He's right."

"Build a fire." They were knee-deep in seedlings leshys had put there. "I don't think we ought to be tearing up any trees, under the circumstances."

"There's the bathhouse," Sasha said. "The furnace will be stone. There's wood left—at least of the walls."

"Cinders," Pyetr muttered, but he was glad enough to hear words like fire and limits. The horses had wandered off from all this shouting, browsing among the seedlings. They both put their heads up and Sasha called to them, "Come on."

No one, in this place, in this night, had any particular choice about it.

Wizardry helped make damp wood catch, in a furnace mostly intact. Its effect against the smoke was minimal so far as Pyetr could see, but a circle of sulfur and salt around the old walls would stay put against any chance or wizard-raised wind—and such of the walls as still stood, helped against the rainy chill.

Pyetr fed the fire and kept an eye on Chernevog while Sasha was outside the walls including the horses in the circle—bending birch seedlings, tying them with mending-cord, and wishing them well: on the whole, Pyetr approved of birch trees, and leshys, and whatever was alive, as opposed to dead; and particularly whatever opposed the sort of magic Chernevog dealt with.

Chernevog was sitting opposite him, against the fire-scorched wall, knees tucked up. His eyes were open, but he had not moved since he had sat down.

"There's the canvas," Pyetr said. "You could wrap in that, you know."

Chernevog gave no sign he had heard. His thin shirt seemed scant protection against the chill in the mist.

Pyetr chucked a stick in Chernevog's direction. If Chernevog was thinking of some mischief he had no inclination to let him do it in peace. "The canvas," he said, "beside you. Or freeze. I'm sure I don't care."

He thought about the bannik, or whatever it was, and tried to wonder about Eveshka and what else it had shown them. He listened to Sasha moving around out beyond the walls, in the dark, and thought, Get back here, boy. I really don't like this.

Chernevog said, suddenly, "I did love Owl."

It sounded like an accusation. A just complaint, what was worse, but he did not want to argue grievances with the man, not here, where memory was so vivid. He kept his mouth shut.

Chernevog said, "I wanted Eveshka. I'd have given her everything she could have asked."

"Shut up, Snake. You'll make me mad if you go on."

"She wanted you. I couldn't understand that."

"I can."

Chernevog said, "I wish I'd done differently by you."

"But you didn't, Snake, you really made me mad. And you're doing it again."

"You want so very little."

"Sasha!"

He could not get his breath for a moment. Then breath came, and Sasha came running.

"Pyetr?"

"Snake, here, tried something." He was still short-winded. "I don't know what."

"I'm very sorry," Chernevog said. "You frightened me."

"*I* frightened you." Pyetr put another stick into the furnace, wanting nothing to have happened, nothing magical to have insinuated itself into him that Sasha might not detect. "Don't put any damn wishes on me. —Sasha, I don't know what he was up to, but he did something."

Sasha squatted and put his hand on his shoulder, but the queasiness in his stomach did not go away. Wishes, he thought, did not necessarily lie *in* someone, they were not there to be found like a splinter or a bruise. They just waited down the road and pounced when the time came.

"It's all right," Sasha said.

"I damn sure hope it is." He shrugged off Sasha's hand, not wanting to worry about it. "Did you finish out there?"

"Almost—I didn't feel him do anything, Pyetr."

So he was being foolish—if Sasha knew everything that was going on, which he hoped, but he was not sure of: nothing seemed sure, dealing with Kavi Chernevog.

"I'm all right, then," he said. "Go on, get back to it. We've got one Snake in here, we don't need another."

Sasha pressed his shoulder, stood up and did something, Pyetr had no idea what: Chernevog put up a hand as if he were about to be hit, and said, "I didn't touch him."

"He evidently didn't," Pyetr said, reluctantly.

Sasha stood there a moment. Chernevog stared up at him with a hard, defiant expression.

That was a fight going on, Pyetr decided. He got up with his sword in hand and said, "Snake, behave or I'll cut your head off. Hear me?"

Chernevog did not look at him immediately. Then his eyes shifted slowly to fix on him, and Pyetr felt a sudden lightheadedness, a chill against his heart.

The stone floor came up under his knee—the sword clattered onto the stones as he saw Chernevog stand up, and Sasha facing him.

"Chernevog!" he yelled.

"Don't fight me," Chernevog said, and even thinking about it was an uphill struggle.

"Damn you," he said, and did struggle—to reach the sword

and pick it up, but it was hard to believe Chernevog meant any harm, to him or to Sasha: Chernevog needed them, and what Chernevog needed was very, very safe.

"Protection enough, your circle," Chernevog said. "Thank you."

Papa had not brought up a fool, to go straight up to any strange door and knock. Eveshka sat at the edge of the woods and listened to the silence. Hwiuur had gone somewhere or Hwiuur was lying as still as he could. Of the shapeshifter there was no sign, either—whether her father had ever been with her, or whether it had been that creature all along. Their absence now meant only that they were up to no good; and if the vodyanoi had told her the truth about Pyetr and Sasha being in Chernevog's company, she had no doubt where that trouble had gone.

She would wish not—excepting it was not a place to be flinging wishes about recklessly or loudly.

Damn, she did not like this strange house under the hill, and she did not like Hwiuur disappearing and she did not like the idea that whoever lived here was—she felt it—aware of her being here.

How not? she thought. Hwiuur would certainly have seen to that.

She locked her hands in front of her mouth, she wanted, as quietly and as carefully as she could, to know what was in that house without having it catch her at it—a small burglary, Pyetr would call it, without touching the door at all.

Ah, someone said to her, there you are.

She drew back, quickly, felt a magic more powerful than anything Kavi had ever used.

It said, Oh, don't be a fool. There's no use sitting there in the dark. Come inside. I don't bite.

She said, Who are you?

But that was a mistake. Curiosity opened a way for it. It said, softly, Your mother, dear. Of course.

20

"Sasha?" Pyetr was saying, "Sasha?" and patting his face, saying, "Damn you, let him go," —to someone else, Sasha decided. Then he realized that Pyetr was holding his head off the ground and the person Pyetr was talking to was Chernevog, who sat comfortably at their fireside.

Pyetr rested a hand on Sasha's shoulder, said, in a low voice: "I don't know what he's up to. He's got his book, he's got yours and Uulamets', and I couldn't stop him. I'm sorry." Pyetr sounded terribly distraught, as if it were his fault—and that was in no wise just.

Sasha asked, "Are you all right?"

"So far."

He made the effort to sit up, winced as the ache in his head became stabbing pain and found himself leaning on Pyetr's arm, everything gone dim again.

"You hit the ground hard." Pyetr said, continuing to support him, which, the way everything was spinning, was more than welcome. But the ache eased when he wished it: it should not have, Chernevog being free—and free of what . . . his addled wits suddenly realized. He looked into Pyetr's anxious face, saw lines of pain unlike him.

God, no! he thought, and he wished Chernevog's heart back where it belonged.

But he felt no change at all; and Chernevog said, with a stinging rebuke, I haven't hurt him, I've no wish to, without taking back what I don't want, personally, to carry. You won't do my heart any harm—not where it sits. So just do what I tell you—no different than with Uulamets, is it?

Damn you, Sasha thought, and quickly restrained his anger, seeing Chernevog smile at him—affording him a moment to think what he might do to Pyetr to teach him a lesson.

Chernevog said, I have no need to. Do I?

No, he agreed, earnestly trying to turn his thoughts to cooperation, at least for the while.

Chernevog said aloud, to Pyetr: "Let's dispense with grudges. Shall we? They do so little good. I won't blame you, you won't blame me, we won't quarrel: that's best, isn't it, Pyetr Ilyitch?"

Careful, Sasha wished Pyetr.

"Isn't it?" Chernevog asked.

"Yes," Pyetr said faintly.

"That's your friend bespelling you, not me. He's very much afraid for you, Pyetr Ilyitch. But we have an agreement, and I'm not sorry for it, I'm truly not. Be agreeable, is that so much to ask?"

"No," Pyetr answered, a mere movement of the lips: Say anything he wants, Sasha wished him, never mind the truth.

Chernevog said, "I really, really have come to envy you two. I don't know I've ever seen two people trust each other."

"You wouldn't," Pyetr said, before Sasha could stop him.

"No," Chernevog said, "I wouldn't. I really wouldn't. But it's comfortable just being with people like you—even if I am a snake." He smiled at them, and shrugged. "This snake can do very well for you, you understand, if you'll only let him."

"He's lost his damn mind," Pyetr muttered under his breath.

"No, no, no," Chernevog said. "I'm very serious. The leshys did teach me something—patience, for one thing. Waiting for things instead of forcing them. They do come. This one did."

"I think I'll have a nap," Pyetr said. "It's late. We're in the hands of a crazy man."

Sasha's heart turned over. He wished Chernevog not to do anything about that; and Chernevog only said, gently, "I wouldn't change him. —We'll talk about 'Veshka tomorrow."

It was a trap, of course. Sasha bit his lip and knew Pyetr

knew it, and knew Pyetr had not the constitution to ignore a challenge.

Pyetr just sat there and stared at Chernevog, that was as far as he went; and Chernevog sat there a moment before saying, with no trace of mockery, "Something's seriously wrong. I've as much magic as I need—but I feel limits I didn't have before. I don't know whether it's something the leshys did to me or whether it's something altogether different. I do know that 'Veshka's north of us, I know she's left the boat, I know old Hwiuur's about . . ."

"Let's get to the point," Pyetr said.

"That is the point. Hwiuur's being—pardon me—a snake. Very difficult to catch. Possibly it's a little last rebellion: he's like that. But it's not the only uneasy feeling I have, and it doesn't, as you say, answer the question what's happened to the leshys, a very major question, in my position. So I do think it's just as well we go north, and find 'Veshka, and explain to her you're with me—because if we don't, she's very likely to fall into the hands of some other crazy person, do you see, and none of us wants that."

Pyetr said nothing. Sasha thought of flowers, thought of bread baking, thought of the garden at home and wondered if it needed weeding. He wished the weeds at least not to prosper.

Chernevog said, "Prudent, but let's all admit she might try to free you, and I've no doubt there are things that will fly straight to her to help her. That's why I want to find her first. That's why I'm sure you do."

Flowers, Sasha thought. Birches and a fieldmouse by the hearth.

Pyetr, don't listen to him.

Chernevog said, "Your friend is speaking to you again. He's trying to advise you be careful. So would I. I'd give him the same advice, of course, but he's trying not to listen to me. —I'll warrant his head's not hurting now."

The pain had gone; Sasha had no recollection when.

"See?" Chernevog said softly. "A safe camp, a safe rest. I can be very easy to get along with, if people are agreeable. —Put some wood on the fire, will you?"

The house seemed larger inside than out—the log walls were trimmed and polished and other rooms were curtained with fine needlework at which one had no wish to gaze overlong, the patterns so caught the eye. Fire blazed up in a hearth of river stone, an oak mantel held silver plates, and herbs hung in chains and bunches beside it.

This was Draga's house.

And the mother Eveshka had not seen from her birth a hundred years ago was young and beautiful, her mother's hair was long and pale, freshly brushed and tied up with ribbons, her nightgown embroidered with blue flowers very like those Eveshka had thought she had made up, to sew about her hems.

It was her nose, her mouth, her chin, except a little cleft. The resemblances both fascinated and terrified her.

Her mother said, "Do come in, Eveshka," and, "Let me take your coat, dear, do sit down, god, your hair's all over leaves . . ."

Eveshka set her pack down by the hearthside bench her mother offered her, and kept her coat on, and stayed standing.

But her mother slipped on a robe, drawing her braids over one shoulder, said, looking at her, "Would you like some water to wash?" —implying, Eveshka supposed, that her face must be dirty. Her hands certainly were. Her boots were muddy from the rain. She would never have let anyone so disreputable besmirch her own well-swept floors, she would scold Pyetr or Sasha or her father right out the door to shed the boots, but she suddenly found herself defending her dirt as her right to be out that door again tonight, very soon, and sooner, if she found reason.

"No, thank you," she said.

"Well, do sit," her mother said, beginning to fuss about the kitchen. "Do."

"You needn't go to any trouble," Eveshka said. "Why did you call me here?"

"Because I wanted to see my daughter. Because you're in danger."

228

"From whom? From you?"

Draga drew tea from the samovar, set silver cups on a silver plate and slipped a honey-cake onto a small dish to set beside it.

Eveshka repeated, wanting a truthful answer: "From you, mother?"

Draga brought the tray to the fireside, set it on the end of the bench. "Your father told you terrible things about me. I know."

"My father's been dead for three years," she said shortly. "Why now, mother? What do you want?"

"To protect you. And my grandchild."

She wanted no wishes about the baby one way or the other until she was sure what she wanted, and she was surrounded by wishes, everyone's damned interference in something happening inside her.

"Does *everyone* in the world know?" she asked sharply.

"You didn't?"

She wanted to know things; she desperately barred her mother's thoughts, that came at her this way and that, persistent as a snake after eggs.

She said, carefully, aloud, "No, I didn't. It can't be far along."

"Mere days. Pyetr's the father?"

"What do you know about him?"

"That he's a common man. That he's very kind to you, and very wise, and very handsome."

That was not the response she had expected. Her father had never had a kind word for Pyetr, and that one of her parents finally agreed with her judgment tempted her to question all the things she had heard of Draga—but she must not be taken in that easily, dammit, no. Her mother had been spying on them, her mother had been sneaking about eavesdropping on their business.

"You're afraid," Draga said. "Here, don't let the tea cool— sit down, sit. God, you've grown so beautiful."

"I was murdered! I spent a hundred damned years as a ghost, mama, where in hell were you when I needed help?"

"Dear, I've had troubles, too."

"You were sleeping with Kavi Chernevog. You sent him to our house, you sent him to rob papa, and to sleep with me, if he could—"

"That was Kavi's idea."

"He was a boy, mama, you were years and years older than he was!"

"A very charming, very dangerous boy. I wanted you, dear, I wanted you to come and live with me, and yes, I sent Kavi: your father would hardly have let me walk up to the door. Kavi wanted me to teach him certain things—I agreed if he'd go and get you away from your father, which of course took your cooperation. Yes, I thought he might try to win you for himself, you're of an age; but Kavi had no intention of keeping his promises. He stayed to learn what he could from your father, he got caught where he had no business to be, and he still had a chance to have kept his promise to me. But he murdered you instead. Do you understand? He killed you because he'd told too many lies, and he knew how strong you were, and he knew you'd tell me too much. He knew if you ever got to me, the two of us would grow closer and closer, until he had no chance against us. So he killed you to keep you from me. And then he had to kill me before I found out what he'd done."

"Did he?"

"He came very close to it. I was very weak, all but helpless. I knew what he was doing—I'd even have offered your father my help, if I'd been able to, but I hadn't the strength. Then—I found out later it was Kavi's fall—something changed quite suddenly, and I could wish myself back, bit by bit."

It was plausible. It was entirely plausible. Draga offered the tea, stood patiently with the tray in her hands, wanting her to take it, and for courtesy's sake, and because her mother seemed disposed to stand there until she made up her mind, Eveshka took the cup from the tray, only to hold in her hands.

"No cake?"

"I'm not hungry."

"Well, well—" Her mother took the other cup, set the tray on the mantel and sat down, patting the bench. "Do sit. God, after all these years. What a lovely young woman you are!"

Eveshka stayed on her feet. "Why didn't you just *tell* me you wanted to see me?"

"Because I wasn't sure you'd come, I wasn't sure you'd want to see me—and because there's more going on than you know."

"Evidently everything's going on that I don't know! I'm having a baby and my dead mother's hiding in the woods—"

"Dear, dear, sit down. And drink the tea. It's not poisoned."

So finally her mother talked about things as they were. Eveshka sat down, coat and all, holding the teacup in her lap, and looked her mother in the eye, saying, "So what else don't I know, that you think I should?"

"A great deal."

"I've an hour or so in mind."

"Aren't you warm in that coat?"

"Let's get to the point, mama."

Draga sipped her tea. "Kavi Chernevog."

"What about him?"

"He's awake, he's looking for you, and he has your husband and his friend prisoner."

"That's a lie!"

"I'd be very careful trying to bespeak young Alexander at the moment. You're liable to get a very unpleasant answer. —Let me tell you, daughter, you're a lovely, intelligent young woman with your father's manners, my wits, and both our gifts in measure enough Kavi finds you very dangerous. I wanted you here. I would have wanted your husband and young Alexander with you, but that part of it your young friend prevented. At least Kavi doesn't know about me yet and Kavi doesn't believe you have any help now that the leshys have fallen asleep."

That, she had not known. The rest of it—

She threw one small item onto the pile, hoping it was harmless. She said, "Hwiuur's loose. The vodyanoi."

"I know him. Where is he?"

"In your woods, mama. Is he yours?"

"No, he's not mine. Hwiuur belongs to whoever scares him. And since Kavi's waked—I've no doubt whose he is. You say he was in my woods. Where?"

CHERNEVOG

"You should know that, mama, you should know it, he was close enough. You knew I was there."

"I saw you. I didn't see him. I don't like this at all." Draga shut her eyes a moment, and *wanted* something. Of a sudden something large stirred beyond the curtains, claws clicked across the boards and a huge bear thrust a nose into the room—came shambling in as if it owned the place.

"His name is Brodyachi," Draga said. "He *is* a bear."

Brodyachi rocked from side to side, swinging his head and managing to look at Eveshka sullenly, eye to eye. He had a terrible scar across his head and other scars that looked like burns, about his shoulders.

"Trespassers, Brodyachi!" Draga went and opened the door.

Brodyachi got up and slouched out of the house into the night.

"I had him indoors tonight," Draga said, "knowing you were very close. I'm afraid Brodyachi's rather a sullen fellow. Be on your guard against him. —Would you like some tea to drink this time, dear? That cup must be cold by now."

"This is fine." She had an idea what Brodyachi was, and that it would be no easy thing to overcome the spells that protected him.

So her mother had her heart well protected. But she had hers in her, and there was nothing but her wishes to defend it.

Her mother said, "Won't you take off the coat?"

They lay down to sleep, with the fire built up, their canvas tied between two rocks and the surviving wall of the bathhouse. It was dry, it was warm, it should have afforded them comfort. But the sight of Chernevog reading by firelight afforded none, and as for what had happened to him, Pyetr felt a decided queasiness about his stomach—not pain, not acute fear: he told himself that nothing substantial had happened, that he still had his own heart, whatever the substance of it was, and Chernevog's could not be that well-used, however old it was.

Sasha touched his shoulder. He turned his head and saw the worry on Sasha's face.

"This time it *is* my fault," Sasha whispered, and wanted something, Pyetr had no idea what, except it upset his stomach further.

Sasha gave up whatever he was doing and looked thoroughly upset.

"Don't believe him," Sasha said. "Whatever you do, don't start believing him."

"Hell," he whispered, "I have trouble enough believing in Babi." He elbowed Sasha in the ribs. "Get some sleep. At least we don't have to keep one ear awake for Snake tonight. We know damn well where he is."

Bad joke. It was the best he could do. Sasha said, touching his brow— "Go to sleep, Pyetr."

Damned dirty trick the boy had, Pyetr thought, opening his eyes in the sunrise.

But he was, all the same, grateful.

21

Eveshka waked face down in a comfortable nest of pillows and blankets and felt a moment of cold fear, having no memory of falling asleep, or having lain down in this bed which was clearly in her mother's house. Somehow she was in a clean white gown, somehow she was washed and barefoot, and with her hair braided with pale blue ribbons. And someone was stirring about beyond the curtains, clattering pottery. The house smelled of breakfast.

"Mother!" she cried, irate. She flung her feet out of bed, looked in vain for her pack, her boots and the clothes she had been wearing. There was only a light robe on a peg and she put it on and stormed out into the kitchen.

Her mother looked at her, mixing bowl and spoon in hand, and said, "Set the table, dear."

"Mother, where's my bag?"

"Breakfast first."

Eveshka walked about the room, peering under benches and behind curtains.

"The dishes are in the cupboard," Draga said.

"Where are my clothes, dammit? Where are my belongings?"

"You sound like your father." Draga nodded toward the other curtain. "Your baggage is there, your boots are clean, outside the door, your clothes are drying. You're quite the slugabed, my dear."

Eveshka went to the curtained closet, drew out her bag and her coat and laid them on the bench by the fire, where her mother was putting cakes on a griddle. She walked to the

234

door, opened it and retrieved her boots, standing in the open door to pull them on.

"Eveshka, dear, you're making a draft in the fireplace."

"I want my clothes," she said, and closed the door and walked out across the clearing in a nightrobe and her boots to collect her clothes off the oak that stood at the edge of the woods.

Thank the god, she thought, her book was on the boat. She could remember nothing of how she had gotten to bed—sleeping like the very dead last night, since she supposed it was her mother who had washed her and braided her hair and dressed her like a ribboned doll.

She reached up to get her clothes from off the tree and heard a loud grunt, looked, still standing on tiptoe, and saw the bear get up from behind the oak and look at her.

"Nice Brodyachi," she said, wishing absolutely nothing at him, knowing how touchy a wizard's companion could be. "That's a good fellow."

She gathered the clothes, backed carefully away, one eye to the bear. It walked with a sullen swing of its head, faster and faster. Moaned in a bear's warning voice.

"Mother!" she yelled.

And dashed for the door and slammed it as Brodyachi charged. She braced her shoulder against it and dropped the latch as he slapped the wood.

Her mother was taking up the cakes.

"Brodyachi," Draga said, rising to her feet, and Eveshka could hear the bear's harsh sigh, hear the boards of the door creak as it sat down against it. Her mother said, "After breakfast, you can feed him a cake or two. That may win him. —Do get the dishes, dear. I'm standing here with nowhere to put these."

They packed up, they picked up the bags and the bedrolls to take out to the horses. Chernevog took the bag with the books and the herb-pots, which answered the question whether Chernevog would turn a hand himself, and certainly what he wanted to keep out of Sasha's reach, Pyetr reckoned bitterly.

He also reckoned very well which horse Chernevog would

want for himself, and when Chernevog wanted to walk out to the horses, Pyetr kept his mouth shut and planned to keep it that way, wishing at the bottom of his heart that Volkhi would have the discrimination to give a sudden pitch and break Chernevog's neck—but the very thought that Chernevog might harm Volkhi or magic the spirit out of him made him sure he wanted to do nothing to provoke him. Volkhi came wandering up to them, and he attached the reins, trying to think nothing at all.

"Pyetr," Sasha said, and he thought, probably not on his own initiative, that Sasha wanted him to ride double with him on Missy; but, "No," he said, shaking his head, and went on tying his knots. He knew bullies, he had met them aplenty in Vojvoda, and if he was the target Chernevog picked this morning, then so be it: better one of them than both and better to keep his head down and take it than challenge the scoundrel to find one and the next and the next soft spot until he felt out where all the telling ones were.

So he finished his knot and lapped the rein-ends over Volkhi's neck, turned to offer Chernevog a lift up. But he thought then that he was supposed to get on and pull Chernevog up, and he found himself eye to eye with Chernevog, not sure what the man wanted.

"Go on," Chernevog said.

He gave a doubtful shake of his head, turned and took a handful of Volkhi's mane.

Fear stopped him then, a cold sudden thought of Chernevog at his back. And something very strong wanted him to go ahead, now, before Chernevog lost his patience.

He turned against Volkhi's side and looked Chernevog in the face, sure that one of these conflicting impulses was Sasha's, one was Chernevog's, and all he could do was stand there with go and stay chasing around his own cold apprehension.

"Can't you just say what you want?" he asked, the way he would ask Sasha, and feared he might be tilting some balance in this silent, rapid warfare . . . might just have done something very stupid, and dangerous to Sasha, and he wanted Chernevog to think about *him*, not Sasha. He gave Chernevog a sudden shove. Chernevog turned and looked him in the face and he could not draw the next breath, absolutely could not get rid of the one he had.

"Stop it!" Sasha cried.

Breath went out of him. He gasped after the next. Chernevog said, "Don't do that again," and Pyetr turned perforce and with his knees shaking under him, found enough strength to get up to Volkhi's back.

Chernevog passed him the baggage Volkhi carried, the bag with the books, too, and wanted his hand then, to pull him up.

Pyetr gave it, leaned, braced his leg, and let Chernevog climb on, with a grip on his arm and his shirt, Volkhi shifting weight from one hind foot to the other. Chernevog settled, and again he felt that queasiness in his stomach that meant two wizards wanted conflicting things of him.

He bit his lip, he did not ask Sasha to stop, the boy knew what he was doing, if it killed him, the boy knew what he was doing . . .

Chernevog's arms came around his waist, Volkhi turned his head and started moving in a direction he supposed Chernevog wanted, all of which passed in a kind of fog. He wanted Chernevog not to hold so closely, he wanted not to have Chernevog up against his back, he wanted not to feel the dark spot he had felt since last night waking up and slithering about in the middle of him.

He thought, It's his heart, whatever that means. It's his damned, shriveled heart—

"Let him go!" Sasha was saying, pulling Missy alongside, but Missy suddenly pitched and shied off. "Pyetr!" Sasha cried and he saw Sasha hauling on the reins, trying to reason with the mare. "Dammit, don't do that to him!"

—but that dark spot just wandered about where it wanted to, and finally found itself a place to rest, after which the acute fear passed, and the dizziness passed, and Pyetr only knew something was still there, so close to where *he* was that he could no longer see it.

"He's perfectly safe," Chernevog said, which echoed strangely in his hearing, and Volkhi, who had jolted them a bit when Missy shied, walked steadily now. "No reason to worry," Chernevog whispered behind his ear. "I won't hurt you, I've no intention at all of harming you . . ."

He felt a deep chill. He was no longer riding through young trees, he was seeing the fireside last night, he was remembering Sasha hitting the stone floor like a sack of flour and himself standing there wondering whether he should want to do something about that. That was how it had hit him: a small dead spot that could see his best friend lying on the ground and ask himself if he really wanted to do something that was going to get him hurt—

Because for a moment it had seemed nobody ever looked out for anybody . . .

As if the last several years had never happened, as if he was the same ragged boy who had had nobody—nobody but a father who sometimes fed him and sometimes got drunk or went off somewhere for days.

Though he had cared, dammit: he remembered hunting for his father and wishing—god, wishing his father would die so he would never have to spend another night scared he was dead in some damned alley—

His father had died, murdered one midsummer's eve. And he had had that same cold dark spot in the middle of him. He had gotten drunk for the first time in his young life, gotten drunk and walked The Doe's roof ridge with a vodka jug, while drunken grown-ups cheered and clapped below—but they cheered their loudest when he almost fell.

They had given him drinks, perhaps out of kindness, until he fell on his face. He had missed the funeral, such as there was for Ilya Kochevikov: the town watch had dumped him in a shallow grave and nobody even marked it.

Not even he had. He had come there the next afternoon to see where it was, and just walked off from it—because his father was through scaring him: that was all he had managed to feel while he was standing there: his father would never scare him any more.

He still dreamed about searching for his father. Then the terror would be real again, and he would think, god, he can't be dead, he can't be dead—for reasons he did not to this day understand.

That was where he was this morning—remembering teetering drunk on that damn roof—he had done it on three memorable occasions since, for sizable bets—and watching the blurry roof ridge ahead of him swaying back and forth, in this numbness that said there was only that narrow a track to walk, and if he fell the whole world would watch and cheer him down—

Walk it with me, Kavi Chernevog? Think you're brave? Think you're good?

. . . He stood in winter woods, *called* to Owl, and Owl came out of the snowy sky, white against white, Owl settled on his arm and took the mouse he had for him.

He could not love Owl now, he could not love anything, he only understood what life and death were. He could know fear, he could know hate, which was tangled with it—he could know his own advantage when he saw it, so it really was not so very different, being without a heart. It was still comfortable to be with Owl. Owl's needs were simple, a mouse or two—no trouble to catch them, wish them still, wish them dead.

Owl when he killed was quick. Owl never thought about killing. Owl just did.

He could wish Owl were free—but he was not: Owl was bound to him and he was bound to Draga. He could escape for an hour or so, he could go out in the white and the cold and call Owl to him and for a while he could forget . . .

No good to run, her voice said. You can try.

No good to wish, she said. You can try that, too.

And one night by the hearth she said, this woman standing in front of the fire, Do you want me to call Owl here? No, he said, and insofar as he was still Pyetr, he saw her pale hair and thought, as one would in a dream, Chernevog's being a fool, it's Eveshka—not Draga. He doesn't know what he's dealing with.

But things seemed to blur then, and he thought, panicked, No, it isn't 'Veshka, it isn't her—before the woman turned her head and looked him in the eyes.

He wanted out of this dream. He wanted out of it, because he knew where it was going. He heard Owl battering at the windows, he felt his heart beating in panic—

Not Eveshka, he kept saying to himself. There was no

likeness, none but the hair, none but the shape of the face, he did not know how he could mistake that even from the back. The chin was cleft, the eyes were not Eveshka's eyes—they were ice, they were winter.

She came close and touched him under the chin—she was so much taller than he; and lifted his face and kissed him on the mouth while Owl battered himself frantically against the shutters and his heart beat in fear. He had no idea now what right was, or where he could go if he ran. She kissed him twice more and said he had never had a secret she did not know, and never would have a purpose but what she set him.

He wanted not to go into that room with her . . . and Chernevog gave him back the daylight and the forest, abhorring his own recollections. Chernevog did not want to be a servant again, he would never be in that position again. . . .

He walked up the path to the ferryman's cottage, passed a gate Pyetr knew, in front of trees long dead—he came up the familiar walk-up and onto the porch and knocked fearfully, guarding his thoughts—or Uulamets might know instantly why he was there, and kill him.

But it was a girl in blond braids that answered the door—the hair was so like Draga's it made his heart jump with fright; but it could only be Draga's daughter—a girl no more than thirteen.

He took off his cap. He knew who she was and dimly knew he was dealing with someone very dangerous to him. He said, in a boy's young voice, "I'm Kavi Chernevog. I've come to see master Uulamets. Is he at home?"

Eveshka let him in.

No! Pyetr thought, wanting desperately not to see this; and Chernevog said, silently, at his shoulder, She's very clever, if she used her good sense—but you can reason with her, can't you? Persuade her to join us: then there's nothing can threaten us, nothing will ever threaten us again.

"No," he muttered. It was hard to think at all. Chernevog's thoughts kept coming at him, clinging like spiderweb. He heard Missy behind them, and wanted help, desperately wanted it. He wanted to rein back, and his hands would not move.

Of a sudden there was a quick thump of hooves, Volkhi

spun, all but unseating him and Chernevog, then stopped—
as Pyetr saw a flash of Missy's retreating rump, green birches,
Sasha's white shirt in the sunlight—

He kicked Volkhi hard then: Volkhi jumped and Chernevog slid, dragging him off, while his fistful of mane kept him
and Chernevog upright against Volkhi's side. He let that go
and bashed his elbow into Chernevog's ribs, spun around and
hit him in the jaw—after which he could not hit him again—
could not: his arm would not answer and the will to act just
would not form itself.

Volkhi had stopped and side-stepped, trod on one of their
fallen packs. Pottery crunched like old bone. Pyetr gazed
helplessly out over the sea of young birches, saw nothing but
sunlight glancing off the leaves. The boy and the horse were
well out of sight in the taller growth now—going somewhere
with something in mind, he told himself. Sasha had not just
run out on him: the boy had suddenly thought of an answer
and he would do something clever and get him out of this.

Even if the feeling at the pit of his stomach recalled with
disquieting immediacy how other friends had run out on him
. . . like 'Mitri Venedikov backing away from him, refusing
to help him, while he was bleeding his life out . . .

His own father saying, when he was in trouble for stealing, Boy, you're not my responsibility . . .

Chernevog laid a hand on his shoulder, pulled him around
face to face with him. Chernevog's lip was cut, blood was
smeared on his chin, and Pyetr could no more lift a hand than
he could a moment ago. He had a long, long moment to realize Chernevog was very put out with him.

Chernevog said, "Is that all it's worth? He's left you."

He said, "He's not left. You'd better worry, Snake."

Chernevog looked at him as if he had lost his mind. He
expected Chernevog would do something very painful, and
on that account it was stupid to have said anything, but it
was like kicking the horse—it kept Chernevog busy and let
Sasha get that much further.

Chernevog walked off from him, stood with his back to
him, looking off in the direction Sasha had taken, and when
Pyetr thought of going for Chernevog again his thoughts slid
away from him like water off a roof. He tried to speak, but

he could not do that either; and that small dark spot in his mind slithered around stirring up that bitter, pain-ridden memory of 'Mitri walking away from him in a dark tavern-yard, starting to run, he was so anxious to avoid a friend in trouble—

Sasha would not desert him. Sasha would be back—in time, he did most earnestly hope. He stood there—he could do little else—until Chernevog turned a cold face toward him and said, "Get up on the horse."

Then he wondered—he could not help it—whether Chernevog had reached Sasha with some spell . . . whether Sasha was even alive.

Chernevog said, "Move, dammit," and had him turning and catching up Volkhi's reins before he even thought about it. He looked back with the sudden remembrance that he was armed, that Chernevog had never taken the sword from him: that was how thoroughly Chernevog had him. He simply could not think of things when they mattered; and Chernevog wanted the sword now. Chernevog said very quietly, "Your friend is being a fool. Give me the sword. Take off the belt and give it to me."

He did that, moving as it seemed in a dream, watching his own actions from some remote place. It seemed to him that there was some reason Chernevog wanted the weapon now—that perhaps Chernevog thought Sasha might indeed reach him and, through him, use it.

It left his fingers. Chernevog said, slinging the belt from his shoulder, "There are creatures that will offer him everything he needs. He has protection I can't break, and I'm not entirely sure he's acting on his own. Do you understand me, Pyetr Ilyitch?"

He tried not to listen. He thought, doggedly, Sasha's not stupid, he wouldn't resort to magic, he swore he wouldn't, Chernevog's lying—but Chernevog said, catching his arm with a painful grip:

"Pyetr Ilyitch, *listen* to me . . ."

They sat in the open doorway, facing each other on benches pulled into the sunlight. Draga's needle flew in and out the blue wool, making flowers, stitching a chain of red. Draga said, "You shouldn't think about going home until the baby's born. Two young men—I'll warrant neither one's ever seen a baby born. Have they?"

"I don't think so," Eveshka said, hands on knees—in her own dress, with which her mother's pale blue ribbons clashed. She thought, I'm not sure this one's going to be born at all. But she kept that quiet: mama seemed definite and stubborn in her ways: papa had certainly had that description right.

"So you should stay here."

One could ask mama to come south and stay, but Eveshka did not find that an attractive thought—bringing mama near Pyetr. Or even near Sasha, who would be patient and try to get along with anyone, but mama seemed all too definite in her opinions even for Sasha's goodwill.

Not to mention mama's companion, Brodyachi, who lay at the foot of the old oak, watching every move she made with yellow, suspicious eyes.

The needle flickered, eclipsed by the wool, sparkling in the sun. "There is no chance that Sasha's the father?"

"No!"

A good many more stitches, before her mother said, without looking up, "Forgive me. But it's very important."

"Damned right it's important!"

"I don't know if there's ever been any wizard with the gift on both sides. Carrying it to a second generation . . ." Her mother paused to tie a knot and bite a thread. "You were difficult enough. A wizard-child of still another degree . . . the god only knows."

That thought led terrible places. Papa used to say . . .

". . . Things sometimes seem to want themselves to happen," her mother said, and sent a chill down her spine, because it was what papa used to say, that she had dismissed with other of her father's unprovable ideas. "It's troublesome, it's certainly troublesome. Your father and I used to talk about it—when we were speaking to each other, when we actually thought—well, your father was very anxious about your birth, your father and I quarrelled—I suppose he's told you this."

"I don't know, until I know what it is."

"Well—" Draga threaded her needle with white. "Your

father was very upset when I conceived you. It wasn't supposed to happen. He tried to make me lose you; I fought him on it, that much I could do." She made the center of a flower, a quick series of knots, and Eveshka waited, biting her lip, because papa had never said anything except that she was her mother's idea and had her mother's bad habits. "I'd have run off. But he was the stronger, in those days. He couldn't make me lose you, but he wouldn't let me leave, either, till you'd been born. Then—" Her mother looked up at her, a troubled, pained sort of look. "The truth is, dear, your father tried to kill me the day you were born. He almost did, but I got away across the river. And I wanted you—oh, I wanted you so badly. But I never could cross the river again."

It filled in gaps, it made plausible sense. It might be at least one side of the truth, she thought—though papa had said her mother had tried to kill him, too—in more than one way.

So she asked, hardening her heart, "And Kavi, mama?"

"Kavi was a very gifted boy, a boatman's son, so the story goes, from a village downriver. The mother died—Kavi was quite precocious, very dangerous. The father left him with a wizard named Lenki—I heard all this from her—a nasty old creature, really, not particularly gifted, entirely unreasonable, the sort of person one hates to see a child with. But she wouldn't give him up: she treated him like a rag doll when he was little, doted on him, spoiled him; kicked him about and worked him like a dog once he'd gotten beyond a baby. One day evidently he'd had enough, and she died. I caught him—caught *is* the word—months later. He'd been living in the woods, alone, like a wild thing. Poor boy, I thought when I found him. I'd lost you . . . I was very foolish just then." Another knot. Draga bit the thread and reknotted it. "Well, well, I knew what he'd done to Lenki, but of course I could civilize him. Pretty lad, such lovely, lovely eyes, and very well-spoken . . . but you know that."

"Thanks to you, mama!"

"He has the morals of a stoat. I did very quickly know he was no child; and of course he swears now I bewitched him into my bed." Another nip at the thread, another knot, a quick flash of the needle in the sun. "Kavi lies to himself on certain points: in fact he was terrified of me; I made him behave, you see, I could make him behave in those days, and anyone who could do that frightened him. So he became quite charming, quite persistent, quite—well, well, I was foolish, what can I say? And I certainly regretted it. —You see, what Kavi fears becomes evil to him. I became evil. He doesn't see it that way, of course, he denies there's any such thing as evil—but I'm certain your father became very evil to him; and possibly you did."

"And you sent him to us!"

"My dear, I didn't know all this then. I certainly didn't know he'd come back and try to kill me. I once thought your father might have done something to him—that was my instant judgment. But over the years I've come to understand the way Kavi thinks—and everything is very reasonable, if you stand where he does. He's the only one right; anything that protects him is right; any position is right if it serves him at the moment. Do you want him to be moral? He will be, as quickly as he can understand what you want—he won't feel safe until he's modeled himself quite on your design. And he'll use it to destroy you. Do you know—" She tied off, replaced the needle in its cushion, looked up with a frown. "I never was disposed to believe a child could be born the way he is. I always thought Lenki mishandled him—and perhaps being pushed to the point he'd killed her—broke something in him; or maybe something essential to humanity fell away from him while he was living like an animal in the woods. But over the years I've come to believe something got to him while he was still a baby, something found him—I don't know how, I don't know what—"

She truly did not like to hear this, but she was all but afraid to breathe, fearing her mother would stop talking down this track and close off what she knew: it was so hard, sometimes, to talk coherently about magic—perhaps that there were no words to compass it; or that certain things— believing her father for a moment—did not *want* to be talked about. . . .

"—but I've come to wonder if he was any boatman's son. I've come to wonder very seriously if he isn't . . . what we talked about, you know—doubly gifted . . ."

She stopped talking then, gazing off into the woods.

Eveshka felt her heart racing, thinking, Dammit, she wants to scare me.

". . . or maybe it was Malenkova. Malenkova was a terrible woman. She taught both your father and me. That's where we met, in her house."

"What happened to her?" Asking that was like lifting a heavy weight. It was a question that did not seem to want to be asked. "Is she still alive?"

"I don't think so. But then—one never knows." Her mother looked distracted, blinked, reached for the needle and a new thread. "I've asked myself . . . if there's any remote chance Kavi was hers."

"She was an old woman!"

"*You're* very old, dear—in some people's reckoning. So am I. And I'd put nothing outside possibility with her. Even—though I much doubt it—that Kavi's your half-brother."

Oh, god! Eveshka thought, thought of Kavi in the cellar, Kavi stopping her at the shelves in the back—

"I certainly didn't think that when I was sleeping with him," Draga said.

"You mean he might be yours?" Eveshka asked.

"No, no, dear, your father's. Your father and Malenkova—"

"My father was only a—"

"Young boy? Not that young. He ran away. Malenkova let him, I suspect. Sometimes she just grew careless. Sometimes she had reasons. Eventually I escaped, and we were lovers. But Malenkova poisoned everything we might have had. Your father had become very bitter. He'd become so afraid, so *unreasonably* afraid—of having a child . . ."

Eveshka felt her heart beating so that she feared she would faint. What was inside her suddenly seemed real, and destructive of everything she most wanted.

"There was a year or so I didn't see Malenkova at all. She was like that—you lived in her house, the very house Kavi had, the one that burned . . . and you did what she wanted; then she would be off in the woods somewhere, I suppose, for months at a time. But the god help you if she came back and there was any least thing wrong. She was a terrible woman. I don't know how old she was. Your father—you understand, he looked his years, well, at least—he looked *appropriate* for them. But he was letting himself age when I joined him. He said—he said, I remember it very clearly—I don't plan to live forever. He wouldn't use magic on himself. He didn't. He'd cut his finger—he'd just let it bleed. I think Malenkova made him a little crazy. And I never, never thought he'd go so crazy when I had you. I tell you, dear, I was terrified—I was terrified he'd drown you when you were born. I thought he'd done that . . . I was lying in bed, he took you away—and I got up and I tried to get you back. But I couldn't. I was afraid he'd kill me in the state I was in. I wasn't thinking very clearly. I was afraid of him. I ran away. That's where all the grief started. Maybe I should have stayed and fought him for you. But maybe I would have died."

"He said you tried to kill him."

"I did try—I meant to, if it would have saved you. Sometimes a mother doesn't think very clearly. I was glad, at least, to know you were alive, I was able to spy a bit, you see. And your poor father—I can say that now—" A knot. A small laugh. "You did run him ragged. His idea of bringing up a child . . . was simply to prevent you doing magic."

Things fell into place, then, papa always wishing at her . . .

"And you being a wizard-child on both sides . . . of course what he was doing to protect nature from you was completely *un*natural: he could only stop you with magic that scared him to work. I think he finally realized how crazy that was. He didn't know really what to do. And for all the harm he did, now, I can forgive him a great deal. Malenkova did terrible things to him. She dealt with deep magic. With sorcery, if you want to call it that, though there's no real distinction except in degree. And if he truly *was* Kavi's father—"

Her mother stopped talking. New flowers chained across the wool, one after the other.

"Mother? —If he was Kavi's father?"

Half a flower more. "Well, the time doesn't work. Although—" The needle stopped. "I don't put *anything* beyond Malenkova. Her magic had no rules."

"Why? Why would she want a child?"

"Dear, I don't know she did—for any reason anyone would like to talk about. She'd—"

"Mama?"

Her mother's lips went to a thin line. She finished a petal. "If that was so," her mother said, slowly, "then he'd be exactly what you are—wizard-born on both sides. More than that: your father discouraged you from magic; but Kavi—"

There was silence. Eveshka waited, watched her mother think and almost eavesdropped, she wanted so badly to know.

"If Kavi was hers," her mother said, "he was conceived for a reason: she was careless—but never in something that inconvenienced her. She was terribly powerful. I can't even explain to you what she did—but she wanted to get *into* the magical, she wanted to go into that realm herself—and I'm far from sure all her absences were into the woods, if you want the truth."

"What would she do with a child?"

"As I said, the time doesn't work. By years. But that's not saying time is the same there. As a matter of fact, I've very strong suspicions it isn't. And I'm not sure where Malenkova *is*."

"God, mother."

"One has time for very strange thoughts in a hundred years. I've turned it over and over and over—what happened, why it happened—where Malenkova is. And how Kavi was so—damnably precocious. That's why I want you here. That's why you mustn't leave and go running off to fight him on your own. You'll lose. And I'm very much afraid—very much afraid that there's something *in* the magical realm with an interest in this world. You have to understand—that's never been true. But it may be, now. To tell the truth, I don't know why you were born. I don't know if you're what magic's arranged to counter Kavi Chernevog—or whether you're something magic's made to be his match—to bear a child we don't want to think about."

Eveshka stood up abruptly, cold to the marrow. Her mother looked up at her, the sewing crumpled in her lap. "Don't panic. You mustn't panic, 'Veshka. Do you understand me? I want you to listen to me. Don't make any wishes right now, not about you, not about me, not about your husband, certainly not about that baby—think about flowers, 'Veshka, think about flowers . . ."

Flowers with thorns. Flowers red as blood . . .

" 'Veshka!"

She caught her breath. Her mother stood up and took her by the arms, looked her in the eyes. " 'Veshka, dear, you and I, understand me? You and I . . . against Kavi. Your father made you afraid of magic. You mustn't be—or neither of us has a chance."

22

✠ ✠ ✠ ✠ Volkhi picked a crooked, trailless course through the young trees, knee-deep in seedlings while the taller, three-year growth was constantly enough to screen anything beyond a stone's throw from their track.

Find Sasha, Chernevog said. So, perforce, they tried. They tried past noon, and into afternoon, taking a general course westward—Sasha had not been at the burned house, had not, which Chernevog had thought might be the case, gone back to Uulamets' grave. After that—

After that they turned north and west, in the not unlikely case Sasha had gone toward the river, Chernevog said. Chernevog searched with his magic and Pyetr scanned the sunlit, fluttering greenwood with ordinary eyes, looking for a white and brown horse, hoping with half his heart they would find no trace at all, hoping that Sasha was clear away and safe—and fearing he was not. He imagined terrible things—things like Missy falling; or vodyaniye and such lurking in ambush to drag horse and rider down into the brook; or Sasha's heart just stopping, on a stronger wizard's wish.

"That's far easier than will happen to him," Chernevog muttered at his back, "believe me."

"Believe you? God . . . let me go and I'll find him. Just go back to the house and wait, why don't you? Snake, I swear to you, if you want him found, if you really, truly do want him found—"

Chernevog said, "If he doesn't have a chance out there, you have less. Or I would do that."

"The hell you would."

250

C. J. CHERRYH

"Believe me."

That was a wish. It smothered thinking for a moment. It suffocated reason.

"You don't understand," Chernevog said. "He's not going to die. That's not the worst that can happen to him."

He felt cold through and through, despite the sunlight. He fought believing anything Chernevog said—but sometimes it was so close to his own apprehensions . . .

"There's no particular good, no particular evil in magic, Pyetr Ilyitch: one either rules it—or one *is* ruled; and he's quite vulnerable. He won't die, but you'll wish he had. He won't be able to. Then you'll wish you'd helped me with more enthusiasm."

"Shut up!"

"My friend, be reasonable."

"I'm not your friend."

"You're not my enemy. I assure you, you're not my enemy."

"I killed your damn owl," Pyetr muttered, and pulled Chernevog's hands loose from his middle. "Keep your hands off me."

"I've no grudges. Owl was very old."

That callousness turned him sick at his stomach. "Don't you love anything, Snake? Didn't you, once? —What do you want, that matters to anybody?"

"Just Owl." They rode up a slope, Volkhi's hindquarters bunching in a quick few efforts. Chernevog held to him again—with cause. "Just Owl. And he's gone. Now you're in his place. He was fond of mice. What do you want from me?"

"I want you to keep your damned hands to yourself!"

"I'll love what you love; hate what you hate—I've given you that power over me. What more can I do for you?"

That's a lie, he thought as they rode along the ridge. —Sasha might have done something with his heart, if he could only have gotten it away from me—

"He can't. It's much too strong a bond: it's magical; and I'm far stronger. But it's true you can command my friendship. Bestow it where you like: that takes no wizardry at all. It's simply the nature of hearts, when they're together long enough. You see how much I trust you."

251

He wanted Chernevog away from him, he wanted help; he was drowning in Chernevog's thoughts. He thought distractedly, looking at the trees, Very soon there's not going to be anything left of me. Sasha won't trust me if we find him. He shouldn't. God help me, I'm losing my mind.

"Of course," Chernevog said, resting his hand on his shoulder, "as you probably do suspect by now—it can equally well go the other way."

Sasha sat tucked up in green shade, beside Missy's feet, Missy being quite content to stand with a patch of sun on her back— Sasha felt it, too, the way he had slowly felt aches in her legs ease and the pain in her gut ebb. It had been hard going for an old horse not used to running and not used to forests.

Eventually the upset in her stomach eased and Missy began to nose the herbage in front of her in some interest; mostly she wanted water, and her chest still burned, and it was not fair she had not been let drink her fill when there was water at hand . . . but now when she thought of it there was nothing stopping her, so she walked over to the little spring that welled up out of the rocks and drank as much as she wanted. There had been bogles and grabby-things; her ears still slanted to listen for them and her eyes still watched all around at once, from the spring under her nose to, still visible behind her own feet, her favorite person sitting under the tree. Sasha saw himself from that unusual, top-blind point of view, and rode Missy's thoughts, not remembering where he had come from or where he was going, just watching the thicket around them and tasting the good, cold water.

The whole woods was still. Very carefully he let go that wide vision and that keen hearing, and saw, from the rear perspective, Missy drinking. Then he could move without fearing he was going to run blindly into something ahead, although down and up still felt confused, and sitting upright made him dizzy for a moment.

He had been Missy for some little time, to judge by the sinking of the sun—the shade was deeper, no direct light at all now in this little water-cut nook where bracken competed with young trees. He had been safe, this while: Missy was not a noisy creature. Missy wanted very little that made a difference in the world.

Missy lifted her head suddenly, pricked up her ears, and he instantly wanted to know what she was thinking—but Missy decided it was only a fox she smelled. Foxes were familiar. Foxes skulked about and were no bother to horses.

Sasha paid attention for a while, and worried Missy: Sasha thought a fox could hide a grabby-thing. Missy found this a disturbing idea, and decided never to trust foxes after this.

But it went away; and Sasha decided not, after all.

There was a danger in sitting like this too long. One could forget what one was doing, either harm Missy with ideas that were frightening gibberish to her; or go a little crazy himself and sit here, the two of them locked together until the next rain waked him or until he wished something truly dangerous for Missy or for himself.

There was danger in wishes of any kind so long as Chernevog might be paying attention in his direction. Chernevog had him far outmatched and Chernevog had Pyetr, and if he thought about what might be happening to Pyetr he could not trust himself to be sane right now, or to do anything reasonable or useful. He had worked very hard to be quiet and to go completely inside himself and Missy, until there was only his own life to worry over: he had drawn that selfishness tighter and tighter and tighter, not watching what Chernevog did, not trying to do anything about it, not wanting to be there—until his not being there suddenly became thoroughly, magically imperative—

It freed him—but not Pyetr.

He pulled at his knee, straightened his leg, rubbed feeling back into his numb foot. Wish nothing unnecessary.

Think nothing unnecessary. Do the natural thing. Learn from Missy. Get up, get the baggage, see about something to eat. There were dangers but they were not here, and as long as he wanted only little things Missy would want they might not impinge on Chernevog's specific wishes; so long as he wanted specific, natural things they might happen, and Chernevog's widest, magic-driven designs might go skewed around them—that was always the hazard in generalities, master Uulamets had argued in his book: that in natural things nature tended to reassert itself, given any reasonable loophole.

So one moved a pebble. One wished, as simply as Missy, for well-being and supper, things that were, after all, *fair*—Missy was very much on things being fair, expecting things that ought to follow, one from another; and things that ought to happen in certain ways, on time, and in due amounts.

One wished, among first things, to make amends for keeping bad and scary company and to share this nice sausage he had with someone who had a perfect right to it. He broke off half—he was very sorry about the vodka; that was at the moment in a place he did not want to think about—but there was this sausage, this very nice sausage, because it was only fair.

An alarming row of teeth snatched the bit from his hand. And vanished, together with the sausage.

"That's a good Babi." He offered the other half.

It whisked into nowhere, too.

Eyes stared at him, faint, gold, vertically slitted, against green forest shade.

"Good Babi. Wonderful Babi. Brave Babi. Babi, do you want vodka? I think it's fair we get it back. That's *my* jug, and my spell on it, after all, and I think I should have it, don't you?"

Babi waddled up on his hind legs and crawled up into Sasha's lap to cling to his coat.

"We can't just go and look for it," Sasha said, stroking Babi's fur. "We need help. I think we'd better get Missy and find the boat and see if we can figure anything out, don't you?"

Chernevog was not pleased: Pyetr had no doubt at all of that while Chernevog was riding behind him, holding to him, wishing at him until he felt his hold on his own thoughts precarious. His own anger and his own grudge against Chernevog had occupied all his attention at the start, but Chernevog kept finding ways past that—little doubts niggling their way into his mind, Chernevog saying, "If we don't find him, he may not see the morning," and: "You can't understand these things, dammit, you don't understand the trouble he's in," and finally, to the point: "Pyetr Ilyitch, you know how he thinks, you know what he'd most likely do. If you don't find him, dying's not the worst that can happen to him, don't you care? It's your fault, isn't it, what becomes of him? He doesn't understand what he's taken on. Don't be a bloody-minded fool!"

"I don't know anything," he told Chernevog. "It's a wide woods—how in hell can I guess where he'd go? You're the wizard."

"He's wishing me confused, damn you!"

"Then how can I resist?"

"Would he wish you in wrong directions?"

He said: "In your company, yes." And Chernevog: "No, he wouldn't. He's a clever lad. It was no little trick to get away in the first place—but that has a certain cost. —I know how he did it. Don't you wonder? Don't you wonder how he could leave you and not let me hear him thinking?"

One tried desperately not to wonder. One could think earnestly about breaking Chernevog's neck, which was hard to think about: one's thoughts kept getting away; and one could be angry about Chernevog's nattering at him, but that always led to the same place; and when one came back from half losing one's mind, exhausted and desperate and still beset, and wrapped about by Chernevog's arms, one concentrated on the trees or looked at bark and such and memorized shapes in the case that Sasha might rescue him and they might have to backtrack.

But that was useless, too—wizards could find their own way wherever they wanted; an ordinary man was no damn help to anyone . . . and he kept losing little bits of their trail anyway, moments that he was thinking of Vojvoda, of being hungry and desperate, of things he was not particularly proud of . . . like what he had done once to pay an innkeeper . . .

"We all have our faults," Chernevog said to him. "And the limits of our pride. Some are less fastidious than others."

He gave a backward jab of his elbow, "Leave me alone!"

It did Chernevog no damage. He was dizzy for a time after that and thought he might fall off the horse, but his body went on balancing the way it knew how to do. He was quite awake: he simply did not remember for the moment how to make his arms move, he scarcely knew how to breathe—

"Let me go," he said finally, discovering he could speak.

And was back in Chernevog's house, with Eveshka sitting in front of the fire with her back to him—and he thought, again, No, it isn't, it isn't her—I know this dream . . . oh, god, I want out of this—

He was standing on the river shore, tall trees grayed with morning mist. He saw a far, dim figure coming down the grassy bank, cloaked against the chill.

Eveshka had answered him, Eveshka came walking down from the house to meet him there. Come back at dawn, she had said. I'll talk to my father.

But there was no hope of reasoning with Uulamets. He knew that. He knew there was none of reasoning with Draga. If he did what Draga had said and brought her Eveshka, then there was no hope for him, either, there was no hope in the world for a young wizard who had (Eveshka knew the truth, but not the significance of what she knew) already betrayed her.

She came walking up to him, she put back her hood. She was sixteen, she would die in that blue dress—Chernevog had already made up his mind that he would have to kill her—

"God, no!" he cried, and kicked Volkhi and tried to carry Chernevog off with him, but Volkhi no more than jumped, and he could not even as lift his arm.

"You don't appreciate your wife's abilities," Chernevog said, holding him on the horse. "I did. I asked for her heart and she gave it to me—to give to Owl. To free her, I said—to put it with mine, where it would be safe. And it was. Do you know how I could lie to her?"

He did not. He did not want to know.

"The same way your friend could lie to us. By caring for nothing else in the world."

Sasha wouldn't, he thought. He couldn't.

Dmitri walking away from him in the yard—

Sasha's not like that, dammit!

He remembered Sasha riding away. He thought how terribly frightened he was in Chernevog's hands, and how des-

perate, and how if Sasha could not hold off Chernevog, and
Sasha had surely known he could not . . .

Dammit, Sasha's doing something, he thought; and wondered, while he tried not to wonder: What *can* he do that
won't involve magic?

Uulamets—giving Sasha his knowledge at his death, leaving too damned much to Sasha . . .

God, no! He tore his ragged thoughts toward pain, remembered old Yurishev, who had run a sword through him one
night.

That for Chernevog's eavesdropping. He realized in vivid
detail how much it had hurt, falling in the stable—

(Sasha had gotten him to safety, Sasha was resourceful,
Sasha would go—where?)

He kicked poor confused Volkhi again and made him run
a few paces, but that lasted no more than the other times;
Volkhi settled back to a walk, snorting and switching his tail,
and Chernevog said against Pyetr's ear:

"You're not my match, Pyetr Ilyitch. Got the old man's
dying bequest, has he?"

He owed Sasha his life, Sasha had risked his neck for
him . . . he said, aloud, biting his lip till it bled, because
thoughts kept getting away from him: "Nobody's ever cared
much about you, Snake. I can't say as I blame them."

"So where are these friends of yours now?" Chernevog
asked. "They ran. He ran. He left you. He's quite desperate.
Where would he go next? Deal with Uulamets' ghost—alone,
with what he already carries? That's not damned smart of
him!"

Eveshka, he thought without wanting to think: he was
not even sure it was his thought. He thought, trying to back
out of it: But he wouldn't trust her by herself. He'd—

He tried to move. Chernevog wished him utterly helpless.
"I have the books, Pyetr Ilyitch. You know there's little I
can't find out from them. I'll find the answers."

"Given time," he said, tasting blood. He had this thing
slithering about inside him, it was scared and angry, and in
his own foolishness he thought about Eveshka's writing in
that book, and Sasha telling him not even another wizard
could change what was written there.

I know you'll follow me . . .

It began to mean something more than ominous. She had written it in Sasha's book . . . not talking to him at all. To Sasha. *I know you'll follow me . . .* Like the bannik's visions—that Sasha said were coming true.

He bit his lip hard, looked at the trees, trying not to think about all the things that might mean. But he went on giving away what, except for him, Chernevog had had no time to find out—maybe no way to understand the way he understood it until he gave it to him . . .

"Has she spoken to you at all?" Chernevog asked him. "She came north. Why? What do you suppose she was looking for, if not me? You expected her across the river. But I wasn't her purpose. What would it be?"

"Wonder," he said though he had no idea either. Chernevog said, distant voice against the sighing of the trees, the sound of Volkhi's moving:

"Sasha's to follow her. To what?"

"I don't know. I've no idea."

I know you'll follow me. I beg you don't . . .

Something had separated them. She had packed quite purposefully, taken the boat—something, the god only knew what, had held her asleep on the river, unable to talk to them . . .

"That much I've gathered," Chernevog said.

He wondered how much else Chernevog had gathered, how much he had told Chernevog in his lapses from reason. He bit his lip to distract himself, and thought, amazingly clear-headed for a moment, Sasha won't leave me. No matter where he is, no matter if he doesn't come back, he won't have left me.

The woods went curiously blurred. There was a pain in his chest. He thought, That damned well made him mad. I wonder why . . .

After which he knew nothing clearly. Chernevog held him on the horse, and the cold spot was wider and stronger. Chernevog said against his ear, "Pyetr Ilyitch, for entirely different reasons, I do hope you're right."

—

"You might eat something," Chernevog said to him—and Pyetr found himself lying on his back on the ground, firelight on the young leaves overhead. He had come up abruptly, he fell back again, thumping his head on the ground, and by the feel of it he had done that before. He looked again and saw Chernevog calmly reading by firelight, Volkhi browsing on the undergrowth.

He really should have done better than this, he thought. Sasha would expect him to have done better than this. His sword, the books, everything . . .

"Supper," Chernevog said, and waved a hand toward the baggage, lying the other side of the fire.

He had no choice about that either. He got up, walked over where the baggage was lying, then bent and started to get the pack with their food in it.

But something was sitting on the brush just beyond his shadow, something that stared at him with red-gold eyes.

He froze in mid-reach.

Chernevog moved suddenly, casting his standing shadow beside his.

The bannik, the fragment, whatever it was—hissed; Pyetr scrambled backward, stood up, while the cold spot in the middle of him—grew colder and colder.

It *wanted* him.

He watched it slowly fade. He took another step back for good measure before he looked at Chernevog—found him nothing but a shadow against the fire; and himself trembling from head to foot, for no reason he could say, except it was *him*, dammit, it was what he was carrying that the creature wanted.

Volkhi snorted, snuffed the wind, made a small uneasy sound.

"A piece of you," Pyetr said when he got a breath. "Piece, is it? Dammit, it wants what you gave me!"

Chernevog said nothing, faceless shadow against the fire—but of a sudden Pyetr thought of the house that had burned, the bathhouse outside.

He hid there by night, he barred the door—he tried to summon up a magic against Draga—by whatever creature would answer him.

259

God . . .

"It didn't work," Chernevog said.

Pyetr looked back to where the baggage still lay, next the bushes. It was stupid to think whatever it was might still lurk there—it was their bannik, dammit, it was something Sasha had not trusted, but they had met it before. He walked over and snatched up the jug and the pack Chernevog had asked for, walked back to the fire and said, if shakily,

"Supper, Snake."

Missy had her misgivings about this trek, in the dark, in a pathless, tangled forest. So did Babi, evidently, who preferred to sit on Missy's rump or occasionally to clamber around to Sasha's lap, and never to go on the ground at all.

Sasha half expected ghosts. But none had troubled them; and beyond that he tried not to think at all beyond his narrow concern for Missy and Babi, and the single purpose of finding the boat. He kept to small, immediate thoughts, rode Missy's senses, and Missy's memories, which at the moment involved The Cockerel's nice warm stable at this hour, and apples—only fair for a hard day's work, Missy thought; but they were here, apples were not likely, and her favorite person thought it would be a good idea to keep walking and get out of this place where he feared bogles and grabby-things.

Missy agreed with that, although she would gladly have had something to eat along the way and she wished she had company.

Which Sasha did not want to think about, damn, he did not.

Babi held to him quite forlornly, and might want him to know things, too, but he never had been able to fathom what Babi was thinking, and he feared to wonder at all deeply about Babi's thoughts, considering the temptations that posed: thank the god Babi had run away and not made himself available when he had been both desperate and foolish.

About which he also did not want to think, so he thought instead about the vodka and how Babi did deserve it, and how Missy deserved all the apples she could eat, when next he could find some.

Missy put a little enthusiasm into her gait, and wondered where these apples were.

She did, on the sudden whim of a breeze, smell water. Sasha could, on his own, eventually, and Babi clambered down Missy's mane and Sasha's leg and dropped down to the leaves.

He hoped Babi meant to stay close. He had a very anxious feeling of a sudden: that was, perhaps, Missy; but it seemed to him he had smelled better places—this one had the flavor of too little light and too much water.

And Babi, wherever he had gotten to, was growling at something in the brush, while Missy slowed her pace, doubtful of this place they were going, which did not smell like what her person wanted and certainly did not smell like the promised apples. It smelled more like old wood and rotten ground, a stable, perhaps, but not a nice one; and Sasha could not tell, riding Missy's senses as he did, whether it was that bad or whether it was simply Missy's keen nose.

Babi turned up, a much larger and more imposing Babi, walking along at Missy's feet, and something plunked into water close at hand—a startled frog, Sasha hoped, and bit his lip to keep from the idea of Pyetr's sword, which was dangerous to want and the god only knew what he would do with it that he could not do with a stout stick. He regretted the one that was standing in the corner at home, where it did him no good . . . a stick was a perfectly adequate weapon. A branch would do . . . except he had no desire to get down to find one.

Another plunk. Another frog, one hoped. Missy felt squishy stuff slipping under her feet and snorted in disgust. She seriously questioned the collective judgment in going further, nothing here smelled nice, and the dvorovoi thought so, too.

But her person insisted there was a grabby-thing after them that was somehow—here her person grew very hazy—going to get them if they did not go through this place and find the big water.

So she wrinkled up her nose and trod right through the squishy stuff, in water up to her knees—no running on this ground, even though her skin shivered at the smell and the sounds of this place.

Willows whispered here. Water sighed. And something groaned and squealed repeatedly as if it were in pain. Missy did not like that sound.

But her person thought of old boards and Missy decided it was after all a stable, but not one where she wanted at all to stay.

"Babi?" Sasha said, but Babi was off somewhere through the trees, and several things went plunk and splash, while that dreadful groaning went on and on with a curious regularity. He could not hear it with his own ears, but he began to find it familiar, began to hear in it the surge of the water, the groaning of wood against wood.

"Babi?" he asked, wishing the dvorovoi would stay close, and with a tiny, unwanted wisp of a wish, wondered if finding the boat meant finding Eveshka.

Dangerous, he thought. Terribly dangerous. He got nothing; and wanted nothing but to be Missy for a while, until he could be closer; he was Missy so thoroughly that riding made him very dizzy, and he shut his eyes and let hers do the work—leaning on her shoulders and wanting her to keep walking toward the creaking sound, little as she liked it.

Grabby-things, Missy was sure. They were going to leap out of where such things always came from, out of the spot between her eyes she could never see—

She saw a white, huge thing coming out of that spot—a huge, flappy thing, and her heart went thump and her legs did a quick step without her thinking about it; but her person said it was safe, it was cloth on a big thing built of boards, and a nice person had brought it there from a place he knew.

She was not sure about her person's judgment. It flapped and it groaned and she approached it very carefully—it smelled suspicious.

The boat was snared fast in willows and the groaning was its hull rubbing against broken limbs—it did look spooky, even to his eyes, the sail still spread, veiled in shadowy willow-boughs, the shape of the bow thrusting out of the trees.

It was only wizardry that could have brought it up this

branch of the river, against the current, it was only wizardry that could have lodged it here.

"Babi," he said softly, slid off and untied Missy's reins, in the case she had to run in this woods—lapped them about his waist, and wished her to stay here.

She shivered, threw her head, clearly hoping her person did not intend to leave her here long.

"I'll be right back," he said, and patted her neck, wanting Babi to take care of Missy. He walked further then, parting the willow curtains, in among the old trees—old trees, indeed, and alive: this shore was past the desolation Chernevog had worked.

But one did not want to think about him.

He heard Missy make a soft, worried sound. But the groaning of the boat against the willows and the flap of the imprisoned sail was enough to distress her. He wanted Babi to take care of her, and he heaved himself up on a willow limb and walked it to the rail of the old ferry, through black, trailing curtains of leaves.

He dropped onto the deck with a thump very loud to his ears. He walked out near the mast and back to the little deckhouse, stopped and looked around him, listening to the flapping of the sail and the sighing and the groaning that gave the boat a voice.

He wanted to know, then, whether Eveshka had left this boat of her own will—that seemed a safe wish. He hoped there might be resources left—they kept the boat stocked with all sorts of things, even apples, and Eveshka alone could not have used everything or carried everything away.

The deckhouse was the first place to look—not the sort of a cubbyhole he was glad to open up and go poking into in the dark, but it seemed worse to him to wait for morning, while things went further wrong elsewhere. "Babi?" he whispered, thinking if Missy could, please the god, take care of herself for a few moments, and Babi turned up on deck, then he would feel very much better opening this door.

Babi did not immediately appear, but he had the feeling Babi was listening, at least; and he turned the wooden latch and pushed it open, hoping if something was lurking in there it would make a sound now.

There was only the flap of the sail over him, and the hull groaning. He sank down on his heels so he could see into the dark by reflected starlight, and gingerly reached in to drag out the baskets they kept there.

He heard Babi growl behind him. He hoped it was Babi. He turned on one knee, he heard a watery sound, he looked toward that and saw a great slick darkness rise up, up and up in the starlight, and grin down above the rail with sharp-toothed jaws.

"Well, well," the vodyanoi said, "young wizard. I was wondering about you."

Sasha felt into his pocket, after the packet of salt he kept there, and wished—

No. He did not wish for the rest of it. He wished the vodyanoi to keep his distance. He said, slowly rising to his feet, "Hwiuur, what do you think you're doing here?"

"Waiting," Hwiuur said. "Of course, waiting. Of course you'd come—but where's your friend, mmmm?"

"Stay back!"

"Mmmm. A horse. A nice fat horse. I might start with it."

"Stay where you are!"

"Stay where I am . . . Where I am is in the river, in my river, young wizard, where you're trespassing, and all alone, aren't you, young wizard? The dvorovoi has no power on the water—but you could wish him to try."

That was a very bad thought. So was the fact that this creature was Chernevog's—and Chernevog might know exactly where he was.

If it was still Chernevog's.

23

✳ ✳ ✳ ✳ Hwiuur said softly, weaving to one side, "A bad position, young wizard, a very bad position you're in."

"Where's Eveshka?" Sasha asked it outright, and *wanted* it to tell him.

Hwiuur leaned slowly to the other side and hissed. "Oh, we want pretty bones, do we? She went walking."

"Where?"

Hwiuur swayed closer.

"Get back!" Sasha cried, waving his hand at it; and Hwiuur drew back with a hiss.

"Rude, rude young wizard. You want my help and you push me back. Is that at all reasonable?"

"With you it is! Mind your manners. Tell me where she went walking. Tell me where she is!"

"Safe," Chernevog's voice said at his back.

He did not stop to think—he dived for the deckhouse door and rolled inside, pulled the door to after him as the whole boat rocked and the rail splintered. He thrust his shoulders back against the baskets and the wall, braced the door with his feet, wishing it to stay *shut* and Missy to run, get away, fast—

He heard someone walking on the deck outside. He heard someone say, definitely in Chernevog's voice, right next the deckhouse door, "It's quite useless."

He trembled, lying there in the pitch dark with a basket crunching between his back and the deckhouse wall, feeling the door shake against the soles of his boots as something kicked it. God, he had wished, he had thrown magic at it—

He heard the slithering of a huge body, felt the boat tip, heard Hwiuur's whisper over the deckhouse ceiling, heard the slither of a huge body over the boards.

"Well, now, young wizard. Perhaps now you'll be sorry you were rude."

And Pyetr's voice: "Sasha?"

For a moment he believed it. Then he thought not, knowing where he had left Pyetr, knowing Chernevog would have *wanted* him out that door with more force than he felt out there, Chernevog could not so conveniently have found him. Chernevog would not have taken second place to the vodyanoi . . .

"Sasha?" Pyetr's voice said. "Sasha, I'm in trouble. I'm in deep trouble. Can we have some help here?"

He squeezed his eyes shut and braced the door. He thought, hearing the boards above him creak with Hwiuur's weight, Everything's a lie. Everything I hear from it's a lie. Pyetr couldn't possibly be here. That's the shapeshifter, that's all it is.

It hasn't a mind of its own, only what it borrows, like the likeness, that's what Uulamets knew about it—

"Sasha! For the god's sake, Sasha!"

Nothing more than an echo. It doesn't know anything, it's no more malicious than its original so long as there's no one directing it . . .

"Sasha! God, *Sasha!*"

Pyetr wouldn't want me to open this door. Pyetr would never call me out into danger. It's a damned clumsy trick. . . . But a shapeshifter had no sense to know that. In its own right it had neither shape, nor mind . . .

"Sasha!" He heard steps running across the deck, heard Hwiuur's weight slide across the boards and the steps stop abruptly.

Pyetr? he thought, wondering, he could not help it, what was going on out there: and something that felt like Pyetr was thinking. Oh, damn! Pyetr had expected help on the boat and ran straight into a trap—

No. He wanted what *Pyetr* was thinking, and got nothing. Dark. Confusion. Pyetr was asleep somewhere, he tried to assure himself of that, the god grant it was only sleep. He heard Hwiuur move, heard Pyetr yelling, "Sasha, dammit, do something—*help me!*"

He kept bracing the door, the whole deckhouse creaking around him as the vodyanoi moved—the baskets crackling against his shoulders as he shoved against them . . .

Baskets.

God.

He reached back over his shoulder and rummaged in the dark, thinking, Fool, *fool!* Salt and sulfur—

Nothing but clothes in the basket immediately behind him. He tried another, arching his back, straining with both his feet against the door, found clay pots, pulled them out and pulled stoppers one after the other. Marjoram. Parsley. Thyme. . . .

"Sasha! for the god's sake!"

Rosemary . . .

"Sasha!"

The missing flour . . . Sasha dumped it, reached after the next, pulled the stopper—

"Sasha!"

Salt—

He drew his feet up, rolled with the jar in his arms, eeled his way out the open door and scrambled upright on the deck under Hwiuur's shadowy jaws—slewed the pot wide and sprayed a wide white cloud of salt at Hwiuur's face and on around, where Pyetr stood with an expression of shock on his face.

Hwiuur hissed and thrashed backward for the water, rocked the whole boat as he went over, dragging bits of the rail with him.

What had been Pyetr melted and ran in little dark threads across the deck and off the edge, like spilled ink.

Sasha sat down hard where he stood, with the half-empty salt jar in his arms, white dust blowing across an empty deck and melting in the puddles of water the vodyanoi had left.

He shook, great tremors that knocked his knees together and made his teeth chatter.

Close, he said to himself, very close. He hoped Missy was all right out there, and that Babi was with her.

Most of all—he hoped Pyetr was all right; but he dared

not think about Pyetr now, dared not, please the god—he dared not.

But—he thought, recalling that darkness he had touched when he had sought Pyetr—the shapeshifter until now had taken the shape of dead people, not the living; and Pyetr had not answered him.

His teeth kept rattling. He told himself it was magical and it would damned well take any shape it wanted, that anything else was only coincidence, only what they happened to have seen it do.

The greater danger had been in reaching out like that. He dragged his mind away from it, he wondered instead after Missy, wondered, still shaking, where she was.

Quite far away and knee-deep in water, as it seemed. He reassured her: it was safer near him. He wanted her to come back now, the bad things were gone; he wanted Babi to make sure she got here safely—but Babi arrived quite suddenly on the deck, a formidably large Babi, a very angry Babi.

"Go see about Missy," he murmured. "It's all right, the River-thing's gone."

Babi did not go at once, Babi marched over to the shattered rail and Sasha wanted him to stop. "See to Missy," he said again, *wishing* Babi, strongly, and Babi went this time without looking over that edge.

Sasha hugged the salt jar against him and stood up, still weak in the knees, still thinking about the shapeshifter and its tricks, and leaned against the deckhouse. The wind blew pale salt across the starlit deck and the sail flapped and thumped against the willows.

He *wanted* to know Pyetr's state of mind, he could not for a moment help himself—it was his heart at work, in the convolute way he had to think of such things. He dragged himself back from that thought and tried to tell himself what he had felt from Pyetr had not been the dark that death was. He had felt that dark silence many times, many times, if he went eavesdropping on people in their sleep—sometimes one overheard dreams and sometimes just a confusion no different than ghosts—

Another shiver came over him, a sudden chill, a breathing

at his nape. He looked across the deckhouse roof to the stern, fearing to see Hwiuur's massive head rising out of the river.

But there was nothing more substantial than a sudden chill, as if the wind had skipped around his shoulders and whipped around into his face. It spun around and around him, touching him with cold.

Pyetr? he wondered with a heart-deep chill. Surely not.

The cold spot passed through him. *Not* Pyetr—thank the god, no. It left him weak-kneed and short of breath and shivering so he had trouble hanging on to the salt jar. He asked it, teeth chattering: "Who are you?" and waited for some manifestation, some pale wisp in the night.

But there was nothing. He stood there looking into the dark, not entirely sure he wanted to hear from it again—and felt an overwhelming anxiousness.

"Master Uulamets?" he asked whatever-it-was. "That's you, isn't it? Misighi said to look for you."

It had shaken him worse than any ghost yet. He was all but certain now what it was—if it remembered its own name. He sensed its anger with him, and that was something he could not help at all—that he was profoundly glad this ghost was dead and Pyetr was alive.

"I'm sorry," he said carefully to the dark, aloud, because it was easier to shepherd spoken words down a single, careful path. "It's not that I'm glad you're dead, understand, I never was. I'm not now."

But it was hard to lie to a ghost, and he was terrified, now that he had found it. This one knew what to touch. What to ask. It had lent pieces of itself to him it might want back with a claim he might not resist—and he needed them and Pyetr did, desperately, this ghost having no love of Pyetr at all.

The boat groaned. There was the soft sound of water. He *wanted* the ghost to show himself, he *wanted* it to behave itself and forgive him that he did not want it alive and could not trust it. Uulamets had never encouraged trust. Quite the opposite.

He only knew he was supposed to take the baskets out of the deckhouse. All of them. Now. Immediately.

As wishes went it seemed harmless. He was not sure it was at all sane. But he pushed the door open and started dragging baskets out onto the deck.

The third he pulled out—

—'Veshka's book—here. Oh, god—

He wanted light. Or something did. He rummaged feverishly in the deckhouse, looking for the lamp they kept there—managed, with many false efforts and desperate wishes, to get the thing lit, while the cold swirled about him and through him. He set the fluttering light down inside the deckhouse door and gathered the open book into his lap, tilting it until he could see the last pages written. He read, first:

I don't know what to wish about the baby. Papa would say—you can undo anything but the past . . .

Draga threw herbs onto the fire and sparks flew, a cloud of stars whirling up the chimney. Draga said, "Many things pass boundaries: not all are changed. Wood and water and iron go into the same fire. Each behaves differently. Does fire frighten you?"

"No," Eveshka said.

"You'd put your hand into it?"

"I could," Eveshka said.

Draga reached into the fire and gathered up an ember. Eveshka thought, It's the same as reaching into the fire—she's wishing the heat away as fast as it comes. But she's very good.

Draga closed her fist about the coal, so there was nowhere for the heat to go. —Where *is* it going? Eveshka wondered. Can she wish it back into the fire?

"I'm not wishing it anywhere," Draga said, and opened her hand. The cinder had become black. It still smoldered. There was soot on Draga's hand. "That's the very simple difference between your wizardry and mine. Your wish would be very modest and constant, very fussy, and if someone said your name you might burn yourself very badly, mightn't you? Because you'd lose your spell at the first pain, and you might not be able to restore it. But real magic doesn't bother to figure out a clever way to hold the fire. It ignores nature."

The ember began to glow again, and burst into fire in the middle of Draga's hand.

"That," Draga said, "is magic."

"A straw actually does as well," Eveshka said, with Pyetr's stubborn pragmatism: her mother was pushing her, undermining *her* way of doing things, and a straw *was* better, not least because it did not tempt one to throw wishes about carelessly.

"Wishes just don't matter. That's the thing, dear, you don't have to be that careful. If you make a mistake you can retrieve it."

"Don't eavesdrop, mama!"

"You don't want me to know certain things?"

"I'm not your echo, mama, and I like my privacy, thank you. —And what happens if you do make a mistake? What happens if you don't understand what else you're wishing?"

"That part is the same. There are consequences. Only some of them happen here, in the natural world."

"Can magic find them out beforehand? Reliably?"

"Some of them."

"Then it's damned *stupid*, mama, doing anything of the sort."

"Shhh. You raise a rainstorm. Do you know every leaf that falls? The law is that leaves will fall. Which leaf is meaningless to know. What you care about is that the rain come— and stop in due course. The difference is scope, dear."

"My husband is no leaf, mama!"

"Neither is that baby."

"I don't know that I want a baby! I don't know I want one at all!"

"The one you don't want, dear, is the one you and Kavi might have had. Or the one you and Sasha might have had. *This* one is manageable. But not, considering your enemies, the way your father managed you." Draga shook ash from her hand. That was all that remained of the ember. "Does it matter in the magical world that a bit of wood burned? No. And yes—if it makes you understand what's essential, it's of extreme consequence there and here. There's no reason by which that bit of wood should have that value. But it may."

"The value isn't in the wood," Eveshka said doggedly, "the answer isn't in the smoke."

"That's Malenkova, did you know that? She used to say that."

She had thought it was her father. She had thought so many things were only his.

Draga said, "The value of a piece of wood, dear, is wherever a sorcerer assigns it. That's the important thing. You can vest a value *in* a thing . . . put a spell on it, if you like. You can command a thing to be *of* a certain value. Or state."

The fire was *out*. There was no light. Suddenly it burned again, as if nothing had happened.

"That wasn't a trick," Draga said. "It happened. Do you believe me?"

"If you can do it you can make me believe you did it, can't you? So it makes no difference. I'll grant you did. *Why* did you do it?"

"You do sound like your father. I did it because I wanted to. Because I can do it."

"Well, why bother with fires? Wish yourself tsarina of Kiev. Wish yourself a dozen handsome men to wait on you and rings on all fingers. . . ."

"I could do that."

"I prefer my husband."

"I've had one, thank you." Draga dusted her hands one against the other, wiped the soot off with a towel. "And of course you're right, nothing's that easy. My little business with the fire was showy—but a straw *is* better, with a little wish to help it, and ten handsome servants might be nice, but then, I've help when I need it."

"What help?"

"Oh, him or her, whatever suits."

"A shapeshifter?" Eveshka was appalled.

"Dear, you *won't* have a dvorovoi or a leshy anywhere near you if you do magic. They don't like demands on them. A shapeshifter's one of the most selfless creatures you'll deal with—if you're careful what you let it be. You have to be very stern with it. And you have to be aware there are creatures that aren't at all selfless, and they'd very happily take any situation and turn it to their advantage. You have to learn your way in magic—and the wizard who's very likely to find serious trouble, my dear, is the one who's doing magic without knowing what he's borrowing from, because a good many of your silly, childish spells are, truly, borrowing from something outside the natural."

A rusalka had no trouble understanding that: Eveshka bit her lip, clenched her hands and tried not to remember that feeling, that flood of life into death—

"A wizard-child does it—and there are always creatures ready to help, unless he's guarded."

"I knew one that wasn't guarded! He had no help. And *he's* not a sorcerer."

"Sasha's very unusual. But Sasha burned his parents to death. Did you know that?"

"He told me."

"So he did make a mistake. It scared him out of doing magic at all until your father got his hands on him. He's very innocent. His wish was not to do harm. And the strength of the innocent in magic is like the strength of children—naive and terribly dangerous."

"How do you know about him?"

"I have my sources. I even know what wanted him. It still does. And of course he'd be very foolish to deal with it. You never deal with the one that wants you most. You deal with something just a bit stronger—and you have to be very stubborn. You can smother a gift the way your young friend did; but it's very unusual for a child to do the right thing. Usually they don't. Born in an ordinary situation, they can do very dangerous things—and very many fall right into the magical world and become—the god knows what. If a child is being attacked—" Her mother caught her hands in hers and held them so tightly the bones ground together, pain she opened her mouth to protest, but her mother said, "As you were attacked, dear. Kavi wanted you dead and you wouldn't die. You fought back as hard as a wizard could fight, you fought him by wanting your life so much . . . so much . . . you pulled at everything in sight, like someone drowning—"

"I did drown, mama!" The pain was nothing. The image scared her. It reminded her—

"You can drown in magic or you can strike out and swim,

dear, you don't have to draw on the natural world. There is a place to get everything your wizardry can use—the right way. It was your father's damnable teaching that made you a killer. You wouldn't do what was reasonable, no, you followed your father and you ended up Kavi's creature—say what you will, Kavi was using you; Kavi's wishes have been, even while he was sleeping, and he'll go on using you, against everything you want for yourself, unless you listen to different advice."

Listening to anyone's advice frightened her. There had been so many lies.

"Kavi has your husband in his hands," Draga said, and squeezed hard, while cold panic swept over her. "Don't wish! Listen! Sasha's run, he's had to, he's completely out of his element. He can't help your husband at all, he's in danger himself, and there's precious little he can appeal to, unless he does resort to magic—alone, untaught, and with your father's ideas to cripple him. I can't reach him. You're the one who has a chance, but you've got to listen to me now, daughter, you've got to believe for once in your life someone is telling you the truth."

Something had happened, Pyetr had no idea what, except it meant they were ahorse again, riding in the dark—he had opened his eyes by firelight with the side of his face stinging and Chernevog holding him painfully by the arm, saying, "Get up, get up, pack up. Move, damn you!"

He still had a wobbly, hollow feeling from that sudden waking, he still had no idea what had put fear on Chernevog's face or what hour of the night it was, but a dream kept coming back to him that Sasha had called his name in profound distress, just before that waking; and he doubted Chernevog would tell him anything but lies.

But Chernevog said, as they rode, "Your friend's found something, or something's found him."

He wanted to know, dammit, he could not help wondering, and Chernevog said, holding to him,

"He's upstream from us. He went back toward the house and doubled back east and north following the river—looking

for Eveshka, I'm sure: it's what he hopes to do I can't figure—
or how much he understands of anything he's doing."

That was a question. Like ghosts, it came at him with
fewer distractions in the dark. Pyetr bit the sore spot on his
lip and tried to tell himself he had not felt Sasha wanting
him, nothing was wrong, that Chernevog was worried was
the best thing in the world, and if Chernevog wanted him to
make guesses what another wizard would do, Chernevog had
to be desperate.

"You felt it," Chernevog said. "You know he's in trouble."

"I don't know that," he retorted, "but if you are, that does
me good, Snake."

Chernevog made him think of shapeshifters then, and his
thoughts jumped to Uulamets' likeness, the creature trying
to lead him—

"Where?"

—east. To the river. . . .

"My old servant," Chernevog said. "But slippery. Damned
slippery."

He remembered Sasha saying—the vodyanoi had corrupted Chernevog, not the other way around.

"Corrupted *me*?" Chernevog asked, and shifted his seat
as if that idea had truly startled him. "Corrupted *me*, god,
no!"

Pyetr thought, And you aren't, Snake?

Chernevog said nothing for a moment, and shifted his
hands to Pyetr's shoulders, both, too friendly for Pyetr's liking. Chernevog's presence was very quiet for a moment—
enough to make a man's skin crawl, and Chernevog:

"Be still."

"Be still, hell." He gave a violent shrug, remembered
Vojvoda for no reason, remembered 'Veshka, remembered the
river and Babi and Sasha and planting the garden, all so rapidly he knew he was not recalling these things for his own
reasons. He grew alarmed—and got the notion—while it was
weaving its way through his thoughts he realized it was not
his either—that Sasha's safety might rely on his willing cooperation.

That's a damned lie, he thought, but he could not make himself absolutely sure of that. He thought—if it were true—

If it were true—

Chernevog said: "If Sasha thinks the vodyanoi's corrupted *me*, then he's mistaken what he's dealing with. He's terribly, dangerously wrong. And so might Eveshka be. You don't deal with a creature like Hwiuur. You don't."

He did not understand, except that no one in his right mind would trust the vodyanoi for anything. He thought, Sasha's not a fool.

"Sasha's not wholly a fool. But Hwiuur's a great liar. He'll try to frighten you. And if you're going to deal with magic, Pyetr Ilyitch, you don't deal with something like him—god, you don't." He put one hand on Pyetr's back, said, quietly, compelling his attention, "Forget about my corruption. It has nothing to do with anything. I'm wanting him to hear you, right now, for whatever you want to tell him, Pyetr Ilyitch."

He thought, It's a trap, it has to be.

But immediately it seemed Sasha wanted assurance of him; and quick as that he wanted Sasha not to trust the vodyanoi, to make no bargains that did not involve Chernevog's guidance—

No! Pyetr thought, but he doubted anyone was listening to him any longer—he knew Sasha was worried about him, and Chernevog was anxious to find Sasha before Sasha made any bargains with anything, because he needed Sasha, he was afraid Eveshka might have slipped into something that would make her—

He could not think about that. He could not even imagine the kind of thing trying to shape itself in his mind, Eveshka would never do that, but Eveshka had never wanted to kill anybody, either.

Then for no reason he could think of, and very frightened, he was sure Eveshka had conceived a baby, and that it was his, and that nothing was safe or sure in those circumstances. When? he wondered, and, Why not tell me? He was wounded, and feared she was running from him—but he decided then Eveshka was not, she was concerned for him—

She wanted him the way Draga had wanted Chernevog, nothing to do with his own good.

That was not so. No. And of a sudden he was aware of Sasha wanting his whole attention, of Chernevog behind him again—it had seemed otherwise for a moment, as if Sasha and Chernevog were face to face—Sasha saying, in words he could almost hear, Pyetr, listen to me, don't listen to him, it's very dangerous for you to listen to him.

At the bottom of his heart he was mortally afraid for his sanity: Sasha was telling him to be wary, Chernevog's hand was holding the reins in his hand and he was leaning against Chernevog with a sense of warmth and ease he told himself was a lie.

Chernevog said, aloud, "Your young friend doesn't want to be found. But he's afraid of your wife—he's afraid of her and he's afraid of the old man's ghost, which I think he's found. At least he's come to his senses. He's very much afraid your wife is gone, Pyetr Ilyitch—at least, that she's fallen into a trap he can't get her out of—and so am I. He's very much worried that you may be particularly vulnerable to her—and he wants me to keep you safe and away from her."

"You're lying, Snake."

"He's going to try to find out what he's dealing with. I hope he survives it, I truly do: *I* want to know what he finds out. Most of all we don't want to lend your wife any help— or any victims. Especially one carrying what you hold. Do we, Pyetr Ilyitch?"

"Go to hell," he said. He refused to believe Sasha had said any such thing, even if it had elements of reason in it, even if it was thoroughly like Sasha to go to help Eveshka and try to keep his fool of a friend ignorant of it—but trusting Chernevog enough to tell him anything about his intentions was not reasonable.

Chernevog had used him to reach Sasha, that was what he had just done, Chernevog was lying to him and he hoped to the god he had not just put Sasha in more danger than he was already in.

"Hardly possible," Chernevog said. "But the danger's not from me. It's not even from your wife, if that gives you any ease of mind."

He felt too calm, too much at ease, considering what he was hearing. He hated it. He hated Chernevog for doing it to him, and he thought of breaking Chernevog's skull—if he could so much as lift a finger toward that purpose.

Chernevog said, "Owl had no pity. He never understood my fondness for him. He did like the mice."

It had come on him suddenly while he read, without warning . . . this *presence* of Pyetr's—and he should have known then, Sasha thought, in one blink of an eye he should have realized that Pyetr could never have caught his attention without magic, and magic never could have gotten to him through his own precautions without Pyetr's need to drive it.

Which meant—if he had had any forethought—Chernevog.

He leaned his elbows against Eveshka's book, thinking— god, he had told Chernevog too much of that as it was, especially the part about the baby. He had thought of that news the instant he had felt he was truly dealing with Pyetr, it was part of his reasons and his heart had led him to admit that without so much as thinking. Now he asked himself what he had done and what he might have agreed to.

If you want to bargain, Chernevog had said, first off —don't take anything the vodyanoi might offer: he's easily any shapeshifter's master, but there are things so far beyond the vodyanoi's reach.

They'll waste no time, Chernevog had said, gobbling him down to get you. If you're going to want magic, young friend, don't be modest: deal only with real power . . . me, for a first instance.

After which Chernevog had added, so slyly and smugly he could almost see the smile, After all, if you think I'm a bastard, what do you think my rivals are?

Deal with me or deal with them—and remember we have at least one interest very much in common. Do you want him free of me? I'm certainly willing to talk about that.

And he, perhaps foolishly: Help me at a distance. I'm not ready to bargain with anything. Keep Pyetr safe, hear me? Don't let him follow me.

—Because he knew, he knew beyond a doubt Pyetr would

be off toward Eveshka if he had the chance; and he was, himself, so scared, so scared *for* 'Veshka and *of* 'Veshka—

Don't deal with Hwiuur, Chernevog had said. Certainly he's not *my* master. He may act completely on his own—I involved him once and it's only natural he take an interest, but how far that interest goes, or if it might involve someone else. . . . Take a lesson from me, young friend, *never* ask for help from subordinates. Some Things are hell to get rid of. . . .

Something was leaning over his shoulder of a sudden. He turned and looked, heart thumping, virtually sure it was Uulamets, terrified that the ghost had been eavesdropping.

God, the old man had hated Chernevog; and more— he had hated Pyetr . . . had feuded with him constantly— Uulamets was angry, he knew that he was.

Cold blasted through him like a winter gale, bringing memories of the house, memories of the lightning, the fire, the vodyanoi, muddy bones, a puddle of weed—dark, deep dark, echoing with crazed voices. He felt his knee hit the deck, felt the deckhouse slide past his arm and snag his sleeve—he was on the boat and the boat went back and forth across the river, travelers came in numbers, and he was running, hiding among them, while something across the river wanted him—

There were too many memories. They tumbled one over the other, shrieking for his attention. He wanted his own, only his own, he tucked down with his arms over his ears and held on to what was Sasha Misurov with the barest awareness of where he was or when or why.

He thought, when, after a long time, the flood had subsided . . . Chernevog is right: he's fragmented, he's not sane— god, he's remembering things all out of order—he can't make sense, he hates Pyetr, he'll never accept any compromise . . .

Bargain with what has power, Chernevog had said. Bargain with *me* . . .

He *wanted* sense out of it. He *wanted* the ghost to find the pieces in right order, the way he remembered them— Malenkova's house, Draga, the river house— It howled at him, it whirled about him and tumbled all the pieces out of order again in rage, frustration, fear— He cried aloud into that gale:

"Master Uulamets, I've no choice—you can't help me and I've no damn choice, have I?"

He felt as if master Uulamets had gathered him up and hit him in the face—repeatedly. He felt cold, and weaker, and weaker.

It was theft—he knew what Uulamets was doing, the same deadly robbery that he had done to the trees, the same that a rusalka did to her victims. He wished it to stop—but he felt the cold deepen, until his jaws locked and his teeth were chattering, the lamp flame making wild shadows about the deck as the wind swirled about him.

"Don't," he said, "master Uulamets, stop . . . stop it!"

The book fell open in his lap, wind blew at its pages.

It *wanted* him to look at it. He could hardly hold the book, he hugged it in his arms and braced it against his knee, cramped up to turn it to the light. A second time the wind whipped the pages, driving the lamp flame in giddy shadows.

He read, *I'm not sure this is the best thing to do—but something's terribly wrong. I've dreamed about water. I dream constantly about water and something wanting me. I know Pyetr's safe now, at least. This time it was so close to taking him, so close—I don't know where, I don't know for what purpose, I only know I can't stop it without going there myself. . . .*

The cold grew worse. Pages escaped his hands, and the wind died. He could scarcely hold the book, his fingers were so cold. The first word his eye fell on now was—

Draga.

24

Volkhi should have been exhausted and footsore by now, carrying two men's weight through this damnable bog. Pyetr thought so—so far as he could think at all—but Volkhi showed no signs of tiring, and that unnatural endurance began to scare him, so far as he could stay awake to worry. He tried—damn it all, he tried to move, if only to inconvenience Chernevog, but every time he succeeded in moving he abruptly fell asleep again in Chernevog's arms—while Volkhi kept traveling and for all he knew, killing himself. Little Chernevog cared for that.

But finally Chernevog said, "No. I'm doing no harm to him. None to us either: blackest sorcery as old Uulamets would have it. Or magic—it's all one. I haven't your young friend's limitations."

"A horse can't go on forever!" he cried.

"While I wish it, he can. And be none the worse for it, I promise you."

He thought about that a moment, in the haze his thoughts occupied, thought about it and began to worry about where they were going, and where Sasha was, and whether Sasha and Missy had a chance of staying ahead of them—

"But I want them to," Chernevog said. "Remember?"

He did not remember. He thought, it's another damn trap. He's playing games again.

"All he'd have to do," Chernevog said, "is be reasonable and deal with me. Remember that, too."

He thought, muzzily, Have anything you want, as long as you want, any time you want? It's hell on Sasha—hell on

281

'Veshka—the god knows Volkhi and I aren't damn happy right now, either.

He felt himself going out again, abruptly, dizzying as a fall. "No," he said, fighting it. But it never did any good.

Perhaps he did sleep. Perhaps it was immediately afterward that Volkhi stopped and Chernevog said, shoving him upright, "You can get down now."

Something vast and pale shone through the trees. His eyes could not make sense of it until he realized it for the flapping sail of the boat.

Chernevog wanted him to find out what the situation was. He needed no order to do that. He flung a leg over Volkhi's neck and slid off to a landing steadier than it had any right to be and a well-being greater than it sanely ought to be. He let the reins fall: Chernevog could fish for them if he wanted to stay ahorse; himself, he was very willing to board the old ferry, hoping—

—hoping for rescue if the boy was there and had his wits about him; and fearing the god knew what kind of terrible discovery aboard; but he tried not to think of that.

Chernevog said, above him on Volkhi's back, "The boy's slippery, if nothing else. Damned difficult to track, but I don't think he's here. Catch!"

Chernevog flung the sword at him. He snatched it by the hilt in surprise, and had instant and uncharitable thoughts of slinging the sheath off and running Chernevog through.

His breath came suddenly short. Chernevog said, "Go on. You haven't all night."

"Damn you," he muttered, clenched the sword in his hand and turned and went toward the boat, where Chernevog wanted him to go. Anger choked him, while that dark cold spot stirred in the middle of him and wanted his attention, now, sharply, to what regarded their mutual survival.

There was ample evidence of a horse on the open ground near the water—Missy, he was well sure. Sasha had gotten this far, Chernevog thought so, too, but when he stood and called Sasha's name there was no answer from the boat. He saw a way to get to the deck, hauled himself up onto a low limb, grabbed a handful of willow-wands and jumped for the boards.

The thump would have waked any sleeper. His shouting certainly should have. He saw the deckhouse door open, and the far rail splintered with a very large piece missing. That was not at all encouraging.

"Sasha?" he called. And in remotest, most painful hope: " 'Veshka?"

The sail filled and flapped, boards creaked and the water lapped at the hull, but of a single sound of any living presence—there was none.

He gave a perfunctory look into the deckhouse, he saw only the expected baskets, he walked around to the stern and saw the securing loop of rope over the tiller bar—that was better news. At least the hand that had last had the tiller had left it in good order, no matter that nothing short of cutting the forward stay might ever get that spar down and nothing but loosing the rest of the stays and unstepping the mast might make it possible to haul the boat free: it felt grounded, rocking on the water, but not quite floating free.

One only hoped . . . god, one hoped that that splintered rail and the boat having come to such a predicament did not mean Eveshka had left the boat before it ever came to rest. That break in the rail was twice Volkhi's girth, at least.

He dropped to his heels, wiped a finger across the boards underfoot—carried it to his tongue. He tasted salt and dust.

There had been a defense.

Chernevog wanted him back, Chernevog thought the questions answered, he had looked, there was no likelihood anyone had hidden and the fact that the horse was gone meant Sasha had left along the shore.

He wished he were utterly as sure of that. He walked to the broken rail, looked over the side there—saw ripples and a sudden roiling of the water, a fish perhaps.

Perhaps not. There was no scarring of the hull to evidence any impact with the other shore. He looked out as far as he could see, and felt Chernevog's insistence pulling at him— worried, not forcing him—but about to.

Only good sense, he thought. Sasha had gone. If Sasha was riding into trouble, and trouble of the sort that had broken that rail, he was willing to follow. He crossed the deck, snatched a handful of willow-wands and vaulted off to a landing on the spongy ground where Chernevog stood with Volkhi.

"Do you know where he's gone?" he asked Chernevog.

"I know which direction he's gone. I'm relatively sure of that."

Perhaps he was losing his last sane thought, perhaps he was terribly misled even to think of finding Sasha when he had no wish to be found—perhaps the thought that the boy was into more than he could handle was entirely from Chernevog, deceiving him. But he offered the sword to Chernevog on what he reasonably believed was his own impulse, saying, "If you can use it, Snake. Or if you can't—"

"Keep it, if you'll refrain from using it on me. Do we agree?"

"I want to find him. I don't like the look of this." He gathered up Volkhi's reins and looked around at Chernevog, wondering and trying not to wonder . . . what was going on with Eveshka and whether—

Whether there was any hope for her—or ever had been— or whether he had loved her enough while there was a chance; or what he had done and not done to bring her and all of them to this.

It was not a confidence he wanted to share with Chernevog. He would have balked at sharing it with Sasha; and now he was not even sure whether his doubts in that intimate matter came from his own heart or Chernevog's at work in him.

She had a baby?

All he could feel was fear.

"You're right," Chernevog said. "You're very right. I'd no notion why this might be happening. Now I do. —Are you absolutely certain that baby's not Sasha's?"

That dark spot wrapped all about his heart. He actually considered that possibility, actually considered it, in one black moment—appalled to realize he would not be utterly surprised nor even irrevocably upset with either one of them—hurt, yes; but he would understand it—the boy becoming a painfully lonely young man, and Eveshka frustrated with a husband who was (the folk in Vojvoda had quite well agreed with Ilya Uulamets' opinion) no fit match for her.

Chernevog said, "If it is his—"

Chernevog tried to make him know something. All it made him was afraid.

Chernevog said, quietly, "If it is his, Pyetr Ilyitch, there'd certainly be a reason he's avoiding us."

"Damn you, it isn't, and you don't know him!"

"If it is—none of us will see it grow up. That's the truth, Pyetr Ilyitch. I lie as a matter of course—but this is the plain truth. I killed Eveshka because I'd gotten myself in a trap—because she'd have killed *me* if I hadn't."

" 'Veshka never killed anything—" —in her life, he started to say, like a fool. But that was the 'Veshka who saved field-mice. In death, she had killed, the god knew she had killed.

"Her mother sent me," Chernevog said. "A child like her, doubly born—that's power . . . until she grows up. Draga wanted her dead when she couldn't get her away from her father. Draga tried to kill her when she was born. I tried to find her father's hold over her. I got caught in his book; I had to get away and I had to kill her. I had her heart. I thought I might hold her—but I couldn't and you know what happened. Now we're here—and she's carrying a child that I hope to hell is yours."

"Why?" Pyetr cried. "What's the threat in a baby?"

But he thought of Sasha saying, 'Veshka's mother was a wizard, her father was, she got her gift from both sides . . .

Sasha saying, Chernevog himself was scared of her. . . .

Chernevog did not answer that. Chernevog wanted him on the horse, Chernevog wanted them on their way with no more questions. Pyetr threw the reins over Volkhi's neck and thought with anguish that if Chernevog was lying, he no longer knew his way out of the maze of Chernevog's reasons. If Chernevog was lying, he feared the last thing he would lose would be himself, Chernevog's, ultimately, like Owl, no damn bit more than that. The god only knew but what 'Veshka was going to fight Chernevog—and he was going to be with him, where Sasha had put him, the god help him.

He helped Chernevog up behind him, he all but lost his stomach when Chernevog took his hand and his arm and used him for a ladder—himself leaning far over the other way and Volkhi shifting under him. He said, between his teeth, "Do me a favor. Sit back, keep your hands off, and don't be wishing at me."

"All I want is your help."

"Stop it, dammit!" he cried, and, drawing a calmer breath, reminded himself how he had had to teach Sasha manners at the first.

He hurt the way he had hurt when an old man's sword had gone through him—only shock at the first, seeing the blade shorter than it ought to be up against his side. He could not even say what had hit him tonight, but he was like that. When he had gotten the old boyar's sword through his side he had gotten quite a ways afterward before the pain had set in—being an ordinary man, and dull as dirt. He patted Volkhi's neck, said, as Volkhi started to move, "I'm sorry, lad."

Chernevog said, "I assure you, I can keep the horse safe. It's not harming him. Nothing I'm doing is harming him."

"What about my wife?" he asked between his teeth. "What about Sasha, dammit?"

Chernevog said, equally short, "One thing at a time. One damn thing at a time!"

So Volkhi and whatever else Chernevog was doing was all Chernevog could manage.

Chernevog had said himself . . . that magic was resisting him.

25

■✹■✹■✹■✹ Don't wish, dear, Draga said, don't wish
yet. . . .

Whatever you do, dear, don't do anything short-sighted,
don't make any decision until you know the height and the
width of it.

Chase away the straying thoughts, chase everything away.
This is the simplest wish you'll ever make. It *must* be the
simplest.

"There's not forever, dear. Not if you sit too long."

Eveshka sat with her chin on her knees, staring desperately into the hearthfire Draga tended through the night.

Wish *nothing* until you're sure.

But Papa said—kept running through her mind. Papa had
said, It's a damned fool who wishes more magic than he's
born with . . .

Papa had been with her on the boat, she truly believed
that had been no shapeshifter—she had thought about it and
thought about it and she had resolved that doubt in her mind.
Papa had not been able to stop her from coming here, papa
was dead and his presence in the world had grown very faint,
but papa had stayed with her and, changed by his death and
being again the kind man of her earliest childhood, had feared
for her, had watched over her on the river, had wished—

Wished her asleep, most of the time.

Why?

To wish things for her and her baby she would not remember?

To wish things against her mother?

"Your father's dead," Draga said, feeding more twigs into

287

the fire, a fistful of herbs, that flew up on the draft, all sparks, into the red-smoked dark. "The dead don't always tell the truth. Your father didn't want you out of his hands either. Don't deal with him. You might be his bridge back to the world. Your child might be. Don't think about him. Forget him. The dead have to be forgotten. Think of what truly matters."

She thought about Pyetr, but that led at once to thoughts of Kavi holding him prisoner, doing hateful things, spiteful, terrible things to him. Her mother said, quickly,

Don't! Think of flowers. Blue flowers, dear, blue and white—

. . . Spells stitched in hems, spells against too much memory, spells to keep the ghosts at bay.

Spells for forgetting the dark, one stitch and the next, blue thread, green thread, colors the dead could recall but never, ever see.

That was what it was to be dead, and she never wanted to die again, she never wanted anything she loved to die . . .

"Flowers!" her mother said. "Be careful, daughter!"

She thought of the garden at home, careful rows, thought of her own front porch and the fireside in the evenings, the three of them happy and snug in that house . . .

"Sasha's coming *here*," her mother murmured, stirring the embers. The smoke smelled of papaver, and hemp, and strong and dangerous herbs, making her nose sting and her chest burn and her eyes swim. "I know that he is. He's running here for help. But he's dealt with Kavi. He's compromised himself already. I know that, too."

"I don't!" Eveshka protested, and for a moment thoughts went scattering and wild. "He'd deal with him only as he had to."

"Kavi asks a great deal. Your young friend has afforded Kavi a foothold. That's all Kavi asks. You know that, dear. That's all Kavi's ever needed. I don't know this young man— you do. But older and wiser wizards than he have made that mistake, haven't they? Deal with Kavi—when your husband's life is in the balance? Kavi seems so reasonable when he wants you to do him favors. He wouldn't hurt your husband, no, the whole world treats Kavi ill, he's only seemed to be a villain—forget he murdered you: he was young, then; he'd not really harm Pyetr. No matter that he's bestowed his heart on him—"

"Oh, god!"

"It's true," Draga said. "It is true, dear. I'm sorry to tell you so. Owl is dead. He flew at Pyetr's sword." Draga wished her calm, wished her to listen and be very calm. "Kavi tricked your young friend, got your husband alone for only a moment within a magical boundary—that was all it needed."

"How do you know these things?" Eveshka cried.

"Hush, be calm, dear, be calm. I know, that's all. That's what magic does for you. I know—and so far my magic is keeping my workings secret, but your young friend is about to break through that veil, soon, now, very soon. He's coming here because he believes he's no match for Kavi and he hopes for your help. What will you be able to give him?"

"Why didn't you tell me, dammit? What *other* secrets are you keeping?"

"Dear, you weren't so sure of me—"

"I'm still not!"

"—and I wanted no wishes that might make things worse. Now at least you have your wits about you. Use them! Your friend is making mistakes. He's unable to rescue your husband—getting himself away was not a coward's choice: you know how Kavi loves an audience."

She was shaking. She remembered the house . . . Pyetr in Kavi's hands . . .

"But it wasn't the only choice young Sasha might have made. He might have fought Kavi. Instead he's running for your help; he's thinking of wishing magic for himself to get here—and that's nothing to do alone, god, no, it isn't. Your young friend is making dangerous mistakes, one after the other. He's young, he's inexperienced even in using what he has, he's trusting your father's advice, and he's already put your husband in terrible danger—"

"Stop it, mama!"

"He's coming here, I'm telling you, and he might do anything. Kavi's right on his heels—Kavi has your husband with him, do you understand me, 'Veshka? You know Kavi's going to use him to get your attention."

She looked into her mother's eyes—blue, lucent as glass by firelight,

"*Believe* me," Draga said.

"Don't *do* that, mother!"

"You'd better believe something, daughter. Doubt is your enemy. Fear is your enemy. Love can destroy you *and* your husband . . . most terribly. All your life's been if-I-dared and someday. Someday's come, 'Veshka. The sun's rising on it. What will you do, 'Veshka—and when will you know your own mind, 'Veshka? Only for regrets?"

"Quit pushing me, mama! I can't think when you push me!"

"I'll forgive you, dear, —but time won't. It goes on just the same. Make up your mind. Do you want me to guide your wish? I will."

Her mother hardly blinked. There was certainty in her. I will, her mother said, strong as a wish. Her mother *wanted* to guide her, her mother *wanted* her not to make the mistakes Sasha was making.

"Eveshka, do you hear me? Kavi's using that boy. He's sending him here, to open the door. He'll follow. And you know how your husband will fare then. What are you going to do, 'Veshka?"

"I can't think, mama, just shut up!"

"You can't stop doubting, can you? Doubt's the enemy of magic . . . and its friend. Doubt keeps our magic from running wild, keeps idle wishes from leaping the barriers of our thought, gives us that little space, that very little breathing space . . . for thinking things through. But you can't let doubt rule your life. Follow me now. Follow me. It's not so far a step."

She wished not. Her head was spinning. Sight and sound came and went, near and far by turns.

"It's not so far," Draga said. "All you have to do is want the strength, really want to have it."

"I can't!"

" 'Veshka. Just follow me. One perfect wish. One wish for everything you want. Is that so hard? Your husband—your home—your young friend—isn't that really what you'd choose, over everything in the world?"

"No!" she cried, and pressed her hands to her mouth, appalled at what leapt out of her—but when she tried to want only Pyetr, doubt came flooding over her, doubt made her wonder if she loved him or if she loved herself more—until her heart ached and she felt herself about to faint.

Her mother said, looking her in the eyes, "You love your husband, don't you?"

"Yes!"

"More than anything else? What's important, 'Veshka? Do you know at all? What are you going to do with it if you get it?"

Everything in the world was in doubt. Eveshka clenched her hands between her knees, and tried to know that answer. Save Pyetr, she thought. But her father would say, Fool!

"When you wish for magic," her mother said, scarcely louder than the crackle of the fire, "be very sure you demand enough—because this is a bargaining. Forever and ever, you'll exist in the magical realm to whatever degree you decide now. And you'll decide now how much of nature you'll keep—you'll have no more than that."

"You're frightening me."

"I mean to, dear. This is deadly serious. Know what you want. Decide how much you need. And for what. Do you want love? Or do you want magic?"

"I want to be strong enough!"

"Are you?"

"I don't know!"

"God, girl! Perish your ambivalence! *What* do you want? *What*, exactly, do you want?"

"I don't know, mama, I don't know!"

"Do you want your husband? Or do you want your freedom?"

Free? she thought. There's this damn baby—

God, what does it mean to it? Or to Pyetr?

"It means whatever you want for the baby," her mother said. "Kavi certainly doesn't want it born—unless he can get his hands on it. Do you want a baby? That's the question. Do you really want a husband? Was it a husband you wanted in the first place, or was it freedom from your father? You have that now. What will you settle for?"

"Let me think!" she cried, raking a hand through her hair that trailed loose about her face. She could not dismiss her unease, nor her misgivings, and the doubt was the same doubt, always the same doubt, that she simply could not make up her mind, ever.

God, I don't know if I want a baby.

"Defend it," Draga said. "Or be rid of it—if it's not more important already than you've wished yourself to be."

"It's my husband's, too—"

"Then defend him," Draga said, "—if you want either. I've kept us hidden. That's ending. All this time, all these years, I've been waiting for you. The two of us can beat him, dear. Two of us with the same mind can raise help enough to beat him."

"What, mama?" she cried. "Shapeshifters and the like?"

"They're quite harmless—if you command them."

"They're vile!"

"Nothing is vile, dear, except helplessness. You've kept your heart—you did decide that, I hope. I hope it wasn't simply lack of decision. Do you want me to carry it for you? I can."

"No!"

"Or Brodyachi could carry two—if that would clear your thinking. Dear we can't wait here for the world to be better. Take it as it is."

"No!" she said.

"Then what will you have it be?"

"Mother, just let me think, let me think!" She rested her head on her hands, she tried to shape her wish, but even thinking of Pyetr she could conjure no certainty, and her eyes burned and her nose ran disgustingly. She wiped at it, and wiped at her eyes, and wanted—

Something shapeless and far-reaching and angry—in a moment at the edge of thought, the edge of exhaustion and smoke-bred dreams.

Wanted—

God!

Her heart jumped, her head came up, she found herself looking into yellow eyes, brown face.

Terror struck her like winter wind. She was eye to eye

with Brodyachi, thinking, Where was he? Where did he come from?

"He's been here," her mother said, touching her arm, compelling her attention. "He's been here all along. Don't be afraid. Kavi wants that. But you don't have to be."

There was something outside the door. She knew that there was something outside the door—and there could not be. Brodyachi was here, quite calm. Brodyachi certainly would permit nothing foreign near her mother.

"You're safe," her mother said. "You're all right, dear."

She looked askance at the door, she listened to her mother speaking to her, telling her not to be afraid—and something was there. She knew that it was, a sense of presence absolute and dreadful.

Out there was what she had called, and it was all Draga had said and all the belief she could muster—

"Daughter?" Draga said.

She had to get up, she had to go to that door, no matter how dreadful the answer, it *was* an answer, it was her answer, once for all. She put her hand on the latch, she pulled it up and pulled the door back—

Wolves met her. The pack surged at her.

Not attacking, no, not snapping at her . . . *accepting* her, swirling about her, tugging at her skirts, her hands, with gentle jaws. Their thoughts were like their movements: everywhere, constantly changing, as Draga stepped back against the fireside, as Brodyachi drew back and bristled up, threatening with a massive paw—

She was not afraid any longer. The wolves were everywhere about her, they occupied the door, they pressed against her legs, they saw everything, wolves, and not wolves—chaotic as leaves in a gale. Nothing could catch them. No single wish could hold them—no single wish could find them all at once, or compass all their darting thoughts.

She looked at Draga—knew, suddenly, there was no question of her mother's ultimate, ineluctable treachery. But her mother said, "Malenkova," and her thoughts whirled and spun, recognizing that name from the inside.

Draga wanted—things that did not interest her. Her own way interested her. What fled her interested her. Mostly she wanted what belonged to her. She recollected—indeed, she had never forgotten—she wanted Sasha. Sasha had to do what he was told, join her, stop thinking he knew everything.

There was thunder in the distance. The wolves heard it, and pricked up their ears, though her own ears could not hear it. She thought, That's Kavi's working. Kavi wants Sasha to come here and confuse us. Kavi's calling on whatever will listen to him.

She wanted what was hers, that was all, she wanted everything that was hers to be where she could see it and watch it—everything she loved, in one place, in her keeping, never scaring her again. That was what she wanted.

No more foolishness. None from Sasha, and none from Pyetr. They would do what she told them, she would take care of them and they would be happy.

And for Kavi, who threatened what was hers—

The anger turned over and over in her, paced on multiple paws, looked through multiple eyes, anger with no limits and no conscience at all. Draga looked at her with a satisfying fear, wanted things of her, wanted certain things of no interest to her, but that was very well, she sensed a clear direction in Draga, interests which made one thing more important than other things. Draga wanted her to listen and understand, but Draga was only one more voice clamoring for her attention, and her consent, and her intent, which had many feet and many directions.

She wanted things of Draga, all in her own interest, and Draga would do them: Draga had tried to escape many times, but Draga was a fragment not much more than the wolves, more determined than the rest, perhaps—able to compel a direction. Otherwise the pieces came together by chance, or when a few purposes coincided. In Draga's presence things did come together. She said, "Go on," because Draga knew what to do, Draga and she quite well agreed on certain things and the rest absolutely did not interest her.

26

✠ ✠ ✠ ✠ Rain drizzled down through the canopy, glistened in gray daylight on forest mold and living leaves, a grim, soggy kind of morning that sneaked through the trees without the cheer of sunlight. Sasha walked, Missy being by now very sore and very tired: Babi rested among the packs she carried, a small black ball with unhappy, wary eyes. Babi weighed very little in that form; and Missy liked his presence there: Yard-things she had known would stay close by stables, and horses outside their yards were outside their watching—but this one stayed right with her, and combed her mane and tail and warmed her back.

Sasha knew this, riding Missy's thoughts, clinging to a lock of Missy's mane for balance, his two feet and Missy's four being damnably difficult to manage at once, not mentioning that Missy thought a great deal about what she was seeing on the ground and around and behind her, and about how her legs ached and her stomach was truly, awfully empty, even considering there had indeed been apples and grain a while ago. Missy was unhappy and worried in this deep tangle of woods, in which anything might hide. She could hear the rain sneaking up on them.

Sasha worried for other reasons, and dared not stay overlong listening to Missy, because there were things he feared Missy's nose might not smell nor her ears and eyes detect.

Babi would be aware of them. And when Babi suddenly growled and lifted his head from his paws Sasha wished Missy to stop and to stand still for a moment.

He put out his hand to comfort Babi, to reassure him.

Babi hissed, scrambled up and bristled, and before Sasha

could draw his hand back, Babi snapped at him and vanished into thin air.

Not that Babi had not hissed at him before—Babi hissed and growled at all his friends—but never with such anger.

And never offered to bite. God!

"Babi?" he said, more shaken now he thought of it than in the instant he was saving his hand. "Babi, what's wrong?"

As if—he thought—it might have been him Babi was growling at, as if Babi had suddenly failed to recognize him, or to recognize him as a friend.

He could not recall now what he had just been thinking, or whether he had done anything that might have offended Babi; or whether—

Whether something had just gone wrong in a way Babi could not accept, something to do with things he had done— like leaving Pyetr.

God, no, he must not think of that, he dared not think about that, dared not, for Pyetr's own sake, and his, and 'Veshka's. "Come on," he said, "Missy, there's a girl, let's just keep going."

Missy was so tired, so very tired and making her go on was Not Fair. The bang-thumps were coming, and the wind, and she was wet and shivery and too tired to run when they got here. It was Not Fair. She had rather stand here and rest till they did. She saw no grabby-things. Was there an apple?

Later, he promised her. "There's no time," he said, and pulled on her reins and led her, promising her apples, promising her a currying if she would only keep going and watch her feet, god, . . . "Please, Missy."

She liked him. It was a good thing for him.

There was nothing left in either of them but aches. He had fed Missy, gathered what he could, not forgetting the salt, which he had dumped in a bag to itself and kept slung from his shoulder. Damn, he wanted Babi back. He did not count the vodyanoi gone in any reckoning: bright sun drove it deep under water or earth, but there was none, and dry land inconvenienced it, but there was damned little dry this morning.

Damn, damn! he did not like the feeling he was having, as if something was out there, pacing him—and ahead of him—

Just ahead was a place that did not match the rest of the forest. He could not decide how it was different: it *felt* like forest, it felt almost like this one, but it—moved toward him—like a cloud boundary coming across the ground: but this was nothing visible: it was a sound, a feeling of coolth or earthiness. He had time to think: I don't like this, —and to take Missy's bridle and to wish them both well before it broke over them like a sudden dizziness, a sudden lack of breath—

"Oh, god!" he cried, wishing *not*, but it widened, sweeping over them and rolling through the woods, well past them before it stopped and held. He wanted to keep breathing, he wanted himself and Missy safe from it, and when he wondered, he could not help it, who was doing this—

Eveshka *wanted* him, right now, Eveshka was—

It felt like echoes, as if Eveshka was talking to him from the bottom of a well and echoing so he could not make out what she was saying, the sense of her presence and her wanting him doing the same thing, wanting the way a horde of ghosts wanted—it felt like that; and Missy started to sink down, her legs buckling.

"No," he wished her, pulled on the bridle and drew up strength out of her body and his, pulled her around and kept pulling at her, step after faltering step. "Come on, girl, come on, keep going, 'Veshka's being a fool—we don't want to talk to her."

Anger echoed around him, a change in the sense of things, at least. His head spun, his heart skipped beats, he had no idea what Eveshka wanted.

But there was the edge in the woods ahead. He pulled violently at Missy's halter, wanted her, dammit! to keep going, he was not going to leave her on this side of the trouble, not going to let her die here. He could feel the edge coming, the place where the magic stopped—but he was so tired, and what swirled around them offered all the answers and all the strength he needed, *if* he would take it—

The strength it was taking it would give back—it promised.

"Come *on!*" he wished Missy, pleaded with her, being only Missy then, only Missy, who, suddenly understanding a way out, called up something on her own, remembering town and the hill and her person shouting to her. She drew up her own strength and shoved with her legs, one heave and another, hauling against the heaviest load and the steepest hill she had ever known—

She went down, not on stone, on soft dirt—threw her head up and tried to get up again.

Sasha wished not, told her she had done it, she was safe—down on his knees himself, and lying on Missy's shoulder, with the whole world spinning and fading a moment.

It did not want to kill him. It had let him know that. It *wanted* his silence and his compliance and his heart.

No, he told it, and he was not sure what it would do, but it was not going to get any of that—no.

The babble started again, near him, and he leaned against Missy's shoulder and tried just to hold on and not listen to it—while it told him he had to listen, it wanted Pyetr, it wanted him, it offered them a refuge where Chernevog could not reach them, and he had to see to that—do something—where his hands could reach and her magic could not.

It said, out of the confusion—he thought it sounded like Eveshka, at least it had her voice: I can stop Kavi. But not while he can use Pyetr against me. Get him out of Kavi's hands. Get him away. Do just one thing right, damn your pigheaded arrogance, and I'll forgive you what you've done.

It said, in a quiet tone: You're nothing but my father's wish, Sasha. You're his last damned wish in the world, and you've made all his mistakes. Don't kill Pyetr for him. Hear me?

And don't come here until you have him.

Rain spattered down, a patter through the leaves, cold huge drops, that hit like blows and left numbness where they struck. But not enough. He clung to Missy's shoulder and held on, eyes shut, with a knot of pain inside that he had to hold, had to go on thinking about—

Most of all, not go crazy with—god, not let it loose—

Aunt Ilenka saying, I know who's the bad luck in this house—

A cracked teacup, that a wish still held—

Missy grunted, moved one leg, another. Missy had a

cramp. She was getting wet and the ground was cold. She did not know why she was sitting here, but she had caught her breath, and this was not comfortable.

Sasha thought, himself, We can't go any further. He thought: Missy needs help.

He got up, he got her reins untangled, he got the packs off her back and shoved hard at her rump, shoved hard a second time as she got her feet to bear. She stood, dropped her head and shook herself, a spatter of muddy water.

He hugged her neck, he said, "Good girl," and patted her shoulder, while the rain came down. The knot had gone from his chest to his throat, and stung his eyes—pain wanting his attention, which was not going to do a damned thing useful with the rain pouring down on them and whatever that had been telling him things that upended everything he had thought he knew. A heart could hurt. He could ignore it or he could let Missy carry it, but he thought, There's time for that: I don't have to listen to it. He gathered up the baggage, he got into the pack with the apples and gave Missy two. He wrapped up in the canvas with a fistful of dried berries and nibbled on them, in the notion that his body had spent too much and that borrowing was also a decision he did not want to make yet.

He thought, testing his reasoning, I've never felt anything like what just happened.

He thought, It's much stronger than I am.

And, carefully: It was this way and that. It wasn't like a wizard, but it sounded like 'Veshka. It said what 'Veshka might say. She would be mad at me. I don't doubt that. But if it is 'Veshka she's not doing well, is she? That's what Pyetr would say. She's not doing well. . . .

She says I'm a wish. So's a rusalka. A rusalka's a terribly strong wish. She's her own wish. In some measure she's her father's. He *wanted* her alive. She says Uulamets didn't know what he was doing. But the leshys never said that. The leshys said, Take Chernevog to Uulamets. . . .

I didn't do that, did I? Things went wrong. Things are still going wrong. And of magical things I'd trust the leshys. I'd trust Babi. Babi just doesn't trust me right now. Why?

He thought, We're on the forest's side. That's all. Maybe

the leshys are gone, maybe there won't be any help, but that's still the side we are. It's not wise to forget that. If I'm anyone's, I'm Misighi's. If he's dead, if they're all dead, maybe I'm the wish they made.

He felt the disturbance in the woods. He felt where the center was, he felt more than one presence there. He thought, *Draga—*

Uulamets had said, *Draga.*

Nothing made sense. One moment riding through the woods in a light drizzle, the next waking in a pouring rain on a horse standing very still, with Chernevog's arms locked about him, Chernevog saying, "Your friend's in trouble. Your friend's in deep trouble."

"Where?" he asked, never mind the rain, never mind his ribs ached where Chernevog had been holding him—he wanted to go there, and he gathered up Volkhi's reins.

But Chernevog said, preventing him moving, "Listen to me. Don't argue. Listen. I want you to go to him. He's not far from us. I want him to come back here. I don't want to quarrel with him. You're my offer of good faith. Do you understand me?"

"No." He did not understand. He sat still, unable to move, unable to do anything but answer. "It's a damn trap!"

"I want you to do this," Chernevog said, "but I'm also explaining to you. If something goes wrong I want you to come back *here*, immediately."

He had no such intention. If something went wrong he knew where he wanted to be, and he tried not to think that, because then Chernevog might never let him go. He *would* do as he was told. Absolutely he would.

Chernevog said, tightening his arms, "My dear friend, you are so damned poor a liar. And I want you back. I want both of you, dear Owl."

"Damn you," he said.

"The best have tried," Chernevog said, and let him go and slipped from Volkhi's back, taking the baggage with him. "I'm wishing you to find him. Follow your vaguest notions. They'll be mine."

He looked down at Chernevog, taking up the reins. Chernevog gave him nothing but that damnable cold smile, and the idea, he was sure it was Chernevog's, that he had finally to let that cold spot in his heart have its way completely—that being his only guide.

He knew his directions, he turned Volkhi that way and went, and Volkhi picked up speed—whether Volkhi's inclination, free of half his burden, or whether moving at a wizard's wish, Pyetr did not know: god, he could not answer for himself any more why he was doing this or whose he was.

The rain diminished again. The heavy drops that splashed in the puddles now were all from the trees. Sasha listened—touching Missy's senses as well as his own, a comforting presence, Missy stretching legs still a little uncertain, and enjoying here and now with a small measure of grain and a lump or two of honeyed cereal. Missy was not much on worry when the woods were quiet, and that was a very good way to think when a young wizard was occupying a very dangerous borderland. He had a little food to settle his own uneasy stomach, and sat wrapped in his canvas, warm against the rain-chill, simply resting and listening to the woods; and reading, to keep his thoughts from straying into noisy wishes, from the only book he had.

When I was a very little girl I used to sit and watch the people going on their travels. I wasn't supposed to talk to them. I was supposed to stay hidden. But I didn't. They gave me trinkets. I wished them well. I wore flower-crowns and ribbons they gave me and I hid the trinkets from Papa—

That made Papa mad when he found out and he said he'd wish the road less convenient. . . .

And, seeking cautiously to know more recent things: *Pyetr really doesn't know a thing about gardens. He planted the beans so deep so I don't think wishes could grow them . . .*

Sasha made me so angry today. There are hardly any wishes in this book. Just things that happen, no matter what he says. I don't even wish our happiness. My father's heir—says not to, as if I'm a fool. I wish he'd quit suspecting me, every time something goes right or wrong. That is a wish. It could even be dangerous. And I'm not sorry. . . .

He thought, carefully, It was dangerous. It is. To be blind to her—god, that's very dangerous . . . Why didn't she talk to me? Why didn't she tell me how she felt?

Maybe she did. Maybe I didn't want to hear. I'm not beyond fault in this, god, I'm not. I should have seen, I should have tried, but she was so damned private about her magic—

The dreams won't let me alone. I'm so scared . . . I can't want them to stop: that's so dangerous. I'd tell Sasha—but I've heard his advice: Papa would say, Find out what you're doing before you do anything. But I don't know the consequences, god, I can't know, because I don't know what I am. I doubt my own life, I doubt my own substance, I want to know what's still in that cave under the willow—and I'm afraid to know, I'm afraid to go there alone. I can't ask Sasha, he can't keep secrets from Pyetr, and most of all I don't want Pyetr to go in there and find out I'm still in that grave. I don't think he thinks about that now—but after that, how could he forget? When I came back from the dead, did the bones come out of that cave? Where did the flesh come from? Or what am I made of? My father's wishes? I wonder sometimes, what terrible thing Pyetr's sleeping with . . . and what I'm still borrowing from, to keep the life I have. . . .

We finished the bathhouse. I tried not to want anything about it. I've tried not to think about it. Nothing happened, thank the god . . .

Missy lifted her head from her search for remaining grains. Her ears were up. Sasha wished her not to make a sound and she stood with a little shiver down her foreleg—listening and smelling.

Volkhi. And the friendly person. Missy was glad.

Sasha was not. He shut the book and got to his feet, thinking of shapeshifters and vodyaniye and wishing to the god Babi would show up now, please the god, he did not want this . . .

It certainly looked like Pyetr coming through the trees. It looked like Volkhi. But eavesdropping could not always unmask a shapeshifter once the creature had gotten well into stolen shape and stolen thoughts.

Pyetr rode up to Missy, slid off and started toward him, but Sasha wished not, and Pyetr stopped, made a small helpless gesture toward him. That hurt. "He sent me," Pyetr said. "He's not far from here. He wants you to come there—"

"What do you say?"

"I don't know," Pyetr said shakily. "I don't know. He's been tolerably reasonable—for a snake." He touched his heart. "It's still with me, you know. He eavesdrops most of the time . . ."

He did not want Pyetr in this pain, he did not want to go back to Chernevog, he wanted Pyetr free, dammit!

"It's a short ride back," Pyetr said, and gathered up Volkhi's trailing reins. "He wants me back. He says—tell you—don't argue, I don't know what's going on. He says—how do you want me to find it out?"

"Don't do that to him, dammit! Don't treat him like that!"

"He says—the question stands." Pyetr gave a twitch of his shoulders, threw the reins over Volkhi's head, looked back. "Sasha, —it's all right. Don't do what's stupid. I thought—you should make up your own mind—I didn't argue. I should have made him work for this. God, don't be a fool—I should never have done this."

"Wait!" He snatched up the canvas and started rolling it, while Pyetr hesitated with his hand in Volkhi's mane. "Dammit, Missy can't carry me, she's had enough."

"He says—says she will." He left Volkhi, came and picked up the heaviest of the sacks, stopped then, looking at him as if he wanted to argue, and was in so much doubt—of himself, of what they were doing and where they were going. Sasha did eavesdrop, he took those thoughts, he told Chernevog go to hell, said, to Pyetr, as bluntly and brutally as he could, " 'Veshka's in trouble. Her mother's alive."

He felt Chernevog's panic; he felt Pyetr's, like a knife to the heart, and said, sharply, snatching up the rest of the baggage, "Don't. I'll talk to Chernevog. If she's wishing you in her direction, everything may be working that way, everything we've done—everything Chernevog's done." He grabbed Pyetr's arm and made him look him in the face. "Pyetr. We're going to deal with this. *He* has to. You understand?"

"Good," Pyetr said in a shaken voice. "Good. I'm glad we're going to do something. I like that idea."

Sasha flung things onto Missy's back, took Pyetr's assistance up, took the reins, prey to shivers himself—the notion that at any moment they might be overheard here. Whatever-it-was might make another try—by whatever agency.

He thought, as Pyetr led off, He's not gone, thank the god, he's not gone— But he tried desperately hard not to listen to his heart again, because there was no reason in it at all right now, only fear, and a willingness to give anything he had to give to get Pyetr free.

Chernevog had stretched one of their two canvases between two birches, made a fire—it was a proper camp Sasha saw when he and Pyetr came riding in, Chernevog rising to meet them. Sasha had his apprehensions that it might indeed be a trap they were riding into—that Chernevog might have some way to use Pyetr and him to his own advantage that his own poor knowledge could not anticipate.

But Chernevog offered no immediate treachery: in truth he looked disquieted and anxious. They dismounted—Sasha held Missy's mane, and slid off the careful way, face to the horse, not trusting his legs for Pyetr's leg-over slide, having nothing of Pyetr's balance or Pyetr's grace—he thought about that at such a moment, that he was not going to grow up like Pyetr, the chance for that was past, growing up had happened and left him a little awkward, a great deal deliberate—

He said to Chernevog, not aloud: What you didn't do—deserves something.

Chernevog said, Everything you can give. And don't ask me to change our arrangement. It's worked so well.

Snake, Pyetr called him. Sasha drew a deep breath, and said, If things were working well, you wouldn't risk him coming after me.

27

✠ ✠ ✠ ✠ It was two wizards standing and thinking at each other in complete silence, that was what went on, for longer than would let anyone think they were sane: Sasha was not happy and Chernevog was not happy—that was what Pyetr saw, standing there with two horses in better condition than they possibly had a right to be.

Two wizards discussing his wife, and him; and the god knew what else of the world's fate.

"Uulamets knew it?" Chernevog had said early in this, and after that, nothing, while Sasha frowned. Something went on that made that cold spot next to Pyetr's heart very disturbed.

He turned his back on it in despair, leaned on Volkhi's shoulder and tried not to think what they might be saying to each other. Wizards did these things, and wizards fought over things that sane people could not even see . . .

And the god only knew, the god only knew whether Sasha was holding his own at all, or what Chernevog might ask or want of them, with him for a hostage and his wife being threatened.

He had his sword. He had his hand on its hilt without thinking he even had it.

But something stopped him—perhaps the thought that they needed Chernevog; and he no longer knew if it was his thought or Chernevog's cynical dismissal of him.

Not a damned chance, that thought said. The dark spot stirred and sent a chill down his back.

He recalled Chernevog mocking him, saying: I'll love what

305

you love, hate what you hate, I've given you that power over me—

Then adding: Of course it can also go the other way . . .

—Damned if it can't, Snake. *Listen* to me!

He thought of Sasha and thought of 'Veshka, not their worst and not their best either, only the way they were; he thought about that cold spot that slithered about in him and that boy that had long ago shed it into Owl, whatever its condition might be now: that boy had known smothering and spoiling and betraying in his life and Pyetr understood that very well—those guilt-driven, terrified searches after a drunken father, as if a grown man's troubles were at all a young boy's fault—

The boy he had been could not have understood The Cockerel's mouse-quiet spook of a stableboy—and damned sure the young man could not have understood Eveshka. He would have walked away from Sasha, once, been a scoundrel with Eveshka . . . he had wasted a good deal of his life in that condition, seeing only the outside of people and missing the substance . . .

You've made the same mistake, Snake. Damned if you haven't. You've missed everything so far.

Snake turned and looked at him—looked straight into him, in a way he only let Sasha and 'Veshka do, in his whole life: but he thought with a shudder, Well, hello, Snake, come on ahead, Snake, I won't stop you.

Snake was not sure what he was up to or what kind of trap it was, but Snake thought curiously—*Will* you not?

Sasha wanted something then. Strongly. Snake did. Pyetr felt it going on, and said, out loud, the only way a plain man was sure things were heard: "Sasha, it's all right. Snake's all right. He's just—"

He felt pain, sudden drowsiness. "—Scared," he said, "aren't you, Snake?"—straight to Snake's pride.

Snake felt Sasha behind him, saw him standing in front, Snake felt surrounded and vulnerable and Snake had made that arrogant, foolish bet with him, in giving him his heart, Snake had said himself—

It can go the other way . . .

Walk the roof, Snake? Walk it drunk and blind with me?

Chernevog's face was ghost-white and grim. But he laughed, then—at least life touched that grimness, his eyes lightened, a dark amusement pulled one corner of his mouth. "I'm ever so much older, Owl. Ever so much older than that boy."

"So am I," Pyetr said.

There was, in truth, a smile—most appalling, a grin. Chernevog gave a twitch of his shoulders, laughed softly and still laughing, walked away from them toward the fire.

"God, Pyetr," Sasha said.

Pyetr wondered that he was not more shaken than he was, and put a hand to his heart, asking himself if that cold spot did not feel a little less uncomfortable.

Chernevog sat down at the fireside, poked up the embers, looked up and grimly beckoned Sasha, not him, Pyetr understood. To him, Chernevog said, a silent voice he could quite well hear,

"Ever so much older, Owl. You can't imagine."

He watched Sasha walk away to that fireside. He stood there thinking there was nothing he could do, and sank down on his heels and watched them there, in that silent conversation—about Eveshka.

He thought, What about her? What's she done? What's going on? He thought if there were any good news they would not be talking like that, without looking at him, and Sasha would reassure him.

But Sasha was not inclined to lie to him. Sasha would not tell him a lie that important, that much he was sure of. That Sasha had said nothing at all about Eveshka, and evaded his thinking and wondering and worrying about her—meant it was not good news he had found.

He thought, She doesn't like to do magic. What's this messing with sorcery? She wouldn't do that. Surely she wouldn't do that . . .

He recalled how she had kept him about the house, how she had worried and fretted over him, near smothered him with her worrying—

And loved him. He was sure she did. She loved him, as far as she was able—one got used to Snake, and one could understand a little more how very careful she had been.

Ever so much older, she might say. Like Snake. Ever so much older, Pyetr. You can't imagine. . . .

I can't be rid of the dreams . . . Eveshka had written. And, with chilling accuracy, *I dream about wolves. . . . Wolves tearing me in pieces. I dream of water. And being under it . . .*"

Chernevog turned the page, thinking,

Draga . . .

He looked up into Sasha's face—a jarring thing still, to see this boy looking at him with such frankness, the way only 'Veshka had looked at him, and he never had trusted. He was afraid now, to take this boy on Pyetr's judgment, Pyetr knowing so little beyond the natural world, so damnably little, and trusting the world worked by what he saw. Pyetr he could believe in, the way he believed in trees and rain and sun. Pyetr was exactly what one saw, and exactly what one believed—and he had relied on that when he had had to rely on something.

Pyetr had not failed him—he believed that at least from moment to moment, more than he had ever believed anything. He thought, How do I know anything? Draga deceived me from the beginning, down to this very day she could lie to me—I could see her die, and not know she was still alive.

He had seen Eveshka die—in dark water, drowning, the way he had died in his own dreams, in Draga's house. He gave that thought to Sasha, the whole ugliness, to stop Sasha's intrusive staring at him.

Sasha said, I know. And said further: Uulamets knew. He lived with her.

He had not given those dreams to Pyetr, had not hurt him to that extent. Sasha knew that, too. Sasha said, the way Eveshka had said to him once—I owe you.

Damn, he hated that. He hated it.

He got up from the fireside, he walked away into the drizzle, saw Pyetr stand up from where he was sitting and look at him anxiously. Pyetr did not threaten him. He felt his fears absurd, looking Pyetr in the face; and absolutely justified, feeling Sasha's presence at his back.

He heard Sasha warn him back from Pyetr, Sasha quite ready to fight him for Pyetr's safety.

He turned around again, preferring Pyetr at his back, even with the sword. He said to Sasha, Don't crowd me, boy. I'm not your friend.

Sasha said, Remember I've read your book. And Uulamets'. And 'Veshka's.

I've seen yours, he said. It's astonishingly short.

Mostly, Sasha said—I've studied. I did like your early ideas—some of them.

He said, I was a fool in those days.

Sasha said, You had Draga. I had Uulamets—and Draga wasn't herself when she came to live with Uulamets. She wasn't the young girl he remembered, wasn't at all the young girl he knew in Malenkova's house.

Chernevog shied away from that thought. And came back to it. If Draga was alive, there was no turning his back on any bit of knowledge.

Sasha said, She was much longer with Malenkova than he was. Years. —What became of her book?

In my house, he said. You didn't find it?

Sasha shook his head. No. No, we didn't. A great deal burned. The rest—the leshys gave us. Hers wasn't with it.

He had a very cold thought, then—the leshys fading, their missing that book, while they turned all their watchfulness on him—

Draga? Sasha asked.

Chernevog looked Sasha in the face with less and less and less confidence in their lives and in what they knew. He said, Right now I'm not sure of anything.

Sasha recalled what he had met in the woods ahead—that confusion, that violence—that spoke in Eveshka's voice—

He thought of Eveshka's book, where she had written, asking, *What am I made of? My father's wishes?*

Chernevog said distractedly, Her *life* is her father's. Heart and soul are hers. The substance? The god only knows. Not mentioning the child . . .

—

Wizard business went on and on with never a word aloud.
Pyetr brushed down the horses, sat and sharpened his sword,
for what good it might be, then gave the horses another currying, all the while trying not to think, trying not to wonder
anything, while Sasha and Chernevog in unsettling cooperation looked through the several books, with a great many
shakes of the head, a good many frowns, and an occasional
stirring of Chernevog's misplaced heart—a slithery anxiousness Pyetr could not ignore.

Chernevog was increasingly disturbed. That was very personally clear.

Pyetr thought, There's something going on. Something
very bad happened this morning while I was asleep. Something changed, something both of them know and Sasha
won't talk about.

Sasha looked his way and said, "Pyetr, you won't bother
us if you get something to eat."

"Do you want anything?" he asked, hoping this meant
answers, and Sasha said distractedly: "That might be a good
idea."

So he built the fire up again and got into the packs and
made supper. Eveshka said he was hopeless at cooking; but a
man could not go far wrong with sausages and hard-baked
bread, which Sasha had gotten from the boat, evidently—
along with Eveshka's book. He recognized it, with its familiar
scars.

And Sasha had said nothing to him about finding it, not
a word. One might be tempted to believe that Sasha was wary
of him in present company—but he bit his lip and distracted
himself from that line of thinking: he wondered nothing
about Sasha's reasons, no, he refused even to consider why
Sasha had come here or what had made him accept Chernevog's offer: Snake was too clever. Snake might well be asking
him questions he could not hear—he put nothing past Chernevog, and nothing beyond his reach.

He did not know, for another thing, what whatever they
were afraid of might be doing out there—Draga, Sasha had
said, the only name he put to it. Sasha had always said that
distance made a difference with wizardry, and Chernevog had

talked about a little further on in this woods being more dangerous than where they were now—but it did seem to him that whatever-it-was could damn well get up and walk a bit and close that gap. Whatever-it-was . . . which involved Draga, and Eveshka's book, and her life, and whatever mess she was in—he was sure it did.

He wanted answers, dammit. And none came. The west was rumbling with thunder again—he listened with a little rising hope, thinking that the storm coming might be their doing, that *something* might be in the making.

But with dusk coming on, and the storm still delaying, he got up and got the vodka jug, and took it back to his place beyond the firelight, beside the horses. He sat down and had himself a drink—had another, and thought—

Babi.

He poured a drop on the ground. Nothing caught it. He tried another, wishing very hard, if that should make a difference. The thunder seemed closer of a sudden, and he wondered if the coming storm *was* on their side. He thought, Damned rotten night coming. He thought about the Things that disliked the light, and he thought about ghosts, and the one they had come here looking for.

It was too much to ask, that the old man put in an appearance.

But something cold did touch him. It brushed his face and whisked away.

No, Chernevog insisted. He did not think it a good idea to attempt Uulamets at this point. No, no, and no, no matter the reason in Sasha's arguments. The old man had no liking for him, the old man would not tolerate his presence, they were likely to get a very unpleasant manifestation—

Afraid, Sasha thought, and maybe Chernevog overheard that. Chernevog gave him an offended look. But it was true—it was fear that made Chernevog pull back and there were things he feared that Chernevog suggested:

Be rid of your heart. Listen to me. You can take it back later. It's not irrevocable, for the god's sake . . . look at me.

Magic and a heart don't go together. You can't do anything against her until you settle that question!

Sasha thought, with the thunder rumbling frighteningly close, Master Uulamets said, Wish no harm. . . .

"God," Chernevog exclaimed aloud, "you're not still listening to that old fool. Wizardry won't help us, boy, it's not going to help—it can't defend your friend and it damned sure—"

Don't, Sasha wished him, for fear of Pyetr hearing: he already knew what else Chernevog thought of that wizardry could not do: it could not overcome what had happened to Eveshka.

How much longer are you going to delay telling him? Chernevog asked, with a thought toward Pyetr. Boy, he has my heart. *I* know the truth. I don't know but what it spills over—I've never dealt with anyone but Owl, and Owl wasn't much on understanding.

It offended him that Chernevog chided him about Pyetr's welfare. He said, It does him no good to lose myself, does it? You don't love anything, you never have. You don't understand how much it hurts.

—Thank the god I don't, Chernevog replied. —And you don't have to. Listen to me, Alexander Vasilyevitch!

No!

For a moment breath came hard. Tempers rose, anger flared, palpable and threatening; but Sasha wished *not*, no quarreling, and Chernevog as strongly wished them both to be calm, saying,

Damned stubborn boy! You'll get us all killed. Quiet!

They had resolved, at least, what creature Eveshka had allied with: one could smell it a distance, one could recognize it, Chernevog said, in his memories of her presence—

Wolves, twenty and more of them. Draga's wolves. Chernevog recalled them all too well, creatures each with names, and more mind each and alone than they had together—

One's bad, Chernevog had said, with a shudder; but it thinks. The lot of them don't think—in any reasonable way. Put your heart in that lot—god knows, 'Veshka never could make up her mind. I'm afraid she's found the one creature that might suit her.

That made Sasha mad, and defensive of Eveshka. But it was also, he feared, true.

Chernevog kept after that thought. Chernevog said, now— Listen, boy, if Draga's alive in any physical way, the power she had is nothing to the power she can get through 'Veshka. I'm telling you simple wizardry won't stop her, I swear to you, it will not stop her. You've met magic. You ran from it. Can *wit* overcome that? Can nature? Are you that damnably, stupidly blind, to go back at it again empty-handed?

Sasha said, back to the point of their disagreement, Listen to me. Give *me* your help—

Chernevog said, with stinging despite: Turn myself over to you? *Boy*, you're not listening! If you want your friend alive, if you want him free—there's a cost, and I'm not the one here begging help, I'm not the one desperate to get a fool girl out of her predicament!

Sasha looked him in the face, jaw set, said: —No. You're the one desperate to *have* my help, Kavi Chernevog, because 'Veshka has every reason to want her hands on you, Draga had you once and she wants you back, and if I go, Kavi Chernevog, and if we go under, at least I'm not damning the people I care about to fight each other—

—No, Chernevog retorted—of course not! You're damning your friend to be hers, *as she is*, for as long as she can keep him alive—or for as long as she can keep him out of Draga's hands, which, between you and me, isn't damned long, boy! If you think a loving, crazy wife is hell, god help you when you meet her mother. I'm not your worst choice—and believe me you've got only two.

Pyetr took another drink, while Volkhi and Missy fretted quietly. The approaching storm had them disturbed. The god hope there was no other reason in the woods around them. He had them tied. He did not trust Sasha's attention to details at the moment. He very much wished for Babi, he even wished for Uulamets. But the cold touch that swept past him from time to time did not seem to have anything to do with the old man, unless it was that damned raven of his—because whatever was bothering him glided in and out again with that kind of feeling; and as the light faded from the sky, when less and less detail distracted a man's eye from what his mind saw—he imagined a wide, winged shape . . .

Continually now, from the direction of the fire, he felt the disturbance of Chernevog's heart, he saw the frowns and felt there was a quarrel of some sort going on over there, a very dangerous quarrel.

Sasha had said very little to him on the short ride to this place: he had talked about the vodyanoi, and how the rail had gotten broken on the boat. About having found Uulamets, and how Uulamets had moved the pages in the book, how he was certain that Uulamets had done the most he could do—

He's not like 'Veshka was, Sasha had said. I don't know if an old man could do what she did—I don't know if Uulamets would. He protected these woods. What she did to it upset him terribly. I don't know that he could have made himself do what she did, no matter how he needed it.

Then Sasha had said, And I don't know if an old man could believe in his own life the way she did. It's not enough not to disbelieve your own death, I think—that only makes a ghost. What makes a rusalka is a kind of believing I'm not sure one can even do past fifteen or sixteen . . .

Like the jug, he had said, inelegant comparison.

Exactly like the jug, Sasha had said, and said nothing else for a few moments.

Then: —I think, dead, Uulamets has found so many doubts, so much that wasn't the way he thought—

Another silence. And:

What I have to tell Chernevog isn't going to make him happy either. He's been tricked—unless he's lied to us all along.

He had said, distressed at that thought: Lied to us—about Draga? He wouldn't have to. If he was hers, he could have turned us both over to her. He could have done it that night at the house—

Sasha had said: Not necessarily. And gone on to say: I'm stronger than might seem. I know that I am.

Somehow that had failed to comfort him. Are you as strong as he is? he had asked.

And Sasha, a very soft voice, very faint, What's happened

to Chernevog is doubt. What's happened to me is certainty. I *know* certain things, I *know* what I want. That's why I won't give up my heart. That's why I can't give it up. That's exactly what he'll want and I won't give it.

He had asked, carefully, scared Chernevog was listening: Can you want me free?

And Sasha, equally carefully: I don't dare. You have his protection. That's not inconsiderable.

That had upset him. It still did. He thought, Dammit, don't I have a choice? He doesn't have to live with this. He doesn't have Snake putting him to sleep any time it suits him. I hate this! What's 'Veshka to think if she does reach me? All she'll touch is Kavi Chernevog . . .

—Maybe she thinks that already—maybe she thinks we've just gone over to Chernevog, that we're his creatures. . . .

And aren't we? Aren't we now? We're fighting his damn fight, we're keeping him alive, we're going right down the track of his wishes, and 'Veshka's his enemy the same as Draga is.

I shouldn't have gone after Sasha. I should have fought him on that point. Snake's using me, exactly the way he said he would. Sasha's over there in a damn dice game—and at any moment Snake's going to switch the dice, I know he is. I know that damned slithery heart of his. He's not done with us . . . he's not done with being what he is, he's only learned how to want *us*, and want company, and want us—

God, he wants us with him, wants us to be his the way Sasha and I have been together, his to keep—to damn well *own*, down to the breaths we take. Only he's not Sasha. He's not any good-hearted stableboy.

That cold touch brushed his face again. He saw it glide away this time, broad wings, broad, pale wings—

Owl.

And beyond the light, a shadow-shape with glowing eyes.

Wolves and tearing jaws—

Eveshka's face, cold and calm—

He snatched up his sword and scrambled to his feet, while the horses snorted in alarm, pulling at their tethers.

Draga's face . . .

And a pull at his heart, so fierce it took his breath away.

"Pyetr!" he heard Sasha cry, a thin and distant voice. He caught a breath, heard a maelstrom of voices, calling to him—

'Veshka's voice among them, saying, *Pyetr, Pyetr, I need you—oh god, I need you—*

The bannik pulled the other way. He felt the pain, felt Snake's heart stirring in wild panic. The bannik flew from where it was and turned up face to face with him, wild eyes glaring, hands reaching, nails like claws, teeth like a rat's—

He struck at it, he tore himself away, with Eveshka shrieking at him, wishing it away from him.

Thunder cracked. Lightning burst a tree in the woods beside him.

He could not hear, then, he could not see—except Volkhi's rearing shape seared into his sight. He thought, My wife, dammit! 'Veshka's doing this!

Damn her, she's our hope—she's the only hope—

He ran, blind for that black shape his vision still held, he grabbed the tight-stretched tether Volkhi was fighting, slung the sheath off his sword and cut it.

He dropped the sword. He needed both hands to get a hold on Volkhi. He wrapped his hand in the tether and hauled himself for Volkhi's neck, Volkhi's shoulder, grabbed a fistful of mane and flung himself in the direction Volkhi was bolting, landing astride.

He had a little vision in his streaming eyes, he ducked low on Volkhi's back as branches raked over them and hoped to the god Volkhi was not as blind.

He *knew* where she was. Volkhi was going that direction. He heard 'Veshka's voice, he knew she was in trouble and he wished to the god he had the sword—but he had enough on his hands, keeping Volkhi on his feet in the dark-hazed woods and telling his wife, the while he did it,

Dammit, 'Veshka, stop it—*listen to me*, hear?

28

✠ ✠ ✠ ✠   "Pyetr!" Sasha cried, *"Pyetr!"*

Thunder cracked. Wind howled through the trees, pelting them with leaves, and Chernevog caught Sasha's arm, wanting him to stop, wait, use his head—

"You've no choice!" Chernevog yelled at him, "you've no more time for dithering, boy! Make a choice—join me or join that! If he puts my heart in her hands we've neither of us got a choice at all! Help me!"

Sasha spun on one foot and tore from his grip, raced through the lightning-seared dusk toward the remaining horse, and Chernevog wished *not—*

Sasha stopped and swung about, in the gibbering chaos about them, the horse struggling and screaming in fright— Sasha wished, fighting his attempt to reason with him . . .

Chaos and magic—wild wishes racketing about the walls in physical form—

Wanting him—

"God!" Chernevog cried, as a white shape flew in his face, buffeted him with icy wings. Sasha had caught up the fallen sword, beckoned him with it, shouting.

"Come help me! Help me, for the god's sake!"

"Nothing we can do!" Chernevog cried. "Dammit, he's giving Draga everything she wants—and a wizard's no help to me! Join me, boy, join me, or I'll be joining her, and then where will you be, where's hope for any of us?"

Sasha squinted in the wind, shielding his eyes with his arm, and cried, "I'm going after him! You can do what you want, Chernevog!"

Thunder cracked. A tree shattered, spun burning frag-

317

ments along the wind. The horse reared, cracking the limb it was tied to. Sasha grabbed after it, hacked at the tether.

Chernevog wanted the lightning elsewhere, he wanted Sasha to listen to him—he no longer knew anything for certain: no longer knew what had waked him or what had brought him here—Draga had shaped his magic, *Draga* had used it—

"Come on!" Sasha shouted at him, *wanting* him.

But a jagged shadow loomed between himself and Sasha, face to face with him—caging him with outstretched arms. He wanted help. It wanted—him. It was—him.

The night he had tried magic on his own, to know enough to free himself—

A wish unfinished, a desire Draga had ripped away and twisted—

"Chernevog!"

"All right!" he yelled at Sasha, waved his arm and swept up the fragment, crazed as it was—

The shadow—the fragment—vanished; but Owl was still there, Owl flew ghostly white and unruffled by the gale as Chernevog ran toward him. Sasha grabbed Missy's mane, wanted her still just as long as it took: he heaved himself onto her back, pulled her about as Chernevog reached him—

Wanting him to stop, wanting up with him—this . . . *Thing* along with him.

It wanted to beat Draga—it *saw* lightnings and a rider on a black horse—

It took his offered hand, clambered up over him and flung itself astride as Missy took out running, held on to him as Missy trampled a rotten branch to splinters and took the hill in a dozen long strides.

He wanted to overtake Pyetr before it was too late. Chernevog offered help. And what he had taken up behind him and what was clinging to his back—he had no idea.

Lightnings cracked, throwing the whole woods into white glare, a broken limb tumbled into their path, Volkhi sailed over it and kept going, along a hollow and up a bank, between two trees so close one bruised Pyetr's leg.

It was 'Veshka's wish guided him, Pyetr trusted that it was, it was her voice he heard wailing over the rest.

Lightning showed an abrupt edge to the ground—it came up through the trees, under Volkhi's feet, and Volkhi plunged down a slope, took a shallow brook in stride and headed up again.

A thunderbolt hit behind, showing brush between the trees. Volkhi crashed through it, under limbs, and Pyetr grasped mane along with the reins, tucked low and held on as branches stabbed his back.

He heard wolves over the splintering of brush and Volkhi's pounding strides, he saw clear ground ahead, lightning lit—a hill beyond a thinning screen of trees.

They came pounding into the clear, under open sky, where lightnings flickered—and Volkhi came to a sudden sliding halt, then laid back his ears and swung about as if something invisible held him.

A bear's warning sounded over the wind. Pyetr saw the moving darkness at the edge of the trees as Volkhi turned. Thunder crashed and rumbled, and Volkhi kept turning, smelling the bear, it was damn sure. He gave Volkhi a gentle kick to make him move, and Volkhi only shivered, making nervous small steps, turning again.

Eveshka stood in front of him—looking up at him.

She said, "Pyetr?" But it seemed a dozen voices were speaking in his head. "Pyetr, get down, come here, do you understand me?"

He *wanted* to get off the horse. He wanted to get down and go to her, but there was that small cold slither about his heart that said,

Fool. Don't trust favors.

Don't trust anything Draga's touched.

He said, with the lightning flickering overhead, casting her alternately in light and dark, " 'Veshka, if you're doing this—make it stop."

The dark spot grew colder, cold that went through all his bones. He did not trust that heart, he did not trust himself

319

near 'Veshka of a sudden, did not like 'Veshka's coldness either, or the way she was looking at him.

He was afraid suddenly of what that heart in him might ask, or make him do—and he reined Volkhi further back.

He heard the bear moaning a challenge at his back—heard a voice very like Eveshka's say, behind him, "Son-in-law, no one means you any harm. Get off the horse. Get off the horse."

Missy was not fast, double-burdened as she was, but she charged through brush and trampled over the debris the gale flung into their path. It was wishes kept her going, it was wishes kept them on her back, and Sasha wished everything she could do. It felt as if Pyetr had just vanished from the world—no sense of where he was, only where he had been going when he had just quit being there.

Don't trust anything! Sasha wished him. Don't believe, don't trust 'Veshka—she's not safe.

Chernevog tried to tell him, it's the wolves that have her heart, Draga's wolves. They've torn it in pieces, and it can't put itself together again—

Missy shied and skidded, almost went down. Sasha caught her neck as she came up, wished her steady.

Lightning showed something glistening in their path, something black and moving, that turned and rose up and up.

"Well," it said, higher and higher above their heads. Lightning flickered on a huge glistening head, gleaming teeth. "My old master and my young enemy. Where are we going, mmm?"

"Run!" Chernevog yelled, and Missy bunched her hindquarters and bolted. Hwiuur's long body stretched across her path. She cleared it: Sasha caught himself on her neck and gasped for breath, Chernevog's hands clenched on his coat. Missy's next stride shook them both back, by luck or wishes, and Missy stopped for nothing.

"Get down," Draga said, and Chernevog's heart shrank at the sound of that voice, saying, No, don't, don't believe anything.

Then Eveshka said, out of the chaos that surrounded her voice, "Pyetr, it's all right."

He looked in that direction—willing to listen—almost, for a moment, forgetting why he had come here, except whatever 'Veshka wanted.

But wolves came from the shadows of the trees, wolves came like shadows and gathered about her skirts.

"The hell it's all right," he said, while Volkhi shivered and backed and fretted in the hold of wishes. "Have you noticed, wife, those aren't dogs? You go running off with never a word, I hear from your old enemy you're having a baby—"

"Pyetr." She held out her hands to him.

He kicked Volkhi hard, but Volkhi could not move.

"Pyetr." Wolves milled about her as she came up to Volkhi's side, Volkhi protesting with a soft, unhappy sound. She looked up at him, and Chernevog's heart turned to ice. "I can free you," she said, but it was the snarling of the wolves that wound around her voice, it was their eyes that looked up at him from the ground. "Pyetr."

Chernevog's heart flinched at her touching his knee. She said, "Pyetr, get down," and it kept echoing.

He shifted his weight, looked down at the wolves looking up at him, looked 'Veshka in the eyes, ignoring the voices that howled and wailed—it was *her* he wanted to find. He took her hand, said, while Chernevog's heart shivered, " 'Veshka, why don't you climb up with me instead? Why don't we just go home? That's what you want, isn't it?"

She hesitated, lips open, lightnings flickering on her eyes. She seemed incapable of speaking then.

He said, "I'm awfully sorry about the garden. But the god knows, the weeds are knee-high by now anyway."

He saw the least flicker within her eyes. But she wanted him down. She wanted him *down*—

"If I do, will you give me a wish, 'Veshka? One wish?"

"What?"

He took a deep breath and slid down among the wolves. "You know what it is," he said: it was her heart he wanted, he was sure she was listening to him thinking, and if she had no idea about that, she had no idea about anything.

"Don't ask me that!" she cried. And: "Mama! No!"

321

He looked around of a sudden as Volkhi shied. He still had the reins. He held on, with an arm around 'Veshka, the other jerked so hard it took his breath.

He heard Sasha shouting something, aloud or in his head he had no idea. He held on, Volkhi swinging about to rear and fight, hauling him and 'Veshka up. Volkhi's knee hit him, knocked the wind half out of him, before Volkhi came down again and his feet hit the ground.

Eveshka *wished* something then. Lightning cracked, blinding him. Volkhi shied, tore the reins from his hand, throwing him and her to the ground among the wolves.

Missy charged into the clearing, right for the middle of things—*run!* Sasha wished her, Chernevog felt it in his bones, and the mare fairly flew, arrow-straight between the wolves and the oncoming bear.

Draga knew he was there. Draga turned her attention *his* way, and Missy stalled and shied up. He felt lightnings gathering, yelled, "Do something!" at Sasha as he let go—slid off the mare and landed on his feet among the wolves, wanting Draga *dead* this time, seeing Brodyachi charging him . . .

Sasha had reined back, wanted his attention, was trying to get back to him.

So were the wolves.

Stop Eveshka! he wished Sasha, and turned his wishes on Brodyachi, wished up Hwiuur's strength, and the river's dark cold, wished age, and smothering, and Brodyachi's other shape—the one Draga lent him at her pleasure.

Pyetr tried to move—the ground had come up hard, and he felt Eveshka wanting him well, wanting other things, dark and violent as the wolves about them. He got as far as his knees and one hand, saw Missy's pale legs bearing down on them, and shoved himself for his feet as Sasha brought Missy to a stop and slid off.

"Let him alone!" Sasha yelled at 'Veshka. "Stop them!"

There was a terrible snarling and spitting, there was *something* in that knot of struggling beasts: Pyetr saw that, trying to stand up. Sasha shoved his sword into his hand and all he could do was lean on it, without an enemy to use it on. He felt the tingling of his skin, recoiled and saw the blade in his hand glow with unnatural fire—

Heard Sasha say, shout, into the roaring wind, "Misighi! Misighi, wake *up*! For the god's sake, wake up! We need you now!"

Pyetr felt terror slithering wildly inside him, felt doubt, felt hate, *felt* the claws and the cold. He yelled, "Dammit, Snake!" because he knew a fool was going to get killed where he was. He got a breath and ran, such as he could. Snake was carrying the whole damned fight by himself, up against the hill where Draga stood, a rolling dark tide of bodies sweeping over her—

Of a sudden all his hair was crackling and standing away from him—he stopped and looked up at the roiling sky with the awful feeling the next bolt was his.

But something went away from him then, so suddenly he felt a piece of him had gone—and the tingling stopped: the bolt hit, over on the hill, splitting the night and shattering the ground.

He could not see, then, he could not see at all, except the shadow image seared into his eyes, a swarming mass of beasts and a man with arms uplifted, calling the lightnings. He could not hear, except that crash still ringing in his ears, and that image drifted over and over again through his sight. If there were wolves left he had no way to know, no way to hear them or know whether anyone was still alive but himself.

"Sasha?" he called out, " 'Veshka?" and started as some-one touched him, as a hard hand closed on his arm and pulled him around, into a man's arms. Then a much softer touch folded itself about him.

He hoped to the god he knew who had their arms about him. He put his hand on a woman's back, felt thick braids. Felt the man's hand, and it was smooth and strong. He said—he thought he said, he could not hear it himself: "I can't see." But that was a lie—he thought he would see that sight for the rest of his life.

Then the image began to fade. Sound came to him, the rush of wind, a horse whinnying, Eveshka sobbing, "God, god,

Pyetr, —" He saw fire, the whole hill caved in and burning as if it had found a source of wood inside.

Sasha said, "They're gone. Chernevog, Draga, both. They're all dead."

A thought leaped up at him, a nonsense thought, terrible as it was: he had no wishes to use at all, he knew he was innocent—but he said, on a ragged breath, hugging 'Veshka tight, "I wish to the god I'd never thought about a bear."

He puzzled 'Veshka. He felt her wondering. But her wondering had only one voice now.

Sasha said, "We're not finished yet," and walked away from them, toward the fire, a figure like the one burned into his memory.

He asked fearfully, "What's he doing? What in hell's he doing? —'Veshka?"

She kept her arm around him and guided him in the same direction, saying, "He's going to send them home."

He had apprehensions about that. He had no wish to come near that fire. But he walked with her. He stood shaking in the knees while 'Veshka and Sasha wished something together—

And flinched at a cold spot going through him, shuddered at another. In a moment ghosts were whirling into the fire like leaves, white wisps shredding on the winds, rising in the smoke.

He heard Uulamets' voice say, out of nowhere, Forgive my wife. She destroyed Malenkova. But Malenkova's beast was too much for her. She was all its purpose . . . ultimately, that's all she was . . .

That shape followed the others into the fire. Eveshka's hand clenched on his.

A white, filmy owl glided past, on broad wings—and a young ghost reached up and let it settle on his hand. That one turned and looked at them, quite solemnly, and whirled away into the smoke.

A spot ached, next Pyetr's heart, the god knew why. 'Veshka held his hand tight, 'Veshka held it till it hurt.

29

Volkhi and Missy had their misgivings about the place. It took, Sasha said, some considerable wishing and a good many bribes to get them back. But they wasted no time in that clearing, with its burned-out house beneath the hill—Sasha on Missy and Pyetr with Eveshka riding behind him on Volkhi, with her arms about him, her head against his shoulders.

She wanted him to know about the child. She wanted him to know, while they rode through the dark, that she would not come home, she would only go with them as far as the boat.

He said, "That's nonsense. That's nonsense, 'Veshka."

"You don't understand, Pyetr."

He put his hands over hers, about his middle. He said, "Chernevog said I'm much too young to understand. But we got along."

One hand clenched and unclenched. He had made her mad. She did not forgive Chernevog. Forgiving, she wanted him to know, did not come easily to her. She would wish him to forget Chernevog and everything about him—except that scared her, disarming him scared her—in the case there was some wish still in him.

He said, "Well, you'd better not stay on the boat, then, had you? You'd better come home and keep an eye on me, to be sure I behave."

That upset her, too. She wanted him to know something very complicated, about wanting things of him and not knowing she was wanting them: she was upset about that, she swore she would never do it again, she wanted him to know that. She had done badly with a husband and she had no idea how she was going to manage a child. "I don't know," she said, "I don't even know what the child might be—"

"A baby, I imagine."

She thought that was stupidly short-sighted. He was doing it deliberately, refusing to see troubles coming. They were fighting again. She cried. She said, "Stop, I want to get off"—angry, afraid of herself and him.

He said, "I was safe with Chernevog. I doubt you'll do me any harm."

"You don't know what I can do!" she cried.

But Sasha said, calmly, riding beside them, "He's much wiser than you think, 'Veshka."

And Pyetr said, "That's all right. I made a bargain with her. She has to pay it, isn't that the way magic works?"

"I didn't make any bargain," she said.

"I got off the horse, didn't I? —Where is your heart?"

She did not answer him. He grew anxious then, wondering if she did in fact have it, or what might have happened, last night.

She said, "I have it."

"So, well?" he asked. "You owe it. You have to pay."

They reached Chernevog's camp, where books lay water-stained and scattered by a dead fire, with their canvas and their baggage. They settled down then to let the horses rest—but there was little of that for them. There was magic going on, Pyetr felt it—felt the anxiety in the air, as if there might be another argument going on; and perhaps he had gotten used to it. He sat with his arms around his knees and waited, not making himself evident.

But finally Eveshka got up and walked off into the dark and stood there. And very slowly he became aware of something furtive and angry next to his heart.

She said to him, wizard-wise and scared, so very scared it made his heart beat faster, You may not like me, Pyetr. But I'll take it back again if that's the case. I'll find some other place to put it.

He got up and walked over to her, stopped at a little distance, feeling her upset. " 'Veshka," he began, wanting to reassure her.

She said, aloud, "My father ran from Malenkova's house. My mother stayed to fight her for her place. It was brave and it was stupid. She beat Malenkova and lost to the wolves. She had to have magic—and it used her."

"Chernevog said as much—about using magic."

"Pyetr, I can't put it down now. If there's a child—I'll have no choice."

He understood that. "We don't want the house to burn."

"Don't—"

"—joke? I prefer to."

For a moment her heart hurt him, the panic was so acute.

"Shush," he said. "Calm down. Calm down. Let me tell you about Chernevog—"

"I don't want to hear about him!"

"I think you should," he said. "I truly think you should."

She stood staring at him, in the firelit dark. Her lip trembled. Tears glistened in her eyes.

"Will you do that for me?" he asked. "Will you listen?"

Winter came. Snows lay deep. Babi turned up in the newly built stable, keeping very much to the horses' company, perhaps that he had taken to his proper job—perhaps that he had renounced wizards and their doings. But he was back, and safe, and seemed content. Occasionally, even last evening, one saw leshys walking. Firewood appeared, miraculously, outside the bathhouse, which nothing haunted, nowadays.

But the baking, this morning, went undone. There were kettles of water, there was a great shifting and moaning of the house-timbers, there were two men trying not to panic, because Eveshka was very close to that herself—they had seen kittens come into the world, and Sasha had seen a calf born once, he said, at which Eveshka burst into tears.

She was scared, terribly scared, Pyetr knew that, having her heart against his own. He did everything he could, he did far better than he thought he could—who had always, always gotten queasy at blood, and flinched at other people's pain. She did not want Sasha there, she had terrible imaginings of what the baby might look like, of birthing something horrid, and deadly—most of all she wanted no one wishing at her.

She cried, I don't know what *I* am, the god only knows what the baby is! I should never have gone through with this—

He reminded her what Sasha said: "You never truly left this world. A rusalka isn't dead. A rusalka hasn't died. That's her trouble, isn't it? You have every right to be alive."

She gave a great breath then. And maybe she wanted the baby born. It happened very quickly. He did all the things Sasha had told him, and held his daughter in his hands.

"Look at her!" he said. "Look at her!"

Eveshka said, worried, he felt it plain as plain, "Give her to me. Give her to me, Pyetr."

Afraid, still. He felt her wishes protecting him. He felt them asking questions a baby had no way to answer.

She wanted him to leave, please, now, let her take care of things.

That stung. But he knew why she felt that way. He felt her fear, inside. He ducked out the door, where Sasha hovered.

"She's all right," he said—but Sasha knew, Sasha knew anything he wanted to, the god help him. Sasha shoved a cup of tea and vodka into his hands, said, "Sit down."

"She's scared," he said, wishing with all his heart he could do something, "she's so damned scared. . . . But if it wasn't right, the House-thing would do something, wouldn't he? He'd let us know."

"He'd know," Sasha assured him.

But something strange happened then. He felt 'Veshka's startlement, that made his heart jump, and he shoved the door open. Something black was lying on the covers of the bed.

The ball of fur lifted his head from his paws, looked up at him with round, solemn eyes, and got up and snuggled next to the baby in Eveshka's arms.

Babi was back. Babi approved of this arrival in the house. Assuredly Babi did.

ABOUT THE AUTHOR

C.J. Cherryh was born in St. Louis, Missouri, but has spent most of her life in Oklahoma. She now lives in Oklahoma City. She has a BA in Latin, an MA in Classics, plus additional language courses; she also qualified in field archeology, but never practiced. She was a professional translator in French, and has taught Latin, Greek, and Ancient History.

Her first novel, *Gate of Ivrel*, was published in 1976, and she quickly became a leading writer of both fantasy and science fiction. She received two Hugo Awards, one for her short story, *Cassandra*, and the second for her novel, *Downbelow Station*. Her novel *Rusalka* was published by Del Rey in 1989.

In her own words:

"I write full time; I travel; I try things out. I've outrun a dog pack in the hills of Thebes and seen *Columbia* lift on her first flight. I've fallen down a cave, nearly drowned, broken an arm, been kicked by horses, fended off an amorous merchant in a tent bazaar, slept on deck in the Adriatic, and driven Picadilly Circus at rush hour. I've waded in two oceans and four of the seven seas, and I want to visit the Amazon, the Serengeti, and see the volcano in Antarctica. I can read history in a potsherd, observe time in a stream-bank, and function in a gadget ancient or modern—none of which has ever cured me of losing my car keys or putting things together before I read the instructions."